GET A FREE BOOK

~

Click here to download The Watcher, a novella exclusive to Ty Patterson's newsletter subscribers

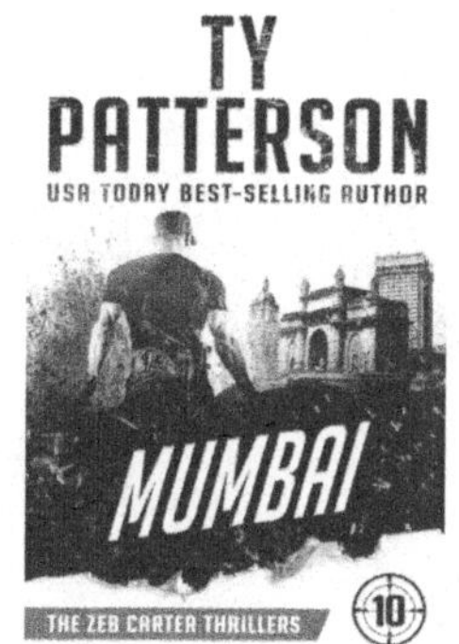

Check out Mumbai here, the next Zeb Carter thriller

Check out Paris, here, the previous Cutter Grogan thriller

Join Ty Patterson's Facebook group of readers, here

ALSO BY TY PATTERSON

Zeb Carter Series

Ten Books in the series and counting

Cutter Grogan Series (Zeb Carter Universe)

Five books in the series and counting

Zeb Carter Short Stories

Three books and counting

Warriors Series (Zeb Carter Universe)

Twelve books in the series

Gemini Series (Zeb Carter Universe)

Four thrillers in the series

Warriors Series Shorts (Zeb Carter Universe)

Six novellas in the series

Cade Stryker Series

Two military sci-fi thrillers

ACKNOWLEDGMENTS

They say it takes a village to produce a book. In my case, many continents have been involved. Sure, an author's job is a solitary one, but writing is just one part of putting out a book.

My beta readers, who are around the world, are my first responders. I owe a debt of gratitude to them for putting into shape all the words I write.

They are:

Dori Barrett, Laura Rachwalik, Jobins MJ, Simon Alphonso, Steve Panza, Maria Stine, Ann Finn, Don Waterman, Kimber Krahn, Robin Eide Steffensen, Blanca Nichols, Loz Yeung, Charlie Carrick, Martin Pingere, Terrill Carpenter, Kathryn Defranc, Dave Davis, Mike Duncan, Donna Young Hartridge, Shadine Mccallen, Shell Levy, Wanona Koeppler, Marion McNulty Hulse, Gerry Kenny, Rob Fox, Dan Gherasim, Toni Osborne, Theresa Ann Kari, JoAnn Cates Lewis, Cathie M Jones, Debbie McNally, Sylvia Foster, Beth Perry, Mike Davis, Pat Barling, Mary Kauffman, John Spiller, Dave Campbell, Mark Campbell, Cathy Silveira, Franca Parente, Jan Fisher, Nancy Schmit, Claire Forgacs, Pete Bennett, Eric Blackburn, Margaret Harvey, Jim Lambert, Jimmy Smith, Suzanne Mickelson, Brad Werths, Allan Coulton, Paula Artlip, Pat Ellis, Linda Collins, Tricia Cullerton, Alun Humphreys, Jimmy Smith and Jennifer Anderson.

Donna Rich, my proofreader, and Doreen Martens, my editor, have been invaluable in polishing the book.

Lastly, a special thanks to Debbie Gallant, Tom Gallant, Michelle Rose Dunn and Cheri Gerhardt, who have supported me since the beginning.

DEDICATIONS

~

To my wife and son for their sacrifices in supporting me

Leave the Devil alone and he might return the favor

1

M*oscow*

Elena Zakharova was scared.

She looked out of her apartment in Ramenki and didn't see anything but kids playing on the common lawn. Her building was on Michurinskiy Prospekt, a wide street with a line of stores fronting it.

GUVD can come only from the street. There is no other way.

GUVD. The Moscow police.

Olga will tell me if they arrive.

She had become close to the hairdresser over the years and was a frequent customer at her salon. They had bonded over failed relationships and a hatred for the government.

The investigative reporter checked her phone again. No signal. She knew that was because her service had been cut. Her landline was out of order, too, as was her gas and electricity. Her bank account had been frozen.

Standard operating protocol for police before arresting someone.

No, she thought fiercely. *This is how thugs operate. GUVD do not work like this.*

Thugs. She shivered. There were several agencies in Russia that wielded enormous power, who could make people disappear, but only one operated in this manner.

SVR, the country's Foreign Intelligence Service.

Gorshky hates me for the articles I have written on him.

The agency's head wasn't someone anyone in Russia would want as an enemy. The man had no lack of resources, tremendous political support, and had been accused of making reporters disappear, killing political opponents and making life unbearable for anyone who criticized the government.

The agency's remit was external, beyond the country's borders, but by declaring investigative reporters as *foreign agents*, the SVR could target them.

Elena went to the window again and swore when she saw nothing alarming.

Stop, she told herself. *Think about how you can get out of this.*

But introspection didn't get her far. She had some cash, but that wouldn't get her anywhere. Every airport and train station would have people looking for her. *It's possible even the taxi drivers are informed about me.*

Her editor had fled his home and gone into hiding.

'Elena, get out while you can,' he'd said in his last message to her. 'When your article is published, nothing can save you.'

She went to the kitchen to salvage some breakfast from her rapidly warming refrigerator, and that was when her door burst open.

Four men in plainclothes lunged at her. One raised a baton and struck her on the head.

At least I sent that message and hid my notes, was her last conscious thought.

. . .

New York

Zeb Carter stared at the message on his phone.

'What's up?' Beth shoulder-bumped him.

She sucked in her breath sharply when he showed it to her.

I am Elena Zakharova. Please help me.

'Zakharova! She's that reporter who has promised to expose Russia's military plans on Ukraine.'

It was news all over the world. The journalist was well-known for hard-hitting reports on government corruption, media harassment and the erosion of democratic rights. In a recent interview, she had hinted at the biggest scoop of her career, one that would reveal the reasons for the government's troop buildup on the Ukrainian border and what its plans were to attack its neighbors.

The segment had been picked up by *The Guardian* and spread around the world, at a time when several countries had little trust in Russia's actions. The country's President had denied it planned to invade its neighbors; its ambassadors around the world made reassuring noises; but those following Russian politics were eagerly awaiting Zakharova's bombshell.

'Her editor disappeared.' Meghan joined them with a worried look. 'A week ago. *The Reality*, their newspaper, is no longer available on the street. Its press was vandalized. By *hooligans*, the police say,' she snorted in disbelief. 'Their online edition has a promo, *Read Elena Zakharova's Article*, but the hyperlink doesn't work.'

'How did she get your number?' Bwana demanded.

'During our last mission,' Zeb replied with a faraway look. 'She was one of several journalists we rescued from that terrorist camp in Syria. She was investigating Chechen fighters in the region. I gave her one of our *front* numbers.'

Any caller to the number was met with voicemail instructions to send a text. Werner scanned incoming messages, verified that they came from authentic numbers, and only then forwarded them to Zeb.

'That *is* her number.' Beth looked it up on her screen. She dialed it, listened for a while and shook her head. 'It's dead.'

She made another call, spoke in Russian and turned to Zeb. 'No one has seen her.'

2

Zeb leaned back in his chair and crossed his hands behind his neck. *That was the first time we met her.*

Moscow

'Keep driving,' he told Meghan softly as she jabbed the horn again and navigated the ambulance through the crowd that overflowed Red Square and spilled onto Ullitsa Llinka, the street that cut through the heart of the city.

Pro-democracy protesters, *he thought bleakly as he watched women and men chant loudly, holding placards and raising fists. A line of armed police kept them from approaching the Kremlin. He could hear the angry shouts and yells over the engine and through the window.*

'How's Chenov?' He leaned to his right to spot the second ambulance following them, in the side mirror.

'He's doing okay,' Roger drawled and waggled his fingers on the

wheel. 'But we need to get to Vnukovo soon. He needs medical attention.'

Petra Chenov, a Russian independent journalist who had exposed the offshore accounts and assets of the country's President around the world. He had fled to the US Embassy when the GUVD went looking for him.

State officials messed up, *Zeb thought bitterly.* We should have taken him right away instead of getting him to stay in a hotel.

The police arrested the journalist in his room and were escorting him away when the Agency crew struck.

Meghan seemed to read his thoughts. 'If we hadn't been around in Moscow, on our way to exfil from our mission, Chenov would have disappeared.'

'Yeah.' Beth nodded. 'Clare got to us just in time.'

They hadn't had any time to prepare for the operation. They had taken out the cops, but in the rescue attempt, the journalist had suffered a couple of broken ribs and a deep gash on his chest.

They had left the cops bound and gagged in Chenov's room, disabled their comms, then stolen the ambulances and slipped into the crew's uniforms.

Beth and Meghan in the front, in the first vehicle, with Zeb behind them on the bench seat. Roger and Bear in the second ambulance, with the rest of the operatives hidden in its back, along with the journalist. The paramedics were with them, too, bound and gagged.

'We need to move faster,' Bear growled in their earpieces from the second vehicle. 'GUVD will know the arrest didn't happen. They'll lock down the city—'

'You want me to run over these protesters?' Meghan snarled. She slammed the brakes when a bunch of people walked in front of the ambulance and gesticulated angrily.

'Please let us pass,' she said, lowering the window and speaking in Russian. 'We are attending a medical emergency.'

'We are blocking all traffic,' a woman said, thumping the door angrily. 'We don't care if people die. What's the point of living in this country if we aren't free?'

'Please—'

'OPEN THE DOORS. LET'S SEE IF YOU HAVE ANYONE INSIDE.' A couple of burly men punched the sides of the vehicle, making it rock.

The cops haven't moved, Zeb thought, checking them surreptitiously. They want to hold their line and block access to the Kremlin.

He had lowered the window to address the protesters when a woman with flaming red hair appeared.

'WE WILL NOT LET YOU PASS!' she yelled. 'WE —'

She broke off. Her eyes widened. She looked past him and took in the twins. Checked out the second vehicle and turned to her companions.

'Step back,' she told them firmly. 'I will deal with this.'

'Elena, we can't—'

'Jakob.' She caught a burly man's shirt and yanked him close. 'I told you, I will handle this. If there are patients inside, or if they are rushing to—'

'You know what we agreed on!'

'I organized this protest,' she hissed. 'BACK OFF.'

She shoved him off, confirmed that he and the other protesters had moved away, and turned to Zeb.

'What are you doing here?' she whispered.

'Trying to get through to Vnukovo Airport,' Beth replied.

Elena Zakharova's eyes narrowed. 'We've been following police radio chatter. Chenov's disappearance ... you are involved?'

Neither Zeb nor the twins responded.

The journalist looked at the second ambulance. Her jaw firmed.

'LET THEM PASS!' she yelled. 'THEY HAVE AN EMERGENCY.'

Some of the protesters yelled angrily, but most obeyed her. The crowd parted to let them through.

. . .

New York

We would have been trapped if she hadn't helped us that day. Zeb straightened and pulled out his phone.

'Ma'am,' he began when Clare came on the line.

'I got a message from Elena Zakharova,' he said, breaking it down quickly.

'Your plans for the main target?'

'Are coming along. If Elena knows something about Russia's war plans—'

'Stopping the conflict isn't your mission. We aren't in that business.'

'What she knows might—'

'It could, but then again, it might not.'

She went silent for so long that he checked his phone to confirm the call was active.

'Go,' she responded finally.

3

Zeb went to the world map hanging on the wall and studied it with his arms crossed.

It won't be an easy operation.

No mission is. We've pulled off hard ones in China and Iran.

He glanced over his shoulder to check out his team. Broker, the eldest in the group, at his usual spot, the golfing strip by the panoramic window. Bwana and Roger, intensely debating the superiority of South Korean cuisine over Japanese. Bear and Chloe, curled up on a couch, flipping through a book. Beth on the phone to her boyfriend, while Meghan was at her screen.

They had trained at Fort Bragg with Delta and at Fort Benning with the Rangers. They carried out joint exercises with elite FBI teams at Quantico.

Yeah. His lips curled in an involuntary smile when Bwana cocked his fist in a gesture that made his biceps strain against his Tee's sleeves. *We are mission ready.*

He went to the games table, picked up a dart and threw it toward the map. It landed on target by sheer luck, its shaft and flight quivering in the air.

His friends came over at hearing the impact and gathered

around him. Beth went to the map and traced the city on which the point had landed.

'Moscow.'

'We're going there?' Bwana cracked a knuckle, the sound loud in the office.

'Yeah,' Zeb replied.

'High time,' Bear growled. Roger nodded, a lean, hungry look on the Texan's face.

'The boss greenlighted it?' Broker raised an eyebrow. 'To get Elena back? She is important to us, but—'

'She's the secondary mission.'

Meghan was the first to catch on. Her green eyes lit up.

'Alexei Gorshky,' she breathed, and Bwana popped all his knuckles, making them sound like gunshots.

4

'SVR is headquartered in Yasenevo,' Meghan explained as she began her briefing. She zoomed in on the map and brought up the neighborhood. She enlarged the district to show satellite images of the outfit's offices. 'Southeast Moscow, half a mile beyond the ring road. Sluzbha Vneshnei Razvedki.' She switched to Russian, knowing all of them spoke it fluently. 'We all know what they do.'

Heads nodded. SVR was the equivalent of the CIA or Britain's MI6. Russian's Foreign Intelligence Service carried out intelligence gathering and espionage all over the world. Its activities didn't stop at running spies, however. It was rumored the agency was behind killing several double agents and opponents to the president. The outfit was also believed to be responsible for the organized spread of misinformation aimed at eroding trust in democracy and public institutions.

'They have hackers,' Meghan continued. 'Teams of them, and they're suspected to be behind the SolarWinds cyberattack, among many others. Technology espionage, malware, ransomware ... all of those are their latest weapons, and they're getting better at deploying them.'

'Gorshky.' She brought up a photograph of the agency head. Dark hair, penetrating eyes, chiseled jaw; the SVR chief had the look of a predator. 'He was involved in the assassination attempt against President Morgan. He has been on our blacklist for a long time, but other missions got in the way. It won't be easy to get him. He has agents with him all the time.'

'Zaslon,' Chloe murmured.

'Yeah. The secretive division within SVR that's responsible for diplomatic security. *Security*,' she scoffed. 'We know they're involved in assassination, too. No one knows how many operatives the agency has. Like other Russian agencies, GRU for instance, there's a lot of deliberate misinformation out there, making our mission even more difficult.'

'You're saying we'll be going in blindfolded, to search for a needle in a bed of thorns, at a time when Russia might invade Ukraine or other countries at any moment and therefore its internal security will be at its tightest,' Roger said sarcastically.

'Yeah.'

'How do we pull it off, in that case?'

'Simple. We get close to him and grab him.'

She grinned at the collective groan. 'There's little we can do from here. Read up on SVR, Gorshky ... everything that we have.'

'And then?'

'We get to Moscow, where we begin.'

'First.' Beth got to her feet, went to the window and looked down at Columbus Avenue. 'We need to deal with our watchers.'

5

'Got a light, bud?' Bwana asked the engineer.

The man, wearing coveralls with the logo of a well-known utility company, straightened up from his toolbox. His partner inside the white van glanced at the operative and Bear.

'Light? We don't—'

Bwana punched him in the belly, caught him by the neck as he doubled up, and flung him inside the vehicle. The second man yelled in anger, his hand streaking to his partly unzipped chest. Bear bounded into the van and body-slammed him, the impact making the vehicle rock on its shocks.

'If we see you again,' Bwana said, crouching next to his gasping victim, 'we'll kill you, rip your body to shreds and drop the pieces into the sewers.'

'You think they'll return?' Bear jumped out of the van and joined Bwana to watch the men stumble out of the vehicle, slam its doors and climb into the cab.

'Nah, their cover is blown.'

'You think they're SVR?'

'Beth and Meg are sure of it. They have good covers; they

are employed by that firm, but they're also doubling up as security agents. The twins traced that firm to the Russian Embassy.'

'I wonder how Zeb is getting along.'

ZEB SAT ON THE BENCH, rolled his shoulders and stretched his legs out. Newspaper Reading Man, next to him, didn't look up from the broadsheet in front of his face.

They were on a broad stretch of sidewalk near Columbus Circle. Behind them was Central Park; ahead was New York traffic. Cabs, trucks, private vehicles and buses all vying with one another, looking to get ahead and beat the next red light. The city's residents hustled to their work places and appointments while tourists snapped photographs. It was yet another day in the city.

Zeb extracted a curved leather case from his backpack, drew out a machete from it and started polishing it. The khukri, gifted to him by a Nepali Gurkha friend, glinted in the light. A passerby gawked, did a double-take and scurried away. Newspaper Man drew a sharp breath.

'If I see you again,' Zeb said conversationally, 'I will disembowel you and feed your guts to the pigeons.'

His neighbor folded his newspaper and put it down next to him. He was clean-shaven, jowly and seemed to be stocky, but Zeb wasn't fooled by his appearance. *We've been watching him for a while. He can move fast.*

Newspaper Man got to his feet lazily, with a scornful grin.

'TERRORIST! HELP! CALL THE COPS. HE'S GOING TO KILL US.'

6

Zeb sat stunned for a moment.

That wasn't the reaction I was expecting.

He sheathed the khukri hastily. 'No—'

'STAY BACK. SOMEONE HELP ME. HE'S GOING TO KILL ME.'

'No, listen—'

Newspaper Reading Man flailed and gesticulated as he shrank away. Someone shrieked, a woman screamed, passersby fled. A squeal of brakes announced the arrival of a prowl car.

'Thank God!' the man half-sobbed and raced towards the emerging cops. 'He's got a long knife with him. He said he would kill me and many others. Please help!'

'Sir!' The officers drew their weapons and aimed at Zeb. 'Put your knife down and surrender.'

'No, there's a misunders—'

'SIR, WE WON'T WARN YOU AGAIN.'

Zeb dropped the khukri and raised his hands in the air. His jaw clenched at the smirk in Newspaper Reading Man's eyes. More patrol cars arrived, and cops spilled out, keeping the onlookers at bay.

'What's going on here?'

His heart sank at the voice.

Gina Difiore, Detective First Grade of the NYPD, on a long-term loan to the FBI, broke through the police cordon. Her shades flashed in the light as they took him in. Peyton Quindica, FBI Special-Agent-in-Charge, her partner, followed her.

Just my luck, Zeb groaned inwardly. *They had to be here.*

'HE WAS GOING ON A KILLING SPREE!'

'I wasn't. I—'

Difiore produced handcuffs and reached out to him. 'We'll take it from here,' she informed the officers. 'He's been on our radar.'

'You have a lot of explaining to do,' she hissed when she got closer.

Zeb spotted the red dot on her chest. It disappeared and then appeared on Newspaper Reading Man's body.

'SHOOTER!' he roared and threw himself at Difiore.

7

'DON'T MOVE!'

'WATCH OUT!'

Zeb heard the cops' voices dimly as he body-slammed into Difiore and brought her down. He yanked at Quindica's ankle savagely and felled her to the sidewalk.

'Get behind the bench!' he whisper-snarled and turned to Newspaper Reading Man, but he was too late.

The first round had slammed into the man's chest; the second blew his head away.

'SHOOTER'S IN THAT VAN!' He pointed to a dark van on the street. He rolled desperately as a shot sprayed concrete chips on his face, heard the whine of an engine, and when he snatched a look, the vehicle was racing away.

'Way to go,' Beth said balefully in his earpiece. 'All you had to do was threaten that man. Good luck in getting Difiore and Quindica to believe you.'

THEY DIDN'T BELIEVE HIM. He could see it in their skeptical expressions.

'I didn't know there was a shooter,' he tried again. 'Wouldn't I have warned you earlier?'

'You're lucky you weren't shot by cops.' Quindica glared at him.

I am.

'Do you know him?'

I can't tell them we were aware of Newspaper Reading Man and the maintenance engineers watching our office.

The FBI agents were aware that he and his team worked in a covert outfit, but that was the extent of their knowledge.

'No.'

'You expect us to believe that?' Quindica scoffed.

'Believe what you want. It's the truth.'

'What was with the khukri?'

'I was polishing it,' he lied.

'Onlookers say you two exchanged words before he started screaming about you being a killer.'

Zeb frowned and checked out the bunch of people who were watching from a distance. Armed FBI officers had taken over from the cops, who maintained a perimeter.

'We didn't speak. I didn't know him. I was—'

'Polishing your machete,' Difiore completed sarcastically. She blew hair out of her eyes and looked at their office, a tall building with mirrored windows on Columbus Avenue. 'Is this related to what you do?'

'We are corporate security consultants,' he replied, trotting out their cover. 'We have business rivals, but they wouldn't hire shooters to take us out.'

'Security consultants.' Quindica shook her head scornfully. 'You know how this will go,' she said, looking at her partner.

'Yeah. He'll stonewall us until Bart gets us to release him.'

Bart Jamieson, FBI Director: their boss, Zeb's friend.

'Did he have a driver's license on him? Any identification?'

'Why would we share that with you?' Quindica put on her shades and ended their conversation.

ZEB RAISED his hands the moment he stepped into their office.

It wasn't enough to stop Beth.

'Gina should have arrested you and carted you off to a holding cell.'

'What were you thinking?' Meghan demanded. 'Why did you have to make a show with your khukri?'

'You were watching?' he asked weakly.

'Of course, we were,' she snorted.

It was standard operating procedure for the rest of the team to be ready to back field agents.

'We got the van's plate.' Broker leaned over Beth's shoulder and brought up an image of the vehicle on a camera feed. Their building had an array of covert and overt CCTV, surveillance and counter-surveillance devices. 'It's a stolen one. Cops found it abandoned a block away. No trace of the shooter or the driver.'

'What about Newspaper Reading Man?'

'Yuri Shalapov. We identified him several weeks ago, but you know about that. He's a clerk in a downtown law firm.'

'We haven't connected him to SVR?'

'Nope,' Meghan made a face. 'Not even to the Russian Embassy.'

'If he was one of Gorshky's men, or even from the GRU, why would they kill him?'

FOOD TRUCK MAN smiled at his customer, who paid him and left with his lunch. He dried his palms and checked that no other patrons were waiting to be served. He reached beneath the counter and drew out an encrypted phone.

'There was a shooting near Columbus Circle.'

'Why would that interest me?'

'Carter was involved.'

8

M*oscow*

Alexei Gorshky put down the phone, crossed his arms behind his neck and stared at the ceiling, as if it had some answers for him.

The call from his case officer disturbed him.

Who else was watching Carter?

It wasn't GRU or any other Russian agency. He was sure of that. Every one of his counterparts had denied involvement in the surveillance or the shooting.

They could be lying, but they won't risk it.

The heads of every covert or overt intelligence outfit in the country knew how powerful he was and of his closeness to the President.

Nyet. It must be some other foreign agency.

Carter had no lack of enemies.

What angered him however, was that his watchers, the

maintenance engineers, hadn't spotted Newspaper Reading Man.

He straightened and punched buttons on his desk phone.

'Vasili,' he barked. 'Where are those men, the ones who were watching Carter?'

New York was eight hours behind Moscow, but the time difference meant nothing to him. He expected his people to take his calls, however inconvenient it was to them.

'In New York, in our embassy,' his case officer replied crisply, as if he was at his desk and not asleep at home.

'Interrogate them again. Find out if they know anything about that man who was shot. And then, terminate them. They got made. We have no use for failures.'

'Da.'

Gorshky ended the call and brooded for several moments.

He had worked hard to get the right surveillance team on Carter.

He'll disappear, now. He'll have tracked those engineers to our embassy.

His fingers involuntarily curled into fists. His eyes fell on the quote framed in his office.

Leave the Devil Alone and He Might Return the Favor.

It was framed in black on thick cream paper and struck fear in first-time visitors, who immediately identified him with the devil.

He recollected the time Carter had entered his office, late at night.

He had been working on a case, with only a skeleton staff around. Even now, he hadn't worked out how the American had beaten his security and gotten inside.

He had gasped when the Agency operative ghosted into his office.

'Don't,' Carter warned him when he reached for his phone. 'I can kill you before anyone gets here.'

Gorshky licked his lips as the American checked out his office.

A thin smile played on Carter's face when he read the quote.

'What if you aren't him?'

'Huh?'

'What if the devil is someone else?'

Gorshky stared at him as he stood there casually, with his hands jammed in his pockets, showing no fear.

Carter left before he could answer, closing the door softly behind him.

He could have killed me. He could have attacked me. The American operative had done neither.

It was only much later that it had come to the SVR head.

He wanted to show me that he can reach me any time. That's why he was in my office.

GORSHKY REACHED for his glass of water and drank it carelessly. The memory faded with the cool trickle down his throat, but his fear didn't.

It intensified when he glanced at his watch and shot to his feet.

He had a meeting with the President—one he wasn't looking forward to.

9

Alexei Gorshky cooled his heels in the marbled hallway in the Kremlin while suited men walked past. A few cast sidelong glances at him, but no one stopped.

Every visitor to the President was made to wait in the corridor. It was a power move by the country's head to show who was in charge. The SVR chief had been to several such meetings, but he still hadn't gotten used to the nerve-wracking wait. He forced himself to stay calm and stared back impassively at the suits.

Kremlin. The name literally meant *fortress inside a city* and was known all over the world as the seat of the Russian government. Inside its brick walls were towers, cathedrals and office buildings, many open to visitors.

The Russian President had his offices all over the city and the country, but the Kremlin was where he attended strategic meetings or had occasion to demonstrate his authority.

'Come.' A uniformed officer approached Gorshky.

Look at him, the SVR chief fumed. *I outrank him but he's behaving as if he doesn't care. He hasn't even greeted me.*

He followed the man silently, however, down the hallway, past several doors until they came to a large one with two guards. He was frisked again, and then the door opened and he entered the President's office.

'Where is she?'

No greetings, no pleasantries, no offers of coffee or other drinks.

Gorshky sat stiffly on the chair in front of the ornate desk and met the eyes of the most powerful man in the country.

'Lubyanka Prison.'

The President's lips twitched in a smile.

'You still use it as that?'

'Da.'

'I like it.'

Lubyanka had been the KGB's headquarters and also housed a prison in which reputed criminals and political dissidents were detained. After the fall of the USSR, the building was occupied by the Federal Secret Service, widely known as the FSB, and Border Control, and the prison had been turned into a museum.

Gorshky, on taking over as SVR chief, had resumed using the building's basement cellars for their original purpose of housing people troublesome to him. Access to the cells was through a discreet entrance, which was heavily guarded. No one questioned the elaborate security, since the building also housed the FSB, the domestic intelligence agency.

Gorshky took great pride in using the building for its original purpose. He housed captives and tortured them right under the feet of visitors, and in the heart of the city.

'She will be safe there.'

It was a statement, not a question.

'Da. She is kept in a separate cell, away from political prisoners. Her guards are vetted and handpicked by my trusted officers. We have cameras on her. Her cell is deep underground. No one will know she is there. She will die in Lubyanka.'

'Nyet.'

The word was uttered harshly.

'She will die only when I say so. Have you touched her?'

He means, have I tortured her.

'I will interrogate her today. We have given her the silent treatment so far, but we need to know what she was going to publish. She said it could change our plans.'

'Nothing will alter those.'

'But, the war—'

'Our plans are going ahead. Continue with her silent treatment. Let her suffer some more, but don't touch her.'

'We need to know what she was going to publish, who her sources were, where her notes are. We found nothing in her apartment or in *The Reality's* offices. Boris Yasimov, its editor, has disappeared. We think he has gone to London—'

'Don't do anything until I say so. You have seen the reaction to her disappearance. People are saying we captured her and have killed Yasimov. There are protests on the street—'

'We can handle them. She has crucial intelligence. If America or Britain get it—'

'Are you questioning me?'

Sweat popped out on Gorshky's forehead, but he didn't wipe it.

'Nyet.' He was glad his voice came out smooth and confident. 'I was merely explaining the urgency.'

'I am aware of that. There are issues I have to deal with. There are some politicians in our own country who are concerned with her disappearance. President Morgan's statement ... I am sure you heard that. But most of all, I want her to suffer some more.'

'Our plans—'

'Are progressing. Don't you follow the news? Haven't you

seen our military might on Ukraine's borders? I trust you to make sure her article is not leaked.'

How can I do that when I can't interrogate her?

Gorshky nodded his head dutifully, however, and when the President opened a file, he got to his feet and left the room quietly.

'Find Yasimov and silence him.'

He nodded at the parting words and, when he was back in his car, swore. He glanced at Lubyanka when they drove past. Elena Zakharova was secure in its cellars. She could wait. He looked contemptuously at the protesters on the street and dialed a number.

'Evgeny,' he commanded another case officer. 'Find out where Yasimov is hiding and send a team.'

10

N*ew York*

MEGHAN RESUMED the briefing when they returned to their office. She outlined logistics.

'We can't go in a group or use our Lear. Gorshky might have more watchers on us. We'll have to split up.'

Zeb was reminded of how briefings were depicted in old-school movies. Dark rooms, a bunch of people crowded underneath a ceiling light that threw shadows on the wall, a flipboard in a corner ... there was nothing old-school about their office or its occupants. A ray of sunshine snuck through the windows and lit Meghan's hair as she walked them through their plans using a wall projector.

He flipped the cover on his tablet computer as his mind drifted to the incident on the street.

'Zeb?'

He looked up at Beth.

'You're not with us.'

'Why did the shooter kill that watcher? Why didn't he take out the maintenance engineers?'

'They left immediately,' Bwana offered, 'as soon as Bear and I made them.'

'Or,' Chloe added, 'he didn't have a line of fire.'

'You don't believe that?' Meghan read his mind.

'He was a pro. Shooting from a van, with moving traffic around him ... that takes skill and nerves. If the engineers were a target, he would have taken them out.'

The elder twin snapped her fingers. 'You think Newspaper Man wasn't SVR.'

'We have to consider it. That someone else was watching us.'

They debated it for several moments, until Beth thumped her table with the flat of her palm.

'This is getting us nowhere. Moscow is our priority. We don't have much time. Gear up.'

THEY FLEW COMMERCIAL.

Zeb, the twins and Broker on one flight, seated apart. He and Broker were traveling as entrepreneurs with investments in Russia; the sisters were tourists, a believable cover since the flow of visitors to Russia hadn't stopped despite the threat of war.

Chloe and Roger took another flight, while Bear and Bwana joined two separate tour groups. 'You both are too noticeable,' the elder twin had said, smirking. 'Gorshky's watchers at JFK will identify you easily. You can blend in with a bunch of tourists, however.'

Zeb grinned at the disguises his friends had come up with. Bear had dyed his hair with a streak of pink and shaved his beard. Bwana had turned to bling. Rings in his ears and on his fingers. A flashy necklace around his neck, a loud Tee and a swagger to his walk.

The changes weren't only superficial, however. They had altered their appearance with sophisticated disguises that researchers at DARPA and NSA had come up with. The prosthetic noses, ears, eyebrows and other facial parts were embedded with chips and emitters that negated infrared waves from smart phones, blurred the distance between nodes and fooled even the most advanced algorithms.

'You think these will work?' Broker scratched his cheek, which bulged from a pad.

'Beth and Meghan greenlighted them.' Zeb shrugged. 'That's good enough for me.'

'They project facial features that are invisible to our eyes, which the cameras pick up on ...' Beth's lips curled up scornfully. 'I could go into the tech, but that would be beyond your IQs.'

'Kids these days,' the elder operative grumbled. 'They have no respect. I taught you and Meg—'

'What you knew. Which was a low base.' She smirked.

'These aren't perfect,' her sister said seriously, looking nothing like her twin. 'We need to combine them with full-face masks when we go hot.'

'Makes sense,' Zeb nodded.

'Will we take Andropov's help?' Meghan drawled in his earpiece.

Grigor Andropov, head of a covert Russian outfit, similar to the Agency. Zeb's friend. The two men maintained a backchannel despite their countries' increasingly hostile stance.

'No.' He scanned the rows ahead of him and spotted her and Beth's gold-brown hair over their headrests. 'It would be a conflict of interest for him.'

'He hates Gorshky,' Beth chimed in. 'And dislikes SVR.'

'Yeah, but we can't ask him to get involved.'

He has the best network of all the Russian agencies. We still might have to go to him if things go hot.

'What?' Meghan asked when he kept quiet.

'Remember China?'

'Yeah, what of it?'

'That was our toughest mission.'

'We know.'

'This will be many times more difficult, and we are going in without a plan.'

'Tell us something we don't know,' Beth scoffed.

'You can opt out. There's still time.'

It was how they worked. Every operative could choose to sit out any mission. No explanations were needed or expected; no judgments were made.

'In your dreams,' Meghan said scornfully.

Moscow

NINE AND A HALF HOURS LATER, into the next day, they landed in Sheremetyevo International Airport, going into operator mode the moment they walked into the concourse.

Heads down, ball caps tight and low to conceal as much of their faces as possible. *It may not fool the cameras, but Gorshky will not be expecting us in Moscow.*

The twins had come up with the decoys several years ago. Body doubles, people whose faces closely resembled the Agency operatives'. Over time, they had settled on a bunch of actors who were paid well to impersonate them at airport terminals and on flights.

Meg sent them to Taiwan. Eight actors, taking individual flights from JFK. The individuals spread themselves in the concourse, making a show of browsing in the stores, *accidentally* exposing their faces to the cameras.

JFK has watchers from several agencies who will spot them. Zeb was confident the sighting would get back to Gorshky. *He will believe we went there.* With China's saber-rattling over Taiwan, it was highly credible that the Agency team would have a mission in that country.

'I'm feeling naked,' Bwana muttered in their earpieces.

Zeb knew what his friend meant. *We are in hostile country, with no weapons and no backup.*

MOSCOW WORKED ON A RING-ROAD SYSTEM. Boulevard Ring was the innermost ring, shaped like a horseshoe, with the Moscow River on the south. It defined the city's center, with the Kremlin, Red Square and many other attractions lying within. It was popular with tourists since it afforded easy access to tourist spots and to the city's famed Metro.

The city was divided into administrative regions, *okrugs*, within which were several districts, all of them organized around the ring roads.

Beth had booked hotels in the Tverskaya neighborhood, right at the heart of the city. Zeb, the twins and Broker in one, Bear and Chloe in another, and Bwana and Roger in a third.

Tourists to the city chose hotels based on location and cost. She had identified theirs based on the ease of hacking into their security system.

She and Meg will make sure their cameras don't store our images.

THEY GATHERED in four coffee shops after a couple of hours of rest.

'I feel naked,' Bwana repeated.

'We heard you the first time,' Chloe groaned. 'Zeb, we're—'

'Basmanny District.'

'What's there?'

'Bwana will feel less naked.'

He put on his shades and adjusted the frame. The lenses lit up with a rear view, projected by nano-cameras drilled into their stems. Beth and Meghan, arm-in-arm with Broker, several feet behind him, and in the distance, far behind, he could see Bear's towering presence.

Zeb went to the Mayakovskaya Metro Station, marveling at the steel and pink columns and the ceiling mosaics. The Zamoskvoretskaya Line, a change at Teatralnaya and the Ploschad Revolyutsii line to Baumanskaya in Basmanny District, in six minutes.

'We could have walked,' Broker grouched when they emerged on the surface.

'Yeah,' Beth retorted before he could reply, 'but in the Metro and in the stations, we could check out if we were being tailed. See this crowd out here? We wouldn't know who was shadowing us.'

Zeb led them to a fast-food joint and joined a line of customers. He gave his order and stood to the side while the server attended to other customers. The manager hustled over and shook his head apologetically.

'Sorry sir, we don't have your drink in stock.'

'I ordered milk.'

'Strawberry flavored. We have run out of it. If you had pre-ordered it—'

'Are you telling me—' He raised his voice, at which the manager took his arm.

'Let's discuss this in my office.'

'You want to discuss milk in your office?'

He went with the manager nevertheless, with his bemused

team following him discreetly. They gawked when the store official shut the door to his large office and wrapped his arms around Zeb in a tight hug.

'Meet Josiah Zahavy,' he said, introducing the manager to his team. 'The best fast-food franchise owner in Moscow. Also, the best Mossad agent in Russia.'

'In the world.' The Israeli grinned.

'Carmen and Dalia will have something to say about that,' Beth said, chuckling, referring to two of their Mossad friends. She side-eyed Zeb. 'Now I understand why you got us to remove our disguises. So that he could recognize us.'

'Yeah.'

'I'm better than Carmen or Dalia, but don't tell them I said that.' Zahavy's smile grew larger. He shook hands with the operatives and winked at the twins. 'I have heard about you. I have taken care of the cameras. Your presence will not be recorded in our system. Now,' he said, turning to Zeb, 'your milk! I have cartons of it.'

He opened a rear door and took them to the warehouse, where he operated a forklift and brought out a crate of milk containers.

He ripped open the covering plastic, removed the first layer of cartons, and gestured *voila* with his hands as he stepped back.

Bwana and Bear opened the wooden crate beneath and whistled in surprise at its contents.

HK416s, Glocks, M4s, ammo boxes, magazines, lightweight, low-profile body armor, knives, grenades, drones—the case had everything they needed.

'Is that a Barrett?' Broker asked, awestruck.

'Not just a Barrett, it's the MK22.' Roger grunted as he lifted it. 'And beneath it is an Accuracy International.'

Bear extracted the second rifle, often considered the best

sniping weapon in the world, then thrust his hand into the crate and brought out a box of 338 Lapua Magnum cartridges.

Zeb stepped back to make way for Meghan, who took the Accuracy, stripped it expertly, put it back, broke it down again and arranged it in its case.

Bwana, Broker and I were the best long-range snipers for a while.

And then the twins had joined their team and the elder sister had taken to shooting like a duck to water, and had easily beaten them.

She would win shooting competitions easily if she ever tried it.

'I can arrange a workshop for you if you want to make your own loads,' Zahavy suggested.

'No.' Zeb shook his head. *Making loads is time-consuming. We will need a shooting range and all that leaves its own trail.*

'We'll use factory stock.'

'You have all this, in Moscow, under the Russians' noses?' Chloe brushed back a tendril of hair.

'What can I say?' Zahavy tried to shrug modestly and failed. 'Mossad. We are the best.'

11

'You're sure about that?' Gorshky asked.

'Da. Our man watched them board flights to Taiwan. They split up, flew with different carriers, and even when they were on the concourse, were spread out.'

The SVR chief nodded unconsciously. He knew good tradecraft when he came across it.

'Get him to stay at JFK. It might be a decoy move. They might return.'

'Da.'

Gorshky hung up and doodled idly on his blotter. *Why isn't Carter in Moscow? Why isn't he trying to stop our invasion?*

The answer came to him instantly.

His agency doesn't take on that kind of mission.

That's why he's in Taiwan. What's he there for, though? He didn't have assets in that country; otherwise he would have deployed them to check the Americans' presence.

It doesn't matter, he thought, mentally shrugging. Taiwan was of no interest to him. *He's not headed here; that's what's important.*

It was as if a weight was lifted off his back.

'Get me Evgeny,' he ordered his aide.

'You said Yasimov fled to London,' he began when his case officer entered his office. 'How do you know? Show me the proof.'

His subordinate placed his laptop on the polished desk and angled its screen towards his boss. He punched keys and brought up a set of images.

'That's him,' he said when a man's profile came up, 'at Sheremetyevo. The same evening that we raided his press.'

Gorshky reached over and scrolled through the rest of the images. 'All of them are side profiles or from the rear. Who took them?'

'One of our agents.'

'Have you found out where he is in London?'

'We didn't have anyone in Heathrow when his flight landed. I am working on tracing his movements.'

Gorshky leaned back in his swivel chair and steepled his fingers. 'Yasimov is smart,' he thought aloud. 'He shook our men easily when we were tailing him. He disappeared whenever he wanted to. Both he and Zakharova have a large network of supporters in this country. Find him in London, but also question all his associates in Moscow. He might be hiding here.'

'Those pictures—'

'Could be someone who looks like him. You don't have frontal images.'

Evgeny nodded and left the office silently.

Could Carter have duped us?

'Vasili, did our man see the Americans up close?' he said when he called his New York man.

'Da. He and that man, Broker, were in the same coffee shop. Our agent got close to Carter, and the others too. I have photographs.'

'Send them—'

'Done.'

The SVR head opened the encrypted folder and flicked through the images quickly. They had been taken from a distance, but there was no mistaking Carter and his team.

'Great work,' he complimented his man. 'Did you interrogate those failures?'

'Da. I got nothing from them. They didn't see that Newspaper Man. NYPD hasn't identified him yet. The shooter is out there, too.'

'Kill them.'

'Done. Their bodies are in the concrete foundation of a building in Harlem.'

Gorshky smiled thinly and cut the call. SVR was built on the backs of men like Vasili.

YASIMOV SIPPED his coffee and watched the TV news. He turned when Igor entered the small living room and hugged him briefly.

'Don't go out,' his friend told him as he pocketed his car keys and shouldered his backpack. 'There is enough food in the kitchen. I will be late. I will use our usual code before I enter.'

'You are risking your life for me.'

'Nonsense. You and I grew up together. If I didn't help you, who would. See that?' He pointed to the TV, which was showing protests in front of the Kremlin. 'Those people are not just against the military buildup on the border. They are there for you and Elena as well. You have huge support in this country.' His face turned bleak. 'Where is she? Did you hear anything?'

'Nyet,' Yasimov said bitterly. 'I am sure she is in some cell somewhere, being tortured. SVR might even have killed her by now.'

'You know it was them who took her?'

'SVR, FSB, GRU ... how does it matter? They are all the

same. Da. I am sure. I have enough contacts. The men who took her were GUVD, but they were acting on SVR orders.'

'What about her article? You can publish it, can't you?'

'Nyet.' His shoulders slumped. 'Elena kept everything close to her chest. She told me she had proof of what the President's plans were for neighboring countries—'

'He plans to invade them and start another Cold War. Everyone knows that.'

'Everyone is *speculating* about that,' the editor corrected his friend. 'Elena had evidence, and now she's gone.'

'She is smart. She must have hidden her notes somewhere.'

'She did. She told me they were somewhere no one would ever think of. But if she is being tortured—'

'Don't think of it.' Igor squeezed his shoulder. 'There is nothing you can do. But you have to stay safe and keep *The Reality* running. If you shut it down and they capture you, too ... then those people'—he pointed at the TV—'they will have lost hope.'

Yasimov watched the broadcast for several moments when his friend left for work. He sighed and went to the kitchen to wash the dishes.

I can't stay here and put Igor at risk.

His initial plan had been to flee to London, where he had a support network. His allies in that country would hide him. He had rushed to Sheremetyevo, using what little tradecraft he had. A long overcoat with the collar pulled high, even though it was summer. Shades and a hat, and his head bent toward the floor.

He had spotted the SVR man when he was purchasing his ticket. He froze, expecting to be arrested, but when no goons appeared, the pounding in his chest subsided. Identifying his tail hadn't been difficult. Over time, he and Elena had built a dossier of Russian intelligence agents, and they had thick files on the leaders of each outfit. They focused their attention on Gorshky in particular, since he had harassed them the most.

He hadn't spotted any other operative in the airport. He thought rapidly, made a discreet call and executed his plan.

He carried on as if he was boarding the flight. He cleared the security check, but while he was on the boarding ramp, ducked suddenly and went down a baggage chute, where a supporter was waiting. He was bundled into a cargo van and delivered outside the airport.

He didn't know for sure if his ruse had worked and that Gorshky believed he was in London.

He had stayed with friends and supporters ever since his escape from the airport, staying a night or two at each apartment before moving to the next one, late at night, heavily disguised.

None of his friends had been harassed, which made him believe Gorshky indeed thought he was in Britain.

Igor's place was where he had stayed the longest, because of their childhood bond.

I'll go today, he made his mind up instantly. *I can't put him in more danger. There is one place in Moscow neither GUVD nor SVR will ever think of.*

12

'Two vans.' Zahavy pointed to the dark vehicles parked in loading bays, bearing the logo of the fast-food chain on their sides. He handed over the key fobs and reached inside his jacket to retrieve a wad of papers. 'And these are your new identities. All of you are delivery people for this company. The vehicles are registered to the company's address. Any calls to—'

'That's a well-known firm.' Chloe frowned.

'It is.' The Mossad agent nodded. 'And there will be real employees answering the phone who will back up your credentials.'

'I don't understand.' Beth frowned, too.

'Mossad owns the company.'

'WHAT?'

He chuckled at her outburst. 'Yes, we have several such investments in Moscow. Not just in Russia, but around the world.'

'Every employee is a Mossad agent?' Bear asked incredulously.

'No, only a handful. The food chain is a legitimate business and it gives us great cover. Like I said'—he winked—'we are Mossad. We are the best.'

Zeb hugged him and tossed a key to Roger, who caught it deftly. They moved the weapons to the vans, where Zahavy had a couple more surprises for them.

'See these logos? You can peel them off like this.' He demonstrated by removing one poster. 'The sidewalls of the vans are hollow. There are several fake signs and number plates in each of the vehicles. You can keep changing their appearance. There are coveralls, too, for each of you, in various combinations. He thumped the floorboard. 'And this is a false bottom. Lift it like this, and you have enough space for your weapons.'

Bwana looked at the van and then at him. He crossed his arms and said, wooden-faced, 'Do you have our target captured somewhere? That's all that's left.'

Zahavy's smile was like sunlight. 'I can't help you there. Who is your target? Aren't you here to stop the war?'

'Nice try,' Zeb grunted and began stowing the weapons in the vehicles.

He hugged the Mossad agent again when they had finished and got in behind the wheel.

'You could have told us about Zahavy and the weapons.' Beth punched him in the shoulder.

'What would be the fun in that?'

He checked his rearview mirror and nodded to himself when the second van came into view with Bear at the wheel.

'Broker,' he called out to his friend, who was in the back of his van with the weapons, 'how are you doing?'

'Comfy seat, snacks, and enough weapons to start a war. Can't complain. Where are we going?'

'To check out Elena's apartment.'

13

Ramenki was off the Third Ring Road and inside the MKAD, the Moscow Automobile Ring Road that marked the outer perimeter of the city. The neighborhood was predominantly a residential district, with tall apartment buildings, a few Metro stops and several stores.

It was dark by the time they reached the neighborhood, and traffic was dwindling by the time they got to Michurinskiy Prospekt.

'There.' Beth nudged Zeb. 'On our left. That's her building.'

Zeb snatched a glance and kept driving, textbook style. Sticking to the speed limit, using blinkers to warn of lane changes, leaving sufficient braking distance. There was no way they were going to risk drawing attention with rash driving.

The Prospekt had two-way traffic separated by central markings, but as they progressed, the road broadened to have a divider in the middle.

He turned at the lights, headed back and completed a U-turn to come up to her building.

'See those stores over there, to the left of the building?' Meghan murmured from behind, indicating a line of shops like a strip mall. 'There are parking spaces. There seems to be an approach road to the building over there.'

Zeb drove to the lot, backed his van into a space and checked out their surroundings.

Elena Zakharova's building was on top of a small hillock, with trees around it. There were no other residential buildings around it. The approach road they had come up had an offshoot to the parking lot as well.

Bear's van backed up into a bay parallel to theirs, his headlights illuminating a mom who came out of a store with her shopping.

They watched her load her purchases into her car while her small daughter stared at the vans with her thumb in her mouth. Bear waggled his fingers at the young girl, who smiled and skipped to the car and disappeared inside.

'Pretend I'm dumb,' Roger mused aloud when the mother's car went down the approach road and joined Michurinskiy, leaving only their vans in the parking lot.

'You are,' Chloe snorted.

'Why are we here?' the Texan continued, ignoring the jibe.

Zeb could almost feel the petite operator roll her eyes.

'Shall I tell him?' she asked.

'Be our guest,' Meghan told her.

'It's like this, Roger,' Chloe enunciated slowly and clearly, as if explaining to a child. 'We know where Gorshky's offices are. We also know where his main residence is, but we can't take him at those locations. There will be heavy security. We know very little of his routine and have zilch on where he hangs out. Does he go to a gym? A massage parlor? Does he have a mistress? He's supposed to be single, but is that really the case? You get the picture? To get at him, we need more intel.'

'And checking out Elena's residence will help us out, how?'

'Jeez,' Beth said scornfully, 'hanging out with us hasn't

helped your grey cells, has it? Elena and Yasimov will have information on him. You can count on it.'

'She isn't here, however, and you can bet Gorshky's thugs have emptied her apartment.'

'We know.' Bwana's voice was a low rumble in the night. 'Still, it's worth searching again to see if she left any files here. We'll also go to *The Reality's* press and check it out.'

'Oh.' Roger paused for a moment. 'I knew all that. I was making sure we were all on the same page.'

Rude noises drowned him out.

Zeb grinned in the dark when he met Meghan's eyes in the mirror. They all knew Roger's dumb act was just that. *He does this frequently. It's his way of confirming our assumptions haven't changed.*

His van shook when the twins, kitted out in coveralls, jumped out and climbed into the rear.

'Bird is in the air,' Beth announced in their earpieces.

Zeb glanced up casually but couldn't spot the drone. He had been specific in his requirement to Avichai Levin, Mossad's director, who hadn't blinked.

'We have those kinds of drones too,' he'd pointed out.

Stealth-painted, with nano-cell camouflage that altered its appearance to blend in with the background, radar, Lidar, night vision, high-definition, and a cell tower, the UAV was specced to a level that wasn't available commercially.

'We have eyes on her apartment,' Beth said, interrupting his musing. 'Seventh floor. No lights from within. Windows to the street and the sides.'

'Apartment seems to be laid out linearly,' Meghan took over. 'Living room, bedroom and kitchen. Bathroom seems to be opposite the bedroom. No outside windows to it. The first two rooms have windows that overlook the yard. She could see the strip mall from there. Kitchen window overlooks the approach road. Parking spaces around the building, with most of them in the front yard.'

Zeb tuned out when he sensed movement in the second van. Roger climbed out, stretched and yawned.

'Where are you going?' he asked when the Texan headed to the line of stores.

'Pizza,' his friend answered. 'I'm hungry.'

Zeb watched him enter the food joint and flash a smile at the takeout clerk.

Smart. He'll engage them in casual conversation and see what comes up.

'SHE'S all they're talking about, by the sounds of it,' he briefed them on his return. 'I said it seemed to be a quiet neighborhood, and the checkout clerk couldn't stop talking.'

'Shall we break into her apartment?' Beth asked him.

'No, we'll return in the morning.'

Daylight will help in dealing with the heavies.

14

They returned the next day after ten am, when the office rush and school runs had ended. Their vans wore new logos and plates.

A first pass on Michurisnkiy didn't arouse any suspicion. No police cars in the parking lot or uniformed officers visible anywhere. A couple of vehicles in front of the stores.

The scene remained unchanged during their second pass, and on their third, he led them to the stores.

Zeb zipped his sleek black coveralls up tight, adjusted his cap over his head, donned shades and climbed out. He was up the hill when he heard his friends follow. He adjusted his lenses and took them in. All of them were similarly attired, the suits flattening the women's curves, their hair pulled back and hidden underneath their caps or collars, to further disguise their gender.

He drew his palm up his chest casually to feel the HK's shape underneath the coveralls and the Glock strapped in his shoulder holster.

'Clear,' he announced when he entered the building's parking lot and scanned the empty vehicles.

He heard the whisper of the drone as it flew over him and inside the entrance.

'One camera,' Beth announced. 'Fried,' she announced a moment later, when the UAV's targeted EMP blast took it out.

That's a low-intensity ray. It wouldn't affect any electronic devices beyond a couple of feet. Their comms and the residents' phones were safe. The drone itself was designed to be immune from its EMP gun.

Zeb removed his shades and drew a mask over his head when he entered the building's lobby, which was small and led to four elevators on each side of the small concrete walkway. He followed the UAV as it flew up the flight of stairs, then heard his team come up the stairs, with Beth or Meghan sounding out *Clear* in their earpieces.

'Camera,' the younger twin warned them, 'on Elena's door. Taken care of.'

'Did—'

'Nope, it didn't see our drone. I fired a precautionary blast, higher intensity, before our bird came into view.'

Smart!

Each floor had four apartments, with the journalist's being the furthest from the stairs. No noise from the other residences.

Empty? Broker mouthed.

Zeb shrugged. It didn't matter. If any door opened, they would show their weapons to send the resident back.

He bent to the reporter's door and pointed to the GUVD seal on it. Bwana made a scoffing sound, ripped it away and picked the new lock that had been installed. The wood around it showed the door had been broken and repaired crudely.

Zeb was pushing the door open to enter the apartment when Meghan tugged his arm and pointed at the small bunch of flowers thrust under the door. A card attached to them with a hand-shaped heart drawn on it. No other writing.

'She's got fans in this building,' Beth murmured.

He nodded, picked up the flowers and stepped inside.

A small living room, a couch, a dining table with three chairs. All of them destroyed, with wood splinters, newspapers and magazines scattered on the floor. The TV was shattered, its remote crushed.

The destruction was repeated in the small bedroom, kitchen and bathroom.

'Ceiling, too.' Bear pointed at the ripped-out lights and cables and loose false-ceiling boards.

'Search,' he told his friends and started with the living room.

An hour later, they gathered in the bedroom and shook their heads collectively.

'If Elena had hidden anything here,' Meghan declared, 'it's no longer there.'

Zeb nodded, absentmindedly. He was aware of the clock ticking. That camera over her door would have been installed by either the cops or SVR. They'd note the feed was down. Calls would be made. There would be some jawing on whether the camera died naturally or had been tampered with. *It could have spotted the drone, too.*

He snapped his fingers, signaling them to depart as stealthily as they had arrived.

The thugs arrived half an hour later.

15

Zeb and his team were back in their vans. He was on his phone, pretending to be on a call, when the first vehicle roared up the approach road.

He spotted a driver, a passenger, a couple more shadows in the back before it went out of sight. Another dark car raced up, and then a third.

'Twelve or fifteen men,' Bear said laconically, 'depending on how jammed in they were.'

Eight of us.

'I'll stay back,' Broker suggested. 'To keep an eye on other arrivals.'

Seven.

Zeb couldn't help grinning at Bwana's hungry look.

'We'll try to take them alive.'

'Sure,' the black operative growled, 'after we break some bones.'

A shopper emerged from one of the stores, seemed to sense something about them, perhaps the sense of menace, then hurried to his car and drove away.

Zeb sprinted up the approach road, and when he reached the building's parking lot, he pulled on his mask.

'Russian, no more English,' Beth reminded them.

'Da,' Chloe replied. Every one of them spoke the language like a local citizen.

The lobby was empty.

Zeb went up the stairs cautiously, his Vibram-soled boots gripping each step firmly. He smelled it first, sweat and cologne and the faint odor of cigarettes. He gestured to his team, crouched low and snatched a glance.

A goon was on the third-floor landing, in a dark combat suit with an AK74 cradled casually in his hands. He straightened. His mouth opened to yell a warning, and then Zeb was on him, ramming him with his shoulder, flipping up and away with his right hand, jamming his left hand against the thug's mouth and smashing his head against the concrete wall.

'How many men?' he grated.

The guard struggled, but his efforts were weak, his eyes dulling from the impact of the head blow.

'How many?' Zeb repeated and cursed when the man slumped.

He flexi-cuffed him swiftly, gagged him and shoved his body down the stairs.

The next landing was clear. No one else until he came to the seventh floor, where two guards turned at his sudden arrival and raised their weapons—but before they could fire, his knife buried itself in one man's throat and another blade, from behind, sank into the second man's chest.

Beth lunged up with him to catch the falling men, who struggled and kicked out but, with the combined weight of the operatives, were subdued.

Zeb stiffened when a man called out from inside. He went to the door's edge and unholstered his Glock.

Beth joined him. Meghan behind her, while the rest of the crew crouched on the stairs to provide covering fire.

'Ivan,' the voice called irritatedly. Footsteps crunched and boots came into view.

Zeb was on him in a flash, slapping his AK74 away, whirling him to face the inside of the apartment, his Glock coming up to jam against the man's temple.

He shoved the man inside the residence, using him as a shield.

'Shoot,' he told the two other thugs in the living room, 'if you want him to die.'

More armed men emerged from inside the apartment, drawn by the sounds of the scuffle and the low voices.

Nine, Zeb counted, *including my prisoner.*

He felt his friends spread out behind him.

'Drop your weapons,' Zeb commanded.

His captive twisted and gasped when the arm against his throat tightened.

'Do you know who we are?' he wheezed. 'You drop *your* guns and surrender. We will go easy on you.'

One of the armed men laughed at that. 'We can kill—'

'I won't warn you again,' Zeb began when Beth hissed.

He sensed a ripple of shock in his friends. The eyes of the thugs facing him widened.

He risked a look behind him and swore inwardly at the sight.

Boris Yasimov stood in the doorway, gawking at the scene.

16

Zeb didn't need to shout out orders. His team reacted like the well-oiled machine they were, each knowing exactly how the others would respond.

Chloe hurled herself backwards at Yasimov, crashing into him, taking him out of the firing zone and into the hallway.

Zeb shoved his prisoner at the thugs and dove to the floor, his Glock triggering, bucking in his hand, the chattering of his friends' HKs filling the room with gunsmoke and death. The shooters fired back. They tried to escape, but they were trapped in the close confines of the living room.

'Injuries?' Zeb snapped when the guns had gone silent.

'I'm good,' Roger drawled.

'Me too,' Bwana replied.

Everyone checked in safe.

He crouch-walked cautiously, covered by the operatives, and checked out the fallen men. One of them moaned and shuddered and went still. None of the others were alive. Head and body shots from his team had neutralized them.

He checked out the rest of the apartment, confirmed that

there weren't any more shooters hiding, and returned to the living room.

'You've been hit,' Meghan observed.

Zeb felt his forehead and inspected his fingers when they came away wet. Beth caught his face, traced the wound and looked down at the floor. She pointed at a concrete chip that had a red edge.

'That one must have hit you.'

Zeb nodded. *It's not serious.*

He looked at the fallen bodies and then at his friends.

'We were faster,' Bear said, reading his thoughts.

'Da,' Bwana replied in Russian. 'They were overconfident, expecting us to surrender. They didn't think we would drop to the floor.'

Still, that was a close call.

Chloe came to the door with Yasimov, who stared at the carnage and turned pale. The editor trembled visibly and raised his eyes to meet Zeb's.

'Who are you? What happened—'

'Not here. Not now.'

He went out of the apartment and checked the guards who had been knifed. Both were dead. He signaled to his friends to follow him and went down the stairs cautiously.

He frowned at the lack of sounds from any of the apartments. *None of the doors have opened. Surely, they can't all be empty.* The explanation came to him moments later. *They are scared. They know Elena was captured. They don't want to get involved.*

He stopped on a lower landing and turned to his team.

'Can we lock her apartment and put back that police seal?'

Meghan instantly guessed where he was going with his question.

'You want to make it look like no one entered it?'

'Yes.'

'We came prepared for every eventuality.' Beth grinned and extracted a roll of GUVD tape from her backpack. 'We'll have to clean up, though. What about that dude on the lower landing?'

Bwana trotted down to inspect and returned moments later. 'Dead.'

'Dead? Did you—'

'I didn't,' he replied indignantly. 'His neck was broken. He must have landed awkwardly when I pushed him down the stairs. I cut his cuffs.' He held them up in the air. 'No need to leave any clues for Gorshky.'

Zeb nodded. *We could have questioned that guard, but it is what it is.*

They returned to the journalist's apartment, carried out the bodies and dumped them in the lobby.

'Yasimov.' Zeb went to the editor, who had been following and watching them in shocked silence. 'Stay here. Warn us if you see anyone coming up the road. If any residents come out and ask you questions, don't reply.'

The editor swallowed. Color returned to his face. 'Who are you?'

His thinning hair was matted to his head with sweat. His glasses kept sliding down his nose from perspiration, but his eyes had regained their sharpness. His dark shirt hung loose over his jeans, and one hand clutched a small carry bag.

'Later. Can you do what I asked?'

'Da.' He nodded nervously.

'Use this to call me.' Zeb gave him a phone. 'There's only one number on it.'

He and this team returned to the apartment and, using Elena's cleaning liquids and detergents, wiped away all signs of the firefight.

All of us are fully suited and gloved. Any fibers we leave behind will be untraceable.

He knelt at the door when they had all emerged and pulled the door shut. *Looks like an average lock*. He brought out a bump key, inserted it into the slot and tried it.

It worked.

'Move over,' Beth told him. She crouched in his place and applied the police tape expertly over the lock.

'What about the camera?'

'Leave it. They know it's damaged already.' She hid a nano-camera in the ceiling light in the landing and grunted in acknowledgment when she got its feed on her screen.

'Who are you?' Yasimov began again when they joined him in the lobby and watched the twins mount a couple more cameras on its ceiling.

'We'll answer your questions, but not right now. We need to leave.'

'Why?'

'Because more men will be coming.'

17

They removed their masks, broke into smaller groups and left the building.

'Some guard you are,' Beth complained to Broker when they arrived at Zeb's van. 'You didn't warn us Yasimov was coming.' She briefed him quickly on the shootout.

'Yasimov?' the elder operative asked, startled. He climbed out of the rear and took in the editor. 'Where ... how ... he didn't come up the approach road.'

Yasimov blinked when all eyes turned on him. 'There's a path over the rise,' he said, pointing toward the trees behind the building. 'I don't think anyone uses it. It's very rough and uneven, with broken branches and logs in the way. Elena and I discovered it some time ago and used it whenever we had to approach her building secretly.'

'Inside,' Zeb ordered and helped him climb into the rear and join Broker. He got behind the wheel, nodded at Bear in the second vehicle, and drove away.

They went far enough to find a deserted road where they switched plates, logos and coveralls, and Zeb drove back to the parking lot while Bear parked his van in a pull-off on Michurinskiy.

They waited.

Meghan who was beside him in the front, sat with a screen in front of her. Beth was in the bench seat behind them, while Broker was with Yasimov, sharing another screen.

The black car raced up forty minutes later. Three men climbed out, casually dressed but hard-faced, eyes alert, their hands close to their waists.

'Yasimov?' Zeb prompted the editor. 'Are those men residents?'

'Nyet,' he whispered. 'I recognize all of them.'

'Who are they?'

'Gorshky's bodyguards. That's Alexei Gorsh–'

'We know who he is.'

'Dmitri Ruslan, he's the one in the middle. The other two are Karel Golubev and Shulga Nikitin.'

Zeb observed Ruslan closely as he led the way to the lobby. *He's an experienced operative.* It showed in the way the man's eyes moved ceaselessly, the hidden cameras capturing his face in high definition.

He sprang back suddenly, gesticulated furiously and turned to his men.

'They found the bodies,' Roger commented. 'These cameras don't have audio?'

'Nope. Those wouldn't have fit in the lights.'

The men disappeared out of view and reappeared on Elena's floor. Nikitin crouched at the door and inspected the lock. He shook his head as if to say it hadn't been tampered with. He got to his feet and yanked down the camera over the door, giving it to Ruslan, who pocketed it.

Nikitin produced a key and inserted it into the lock while Ruslan and Golubev stood at each side of the door, guns in their hands.

Nikitin opened the door and dove in. He called out, after which the two men entered.

The three men emerged half an hour later, locked the door, reapplied the tape and knocked on neighboring doors. Only one opened, to the right. They saw a woman's silhouette briefly, and then the men crowded in and shut the door behind them.

They emerged several minutes later, went to the lobby, jawed and hung around until a police van appeared.

That woman must have said she saw or heard nothing; otherwise Ruslan would have called for his team and not the cops.

'Talk,' Zeb told Yasimov, who had been outfitted with an earpiece and collar-mic. 'Why did you come to Elena's apartment?'

'You first.' The editor had found his courage. 'You call her Elena. Do you know her? Who are you? You can't be GRU, FSB or SVR. Which agency are you from?'

'That isn't important—'

'You want information from me but you won't identify yourself?'

'Correct. We could have given you up to those shooters. We didn't have to save you. That should tell you something.'

The editor fell silent for a moment. 'Are you here to rescue her? You know who Gorshky is.'

'All you need to know is we are allies.'

Will that be enough to make him trust us?

'Elena and I last spoke a week before she was captured,' Yasimov thought aloud. 'She said she knew some Americans who could help her. But you aren't them. The way you speak Russian, you must be local.'

'Boris Yasimov,' Chloe burst out impatiently, 'you will never guess who we are. Don't get fooled by our appearances. We removed our masks, but this isn't how we really look. We might be able to help Elena, but for that you have to help us, and every minute you waste is one less for her. She might be getting tortured even as we speak.'

'I came to hide in her apartment. I thought it would be safe there. I didn't expect those killers there. When did they get there? If you hadn't been there, they would have captured me.'

The words spilled out of him as though a dam had broken. Zeb listened with one eye on the screen, on which he could see police knocking on residents' doors. Ruslan stood in the lobby, giving instructions, speaking into his cell phone, not making any attempt to hide that he was in charge despite the cops' presence.

'What about her article?' he asked when Yasimov drew a breath. 'Do you have it? Will you be publishing it?'

'Nyet! I wish I had it. But Elena never sent me even a draft copy. Only she knows where it is, and maybe Gorshky does too by now.'

'He doesn't.'

'How can you be so sure?'

'Look at those bodies. Would he have sent those men or Ruslan if Elena had confessed everything? She's still alive.'

'Do you know where she could have hidden her notes?'

'Nyet.'

'Do you know what she was going to publish?' Chloe sighed.

'The invasion—'

'Da, but the whole world is already speculating about that. Why would Gorshky or your President bother about it? They could deny the article once it was published.'

'I trust Elena,' the editor said stubbornly. 'If she said it was going to be explosive and world-changing, it would be.'

'She said that?' Zeb sat up straighter. 'World changing?'

'Her exact words.'

There is more to her article, in that case, than just Ukraine.

The police van departed. Ruslan gestured at his flunkies, who hotfooted to the line of stores and went inside.

To question the managers and customers.

They emerged several minutes later, looked briefly at their vans and went up the road to join Ruslan.

'Why didn't they interrogate us?' Beth wondered aloud.

'The shopkeepers must have told them we arrived a few minutes ago,' her sister replied. 'They might have noted our previous number plates—'

'I'll warn Zahavy to expect a call or visitors.'

Zeb watched Ruslan jam his hands in his pockets as his men briefed him. The SVR man nodded at their vehicle, at which they climbed inside and drove away.

'Yasimov,' he called out to the editor. 'How close is Ruslan to Gorshky?'

'Please call me Boris. Dmitri Ruslan is not just his bodyguard; he's also the team lead for the security team.'

Gorshky must have gotten him to capture Elena.

A plan began to form in his mind.

'How much do you know of the protection detail?'

18

'WHY DIDN'T ANYONE TELL ME THE MOMENT IT HAPPENED? Gorshky roared.

Dmitri Ruslan didn't move a muscle. He stood impassively, with his hands clasped behind his back. The SVR chief's aide flinched.

'I myself didn't know—'

'I AM NOT TALKING TO YOU.'

'I was alerted when the camera on Zakharova's door failed,' Ruslan began. 'I figured it was some mechanical problem, but I sent some men just to be sure. I went out myself when they didn't respond and found their bodies.'

Gorshky paced the room as his bodyguard narrated the events.

'No one saw anything?'

'Nyet. We questioned the neighbors. Only one apartment was occupied at that time. A mother and her baby. She said she heard the shooting but was scared to go out and investigate. She didn't even look through the peephole.'

'She could be lying.'

'We slapped her several times. We threatened to rape her. I

am sure she was telling the truth. We interviewed the shops near her building. They don't have cameras and the managers didn't see anything either. The police questioned the residents too. They got the same answers.'

'TWELVE OF OUR MEN WERE SHOT, AND NO ONE SAW OR HEARD ANYTHING?'

Gorshky slammed his palm on his table. Water spilled from his glass and spread on its polished surface. His aide darted forward and mopped it quickly with a paper towel.

The SVR head drew several breaths to calm himself.

'What do you think?'

'No one likes us. No one wants the war.' Ruslan shrugged. 'On top of that, Zakharova is very popular. It is possible her supporters took out our men.'

'A bunch of protesters killed our highly trained agents?'

'The journalist has fans all over the country. Even a lot of soldiers like her. We know the rioters have become more and more sophisticated. They have weapons—HKs, AKs, M4s. They train like commandos.' The bodyguard made a face. 'I wouldn't be surprised if our men were overconfident and got careless.'

'Send more people to the building. Threaten every resident if you have to but get answers.'

Ruslan nodded and was about to move when Gorshky stopped him.

'Wait.' He frowned and watched the muted TV for several seconds. Another protest was being covered by the cameras. 'Don't do that. We don't want more bad publicity. Investigate quietly. Those killers must have come up in some vehicle. Check the cameras on Michurinskiy.'

'Da.'

'And you,' Gorshky barked at his aide, 'get me the boss of that TV station on the phone. Don't they have anything else to cover?'

. . .

RUSLAN WENT to the neighboring office, where four agents were relaxing. He removed his jacket and threw it on a chair and turned to them.

'Karel, you and Shulga go to Zakharova's building. Keep watch on it and see if any strangers come to it.'

'What about the boss? We need to be with him.' Karel tossed away the lurid magazine he was reading.

'I'll take care of that.'

'The five of us are always around him wherever he goes.'

'It's just for a day. You've seen the boss's schedule. He'll be in the office for a couple of days.'

'He'll be going home—'

'I said I will deal with it!' he said through gritted teeth. He softened his voice instantly when Karel stiffened. 'I will tell him you both are not feeling well—'

'He has not sanctioned this, has he?' Shulga grinned. 'Otherwise, you would have replaced us with two men in the pool.'

'Da. He doesn't know about this. We will work with GUVD to see who those killers could be, but we need eyes on the building.'

'You think the killers will return?'

'I don't know.'

'How will we identify them? That building has more than fifty families. They will have visitors, vendors, delivery people …'

'You'll know when you see them. They will be lean, fit, eyes alert … they will be just like us.'

19

'Alexei Gorshky has five men with him at all times,' Boris Yasimov briefed Zeb, Meghan and Chloe in a restaurant in the nearby Yasenevo District. Beth and Broker were at another table, while the rest of the operatives were scattered in surrounding joints, all of them listening in.

They had changed to casual clothing in their vans, and while the editor had taken them in carefully, he had made no comment.

He began briefing them with the attack on *The Reality*, his decoy moves at Sheremetyevo and to his appearance at Elena's apartment. He talked freely without holding back, instinctively trusting them.

'Those five include his driver, Tony the Tank—'

'That's what he's called?' Beth interrupted.

'His real name is something else, but everyone calls him that because of how he's built. Large and squat, all muscle. No one should underestimate him. He might look slow because of his size, but he moves faster than a snake. I have seen him.'

He took a breath and resumed. 'Ruslan is next to his boss whenever he is outside the office, except when he goes to the

Kremlin. Gorshky has only Tony during those visits, but Ruslan and his team follow in a second car. The team leader decides who makes the team. He rotates the protection officers every month, but he is always there. He is like Gorshky. He has no family. He and all the security men are from Zaslon. That's—'

'We know about it,' Chloe interrupted him.

The editor looked at her keenly and then at Zeb and Meghan. He nodded, adjusted his glasses and resumed. 'All of them live with Gorshky in his house in Yasenevo, which is almost next door to the SVR headquarters. Da, we are in the same district right now ... you know that, too.'

Meghan nodded.

'Where does he get the replacements from?' Zeb asked him.

'There is a pool of five men ready for active deployment at any point in time. They are based in the SVR campus here.' He jerked his head in the general direction of the headquarters. 'Those five are exclusively for Gorshky's protection. There are similar teams for other senior officers, ministers and diplomats. The President has his own team, which are separate from Zaslon. Ruslan picks men from that pool for each monthly shift. There is a wider pool of men if anyone falls ill or has to be absent for some emergency.'

'How do you know all this?' Bear growled.

'I'm a newspaper editor. It's my job to know.'

He caved in when they kept silent. 'Elena, I and hundreds of others are part of the Resistance movement. For democracy. We have been watching SVR, FSB, GUVD, all the major agencies, ministers, politicians, for years. We have informers and supporters all over the country. Many army officers are with us. We have files,' he concluded.

'Why are you asking me all this?' he asked when none of them responded.

'You said you have files,' Zeb said, dodging his question. 'You have them on Ruslan and his team too?'

'Da,' the editor said proudly.

'Where are they?'

'In the cloud.'

'Not paper files?' Zeb asked, surprised.

'*The Reality* is a small newspaper, but we are not that backward, *moy drug*.' My friend.

Zeb raised his hand apologetically, feeling the twins' and Chloe's scornful eyes.

'Can you share those with us?' the elder twin asked, smiling at the editor.

'Da. If you are planning what I suspect you are, whatever I have is yours.'

'Doesn't Ruslan have any hobbies?' Roger drawled. 'A girlfriend? Does he go to nightclubs?'

'Da. He goes to Gypsy every weekend.'

'Gypsy?'

'A nightclub on Ullitsa Paustovskogo. He goes at seven pm and is there until three am. One of the dancers is his girlfriend. I don't think she thinks of him like that, but he spends money on her ...'

'With such detailed information as you have, I'm surprised no one from your Resistance has tried to attack Gorshky.'

'A few protesters tried last year. They came to him as he was leaving an event. They were killed. Ruslan shot them in the head. After he tortured them. Ever since that attempt, I share my intelligence with only a close circle.'

He looked around the restaurant. 'Is it safe for me to stay in Elena's apartment?'

'Da, but take provisions with you,' Zeb replied. 'We will reseal the door from outside. You should not come out for days.'

'I wasn't planning to. I have everything I need in my bag to keep *The Reality* going.'

'What's on your mind?' Meghan challenged him when Yasimov went to the bathroom.

'I need to see who those four men with Ruslan are and who the replacement team is.'

'Why?'

'They are close to Gorshky.'

20

They drove Yasimov back to the apartment building, and while Zeb hung out in the parking lot, Meghan and Chloe took the editor to the residence.

He gave them the access details to his cloud account. 'It is a site in the dark net. No one—'

'Da.' The petite operative smiled at him to take the sting out of her interruption. 'We know how that works.'

They left a spoofing device with him that would enable him to get onto the internet without leaving a trail.

'That phone we gave you,' the elder twin told him, 'use it to call us.'

'Whom should I ask for?'

She smiled at his attempt to fish out their names. 'One of us will get back to you.'

'Is this the only place you can hide?' Chloe asked him.

'Da. I cannot risk staying with my friends. I know what you mean. If SVR or the police come here, it will be too late for you to help me, even if I call you.'

'You know what will happen if you are captured? You will disappear like Elena did.'

'Da.'

'Don't you have a wife and daughter?'

'Da. We are separated, however. They are in St. Petersburg.'

'Police will harass her.'

'They have already done that,' Yasimov said bitterly. 'They stopped finally when they realized I have no contact with them.'

It came to Meghan instantly. *The way he speaks of them, his eyes lighting up …* 'That separation,' she said slowly, 'was for show, wasn't it?'

Yasimov's eyes widened. His jaw dropped. 'No! We are—'

His shoulders slumped under her steady gaze.

'How did you guess?' he mumbled, sweeping back his hair with his fingers. 'Only Elena knows. Not even my friends are aware of it. Magda and I have kept up that pretense for years. Shura has grown up without my seeing her. Our plan was that one day we would reunite. I don't know when that will happen.'

'You said Elena knows this,' Chloe chipped in sharply. 'If she is tortured—'

'Magda and Shura have escaped the country to Germany. I arranged that as soon as Elena was captured. They are safe. Only I know where they are.'

He wiped his eyes on his sleeve and regained his composure.

'What are you planning?'

'Stay here.' Meghan squeezed his shoulder and left the editor in the living room.

Zeb listened silently when she and Chloe told them of Yasimov's family.

'Ruslan might return.' Broker followed his gaze to the apartment building.

'He won't, but he will send some men to watch it. That's what we would do in his position.'

'We'll keep watch,' Meghan said. 'Beth and me. No one will think anything of two women in a vehicle at a shopping center. We'll warn Boris if they approach the apartment, and if they enter it, we'll go to his rescue.'

'Do that,' Zeb agreed. 'I need to see someone.'

'What about?'

'To confirm Elena is still alive.'

21

It was evening by the time Zeb reached the fancy hotel in Tverskaya. He backtracked several times and window-shopped aimlessly until he was sure he wasn't being tailed.

Gorshky thinks we are in Taiwan, he reminded himself. Nevertheless, mission security and precautionary measures couldn't be compromised.

He entered the lobby and spotted the sentry instantly. The man was in a suit and made no attempt to hide who he was. A watcher.

Zeb went down the hallway and in its polished mirror saw the man whisper into a collar mic.

The second guard was armed with an AK74, held in his hands as if the weapon was an extension of his body. He stopped Zeb with a raised palm, wanded him, took his phone and nodded at a door.

A body slammed into Zeb as soon as he entered it, and arms wrapped around him tightly.

'It's been a long time, moy drug.' Grigor Andropov hugged him tightly and thumped him on the back.

Zeb grinned and clasped his hand warmly when the Russian spymaster released him.

'You look the same.'

Andropov was still lean, wiry, with his brown hair neatly cut, clean-shaven, sharp, dark eyes observing the world. Only the lines around his face and eyes and the wrinkles on his wrists indicated his age and the responsibility he carried.

'Ach.' His friend waved a hand dismissively. 'I survive. That's a blessing every day. You haven't changed either. Still the panther.'

He poured coffee into two porcelain cups and handed one to Zeb while they caught up and talked of past missions and friends lost.

'You are in Russia on business?'

'You know I can't answer that.'

'It's a dangerous time to be in my country.'

Zeb kept quiet.

'Your mission ... will it affect me?'

'Nyet.'

'I heard you were in Taiwan. I was surprised when I got your message.'

Zeb smiled. 'Yeah, we wanted to make certain people thought that. Looks like it worked.'

'You can't take out my President,' Andropov said flatly. 'Da, I don't agree with his politics and approach, but that's between us. My agency will come after you—'

'Nope. He's not of interest to me. You know I don't do that kind of work. Executing state leaders ... it isn't a mission I'd take on.'

'Taking him out is the only way to stop his military ambitions.'

Zeb didn't respond.

Andropov probed him with his dark eyes for long moments, and then sighed and relaxed.

'I know you don't do assassinations of that kind,' he said apologetically, 'but I had to ask. Tensions are high in the world, and I am sure President Morgan must be desperate to de-escalate the situation.'

'He is, but my business has nothing to do with your president.'

'I will be arrested if anyone in my government knows we are friends. If they find out about this meeting ... FSB, SVR, GRU, they all dislike me and my agency. They are envious of our success. They would like nothing better than for me to disappear.'

'Da, I know.'

Andropov was unique among all the covert intelligence outfit heads in Russia. His politics were moderate and he strongly disagreed with the President's strong-arm policies. Only a select circle knew of his views however, Zeb being one of them.

He's the best spymaster Russia has. He's carried out more successful missions than the bigger agencies, but they get the credit.

'You want weapons? Safe houses? Papers? Vehicles?'

'No.' He shook his head. 'I want information.'

'On whom?' Andropov stiffened again.

'Elena Zakharova.'

The Russian's posture eased. He nodded thoughtfully. He sipped his coffee and wiped his lips. 'I was asked to wiretap her, follow her, abduct her and her editor. I refused.'

'No, not directly,' he added, smiling grimly at Zeb's stare. 'I made up some excuse that my people were busy on other, more critical missions. The Kremlin gave the mission to another agency.'

'Which one?'

'There's only one man in Russia who has a devil quote in his office.'

Gorshky! He's confirming Gorshky grabbed Elena.

'I don't know who that is.'

'Zeb, we go way back. We have worked on some joint missions that our countries aren't even aware of. You have saved my life more than once and helped me many times. Let's not play games. I am sure you know who I'm referring to. You have thick files on every intelligence agency in Russia.'

Files. Zeb couldn't help grinning at the word. *Andropov's outfit is as technologically advanced as ours, but he's still old-school.*

'You got me,' he acknowledged. 'I know who you mean.'

His smile faded. 'Is she alive?'

'Makes sense. Your rescuing her would change the world political equation if her information is as good as she claims.'

Zeb remained wooden-faced.

'You know, I met her several times. Elena. She tracked me down when I was in my gym. Me. One of the most protected people in the country. The average Russian does not know of my existence. Most politicians and ministers don't know of my agency's existence. But Elena identified me somehow, slipped past my security and confronted me in the gym. She wanted to know what role I played in killing political opponents. You know those incidents. Polonium poisoning.'

Zeb nodded.

'I told her I was a businessman. That I exported the finest Russian vodka to countries all over the world. I didn't know what she was talking about. She was persistent, however. She slipped past my security a few more times and kept badgering me until I took her on a factory tour of our distillery. I don't think she was fully convinced, but she stopped accosting me after that. We talked a lot that day. She and I sampled our drinks. She spoke of her dream to have more democracy in our country. She was deeply committed to the protest movement.'

Andropov resumed after a brief silence. 'I didn't record any of our conversations or that tour in our system. My guards are trusted men. They won't talk. To your question ... she is alive.'

'You know—'

'Don't ask me how. She is alive and unharmed, but I don't know how long that will last. Certain people want what she has in her mind. That article.'

'Where is she?'

'In a place even you can't get her out of. Lubyanka.'

Gorshky is still using it as a prison, Zeb thought bleakly. *Andropov is right. It is a fortress. We can't break into it.*

'If you can't go in there, you must make her come out of it.'

Zeb looked at the spymaster in confusion.

His friend smiled enigmatically. 'I am sure you'll work it out.'

He got to his feet and hugged Zeb again and looked hard into his eyes.

'Be successful. The world needs Elena.'

22

'That's Nikitin and Golubev,' Meghan murmured and nudged her sister with her shoulder. 'They were with Ruslan in the morning.

The two men stood out sharply in her night- vision goggles, NVGs, leaning casually against their dark car. It was parked in front of the building, and the men made no attempt to hide themselves.

'Yeah.' Beth nodded after a while. 'They checked Elena's apartment was locked and sealed, from the stairs.'

Meghan squirmed on the grass to get more comfortable and tossed away a pebble from beneath her body.

'Boris was right. No one seems to use the path through these trees. We've been here for a few hours now and haven't seen a single person.'

She turned to Beth when her sister didn't reply and saw her flicking through images on her handheld screen.

'What are you—'

'Karel Golubev is the taller one, Shulga Nikitin is the other dude. Both are single. Zaslon. Expert in weapons ...' she read out their intel on the men.

'Boris and Elena.' She shook her head in amazement when she had finished. 'He named them earlier today, but I thought he was bluffing when he said he had files on Gorshky's security team.'

'Not just on them,' she continued after a pause. 'He has photographs and files on every resident in Elena's building. They must have done background checks to confirm no one was spying on her.'

'Who is the third man in Gorshky's security detail?'

'Nikola Galkin.'

'Are there backup names there?'

'Yes, and intel on them too.'

Beth turned off her screen, slipped it into the pocket of her cargo pants and put her NVGs to her eyes.

'Why are they out in the open like that?'

'It's a warning to strangers to back off.'

'You think they bought what we posted?'

'Our fake messages on social media claiming to be protesters who took revenge on SVR? You bet. That's one reason those dudes are lounging like that. They want to show they aren't intimidated.'

The twins had set up several false, untraceable internet accounts through which they had boasted about killing Elena's attackers. They had revealed enough details to make the posts credible to SVR.

We learned this from the Russians. They used social media to manipulate our elections. We use their techniques against them.

Meghan's grin faded when the men straightened and set off down the approach road towards the stores.

'Shall we—' Beth began.

'You bet!' She got to her feet, dusted herself off and hid their backpacks beneath a bush.

She checked herself and her sister. They carried only their

Glocks beneath their loose, zipped-up jackets, and their earpieces and mics.

'We want to overhear them,' she warned her twin. 'That's all.'

'Gotcha.'

They emerged from the trees behind the building cautiously and raced towards the approach road. They slowed once the men were in sight and followed at a distance.

Golubev and Nikitin entered the convenience store, which was sandwiched between a hair salon and a pharmacy. Meghan split up from her sister and went down one aisle, while Beth sampled perfumes in a parallel one.

'We are wasting our time here,' she heard one of the men murmur.

These shelves are not tall. Beth and I can look over them if we stretch on our toes.

'Da. Those protesters will not return.'

'Did you read what they posted?'

'Those *ublyuduki*,' the second man cursed. 'They won't be posting anything when we get our hands on them.'

Meghan peered over the aisle when they fell silent.

What are they looking at?

She craned her neck to follow their eyes.

A woman.

Her lips curled in disgust. She took in the woman, her gaze sharpening when she noticed her puffy cheeks and bruises.

'It's her, isn't it?' Golubev nudged Nikitin. 'The neighbor.'

Neighbor?

She stifled her gasp when she recognized the woman from Boris's photographs. *That's Grusha Lebedev! She lives next door to Elena. They interrogated her inside her apartment.*

The men went towards the woman.

She tracked them in her aisle.

'Remember us?' Golubev's voice was audible through the cartons and cans stacked on the shelf. 'We should have spent more time on you.'

'Da. You slipped the flowers under her door, didn't you? If our boss hadn't called us off, we would have done more to your face.'

'Much more.' Golubev leered. 'You have a shapely body. We would have shared it.'

Meghan heard the sharp tap of heels, and when she risked a glance, Grusha was walking down the aisle, her head down, the men sneering at her.

She went to the end of her aisle and met the woman as she emerged.

Grusha didn't meet her eyes. She mumbled an apology as she made her way past and reached blindly for a cereal carton, knocking it to the floor.

Meghan crouched, picked it up and handed it to her.

'Are you okay?' she asked softly.

The woman nodded, thanked her in a whisper and went to another shelf quickly.

The older twin checked the rest of the aisles.

The men weren't around.

She went outside, where Beth was waiting. Hard-faced, grim.

'You heard?'

Meghan nodded, her eyes scanning the parking lot.

There they are, returning to their car.

'They beat that woman.'

'I heard,' she repeated.

'They were talking of raping her. Are we going to just watch them as if nothing happened?'

'Do you have your balaclava?'

'Yeah.'

'Gloves?'

'Yes.'

'Let's go.'

They slipped on their masks and gloves when they were away from the parking lot's lights and hurried up the approach road.

'No killing,' she warned softly.

'You're such a party pooper.'

They spread out, walking casually, their shoes crunching on loose stones.

The men heard them and looked their way.

We are some distance away, still. They can't see our masks.

They got close enough to see the frowns on their faces.

'Got a light?' Meghan asked, quickening her steps. She held up her fingers to show the cigarette between them.

She lunged forward as Nikitin reached for his pocket instinctively. Her fist crashed into the side of his face; her body slammed into his and sent him crashing against the car.

She heard Golubev's *nyet* to warn his partner, but Beth was on him as well. She stopped thinking of her sister as Nikitin fought back. *She can handle him.*

His knee came up. She smashed an elbow against its fleshy part, winced when his punch caught the side of her head, but caught his retreating wrist, twisted it and crashed it against his lips to foil his headbutt.

She kept her body moving, twisting, to make it harder for him to grip it or throw a punch, and when his knuckles sped back at her throat, she saw her opening. She stepped back to make room. Saw his eyes flare in triumph, thinking she had made a mistake. She twisted out of the way of the incoming jab, blocked his second hand, caught his right shoulder, locked her wrist around his right hand, pivoted to carry his body and smash it against the car again. She grabbed his hair before he could recover and crashed his head against its roof until she felt his body go limp.

She confirmed he was unconscious and then spun on her heel to check on Beth, who had crushed her knee in Golubev's groin savagely and knocked him out with a headbutt.

'I could have finished before you,' her sister panted, 'but you were in my way.'

'It wasn't a competition.' Meghan grinned. 'Did he—'

'No injuries. We surprised them. If we had been slower to attack, they would have fought differently.'

'Yeah.' The elder twin patted Nikitin's body and came up with his phone.

'Get our backpacks. I'll keep their phones from locking out.'

She checked out the parking lot and building when Beth raced away. Several apartments were lit up and loud music came out of a window. The fight had lasted just a few minutes and wasn't loud enough for anyone to hear. She doubted any resident would come down to investigate, even if they had seen it from their window. *They are scared.*

Beth returned and dropped the backpack on the ground. She zipped it open and brought out a cable, one end of which went into Golubev's phone and the other to her screen. She punched in commands, getting a software program to copy the device's data to her tablet.

Meghan searched the thugs' bodies. Wallets with driving licenses. She extracted the SVR's identity card and waved it at Beth. 'They aren't hiding who they are.'

'Why would they? They're on Gorshky's security team.'

Loose change and car keys in their pockets. Nothing else.

'Should we insert a tracker in their phones or clothing?'

'No.' She shook her head. 'They'll find it and then they'll know we aren't protesters.'

They returned the men's phones to their jackets, got to their feet and went down the approach road as silently as they had arrived.

'Golubev might never have kids.' Beth chuckled as she fired up their van and drove out. 'What do you think they'll tell Ruslan?'

'THAT THEY FELL ON THE STAIRS,' Meghan guessed. 'They won't admit that two women defeated them.'

23

Dmitri Ruslan stared at them when he came into his office the next day.

'What happened to both of you? Have you been fighting?'

'Nyet,' Golubev protested. 'Those residents are like sheep. All of them stayed indoors. Who would we fight with? There was soap water on the stairs. Someone must have been washing them. We slipped on the steps and fell.'

'Both of you?'

'I was in front. I fell first and brought Shulga down and we both slid down several steps.'

'That can cause so much damage?' Galkin asked curiously. 'Your eyes, your neck—'

'Try falling on steps and see for yourself,' Nikitin snapped at him.

'Your looks have improved,' Galkin said solemnly and chuckled at the glare he got in return.

'Did any strangers come to the building?' Ruslan asked.

'Nyet. There were a couple of food delivery men. We confirmed they were genuine, but no one else. Zakharova's apartment is locked, and the seal is unbroken. Shall we return today as well?'

'No. Have you seen what's on social media? The protesters are claiming a great victory against us. They're not hiding that they killed our men. They say they will stop only when we free Zakharova, stop their oppression.'

He shook his head angrily. 'The boss isn't happy. SVR is being humiliated. He is under pressure from the Kremlin.'

He snapped his fingers. 'We need to find those killers. Our men were killed by HK rounds. Those protesters must have bought them in the black market, from some bratva gang. Make calls. Talk to the Zaslon and SVR technology people. Ask them to dig into their databases and see if they have any information on arms deals. I'll talk to GUVD and see if they have any intel as well. Some of you check the cameras, see which vehicles—'

'Isn't this a job for the police?'

Ruslan glowered at him. 'Are you new to Zaslon or this team? You know how we work. We carry out our own investigations. We have time. The boss will be in his office all day. Get to it!'

He went to his desk but didn't turn on his screen. He brooded for several moments as he thought of the dead men.

Those weren't my A-team, but they were good operatives. They were killed by professionals.

He reached for his keyboard, logged into the Zaslon system and ran a search for all armed forces personnel who had retired or quit in the past five years. He filtered the results by age. *They will be young. Not more than forty years.*

He got more than a thousand names. He grimaced.

What about Special Forces? Those men would have the training. They would be as good as my agents.

He filtered down the results by Special Operations Forces. GRU, FSB and SVR had their own elite units too, but he didn't search for them. *They track their former soldiers. They'll have flagged any officer who became a protester. Nyet, these killers have to be from the wider armed forces.*

He grunted in satisfaction when fewer than thirty results came back. He clicked on the first soldier's name and began reading.

'THEY HAD IT COMING,' Beth flared when she and Meghan had finished briefing the team.

Zeb raised his hands defensively. 'I didn't say anything. Only—'

'You don't want Ruslan or Gorshky to suspect there's some other party in play here?' Meghan guessed.

'Yeah.'

'They won't. Those men will never admit they were attacked.'

'It'll hurt their egos.' Chloe smiled. 'What did you find out?'

'Nothing from their phones,' the younger twin said dejectedly. 'They use them only for calls, and those numbers are anonymized. They must have some software on their devices that unscrambles the numbers so that they can recognize the callers, but when we copied them, all we got was the anonymous ones.'

'That's what we have on our phones, too.'

Zeb met her eyes across the table in the restaurant. Bear's back was to him. Breakfast in a large joint near the Kremlin. Broker was with the sisters at a distant table, while Bwana and Roger were outside.

The decision to dine in the same restaurant was a calculated risk. *We're still good. Gorshky isn't looking for us. Bwana might attract attention, but there are lots of tour groups in Moscow, with diverse travelers. Heck, this joint has three other black men in it right now.*

'Elena is still alive. Unharmed.'

'You're sure?' Meghan asked tautly.

'Yeah.'

He heard several sighs of relief.

'Where is she?' Roger demanded.

'Lubyanka. In the basement prison, deep down in the cellars, which Gorshky apparently has restarted.'

'There's no way we can get her out of there,' Beth said disappointedly.

'Yeah.'

'You don't sound upset.'

'I'm not.'

'What are you working on?'

'Getting her out of there.'

'How?'

'We'll need Yasimov's help.'

Silence and then a Texan drawl. 'That back and forth was nice to witness, but aren't you forgetting our main mission?'

'I haven't.'

'What are you doing about that?'

'I will be going clubbing.'

24

Evgeny Laskin was young, ambitious and determined to make a name for himself in SVR.

I'm thirty-two. I have my life ahead of me. I am in Moscow, close to the boss. He had several advantages over many other case officers, but he was also aware that Vasili, the man in New York, was the flavor of the month.

Just because he tracked down Carter, he thought sourly. He stiffened when Gorshky walked past the hallway and entered his office. *I can do better than him.*

Yasimov. That was his assignment.

He called the SVR agents in Heathrow and asked if they had spotted the editor.

None had.

'Are you sleeping on the job?' he hissed angrily at one of the agents. 'He is one of our most wanted people. We have sent out his photographs, everything on him ... he boarded a flight to—'

'I didn't see him. Hundreds of thousands of people come to Heathrow every day—'

'I gave you his flight details, *durak*,' he cursed the operative.

'I didn't see him.'

Laskin slammed the phone down and rubbed his temples. The agents he had to deal with! *He must have been watching women the whole time!*

He was smart, however, and once his rage had dissipated, he started thinking.

What if Yasimov was disguised?

'Did you record all the passengers who came out of that flight?' He called the agent again.

'Da, as they entered the concourse.'

'Send the video to me.'

Laskin went through the clip when he got it and nodded to himself. No Yasimov. That didn't mean anything, however. *He must not have recorded all the passengers.* In any case, it was difficult to say which passengers came from which flight. *They don't wear tags around their necks.* The agent had made a judgment call when recording the arrivals, based on when their bags were unloaded.

He made another call, this time to the London Station officer.

'Ask our drivers if any of them picked up Yasimov or saw him.'

The Russian agencies had several cab drivers at prominent transit points on their payroll. At airports, railway stations and even at harbor ports. Many of those drivers were Russian themselves, either low-level agents or just people who believed in the cause.

The reply came an hour later.

No one had seen or picked up Yasimov.

I wish we could tap into Heathrow's cameras. SVR kept doing that, but British counterintelligence kept detecting their worms and took preventive measures. He had footage from when they had last infiltrated the CCTV system, but it was of no help. That was before Yasimov's escape.

Which reminded him. He fired an angry email at the technicians to get them to repenetrate the airport's surveillance cameras.

What if Yasimov didn't board the flight?

The thought came to him when he was in the dining room, overhearing Gorshky talk of Vasili to other officers.

No, that's not possible. Our agent captured him boarding the flight.

The thought didn't leave him, however, and after finishing his meal, he rushed back to his desk, where he logged into his system and brought up Sheremetyevo's camera footage.

No Yasimov exiting the airport.

That proves it. He was on that flight.

No, he argued with himself. *Unless I have seen Yasimov in London, it proves nothing.*

He knew Sheremetyevo well. He closed his eyes and visualized how *he* would escape.

The emergency exit at the walkway!

Every airbridge to aircraft had such an exit. A door that opened to rolling stairs that would lead passengers to the runway and the safety of the terminal.

That's how I would get away, and if I had a friendly baggage-handling driver, I would climb into their vehicle.

Yasimov had no lack of support. *The Reality* was read by all kinds of Muscovites, from street-food vendors to army generals.

Excited, Laskin searched for the baggage drivers attending Yasimov's aircraft. Four of them. He looked up their files. A drunk-driving offense for one of them, minor traffic violations for another one. None had a criminal record.

All of them lived near Sheremetyevo, either in the suburbs or in dormitories. Two of the men were living with families, one was a divorcee and the fourth was single.

Laskin drummed his fingers on his desk. Family men had a lot to lose. He moved them down his list. The divorced man made monthly payments to his former wife. He had a child with her.

I'll start with Vlad Belsky, the single man.

His bank records didn't turn up anything. Salary. Outgoing expenses, rent. His phone records showed several repeat calls to the same numbers.

The case officer had the entire apparatus of SVR at his fingertips. No records were secret or sacrosanct to the agency. He ran a search for the numbers, and they turned out to be friends and parents.

Laskin's second idea struck him when Gorshky's door opened and he heard his boss laugh. *I bet he's talking to Vasili,* he thought bitterly and settled into his seat.

A map!

Inspired, he brought up the city map and superimposed Belsky's phone's movements on it. Work commute, restaurants, playgrounds, vacations outside the city … but there were significant times when the phone appeared to be turned off. Those were usually on the baggage handler's days off.

Laskin cross-checked those times with protests and demonstrations in the city and couldn't help giving a shout of exclamation.

He settled back in his seat when his coworkers looked at him curiously.

There was a correlation!

He must be joining those demonstrations, he thought excitedly. He brought up video footage of the ongoing protests outside the Kremlin and ran a facial-recognition search on the crowd. However, there were too many people, and the software brought back too many false results.

No matter. He had something. He couldn't go to his boss with it, but he could act on it.

He called the airport and was told Belsky hadn't showed up.

He put on his jacket, went down two floors and entered the office where the heavies worked.

'You two.' He beckoned at two thugs. 'Come with me.'

The low-level soldiers were competent at breaking-and-entering, conducting searches and planting surveillance devices, among other talents. They could be violent as well.

The men dumped their coffee cups in the trash can and followed him obediently.

'Where to?'

'Sheremetyevo.'

'We are going somewhere?'

'We are going to make sure someone doesn't go anywhere.'

25

Zeb picked up the tail during his afternoon jog.

He was running down the Boulevard Ring, named for the ten tree-lined boulevards that joined one another, unbroken.

Leaves crunched under his feet as he ran down Nikitsky Boulevard. He was in a loose hoodie and track suit, a Glock his only weapon in its kydex shoulder holster.

A flash of light caught his eye on the sidewalk. He retrieved a piece of broken mirror and was dumping it in a trashcan when his tail turned his head away quickly.

Zeb didn't react. He pretended he hadn't noticed the abrupt movement. He retied his shoelaces and resumed his run.

Nikitsky turned into Tverskoy Boulevard. He brought out his shades, which had been hooked into his zipper, and put them on. The screens lit up with the rear view. He turned his head fractionally to take in the rear.

There was his shadow. A large man who wore a dark hoodie, too, and was running easily.

Don't recognize him.

Zeb paused to read a poster advertising a play, and in its

polished reflection saw the man come up and go past him.

The man didn't let himself be followed. He sat on a bench and spoke into his phone, not looking up when Zeb jogged in front of him.

More evasive maneuvers didn't shake the man. *He's tailing me for sure, and not doing a great job of hiding. He can't be an SVR man. Gorshky's soldiers are better. That watcher who was shot in New York ... is my tail related to that bunch?*

There was only one way to find out.

He stopped at the next bench and rested his shoe on it to loosen its lace.

The tail came up from behind. *No one else nearby.* The shadow was three feet behind when Zeb straightened, lost his balance and flailed wildly.

The hard edge of his calloused palm struck the man in his throat.

'Izvinite!' he exclaimed in apology. He caught the gasping man's shoulder and squeezed his clavicle pressure point, making the man stumble.

'Here, sit down.' He helped the tail to the bench, caught his right arm solicitously and broke a finger.

'Scream if you want to,' he told the shadow conversationally. 'I'll tell the police you were following me.'

The tail attempted to struggle and gave up instantly when Zeb pulled back his remaining fingers to the breaking point.

'Who are you? Why are you following me?'

The man didn't reply. Sweat poured down his face, which was twisted in agony. His breath came in harsh pants, his eyes squeezed to slits.

'Once I break your fingers, I'll puncture your ribs and your throat. I can do that with my bare hands. You see anyone nearby? That family is way down the boulevard. By the time they come to our bench, you'll be dead and I'll be gone.'

'Pushkin,' the man wheezed. 'Pushkin sent me.'

26

'Illya Pushkin,' Meghan reflected. 'Leader of the Pushkin bratva, one of the most vicious gangs in Moscow. What does he want with you? How did he know you're here?'

'He doesn't know.' Zeb frowned. 'The man was just a messenger. He got a call from Pushkin to follow me. He was told where I would be.'

'You were—'

'No. No one followed me. I'm sure of that. I shouldn't have removed my disguise,' he said disgustedly. 'The one day I do that, I get recognized.'

The phone in his hand rang. He held it up to show it to his team, who were scattered around the restaurant. 'The messenger gave this to me. Told me to expect a call.'

'Da?' he growled in the device.

'A car will be waiting for you on the southwest corner of Red Square. A black Mercedes,' a guttural voice replied. 'Get into it.'

'Why?'

'It will take you to meet Pushkin.'

'Why? I am not—'

'It will be in your interest. Be there in half an hour.'

'What was that about?' Beth spoke up when the caller hung up.

'I have no clue.' Zeb shrugged his shoulders. 'We haven't come across them.' *Bratvas and local criminal gangs aren't our targets unless they have something to do with our national security.*

'The Pushkin Bratva,' Meghan read aloud from her screen. 'Not the largest criminal gang, but the most vicious. While their base is in Moscow, they operate in all the major cities and have their outfits in surrounding countries, too. Ukraine, Belarus, you name it, they're there. Financial scams, extortion, real-estate, drugs ...'

'What do they want with us?' Broker exclaimed. 'And how did they find you?'

'Only one way to get answers.'

'ONLY ONE PERSON,' the driver told Zeb when he climbed inside the Mercedes with Beth and Meghan.

He followed the twins out and bent towards the driver's lowered window.

'Bye.'

'Wait,' the driver cursed. 'Get in. Pushkin says you will be safe. If we wanted to kill you, you would already be dead.'

He pulled out when his passengers showed no reaction to his words.

'He's alone. No other goons,' Beth murmured. 'We aren't blindfolded ... looks like Pushkin isn't trying to hide his location from us.'

'We're behind you,' Bwana spoke in their earpieces.

Zeb nodded unconsciously. *Does Pushkin know about my team?*

The question remained in his mind as the car drove outside the city's center, crossed the Garden Ring, the second beltway in the city, and slowed as it drew close to a building near the Moskva River.

Looks like one of the old pyatietazhki. The five-story apartment buildings had been constructed decades ago, but most of them had been torn down and new residential construction had come up in their place.

'It's been made over,' Beth murmured. 'Looks modern. I can see cameras all over, satellite antennas ... this could be Pushkin's headquarters.'

The iron-grille gate opened automatically on their arrival. An armed guard stared at them impassively as the Mercedes went up a curving driveway past a well-maintained lawn, between ponds and statues. A peacock crossed the road, while in the distance another armed guard patrolled with a dog.

'Welcome to bratva life,' Beth said drily.

The Mercedes rolled to a stop beneath the fancy mirrored roof over the driveway. Two guards opened the door and escorted them inside, where they were searched and their guns and phones taken.

'You will get them back when you're going out.'

So, we are getting out alive!

Zeb's lips curled in a smile when he read the twins' thoughts.

They went down the polished floor, past Greek and Roman sculptures and into a library. Floor-to-ceiling wooden shelves stacked with books. An oak reading table that looked like it must have cost more than a luxury car. Several comfortable couches scattered on the expensive rugs beneath their feet.

Ilya Pushkin on one of them, with three men behind him.

The gangster was dressed in a white shirt tucked into dark trousers with razor-sharp creases. Polished boots on his feet.

'Welcome to my humble house,' he greeted them in flawless English.

'Why are we here?' Zeb demanded.

'I can help you.'

27

Zeb blinked.

That wasn't what I was expecting.

'How did you find us?' Beth demanded before he could reply.

Pushkin gazed at her with a frown. 'I'm trying to work out who you are. I know there are eight of you—'

He won't recognize Beth or Meg. They haven't removed their disguises.

'How do you know that?'

'Remember that man who was killed in New York?'

'He was yours?'

'Da. He was watching you.'

'Speak.' Meghan sat on a couch. Beth joined her while Zeb poured coffee from the flask in front of Pushkin and handed the cups to the sisters.

Those men haven't moved from their positions behind Pushkin. They have guns at their waists. They are confident we are no threat to their boss. He had checked out the room discreetly on entering it. *There will be a hidden exit behind one of those shelves in case Pushkin has to escape.*

He focused on the bratva leader's explanation.

'A few years ago, one of the Russian agencies farmed out some work to one of the bratvas. The job was to kill you in New York.'

'You were involved in that?'

The men behind Pushkin stirred, sensing the menace in Meghan's voice. The bratva leader was unperturbed, however. He raised his hand placatingly.

'Nyet. We don't take jobs from anyone in the government. We have our spies in the other gangs, and from them we got your files. How you look, where you are based.'

We didn't change our office or take down our security consulting front after that attack. There was no need. Their building was one of the most secure in the world, and despite the failed attack, very few people knew who they were or what they did.

'That explains how you know us,' Beth growled. 'Why were you watching us?'

'My man's job was to find out your routine and inform me so that I could meet you. But,' Pushkin said, smiling, 'Carter made him before he could call me.'

'That was your shooter—*you* killed him!' Meghan connected the dots.

'There was no choice. We couldn't let him be questioned by the police. We also found out SVR was watching you. We couldn't risk that agency knowing my man was there.'

His smile broadened at their stares.

'You killed your own man?'

'Da.' Pushkin shrugged. 'Everyone who works for me knows the price they might have to pay.'

'Who was the shooter?' Zeb asked softly.

One of the bodyguards made a gun with his fingers and pointed it in their direction. His thumb cocked.

Zeb lunged at him, grabbed his shooting hand, and broke his wrist. He twisted the arm and shattered his elbow. He was a blur as he shoved the thug onto a second bodyguard and crashed their heads together. He snatched his captive's gun from his waist and aimed it at the third guard, letting the two thugs fall to the floor.

The shooter's gun was half-drawn from his waist. He kept his hand on it, flicked his eyes at the men on the floor and then towards his boss.

Pushkin didn't hide his shock. He swallowed. 'This house is filled with my men. You can't get out alive.'

'If we wanted to kill you,' Zeb repeated the driver's words, 'you would already be dead.'

'Why did you attack Igor?'

'His rounds could have struck some of my friends. He could have killed innocents.'

'His orders were to kill our man. He did that.'

'He fired recklessly. If he was that good a shooter, he didn't need to fire more than two rounds.'

He stomped Igor's head brutally and tossed the gun at the third guard, who caught it reflexively.

Zeb joined the twins on the couch and gestured at Pushkin.

'Continue.'

The bratva leader looked at the fallen men and whispered instructions at the third guard, who summoned helpers and dragged the men away.

Pushkin had put his game face back on when he turned to them.

'You are as dangerous as your files suggest.'

'You had better believe that,' Beth warned him.

'Finding Carter on the Boulevard Ring,' Pushkin said, clasping his hands, 'was a coincidence.' He nodded at Zeb. 'You looked into a travel agency's window on Nikitsky Boulevard. That's one of my businesses. Its manager is a trusted lieutenant. He recognized you from your file and called me.'

I did look into that store window. Zeb went through the bratva leader's story to find holes in it. *It sounds plausible.*

Meghan and Beth's barely discernible nods told him they believed it, too.

'Why do you think we need your help?'

'I don't. But my entire organization is at your disposal if you need it.'

'Why?'

'You are asking the wrong question, Carter. You should have asked why we didn't take the hit job on you.'

'Why didn't you?'

'Because I despise this government and all its agencies.'

'You do business with politicians. You have high contacts in the Kremlin,' Meghan reminded him.

'Da, that's part of business.'

'Why do you hate them so much?'

'Because we are Ukrainians.'

28

That isn't in our files.

'No one knows that,' Pushkin said triumphantly. 'All of us have false identities. The police, the FSB ... everyone thinks we are a Moscow gang.'

'You don't like what the Russian government is doing to your country?'

'Like?' Pushkin shouted. 'If the Western countries don't do something, Russia will invade Ukraine. That's my homeland. I might be a criminal, but—'

'You are a Ukrainian one,' Beth finished.

'Da. When I found out you were in Moscow, I knew you were here on some kind of mission. If there is something we can do'—he snapped his fingers—'just ask. Use that phone my man gave you. Your call will get to me immediately.'

'Aren't you worried we might go to the police?' Zeb asked him curiously. 'You have admitted you head a bratva.'

'What will you tell them that they don't know?' Pushkin waved dismissively. 'I can say whatever I want, but proving it is a different matter. Besides, I own most of Moscow's police. They will not act against me. … You have to be somewhere, Carter?' he asked, noticing Zeb glancing at his watch.

'You might have to. Ask your men to check our phones.'

Pushkin looked at him and cocked his head at the remaining guard. The sentry went out and reappeared with a concerned expression and whispered in his boss's ear.

'Your phones have some kind of timer on them.'

'Da. When those get to zero, this building will blow up. The only way to prevent that is if we turn off the clock or we leave this building unharmed.'

Pushkin stiffened. 'You are bluffing. No one has planted any bombs here. Our security is the best in the world.'

'Believe what you want.' Zeb sipped his coffee and crossed his legs.

'You were with my driver. He said you didn't make any calls. There was no time for you—'

'Do you know where the rest of my team are? Some of them are watching it as we speak. If they don't see us come out—poof.' He snapped his fingers.

'Besides, we don't need to plant bombs. An Armata tank could be rolling down the street as we speak. I'm sure you have equipped your building with bulletproof glass, you have escape tunnels … but can you imagine what a few armor-piercing sabot rounds can do to it?' Zeb grinned, enjoying himself. 'Or, there could be helis heading here right now, carrying MK-82 bombs. There will be nothing left of your building once they land.'

'You too will die.' A sheen of sweat appeared on Pushkin's forehead.

'Da. But the rest of my team is still out there. They will take you, even if you escape.'

'You are lying. You don't know what I am capable of. If I snap my fingers, my men will drag you to the basement and extract answers from you.'

'Go ahead. We won't break easily, which means you'll lose time. If you want to escape, you had better get started. Meanwhile, post some of them to watch out for choppers and tanks. What weapons do you have against those?'

'What do you want?' Pushkin hissed.

'From you? Nothing, for now. This is a warning. You have some intelligence on us, but it doesn't tell everything about us. Don't mess with us. Otherwise, we'll burn down your bratva so fast you won't have time to remember you're Ukrainian.'

He got to his feet and followed the twins out of the library. None of the guards stopped them when they reached the front door, where they picked up their belongings and made a show of turning off the timers.

Zeb turned to Pushkin, who was in the library's doorway.

'Don't tail us. Don't try to find out what we're doing. That way, you'll live longer.'

'You won't have time to remember you're Ukrainian?'

Beth mocked him when they were back in the restaurant. 'Is that the best you could come up with?'

'It worked,' Zeb said defensively.

'I bet.' Meghan chuckled. 'Pushkin's got his men to search the entire building and its gardens for bombs. He'll post people on the roof to watch for choppers. I'd like to see his face when he finds it was all a hoax.'

'Is it true?' Chloe bobbed her head in the general direction of the bratva's headquarters.

'That he's Ukrainian? We got Werner to dig into that, but there is nothing to show that.'

Andropov might know, Zeb thought. *I'll ask him.*

'He could be bluffing.' Roger flashed a smile at a server, who beamed back at him.

'He could.' Zeb nodded, stifling a grin after seeing Beth's

eyeroll at the exchange. 'But what does he gain by that? If he wanted to kill us, they would have done that when I was joining him, or in his building.'

'He might want to know why we're here and sell that information—'

'We aren't being tailed,' Meghan interjected. 'Beth and I hacked into that travel company's systems. There *is* a connection to Pushkin. They use offshore banks, one of which we know has ties to his bratva. We also hacked into the street cameras—'

'Whoa!' Bwana exclaimed admiringly.

'What can we say?' Beth smirked. 'We can't help being danged good.'

'Their tail,' her elder twin continued, 'appeared *after* Zeb peered into that store's window. Pushkin wasn't lying about that. No one,' she held up her phone discreetly, 'inside or outside this restaurant is shadowing us.'

She and Beth are monitoring the street cameras on their phones and tablets.

'Assuming what he said is true,' Chloe said, pursing her lips, 'are we going to take him up?'

Zeb shrugged when they looked at him. 'I don't know. Our plan has a lot of moving parts, none of which have fallen in place.'

'When will they do that?' Bear sighed theatrically.

'When some of Ruslan's team get replaced.'

29

Laskin jumped out of the car before it had even stopped.

'You.' He pointed at the driver. 'Stay here. Alert me if you see Belsky.'

Without waiting for a reply, he went inside the dormitory, with the second man on his heels. They took the stairs, hustling, shoving startled residents out of the way, until they reached the third floor.

Laskin wrinkled his nose at the smells that came out of apartments. Cooking, perspiration, body odors. Lines of clothing hung out to dry in the passageway. Children's toys scattered on the concrete floor. Loud music blasting from one residence.

'How do people live here?' he muttered.

'Not everyone can afford fancy apartments,' his goon replied. 'I live in a dormitory like this.'

That's because you aren't good enough to be promoted, the SVR operative thought, smirking inwardly.

The building was square, with its interior hollowed out to make room for a playground at the bottom. A man puffed on a cigarette and watched them as they turned a corner. A woman brought out her washing and began to hang it up.

Laskin's skin prickled. Each apartment seemed to fall silent as they passed its door. He felt eyes on their backs, but when he looked back, there wasn't anyone behind them. A child cried out somewhere and was hushed instantly.

'It's our suits,' the heavy whispered. 'We don't fit here. They know we are from the government, here to harass some resident. That's how they think of us.'

Laskin reached Belsky's door and pounded on it.

No reply.

An apartment door opened and an elderly man came out. He yawned widely and scratched his armpits as he watched them.

Laskin tried again and got the same response.

More residents hung out in the passageway.

'He isn't there.' Old Man sniggered.

'Break the door.'

Wood splintered around the lock when the thug kicked it. Laskin rushed in, drawing his handgun, and checked out the single-room apartment. It was empty. Dirty dishes in the kitchen sink. A pile of used clothes in the bathroom. Well-stocked refrigerator humming away.

'He might be at work,' the thug said helpfully.

'Don't you think I thought of that?' Laskin snarled. 'I called the airport before coming. He has taken a day off. Search it.'

They tossed the residence. They tore open the mattress and pillows, broke the wardrobe to see if there were hidden compartments, destroyed the bathroom sink and the toilet, smashed the lights, but found nothing. No files, no photographs or laptops or hidden papers.

Laskin kicked the trashcan savagely and stomped out of the apartment.

'WHAT?' he roared at the watching residents.

He brushed past them, ran down the stairs and took deep breaths when he emerged.

He dialed Ruslan.

'I have been investigating Yasimov's disappearance,' he explained.

'Da?'

The case officer swallowed his intense dislike for the Zaslon man and explained what had transpired.

'Have you traced his phone?' Ruslan asked after listening silently.

Laskin gripped his device so hard that his knuckles turned white. *Why didn't I think of something so basic?*

'No,' he mumbled.

His ears burned at the silence at Ruslan's end. He could picture the man's expression of smug superiority.

'Hold on,' the team lead told him. 'Let me check where his phone is right now.'

'It's in a restaurant,' he said after a moment. 'In Dolgoprudny in Moscow Oblast. That's about half an hour from you in this traffic. Who is with you?'

Laskin gave him the thugs' names.

Ruslan made an irritated sound. 'They are door kickers. Leave them there. Belsky might be smart. He might have given someone else his phone. Ask them to call you if he shows up. You go to the restaurant. I will send two men to back you up.'

'Who will you send?'

'Nikitin and Golubev.'

30

Nothing happened in the dormitory that residents didn't know about. Laskin's arrival had sent a ripple through the apartments as soft calls were made from floor to floor and door to door.

They didn't know he was SVR, but they knew his type. Fancy suit, polished suit, government car and two thugs meant only one thing.

Trouble.

Rostov, Old Man, made the call to Belsky.

'You had visitors today,' he briefed quickly. 'Those thugs are still here, but Government Man took a taxi and went somewhere.'

VLAD BELSKY THANKED him and hung up. He smiled absently as his young niece chattered excitedly about her day. He had picked her up from school to take her to dinner, a birthday treat for her, and the plan was to drop her back at the home of Lara, his sister.

He had always hoped his role in Yasimov's escape wouldn't

be discovered, and as days passed, he had grown more confident.

He forced himself to stay calm.

I can't go back to my apartment. I can't go to the airport either.

He patted his niece and made another call to a number he had received anonymously.

'They are on to me. I need help.'

'DITCH THE PHONE IMMEDIATELY,' Yasimov ordered him. 'Take your niece and go to a nearby restaurant. Did you drive?'

'Da.'

'Leave the car as well.'

'I can't put Petra in danger.'

'She won't be. Can you steal someone's phone?'

'Steal?'

'Da. Don't waste time. You are in a busy place. Many people will have their phones on their tables. Grab one, take Petra, go out and call me.'

BELSKY LOOKED AROUND. His eyes lighted on a bunch of teenagers who were two tables away. They were laughing as they ate. One girl hung up from the call she was making and placed her phone near the edge of the table.

'Petra,' he told his niece, 'come, we have to go.'

'But I haven't finished—'

'Mama called me. She has baked a cake for you—'

'A cake!' Petra slid out of her chair instantly, her meal forgotten.

Belsky wiped her fingers with a napkin, caught her hand and weaved through the tables. Years of handling bags had made him deft. He palmed the teenager's phone discreetly and, when he was outside, quickly changed the screen-lock password before it died. He crushed his own phone beneath his heel and kicked it beneath a parked vehicle.

'What happened to your car?'

'It's dead, honey,' he told his niece. He crossed the road and went to the parking lot of the neighboring restaurant. 'We will have to call a taxi.'

He called Yasimov once they were in the darkest part of the lot.

'I am out,' he said.

'STAY THERE,' Yasimov told him. 'I will arrange for you to be picked up.'

The editor looked out of the window at the growing darkness. *Vlad ... I can't repay him enough. I have to get him out of there. I can't ask my friends to help, however. They have done enough for me.*

He could send a secure message to the Resistance movement. The protesters would come to help, but it would take time.

He glanced at his phone and dialed the number on it.

'It's me—'

'Da. What's up?'

He recognized her voice. She and the other woman had put up the cameras.

MEGHAN WALKED over to Zeb's table and dropped the phone in his outstretched palm casually.

'It's Yasimov,' she whispered and continued towards the bathroom.

'We need your help,' Zeb told the editor.

'I will do whatever I can, but you need to help me first.'

'Hold,' Zeb told him after listening. He muted the phone and looked in Beth's direction.

'Vlad Belsky—'

'The baggage handler who helped him escape?' Bwana finished.

'Yeah. He's in trouble. Some men went to his apartment and broke it down.'

'SVR.'

'Could be. He's in the parking lot of a restaurant in Dolgoprudny. He needs extraction.'

His team got up instantly. They threw bills on the table and went out of the restaurant.

Zeb went to his van and got behind the wheel.

'SVR will track his phone.' Meghan buckled in. 'They'll search the neighborhood once they find out he isn't in the restaurant.'

Zeb wheeled out and floored the gas.

31

'I want to punch him up before we take him to Ruslan,' Nikitin announced as he weaved through the traffic.

'Me too,' Golubev snarled. 'Someone has to pay for the attack on us.'

'We have to be careful, though. Dmitri doesn't want him hurt.'

'We know hundreds of ways to hurt someone without leaving marks,' his friend gloated.

They drove through Moscow's traffic, through the beltways, and had to slow down once they hit MKAD.

Nikitin hit the siren on their government car, but it didn't make much difference. Traffic was bumper-to-bumper; no one wanted to make way. Their snarling and threats didn't help, either.

They got lucky when an ambulance rolled up, for which the traffic parted. Nikitin squeezed behind it and breathed a sigh of relief when they exited the beltway and made faster progress.

'It should be here.' Golubev scanned the streets as they entered Dolgoprudny.

'There!' he pointed to the brightly lit restaurant.

'Be casual,' Nikitin warned as he drove into the parking lot and backed into an empty space. 'We're in our suits. That place looks like a family joint.'

They checked out every parked car to confirm Belsky wasn't in it and then headed to the entrance.

A shout made them whirl. They had started to draw their guns when Laskin reached them, panting.

'Evgeny.' Golubev's lips curled. Gorshky's CPO team looked down on every case officer. *It's not just us, all Zaslon agents don't think much of them.* 'You took your time.'

'I had to take a taxi.'

'Follow us. Don't make a scene,' Nikitin said brusquely.

'Belsky is my—'

The Zaslon agents didn't wait for him to finish before entering the restaurant. They split up automatically, heading left and right each, their hands near their waists, their eyes scanning the seating area.

Golubev caught Laskin's eye and jerked his head irritably as if to say, *get inside, start searching.*

The case officer read his expression and went down the middle passageway.

Sounds and smells assailed them. Laughter, the clink of cutlery, servers' requests to the cooks, the manager at the till.

Vlad Belsky wasn't in sight.

Golubev checked out the bathroom, while Nikitin went into the ladies' one, ignoring the shrieks of protest.

'He's not here,' Laskin said in despair.

Golubev watched a bunch of teenagers huddled at a table. One girl looked teary-eyed.

'Shulga,' he ordered, 'go to the manager and check out if they have CCTV cameras.'

'What happened?' he asked the youngsters.

They took in his appearance and voice for one of authority.

'My phone,' the tearful girl's voice quavered. 'Someone stole it when we were having dinner.'

'When was this?'

'About ten, fifteen minutes ago. I had put it here, to the side, and was talking to my friends ...'

Golubev tuned her out. *It could be Belsky! He could have stolen it.*

'What is the number?'

He wrote it down on his palm and turned at Nikitin's hurried approach.

'He was here with a young girl.'

'Da. He stole this woman's phone.'

'Will you get it for me?' the teenager asked excitedly.

Golubev flashed his warmest smile.

'Da. Enjoy your dinner. We will get it back to you before you finish.'

He hustled Nikitin and Laskin out of the restaurant and scanned the surroundings.

'Ping that phone,' he ordered his friend as he searched the darkness.

I would arrange a taxi or get a friend to pick me up if I was escaping.

'Laskin, go to the manager and see if any taxis came up in the last fifteen minutes. Some of their cameras point to the street as well.'

The case officer disappeared inside.

Apartment buildings to the left and right. He wouldn't go there. They will have cameras. He stretched on his toes to peer through the lights across the street. A line of shops and a restaurant.

'No taxis,' Laskin said as he emerged from the restaurant.

'HE'S THERE!' Nikitin yelled, pointing across the street.

Golubev sprinted across the road, holding his hand out in warning. A driver honked angrily; another man lowered his window and cursed. He ignored them, climbed up the grassy bank and gestured silently at Nikitin and Laskin to split up.

'He won't be inside. He'll hide in the parking lot.'

Golubev drew his Glock 17 out and moved stealthily to the line of cars. Zaslon operatives could choose their own weapons, and while many went with Tokarevs or Grachs, he preferred the Austrian weapon.

The first car was empty, as was the second. In his peripheral vision he could see Laskin and Nikitin checking out vehicles at the far end of the L-shaped lot. A family in the third vehicle. The man turned on his lights, momentarily blinding him, and drove away.

Golubev cursed and waited for his night vision to return. The parking lot had street lamps, but none of them were working.

He checked out a truck, reached the intersection of the L's arms and was headed for the next vehicle when he heard a sniffle.

He tracked back and looked beneath the van he had already checked out. No one there. He went to its rear, and then it struck him.

He climbed to the roof of the neighboring car and snarled in triumph.

Belsky and the girl were hugging the van's roof.

32

Zeb cut skillfully through the traffic, passing close to vehicles and leaving frustrated commuters and angry honks in his wake.

'We're right behind you,' Bear announced in their earpieces.

'How far are you?' asked Yasimov, who was patched in on their comms.

'I am on the roof of a black van.' Belsky, conferenced in, couldn't hide his trembling. 'With my niece.'

'Turning into the approach street,' Zeb said, his teeth gritted. He nodded at Beth's pointed finger at the strip of stores, eased to a stop behind a parked vehicle and jammed the brakes.

We'll park on the road for a quick getaway.

He jumped out, but Bwana and Roger were faster.

'Our turn,' the Texan said, smiling, as he pulled down his mask and disappeared into the darkness.

'Spread out,' Zeb told his team. 'We'll back them up.'

. . .

'Let her go,' Belsky pleaded.

'I got them!' Golubev yelled. 'Shulga, get the car!'

'GET DOWN!' He snarled at the baggage handler, grabbed his Tee and yanked him to the ground.

He swore when the girl screamed. He slapped her and pulled her down as well.

A pair of headlights lit them up.

Nikitin, who leaned out of the window. 'Do you need any help?'

'Nyet.' Golubev jammed his Glock tight against Belsky's back and shoved him to the car.

'Laskin,' he ordered the case officer, 'open the trunk. We'll dump them there.'

They pushed their kicking and yelling prisoners at the vehicle.

'Please,' Belsky pleaded. 'She is—'

Golubev punched him in the belly, picked up the girl and tossed her in the trunk as if she weighed nothing.

'WHAT'S GOING ON?'

A burly man called out

'We are the police,' Golubev warned. 'Mind your own business.'

The man seemed to sense the menace radiating from the Zaslon agent and slunk away.

'Good work.' Golubev gloated at Nikitin and Laskin when he joined his partner at the front. 'We'll extract answers from him.'

Nikitin was about to floor it when a body crashed into the windshield.

33

'Saw that?' Roger asked Bwana as they raced across the parking lot, his hands curled into fists at the sight of the men beating up Belsky and the girl.

'Sure did, bud.' Bwana's voice was dark, foreboding, promising immense violence.

'That's Karel Golubev,' Beth identified the attacker. 'And that dude driving the car is Nikitin.'

'They didn't learn their lesson,' Bwana growled. 'Who's the third man?'

'Must be the case officer who went to Belsky's building.'

Roger didn't have time for any elaborate plan. *Can't draw my gun. That will attract attention.*

The SVR car started moving towards the exit, with its captives in the rear.

There was only one way to stop it.

He threw himself against it. *No risk. It's barely moving.*

He relaxed his body at the moment of impact and rolled smoothly over the roof and fell to the ground on the passenger side.

He grabbed the door handle, pulled it open and punched

Nikitin fiercely in the side of his neck. Bwana, big as a barn door, was on the driver side, his face lean and mean as he snapped open Golubev's seat belt, pulled the man out and back-handed him, almost lazily.

Nikitin was fast and vicious. He let his body fall on the Texan's. His hand snaked to his belt.

Not so fast, buddy.

Roger finger-jabbed him in the throat and smashed his head against the side of the car repeatedly. The killer kicked back with his heel, got him in the belly and sent him sprawling to the ground.

Roger swore. He caught the retreating limb, reared up and punched him in the groin.

The SVR man howled in the darkness, his scream cut off when the Texan knocked him out cold.

'You need help?' Roger panted.

'Me?' His friend's teeth gleamed. He dragged Laskin out of the car and knocked out the struggling case officer with a single punch.

Zeb reached the car with the twins and Chloe, while Broker and Bear remained in the shadows to warn them if GUVD or more SVR agents arrived.

He heard the thumping from the trunk and opened it.

He easily deflected Belsky's punch.

'We were on the call with you. Boris's friends.'

'How do I know that? You are wearing masks.'

'It's for our protection. We don't want to be recognized.'

'You could be SVR—'

'Do you think we would go to this trouble to save you if we were?'

Belsky opened his mouth, clamped it shut and reached out a hand.

Zeb helped him out, while Beth reached inside to pick up the girl gently. Rage swept over Zeb when he saw the bruises on her face and heard her sob and hiccup. He felt movement behind him. Turned to see Chloe pirouette like a ballet dancer and bring her heel down on Golubev's face.

'Let's go,' he told his friends. 'Take them with us.'

He helped Belsky limp towards their van, with Beth carrying his niece. Bear rolled up in his van and the rest of his team loaded the unconscious men into it.

'Where to?' Broker radioed when he got behind the wheel.

Zeb looked in the mirror as if he could see his friend in the back of the van with Belsky and his niece.

'A safe house.'

'I got her phone!' the baggage handler spoke up.

'Whose?'

'That girl's. I have to return it to her.'

'We have to get away.'

'I don't steal. I don't keep other people's property.'

Zeb couldn't help smiling at his stubbornness.

He drove towards the restaurant and into the parking lot. Breathed in relief at the sight of the teenagers outside, consoling a crying girl.

He heard the van's side door open, Broker whistle out and saw the phone fly in an arc at the youngsters, and then he was out of the parking lot, with Bear close behind.

'His sister and niece have to disappear,' Beth told him when he reached a traffic light. 'And we need to find a safe house for our prisoners.'

Zeb nodded.

'Broker—'

'I heard. His sister is a single mom. He's calling her right now. Hold up.'

Zeb thumbed his phone when the light changed. He was scrolling down the recent calls when his friend spoke up.

'She and Petra can disappear for a couple of weeks. I have sent their address to you as a pin.'

Meghan took his phone and entered the coordinates in the van's satnav.

'It's just a few minutes away. What about the safe house?'

'I'm onto it.'

'Josiah,' he said when he called the Mossad agent, 'I need two safe houses.'

'For how many guests?'

'One of them for one guest and the other for three. Of those, at least one of them might be badly injured.'

'Are they friends or hostile?'

'The first one is friendly, not the rest.'

'Where are you?'

'Dolgoprudny.'

'Go to Sheremetyevo, to the cargo area at the back of the airport. Are you driving my vans?'

'Yeah.'

'My men will meet you at the entrance of the cargo area. You don't need to go inside.'

'How will we recognize them?'

'You can't miss them. They'll be wearing the fast-food uniforms.'

THEIR FIRST STOP was outside a convenience store beneath an apartment building, where Belsky's sister waited, clutching a roller-case. Her face was pinched, nervous, and when Zeb drove close to her, he could see the sheen of tears in her eyes.

She choked back a sob when the panel door opened. She climbed into the rear, and at Broker's thump, Zeb drove away.

'Lara's asking if we punished the men who hurt her daughter,' his friend's amused voice came on.

'We did,' Bwana replied.

'Sure as heck we did,' Chloe added.

THEIR SECOND STOP was a motel in Odintsovo. It was plain, nondescript, with faded signs and a single flickering light at its entrance.

Zeb looked doubtfully at the twins. 'That doesn't look hospitable.'

'That's the address she gave us,' Beth shrugged.

Belsky came to his window with his sister and niece behind him.

Why's he staring at us?

Our masks! We didn't remove them.

'Will she be—'

'It's her sister-in-law's. They are still close despite the separation from her husband. No one knows about this place. It is recorded in different names ... for taxes.'

Zeb flicked his eyes at the sister, who gave a small finger wave and smiled hesitantly. The young girl skipped on one foot and tugged impatiently at her mom's hand. It looked like she had forgotten her travails.

'What did you tell them about those men?'

'The truth. She knows of my involvement with the Resistance. I didn't tell her about helping Boris.'

The young girl darted to them suddenly, rose on her toes and looked at Meghan gravely.

'I like you,' she said and ran back to her mom.

'We like you too.' Beth grinned. 'We should have killed Golubev,' she said under her breath as they watched Belsky lead his sister and niece inside the motel.

ZEB SLOWED when they reached the cargo approach to Sheremetyevo. A metal barrier was across the road to bottleneck the traffic, beyond which was a construction truck. A man in coveralls and helmet came up when he reached the roadblock.

Zahavy's grinning face was beneath the headgear.

'You!'

'Yes. We are men of many disguises,' the Mossad agent said smugly. He eyed their masks but didn't say anything. 'Park your vans next to those trucks. No one will come here for forty minutes. We are safe.'

He whistled sharply, at which several men came from behind the construction vehicle.

They asked no questions and showed no expression when Bear and Bwana carried out their captives.

Zahavy froze momentarily, however.

'Golubev, Nikitin and Evgeny Laskin!'

'You recognize them?'

'Yes. Should I ask how you got them?'

'No.'

'Can I interrogate them when they wake up? I'll share whatever they reveal.'

'Be my guest. Golubev might not survive whatever you do to them.'

'Will that be a loss?'

'No,' Zeb said coldly as he recalled the young girl's injuries. 'None of them will be.'

'And this is the friend?' The Israeli cocked his head at Belsky.

'Yeah.'

'We will keep him safe. You, my friend,'—he clapped the baggage handler's shoulder—'are going to enjoy your stay with us. Have you heard of this joint?' He mentioned the fast-food brand.

'I love it.' Belsky smiled.

'Then, you are going to have the time of your life.'

His smile disappeared when he turned back to Zeb. 'Those three men. Is this about—'

'Ask not and you shall get no lies.'

'That isn't how the saying goes, but I get it.'

'What's that?' Zeb frowned when Zahavy's men loaded several rolls of some type of film into the vans.

'That's colored film you can apply to the vans. You can make them look white, blue, red, whatever shade you want. With that and the different logos and plates, you will be undetected.'

Zeb was about to thank him when the Mossad operative waved.

'Avichai Levin, Carmen and Dalia swear by you folks. It is my honor to help you.'

'BACK TO THE HOTEL?' Beth asked when Zeb reversed and drove away from the airport.

'Yeah, and then I need to go out.'

'Why?'

'To meet Yasimov.'

'What for?'

'To ask him about the help we need.'

34

Zeb wanted to go alone, but his team wouldn't have it.

'You're a magnet for trouble,' Broker told him. 'You need minders.'

'We can't all go to his apartment.'

'We'll be outside, spread out.'

'Beth and I will be with our long guns in those trees.' Meghan bumped his shoulder.

Zeb gave up.

They drove the vans to a garage that was open despite the late evening hour.

'It's a Mossad front,' he whispered when they rolled in.

The uniformed mechanics paid them no attention as they unwrapped two rolls of film and colored Zeb's van in blue and Bear's vehicle in grey.

They rolled up Michurinskiy, and while Bear stopped in the pull-off, Zeb entered the store's parking lot. He turned off the engine and waited for several moments, feeling the night.

'Clear.' Beth looked up from her screen. 'Nothing on the cameras.'

He climbed out and walked up the approach road with his

head down, mask in one hand. He took the stairs swiftly, sensing no threat, and reached Elena's floor.

Faint TV sounds came from Grusha's door. His belly rumbled at the smell of dinner cooking in someone's home. He slipped on his mask, peeled off the tape carefully and unlocked Elena's door.

He sensed the incoming strike and ducked swiftly. Blocked the baseball bat and chuckled at Yasimov's expression.

'You didn't knock before entering. I thought you were—'

'I wanted to check how alert you were.'

'I would have hurt you.'

No, you wouldn't.

'You didn't,' Zeb told the editor as he surveyed the apartment swiftly.

Yasimov was a neat occupant. No trash on the floor or on the table. The furniture was neatly arranged, with nothing out of place.

'Thank you for helping Vlad.' Yasimov reappeared from the kitchen with two cups of coffee.

'He will be safe.'

'I tried calling—'

'His phone is deactivated. He won't be reachable for a few days. But he is with good people. They will protect him.'

'Thank you again. You said you needed my help. What can I do?'

'You have contacts in the protest movement?'

'Da. I'm like a central figure in the Resistance.' The editor smiled in embarrassment. 'Elena too, when she was there.'

'I know where she is.' Zeb sipped his beverage, savoring the brew. 'Lubyanka.'

Yasimov's eyes widened. His jaws slackened. 'That's not possible. It's a museum.'

'Gorshky has put its basement to its original use. A prison.'

'You are sure?'

'Da.'

'Is she—'

'She's alive. I'm sure she has been questioned, but she hasn't been tortured.'

'That's not like Gorshky.'

Zeb smiled thinly. 'Da, I agree. But he holds all the cards. With her in prison, there's no way her article will be published.'

'You have got to get her—'

'This is Lubyanka we're talking about. No one can breach it.'

'You said you would help!'

'Da. We're working on it. We can do something once she's out of that place.'

'How will you ...' Yasimov trailed off. His eyes lit up. 'You can attack once she is in transit.'

'Correct.'

'Gorshky will move her from Lubyanka if he thinks there is a threat there ... the protesters! Their rioting or attacking the prison will make him move her.'

'You figured it out.'

'I can make that happen right now.' Yasimov darted to the couch and grabbed the secure phone. 'I will call—'

'Nyet. It's too soon. We need more time to prepare.'

'Time? Elena is running out of it.'

'I'm aware of that. But even rescuing her from her transport convoy won't be easy. Several more pieces have to fall into place first.'

'We can't leave her there for long.'

'We won't. Gorshky's bodyguards,' Zeb said, changing the subject. 'How do the backup agents get selected?'

'You mean if something happens to his current team? It will be based on seniority.'

That would be Kostya Bortnik and Magar Orlov, replacing Golubev and Nikitin, Zeb recalled from Yasimov's files.

'And what if something happens to Ruslan?'

The editor frowned at him. He went into the bedroom and returned with his laptop. He logged into his cloud account and brought up the list of names.

'Dusan Smirnov,' he looked up. 'He will take over as team leader.'

Zeb fist-pumped internally at that.

35

'Ruslan is in the building!'

Zeb cocked his head at Beth's warning in his earpiece.

'You didn't spot him?' he asked in Russian.

He pointed his device at Yasimov's expression and checked the camera feed on his phone.

'He walked up the approach road. We didn't recognize him in the darkness.'

'He's alone?'

'Yeah.'

'No one in the parking lot,' Broker checked in.

'No police vehicles or anything out of the ordinary on Michurinskiy,' Bear confirmed.

'We're around the building,' Bwana said. 'Other than for Broker and Bear. He's alone.'

Zeb saw the Zaslon man enter the lobby. His face was hard, his lips tight as he climbed the stairs, swiftly disappeared out of the camera's frame and appeared on the stairs leading to Elena's door.

'Go to the bedroom,' he told Yasimov and drew his Glock.

'Trouble?

'Nothing that we can't handle.'

Especially if Ruslan is alone.

The team leader didn't stop or even glance at Elena's door, however. He went straight to Grusha's apartment and pounded on the door there. He grabbed her throat when she opened it, pushed her back inside and disappeared from the camera when the door closed behind them.

Zeb stared at his screen as rage washed over him.

Why has he gone to her?

He thinks she's part of the Resistance, he answered himself. *He's found out Golubev and Nikitin disappeared and thinks she knows where they are or what happened.*

'Stay inside,' he told Yasimov and went to the door with his phone in one hand.

He stopped when Grusha's apartment door opened. Ruslan appeared in the door frame, his hand grabbing her around the neck. He smashed her head against the wood, flung her inside, slammed the door and stomped down the stairs.

Zeb went out quickly, sealed the apartment behind him and started down the stairs cautiously. He slipped on his mask when he reached the first landing, straining to hear Ruslan's footsteps.

He thought he heard the scrape of a shoe and crouched low —which was when the Zaslon operative lunged from around the frame of the steps, his gun in hand.

'WHO ARE YOU?'

36

Ruslan was moving too fast for his Glock to stay centered on Zeb, who lashed out with his left hand to deflect the gun and charged at the team leader.

The Glock clattered on the landing, and his impact took them sliding down the steps, with Zeb on top.

Zeb saw the flash of metal appear in Ruslan's hand.

Knife!

He caught the wrist and twisted it hard at an almost impossible angle, to bring the point to the Zaslon's belly, but a hard slide over the stairs loosened his grip.

Ruslan yelled in rage and reared up for another strike. Zeb trapped his wrist with both hands and, using the momentum of their slide, turned to take his weight on his right shoulder; with a fierce pull-heave, he flung the Russian to send him skidding on the lobby floor and out into the yard.

He dove at the Zaslon man with the knife in his hand, just as a car burst into the building's lot with its window rolled down.

Zeb glimpsed the gun pointing at him and threw himself to the side as rounds spat into the concrete wall behind him. He took cover behind a pillar, snatching a look a moment later when tires squealed and the vehicle drove off, flinging up a spatter of rubble.

Ruslan got away! That must have been his driver.

He raced down the approach road to see its taillights disappear around a bend.

'We saw it coming but didn't warn you,' Meghan commented. 'It would have distracted you.'

'Where was the car?'

'It wasn't anywhere nearby,' Bear said. 'I saw it coming up Michurinskiy, but by then you were wrestling with him.'

Grusha!

Zeb sprinted back into the building and knocked on her door. He lowered his head to show only his hair when he sensed movement at the peephole and, when it opened, raised his hands in a non-threatening gesture.

'I am a friend of Elena's,' he said immediately. 'The mask is to protect my identity.'

He smiled beneath his balaclava when she brandished a knife.

'I mean no harm. I am not here to hurt you.'

The blade remained in the air.

'Ruslan—that man who came here—what did he want?'

The knife wavered, but her eyes remained suspicious.

'I saw him grab your throat. I would have come to help, but he came out very quickly.'

He eyed the bruised lump on her forehead and the split lip.

'What did he want?'

She took him in: his balaclava, his combat trousers, and the way he stood easily. Her knife hand dropped, though her expression remained wary.

'He wanted to know who attacked his men today. I told him I didn't know anything about that. I said I wasn't involved in the protests. All I did was place those flowers at Elena's door. She was a good neighbor.'

She sniffed and brushed away a tear.

'He and his men beat me up the first time as well. Yesterday. And in the evening, his men threatened me in the store.'

'They won't bother you again.'

'You can't say that,' she flared. 'You don't know anything about them.'

'I know a lot. Those two men who were rude to you in the store will never be seen again.'

'Who are you?' she whispered.

'A friend. Why did Ruslan leave so quickly?'

'I had only one way to convince him I was speaking the truth. I offered myself to him. I told him to rape me.'

The rage consumed him instantly, filling him with so much darkness that for a moment he could see or hear nothing. She had shut the door by the time he recovered.

He went down the steps and into the lobby, hoping Ruslan had returned, wishing he had smashed the man's head to a gory pulp against the concrete steps.

Cool air swept over him, dried the film of perspiration on his face and lowered his pulse. His fists unclenched gradually as he returned to the parking lot. Heard footsteps behind him and knew it was the twins.

'What did she say?' Beth asked him when he reached their van.

Her face tightened at his reply.

'What do you intend to do?'

'Take care of unfinished business.'

37

It was a repeat of the previous meeting.

Alexei Gorshky cooled his heels on the marble floor of the Kremlin building while suits passed him with a supercilious air. As before, no one stopped to talk to him or offer him any drinks.

They are scared of my power, he told himself.

Finally, an aide approached, looking up from his tablet as if the SVR chief was a nuisance.

'Come, you don't have much time.'

Gorshky followed him, wondering how he could get the man transferred to SVR so he could make his life miserable. A sharp knock on the door brought him to the present. He entered the room, strode smartly to the President and stood at attention.

'Gorshky.' The most powerful man in the country regarded him through half-lidded eyes. 'I have supported you for a long time. I have given you whatever budgets you asked for. You have a lot of enemies. They keep telling me you are arrogant. That your power has gone to your head. I've never listened to them. But now I wonder. Are they right, Gorshky? Have you forgotten who appointed you?'

'Nyet. I owe everything to you.'

'Is that so? Why have you let this continue?'

The SVR chief thought of asking: *continue what?* But the way the President looked at him, like a reptile ready to pounce, made him reconsider.

'Your agency is being humiliated by these protesters. What do they call themselves? The Resistance. What are they resisting? What are they fighting for? Democracy? More democracy? More freedom? Pah! Have you found out who killed your men at the reporter's apartment?'

'We are working on it—'

'Why are you allowing them to post on social media?'

'There are so many accounts. We think many of them are bots—'

'Did I ask for an explanation?'

Gorshky bit his tongue.

'Everyone is laughing at your agency's incompetence. Which means they are laughing at Russia. You have allowed a bunch of rioters and protesters to disrespect us.'

'If we interrogate that reporter, get her notes, we can finish—'

'You think those people'—the President waved in the direction of Red Square—'will go home once she is dead? They will make her a martyr. More people will join their movement.'

'Our Ukraine plans—'

'Do you know more about them than me?'

'Nyet, but if her article leaks somehow, America, Britain, NATO ... they may stop us.'

'Do your job, then. Stop the leaking.'

'I'll question her—'

'Nyet. I told you once. She is off-limits until I give you permission.'

It might be too late by then.

He held his tongue, however.

'Did you find the editor?'

'We are working on it—'

'I am beginning to wonder what exactly you are working on.'

Gorshky left the President's office in a cold rage. He fumed as his car drove through Red Square, with protesters lining up on both sides of the road. He was tempted to tell his driver to run over some of them, but sanity prevailed.

He reached his office and crooked a finger at Dmitri Ruslan.

'What progress have you made?' he asked his CPO team leader when the man entered his office.

'We have a few leads. I suspect—'

'Leads? You suspect? Do you know anything? Have you captured anyone?'

'Nyet.'

'You and your team are supposed to be the best ... it doesn't feel like that. Where are Nikitin and Golubev? I saw new faces in your vehicle.'

'They are sick. Bortnik and Orlov are the new men. Good agents.'

'They are sick at the same time?

'Da. They picked up some bug.'

'Why are you still here? Find those killers. Bring me some good news. Send me Evgeny. He was working on finding Yasimov.'

'He's off sick, too.'

'SICK? This is the SVR. How can people fall ill! Do I have to do all the work myself?'

Ruslan listened silently as his boss ranted and let himself out when Gorshky had finished.

I can't tell him Golubev, Nikitin and Laskin have disappeared.

Not until I know what went down. That baggage handler is gone, too. He hasn't shown up to work.

He went to his office and snapped his fingers. Galkin, Bortnik and Orlov came to him.

'What I am about to tell you should remain with you only. Even the boss does not know about this.' He briefed them quickly on Laskin's investigation, Belsky, and his sending Golubev and Nikitin to help.

'All four of them are missing,' he said grimly. 'Our men's phones were at a restaurant opposite the one Belsky was in. I called their manager, but their cameras are down. That can't be a coincidence. Split up the work among yourselves. One of you go through Laskin's files and find out everything you can about Belsky. Go to that restaurant. Question its employees. Get me results.'

'Could it be the protesters?' Galkin observed.

'Who else could it be?' Ruslan snarled.

He sat down when they had left and winced at the shooting pain in his back.

I'm not going to tell them about that masked man in Zakharova's apartment.

The man had been fast, brutal in his punches, and knew all the moves. *Was he alone?*

The team leader hadn't seen anyone else, but when his car turned up, he had taken the opportunity to escape. He couldn't let himself be captured by the protesters.

He tried to remember the attacker's details, but all he could recall was dark clothing and piercing eyes. *Were they black? Brown? Grey?*

He swore when he realized he hadn't noticed their color.

Will Lebedev know anything about him? Was he waiting in the building for me?

Da, he decided. *He must have been up the stairs and someone must have warned him when I arrived.*

Did that mean Mystery Man and the other attackers lived in the building?

Nyet. He shook his head. *We questioned every resident. They are scared of us. These protesters are too smart to stay there.*

It looked like the Resistance movement had established a protective ring around the building.

I can organize a team and flush them out, but they might see us coming. Besides, Ruslan didn't know how many informers the protesters had.

No, it was better to identify the attackers and track them down.

That man had military training. Ruslan was sure of that. No civilian could hit that hard or react that quickly.

He opened the files he had been reading and began going through them again.

'ANY UPDATE?' he asked his team when evening had fallen.

They shook their heads.

'Stay on it,' he growled and looked at his watch.

'Nikola, you are in charge. I am off.'

It was Friday, and with the day he'd had, he knew where he was going to spend the evening.

His steps quickened when he thought of Katerina at Gypsy.

38

Zeb began his stakeout at five pm. He was dressed in a dark shirt hanging loose over his jeans. His Glock and Spyderco knife were on him, but no other weapon.

Meg and Beth are checking out the various roads around Lubyanka. Broker is going through the security team's files. Bwana, Bear and Chloe are checking out attack points outside the SVR office.

None of them knew what he was planning. He had told them he had to meet Zahavy and had slipped out of his hotel. He had taken a taxi to the Gypsy and checked out its exterior.

The outside of the nightclub was unimposing. It was in a squat, concrete structure in front of an apartment building. A bowling alley, a pizza joint, and a retail store were the other occupants in the commercial establishment.

The Gypsy had its main entrance facing the parking lot. The only signs that this was a nightclub were a steel door with a costumed man painted on it and a pair of lights above.

The side of the commercial building had another steel door, and guessing from the crates, alcohol bottles and refuse bags stashed beside it, it had to be the service entrance.

Can't see a fire escape.

The door lights went on at six pm, and half an hour later, two bouncers appeared at the door.

Zeb went inside the Gypsy.

'SHOULD WE FOLLOW HIM?' Bwana asked.

'Nope,' Meghan drawled.

She was sprawled behind the wheel in her van, parked on Ullitsa Paustovskogo. Beth and Broker were in the back, while the rest of the crew were in the second vehicle at a nearby pull-off.

'He doesn't know we've rigged his phone and turned it into a listening device,' Meghan said as she grinned and stretched her legs.

'Check out the exit routes,' Beth scoffed. 'Find out choke points ... how long did he think that would take us?'

'Taking Gorshky outside the SVR office ... we shot that idea down back in New York,' Chloe agreed. 'Did he think we would fall for it?'

'He must have forgotten he told us he would go nightclubbing.' The rasp of Bear running his fingers through his hair was loud over his earpieces.

'Why do you think he's here?' Roger mused aloud.

'You know what went down at Elena's apartment,' Meghan replied. 'Can't you put it together?'

ZEB ORDERED a juice at the bar, ignored the server's raised eyebrows, collected his drink and went to a corner table.

The joint was filling up slowly. Young people from an office came in, boisterous, joking, gesticulating. They went to the bar and placed their orders. The volume of the music rose. A dancer entered a cage that was hanging from the ceiling and started swaying. More customers entered. The lights dimmed.

A spotlight appeared on the stage and applause broke out when a singer entered its glare.

'Do you have private rooms?' he asked, approaching a suit who appeared to be a manager in the establishment.

'I'm CEO of a construction company. I hire rooms to entertain my clients,' he explained when the man looked him up and down.

'Da.' Suit's lips parted in a smile. 'We have a few such rooms. We can serve food and drink there and even send some dancers.' His eyebrows danced.

'Can I see them?'

I need to confirm Ruslan isn't already here.

Zeb strode alongside Suit, who explained the various rooms, how they were priced and how they could be booked. They went down a hallway past the dance floor, where the sound dropped off. The manager opened a door and gestured at the leather couches, dining table and soft lighting in the room.

'We can arrange the furniture in whichever way you want. A table for playing cards, or more chairs, whatever you need can be done.'

Suit showed two more rooms and pointed at the fourth. 'That's the last one we have, but it is occupied. It is our largest. DON'T GO—'

Zeb flung it open with his left hand, his right near his chest. A bare-chested man was groping a woman. No one else inside.

'Prostite!' he apologized. 'I thought it was empty.'

He turned to the glowering manager and peeled off several bills from a wad in his pocket. 'I'll book that one.'

A grin replaced Suit's anger. He counted the money swiftly and made a note in a notebook. 'Come to my office, we'll—'

'What's over there?'

Zeb pointed to two more doors at the end of the hallway.

'Bathrooms,' the manager said, 'for men and women. And

this one.' He opened a concealed door in the rear wall, which led to the parking lot. 'This is for VIPs. You and your guests can use it.'

The hidden exit was some distance from the service entrance and was set flush in the outside wall.

'We can have a bouncer here if you wish, along with a red carpet. But many of our guests prefer to enter anonymously.'

Ruslan will use this entrance. Zeb was sure of it. He checked above the door discreetly. *No cameras.*

'How does it open from outside?'

'Here,' Suit pushed against a pressure pad and the door swung open. 'It has to be unlocked from the inside, though. Some of our regular VIPs are coming today, so we have kept it unbolted.'

'What if strangers use it?'

'We have cameras inside. Our security team will see who has entered. Our bouncers will turn away unauthorized customers.'

Zeb looked at the CCTV device in the ceiling as they walked back to the bar. *That will have to go.*

'Who are your best dancers?'

'The ones on the stage.' Two women were writhing suggestively against a metal pole, smiling at the customers' cheers and whistles. 'Tatiana and Nadia will do more for our customers, for the right price.'

'Only two?'

'We have a third, Katerina, but she is booked today. There she is, behind the bar. Da.' He nodded at Zeb's confusion. 'All our girls help out with serving and bartending in addition to their other duties.'

Zeb took in the woman's Slavic features and tinted blond hair. She met his eyes curiously for a moment and turned back to a customer.

'I have everything I need,' he said, handing Suit a business card. 'I will call you to fix a date.'

'Any time. We will give you the best experience. Your customers will not be disappointed.'

'I'll go out through the VIP entrance.'

'Da.' Suit smiled at him.

Zeb went down the hallway, removing an EMP gun from his pocket. He triggered it at the cameras as he walked past them and went outside to the parking lot.

Will the Gypsy's maintenance team replace them immediately?

There isn't much I can do if they change the cameras. I can't delay taking down Ruslan. He might stop coming as we ratchet up the pressure.

Zeb changed into combat fatigues and a loose jacket in his van and parked it in a vacant spot from which he could watch the main entrance as well as the VIP door.

He reclined his seat and settled down to wait.

The dark vehicle appeared at nine pm.

39

Zeb noticed it immediately, since it didn't ease into a space right away. The vehicle drove around the lot, making several passes.

If Ruslan is inside it, he's checking out the vehicles. His combat outfit had a custom lining that eliminated a heat signature. His hoodie was pulled over his head with its front zipped up, with a transparent seal through which he could observe.

He didn't move when the car crawled past his van slowly, confident that he couldn't be seen. He straightened when it drove past and followed its taillights as it backed into a far corner, where it was darkest.

He'll watch the parking lot for any unusual activity.

The car's door opened and a shadow emerged.

Zeb squinted in the darkness as the figure moved languidly and sucked his breath sharply when an overhead light illuminated Ruslan.

The Zaslon agent's head turned ceaselessly as he checked out the parking lot and headed for the VIP door.

He's alone. No backup. Makes sense. Gorshky or his team might not know about Katerina, and he wants to keep it that way.

Zeb unzipped his hoodie, removed the prosthetics from his face and pocketed them, and hustled out of his van when Ruslan opened the VIP door and slipped inside. He rotated his shoulders and flexed his fingers as he sprinted and jammed a hand in the closing door.

'Excuse me,' he said, smiling politely at Ruslan as he slipped inside and bolted the door behind him.

Time seemed to freeze.

The Russian's dark eyes bored through him, a small frown on his face. Katerina in a cocktail dress, behind him, her smile fading. No one else in the passageway, across which a rope barrier had been placed to prevent customers from entering it.

Ruslan's eyes flared in recognition. He made a small, inarticulate sound as his hand streaked towards his waist.

'Carter!'

Zeb crashed his shoulder into his, caught the emerging gun and twisted it away. The force of his slam sent them crashing against the private room's door, which swung open from their weight.

'Go!' he yelled at Katerina. 'This has nothing to do with you.'

Will she scream? Will she call the security team?

He didn't know. He didn't have time to find out, as Ruslan yelled in rage and headbutted him. Zeb turned just in time to take the impact against his cheek and grimaced at the shock that ran through him. The Zaslon operative was strong, wiry, fast, and filled with fury. He struggled to free his gun hand, but Zeb had trapped it with both hands. His left hand streaked to his thigh and came up with a wicked-looking blade.

Knife!

Zeb dug his fingers into Ruslan's wrist with all his strength, which made the gun slip out of the Russian's hand.

He scrambled back as the Zaslon killer thrust the blade at his chest.

'It was you all along,' the team leader snarled. 'You and your team. You made it look like the protesters.'

He jabbed and thrust, feinted and slashed at Zeb who could only duck and evade, so fast was the attack. He retreated until his back hit the wall.

Ruslan's lip parted triumphantly. 'I will cut you open slowly —' He thrust savagely.

Zeb dropped his knees to the floor and punched Ruslan's groin, twisted his body to grab the knife hand, which was heading towards his back, and yank-pulled the team leader to smash his head against the wall.

Can't give him room. Can't even draw my Glock or knife. That will give him time to attack.

He knuckle-punched the Russian's neck and winced when a return jab smashed into his ribs with the force of a battering ram.

Zeb staggered back when Ruslan heaved off the wall. He stumbled on the carpeted floor and jumped back when the blade missed his belly by a hair's breadth.

Can't let myself be trapped again.

He dove to his right, caught a chair, and hurled it with all his strength at his attacker. Gorshky's team leader ducked lazily, but before he could recover, Zeb was lunging forward in a feint, which drew the blade. He ducked beneath it, caught the flashing arm and twisted it to get Ruslan to drop the blade.

He didn't let go of the arm, however. He kept twisting, curling his body to wrap the limb around it, ignoring the pile-driver punches to his ribs.

He felt the Russian's breath on his neck, sensed his intent and reared his head sideways and up to split his attacker's lips.

Ruslan's shoulder dislocated. He shrieked and brought his right foot up with balletic grace to kick Zeb's face, who let go of the killer and jumped back and spin-kicked the SVR man's neck.

The Zaslon agent groaned as he slammed against the wall. But he recovered and dove with blinding speed towards his gun.

Zeb was expecting the move. He was there a fraction of a second earlier. Caught the gun with his right hand, sent it skidding across the floor and smashed his elbow in Ruslan's face. He felt the killer's teeth break. Blood spurted from his nose. And then fury washed over him when he recalled Grusha's face.

He didn't retreat from the Zaslon's punches. He absorbed them, moving only his head to evade blows to his face as he rained blows on the man's exposed throat. He felt Ruslan shudder and gasp, but he didn't let up and kept hammering away until the Zaslon man fell to the ground.

Zeb elbowed him in the throat and leaned down with all his weight until the man's struggles grew fainter and his hate-filled eyes dulled and his last breath escaped him in a rattle.

Zeb lay on him for long moments as the earth spun on its axis and he got his breath back.

He got to his feet unsteadily and leaned down to search Ruslan's body. He pulled out his phone and tried to unlock it with the man's face, but it didn't respond.

Beth or Meg might be able to crack it open.

The door opened.

He dove to his left, his Glock appearing in his hand to cover the figure at the entrance.

Katerina looked at him and the body on the floor. She entered the room and shut the door behind her.

'You could have shot him with your gun.'

'You were watching?'

'Da. I cracked it open an inch.'

'He didn't give me time. Besides, I wanted to kill him with my hands.'

Zeb lowered his gun, watching her curiously.

'Nyet. I didn't call the security people.'

'Why not?'

'Dmitri thought I cared for him. He thought wrong.'

I was hoping for that.

Her face twisted. 'If you hadn't killed him, I would have. He would have been weak from the fight. I would have broken a bottle and ripped his throat out. He used us,' she said bitterly. 'He treated me like a prostitute. He didn't give me a choice. I had to be his woman or he would send my parents to prison on some false charge. It is like that for all the women in this bar. We are some government man's property. We can't protest. No one will listen to us.'

She bent down and spat on Ruslan's body.

Her face was composed when she looked up.

'He called you by some name. Are you American?'

'You should forget it.'

He turned his back to her, put on his disguise and faced her.

She took in his changed appearance expressionlessly.

'GUVD will question you,' he said.

'I will say what I saw. That a stranger entered through that door and attacked Dmitri. I will say you were masked.'

'Why didn't you call for help?'

'He had a gun with him. He forced me to enter this room and made me watch as he killed Dmitri.'

'You could have escaped.'

'I was scared that the man would come after me. In any case, the fight was over so fast that I didn't have time to think.'

'Do you know who Ruslan was?'

'Da. SVR.'

'You should fear the organization.'

'I am scared of them. I know they will interrogate me even more than the police, but I will tell them the same. What about you? They will see you on camera and identify you.'

'Will they?' He smiled.

'They are not working?'

'Something happened to them.'

'Who are you?'

'Someone you should forget.'

'What about your fingerprints?'

Zeb held his hands up to show the flesh-colored gloves he had been wearing. They were designed to let the skin breathe, absorb sweat and at the same time give a firm grip. He had a transparent film over his head too, which fitted snugly to prevent loose hair from falling.

My sweat and blood traces will be on the floor and on Ruslan's body. But he was sure no Russian agency had his DNA.

Footsteps pounded on the hallway floor, and the door burst open. Zeb turned instantly to the wall and slipped on his mask. Two hard-faced bouncers crashed into the room and took in the scene.

'WHAT HAPPENED? IS HE DEAD? WHO DID THIS?'

One heavy shouted.

'WHO IS THAT MAN? REMOVE YOUR MASK.'

Zeb pivoted on his heel and brought the chair he had been holding down on the first bouncer's head, then threw it against the second man, who, unable to duck out of the way, lunged forward and pounded his skull against the wall.

'They will be your witnesses,' he told Katerina. 'They will back you up.'

'Will I see you again?' she called out as he left the room.

'No.'

He went out through the VIP exit, removed his mask when he was out of the glare of the lights and drove out of the parking lot.

'Did you burn it down?'

He grinned at Beth's voice in his earpiece.

They're out there somewhere, watching me, ready to come in hot and heavy if I needed backup.

'Weren't you going to check out the exits from Lubyanka?'

'Pshaw! You really thought we would fall for that? Oh, and you're welcome.'

'For?'

'For erasing your presence in the Gypsy's security system.'

'I fried the cameras.'

'But they would have recorded your presence until that point.'

'Thanks.'

'Like I said,' she chortled, 'you are welcome.'

'What did you find?' Bwana asked him.

'Ruslan.'

Bear whistled softly. 'And?'

'He's dead.'

'How will that help us?' Chloe filled in the long silence that followed.

'A jigsaw piece has fallen in place.'

40

Alexei Gorshky was still awake when the call came. He was in his office going through case reports and finishing the bureaucratic work, which was necessary though he hated it.

The message shocked him.

'Are you sure?'

'Da. There is no doubt.'

'I will be there shortly. Keep a perimeter. Keep reporters away.'

'Da.'

He sat motionless for several moments as he digested the news and then shot off his chair with an oath.

'Come,' he snapped at the rest of his CPO team, who fell in behind him silently.

Galkin got into his vehicle next to Tony, who met Gorshky's eyes in the rearview mirror.

'The Gypsy,' the SVR chief said flatly. 'I am sure you know where it is.'

'Something has happened?' Galkin swiveled his head to look at him.

'Da. Dmitri is dead.'

GORSHKY, surrounded by his security team, hustled to the Gypsy's VIP entrance once Tony had parked his armored car in a reserved spot.

The lot had been cleared of civilian vehicles and was filled with police vans and ambulances. Armed, uniformed officers were stationed around the nightclub, and when the SVR chief arrived, a suit broke away from a bunch of men and came towards him.

'This is shocking—' Denis Turgenev, the GUVD chief, began.

'Take me inside and tell me what happened,' Gorshky cut him off.

The head of police nodded at a senior officer, who took them inside the Gypsy.

More officers inside. Forensic technicians and medical personnel. A bunch of nightclub employees down the hallway, held back by the barricade and a cordon of policemen.

Gorshky stopped at the door. His face tightened as he took in Ruslan's body and unseeing eyes.

'What happened?' he hissed.

'She knows. She saw everything.' The senior officer nodded at a weeping woman a few feet away. 'That's—'

'Katerina, a dancer.'

He felt Galkin stiffen beside him.

'I am the SVR chief,' he growled. 'You think I didn't know about Dmitri's girlfriend, where he went most Fridays? There is nothing about any of you that I don't know.'

'What went down?' he demanded of the dancer, then listened without interruption as she told him about the masked man and the fight.

'Did he say anything to you?'

'He said he would kill me if I escaped. He had a gun in his hand.'

Gorshky searched the floor.

'We found Ruslan's gun, no other weapon,' the officer said. 'These two bouncers accosted him,' he added, nodding at the two heavies being escorted by officers. Their faces were swollen and bandaged, and they winced as they walked.

'We heard crashing sounds,' the larger man said hoarsely, 'and when we ran inside, Ruslan was on the floor. This man had his back to us, and when he turned, he threw a chair at me and attacked Willem.'

Willem, the second heavy, corroborated the first bouncer's account.

'How tall was he? What was he wearing? Did he speak Russian? Did he have any accent?'

Gorshky fired his questions in a staccato burst.

'Maybe over six feet tall. He was light on his feet. Dark clothing.'

'Da,' Katerina agreed with a quavering voice. 'Some kind of combat clothing. He spoke Russian fluently. I think he is from Moscow, from his accent.'

'How did he come in?'

'I don't know. Dmitri and I were in the room when he burst in.'

'Did you see him escape?

'Nyet. I went to Dmitri as soon as he left the room.'

'We were unconscious,' Willem replied when Gorshky glared at the heavies.

The SVR chief bit back a curse and looked at the camera in the ceiling.

'Not working. Looks like it has been burned in some way. We are still investigating.' The police officer read his glance. 'The last recording shows some VIPs using another room. That was more than half an hour before Ruslan entered the Gypsy.'

'Check every customer in the nightclub,' Gorshky rapped out. 'Investigate all of them.'

'Da.' The officer nodded. 'We have not let anyone leave.'

'My people will conduct their own investigation as well and coordinate with you.'

'Da.' The GUVD man knew his place. He was aware SVR greatly outranked Moscow's police.

Gorshky looked down at Ruslan's body impassively. His former team-leader hadn't been a friend. The SVR chief didn't get close to any of his staff. However, the man had been extremely capable, seemed to read his boss's mind, and had been a very good investigator.

He would be replaced by another team leader from Zaslon, but his killing could not go unpunished.

'I want daily updates.'

'You will have them.'

They turned at the voice. The new arrival was smartly dressed in a suit and polished boots, with buzzcut hair. He stood easily, his arms loose and ready.

'Smirnov.' Gorshky recognized him. He turned to Galkin. 'Nikola, meet Dusan. He will be the new team leader, taking over from Dmitri.'

'Da.' His bodyguard nodded. They were all professionals. They knew how the replacement system worked and how the backup pool operated.

Gorshky headed back to his vehicle and was joined by Smirnov a couple of moments later.

'Dmitri was a good man.'

'I am better.'

The SVR chief looked sideways at the quiet confidence of the new team leader. He was a shade over six feet but shorter than Ruslan. *That's good. Dmitri's height made him noticeable. That isn't good in this business.*

'And I will find who killed Dmitri.'

'Take over everything else that he was investigating.'

'Da.'

Gorshky stared into the darkness as Tony drove him back to his office.

Dmitri was targeted. But was that over some personal enmity?

His former team-leader had been ruthless and cold-blooded. Had someone from his past killed him?

It didn't matter, Gorshky decided. He had to assume the killer was coming for SVR. That was the only way the organization could protect itself.

But who could it have been? The killer seemed to have some kind of military training. *He had to! No civilian could take down Dmitri.* He also had planned for the cameras and knew the former team-leader's routine.

The killer was clearly formidable, an enemy to be wary of.

Mossad, MI6, CIA ... any of those organizations would have such operatives.

There's Carter as well, but he isn't in Moscow.

That was Gorshky's only consoling thought as he sped through the night.

41

'What did you mean by *jigsaw piece*?' Beth demanded the next day.

Zeb adjusted his shades and spotted the twins jogging some distance behind him on Boulevard Ring. The rest of his team were spread out, positioned so that every one of them had at least one other operative in sight.

'I'm working on a plan.'

'He's working on a plan,' the younger twin quoted. 'When will you enlighten us with it?'

'Soon. I heard from Zahavy. He's moved Golubev, Nikitin and Laskin to Tel Aviv. They will be interrogated there.'

'Whatever they know might not help our mission.'

'I am assuming that,' Zeb acknowledged.

'What did you achieve by killing Ruslan?' Meghan asked sharply.

'That he *could* take him out,' Bwana chuckled.

'Was it just that?' Chloe's voice rose.

'I said there is a plan,' Zeb said placatingly. 'You will have to be patient.'

'What's next in this great plan of yours? Other than running around Moscow?' Broker asked sarcastically.

'We'll check out Frunzenskaya.'

'What's there?'

'The Ministry of Defense building.'

'And why are we interested in that?'

'Gorshky is giving a speech in the afternoon. It's one of his few public appearances.'

'Is everything in place?' Gorshky asked Smirnov when his team leader entered his office.

'For the afternoon? Da.'

'Any update from the police or your investigation?'

'We are looking for a van that left the parking lot shortly after the killing. It is either blue or black in color—'

'It will have false plates, if that's how the killer escaped.'

'Da, that's my guess, too. But we have to try. It doesn't look like any of the customers were involved. We interviewed them throughout the night, and no one came to the room. There's something, though. A businessman came to the manager earlier yesterday and asked to check out the meeting rooms.'

'The address and number he gave are false, and he could have been wearing a disguise.'

'Da. We found his wig in a trashbin. We are checking it for DNA—'

'You won't find any traces, and even if you do, he won't be in the system. And if he is, it will be a false identity. He probably threw that wig out deliberately to waste our time. We are dealing with a pro.'

'Da. We checked the cameras, and this mystery businessman isn't on them. Someone tampered with the recordings and deleted his image. We have only the manager's description to go by, which isn't of much help. Do you know where Laskin is?'

'Evgeny?' Gorshky frowned. 'Isn't he outside?'

'Nyet. He is missing. Dmitri might have known where he is, but there's nothing in his emails or call records. The case officer isn't at home—'

'Check it out. I certainly didn't send him anywhere. I had asked him to find Yasimov—'

Gorshky broke off.

'Yasimov. Dmitri. Evgeny ... could the resistance be behind Ruslan's killing?'

'Dmitri was reading up on Spetsnaz officers, retired ones. Their files were on his computer.'

'Follow that up. All these killings and attacks have been extremely organized. It is possible former special forces soldiers could be involved. They could have joined the protesters and trained them. I am sure that's what Dmitri was looking into.'

'Da.'

'Are you ready for the afternoon?'

'I don't think you go. You should minimize your—'

'That's what Dmitri said, too. However, the event at the Ministry of Defense is a prestigious one. There will be international agencies. I am presenting on global security threats. If CIA and MI6 will be represented, I have to be there, too.'

'Do you have one of those lapel cameras?' Zeb tightened his shoelaces and wiped sweat from his face.

Chloe was practicing spin kicks on Bear in a park in the distance, while the twins were stretching. The other operatives weren't in sight, but he knew they were around.

'Yeah,' Beth panted. 'Zahavy's gear has everything we need. Why do you want it?'

'I want to see who has replaced Ruslan.'

'Dusan Smirnov. It's all there in Yasimov's files. Tell us again what you achieved by killing Ruslan, if another operative has taken his place?'

'It will come to you. You're smart—'

'Smarter than you.'

He grinned as he pictured her annoyed face. *They haven't joined the dots yet, but they'll figure it out.*

'How are you going to see Smirnov?' Roger demanded. 'He'll be in Gorshky's car, which we might not spot.'

'We will. They'll drive down Frunzenskaya Naberezhnaya and turn in to the side entrance to the MOD building. We know the car.'

'Won't he take some other route?'

'No. Catlyn Feder and Sir Alex Thompson are at that conference. Gorshky's ego will not allow him to arrive through a back route when the CIA and MI6 directors have taken the main one. It's a matter of appearances for him.'

'How are you expecting to watch Smirnov? He won't get out of the car,' Broker observed.

'He will.'

Yasimov has promised to make that happen.

He didn't know what the editor had in mind, but he trusted him.

'Smirnov and Gorshky will recognize you if you get close.'

'They won't. You're forgetting we're all disguised.'

42

Yasimov underestimated the size of the crowd, Zeb thought with a chuckle when they came to Frunzenskaya Naberezhnaya.

The road along the Moscow River and leading to the MOD building was packed with protesters. They waved *Free Elena Now!* placards as they chanted her name. Several beat drums and blew trumpets.

They were bunched behind a line of metal barricades on the sidewalk while armed police patrolled the road.

Security is tight. The police presence was reinforced by military personnel, who watched the resistance participants impassively.

'You can feel the tension in the air,' Bwana growled. 'It only takes one mistake, say a protester breaking through the barrier and running onto the road, and the cops will start firing.'

'They won't,' Bear argued. 'They've seen these kinds of crowds. They know how to handle them.'

'Can you feel the anger in the air? The soldiers might not open fire, but they might club that protester, and if that happens, more folks will—'

'There will be rioting,' Meghan said soberly. 'And then anything can happen. Zeb, did you get Yasimov to set this up?'

'Nope. The protest was organized a long time ago.'

He slipped inside the crowd and adjusted his lapel to give the small camera the widest possible field of view.

'Don't touch it,' Beth snapped irritably. 'We can control it from here. You do what you have to and leave the rest to us.'

He tapped a burly man who was holding a board and asked if he could borrow a spare one lying on the ground.

'Da. The more of them in the air, the better for Elena.'

'This protest may not do much for her.'

'If it doesn't,' a red-haired woman snarled, 'we will start rioting. We are ready to die for her freedom.'

'She's a reporter. She's not—'

'Are you new to Moscow? Are you even Russian?' She whirled on him and jabbed his chest with her finger. 'Boris and Elena have continued to report independently despite the government threats against them. *The Reality* is the only publication that defies the Kremlin. We aren't protesting just for Elena's release. We are fighting for us. For our right to dissent freely. To have free elections where opposition candidates are not jailed or killed. If you don't believe in all of that, you shouldn't be here.'

'Careful, Zeb,' Beth sniggered in his earpiece. 'She looks like she might swing at you.'

The protester glared at him for a moment and then stormed into the crowd. He followed her as the force of her anger parted the protesters. They reached the side road that led to the gated entrance of the MOD, where a line of sharp-eyed soldiers stood guard.

'RELEASE ELENA!' the woman screamed as she leaned over the barricades.

'RELEASE ELENA!' Zeb bellowed as he squeezed behind her.

The crowd roared, directing their rage at the soldiers, who didn't react.

'You're too close—' Bear began.

Zeb's eyes scanned the protesters, taking in his friend, who was next to several bearded men. *Bwana is in the van in a side street, with Broker. He'll be too noticeable in this crowd.*

'I am where I need to be,' he replied and brought out his phone when it buzzed.

Gorshky's left his office.

'He's on his way,' he whispered into his collar mic.

'How do you know?'

'Yasimov. The Resistance has watchers outside the SVR's office. The editor is plugged into the intel.'

'How will you get Smirnov out of the car?'

Zeb looked at the crowd and the red-haired woman, who was still yelling.

'Something will happen.'

I hope it doesn't result in any killing.

43

The crowd's shouts grew louder. An electric current seemed to go through the protesters, energizing them.

Zeb spotted the reason an instant later when a dark car rolled down Frunzenskaya Naberezhnaya. It had darkened windows, rolled low on its shocks, and sunlight gleamed off its hood as it approached.

That's Gorshky's ride.

He could make out the silhouette of the driver and another person at the front.

Dusan Smirnov.

The car slowed as it came near the side entrance. The chanting, the drums and trumpets grew louder.

'FREE HER!' Red-Haired Woman shouted.

The people around her took up the call. They added their voices as the car turned in to the approach road.

The woman leaned over the barricade and waved her placard angrily at the vehicle. A soldier gestured at her, which fueled her anger. She bent forward further, lost her balance and brought the barrier to the ground. She stumbled onto the road but didn't retreat. She ran towards the car, waving her sign. A few more protesters followed her.

The car stopped. Its door opened. Dusan Smirnov climbed out but stood behind it, exposing only his face. His face was inscrutable as he took in the woman, and then he nodded.

'ZEB!' Meghan yelled in warning when a soldier rushed towards Red-Haired Woman, his rifle raised.

'On it.'

He lunged forward as more soldiers came forward and clubbed the protesters.

Zeb evaded the first uniformed man.

'STOP!' he yelled at the woman.

He grabbed her waist and pulled her back, just as the soldier brought down the butt of his weapon. He was close enough to see the guard's flat eyes and expressionless face. He turned the kicking and struggling woman away, deftly slipped his left leg around the soldier's ankle and yanked hard, which got the man to lose his balance.

The rifle butt missed the woman's head and crashed into Zeb's shoulder. He grimaced at the impact and retreated with the furious protester and got behind the barricade.

The soldier looked down at his shoe with a perplexed expression. *He's wondering if he was tripped by the woman who was kicking out, or by me ... or whether it was an accident.*

Zeb and the woman were safely engulfed in the throng by the time the soldier looked up, and he decided to take no action.

The protesters didn't break into a riot. They gathered their fallen people, all the while shouting at the soldiers and the vehicle, and got behind the barrier. The armed guards let them retreat and went back into formation in front of the gate.

Smirnov watched for long moments and then, at a word from inside the vehicle, got back in. The car resumed its drive to the entrance.

Zeb watched the security man, who searched the crowd and locked eyes with him. The thick window, several feet and many protesters were in between them, but he could feel the weight of the man's stare, and then the car was inside the MOD compound.

Red-Haired Woman slapped him.

'Why did you do that!' she raged. 'Why did you stop me?'

'That soldier would have hit you.'

'So what?'

'It could have led to a riot.'

'So what?'

'The soldiers could have opened fire.'

'So what! You think I am scared of dying?'

Zeb took her in fully. She was shorter than him. Piercings in both eyebrows. Studs in her ears, rings on her fingers and tatts on her forearms. She was anger personified.

'I don't think you are scared of anything,' he replied honestly.

'Dasha.' A protester laid a hand on her shoulder. 'Leave it. He did the right thing.'

She shrugged his hand away, glared at Zeb and the protester, snarled, 'Men!' and stalked away.

'I GOT THAT ON MY PHONE!' Bear laughed uproariously as Zeb squeezed through the crowd and went past him. 'She packed a lot of power in that.'

'Yeah,' he admitted ruefully as he cupped his cheek.

'Your shoulder?' Beth asked worriedly, when he went past the twins.

'His strike was weak. Besides, I've got padding beneath my jacket. Did you—'

'Yeah.' Meghan and her sister fell in behind him as he left the protesters' crowd and went down to the Moscow River.

'We got Smirnov on video. We zoomed in to get closeup shots.'

Roger was on a bench, sipping coffee and browsing a magazine. He got to his feet casually and stretched when they passed him.

'He looks to be the same build as you,' Meghan continued. 'His features, too—'

She stopped abruptly and then hurried to plant herself in front of him.

'*That's* your plan? It's suicidal!'

44

Gorshky was in his office when Smirnov knocked on the door and entered.

The SVR chief was content. His speech had gone down very well and his barbs at the CIA and MI6 had received thunderous applause. He had received several congratulatory messages from ministers, military and agency heads.

'Tell me,' he commanded his security team leader.

'That woman—she's a known troublemaker. She wasn't armed. GUVD questioned her later. None of the protesters were carrying weapons.'

'What about the man who saved her? He looked competent.'

'Da. I was watching the scene. He tripped that soldier, though the officer didn't realize it. He moved very fast, took the right action and saved her from a brutal blow. Unfortunately, he has disappeared.'

'He's just a protester,' Gorshky said, waving dismissively, high on the plaudits he had received. 'Where have you got to with Ruslan, Evgeny and the various investigations?'

'They are troubling me. It's not just Laskin who is missing. Golubev and Nikitin have disappeared, too.'

Gorshky's euphoria vanished instantly.

He rocked forward in his chair, his eyebrows coming together in a straight line.

'Disappeared? What do you mean by that? Our agents cannot—'

'They are related to Belsky.'

'Who is that?'

'A baggage handler. From Laskin's notes, it looks like the man helped Yasimov escape.'

'Yasimov is in London. Evgeny was sure of that.'

'It seems Laskin had second thoughts about that.'

'Where's this Belsky?'

'He's gone, too.'

'Belsky is gone! Evgeny is gone! Dmitri is dead! What are you here for if you have nothing positive for me?'

Smirnov didn't react to the angry outburst. He stood patiently until Gorshky expelled a deep breath from his mouth and sighed.

'Get onto it,' he said. When the team leader had left, he brooded for several moments.

He stopped himself from looking at the quote on the wall and finally reached for his phone and dialed a number.

'Sergei, it's me. Have you heard of any soldiers joining the protesters?'

'Nyet.'

'Find out, and get back to me.'

'Da.'

He ended the call, reassured that Sergei Goncharov, pakhan, leader of the Goncharov bratva, the biggest criminal gang in Russia, was on his side.

45

'You have got to be kidding me!' Chloe exploded when they gathered in a park. A family kicking a football turned to look at them and returned to their game when they found nothing of interest.

'How else can we get close to Gorshky?' Zeb reasoned.

'We don't have to,' Broker scowled. 'We grab him at—'

'He doesn't do public events. Even that MOD event ... you saw how tight security was. Attacking his armored car—nope, that won't work either. We need to be inside his team, which means Dusan Smirnov.'

'How do you plan to achieve that?' Meghan regarded him. A stray hair fell over her face, and she swept it aside, her green eyes cool and calculating.

He grinned. *She's worked it out already but wants to hear it from me.*

'You know the time I broke into his office and accosted him?'

'That was years ago,' Beth said disparagingly. 'We created a lot of distractions—bombs in Moscow, burning vehicles—that would suck up the police and every intelligence agency's attention.'

'The power outage in the city helped us, too,' Roger drawled. 'We may not get that kind of luck again.'

'And you can bet,' Bwana said, kicking the errant football back to the family, 'that Gorshky would have tightened his security by several notches.'

'We will need some luck,' Zeb admitted, 'and some friends.'

He explained his plan, and when he had finished, Broker smacked his palm against his forehead.

'That's the best you came up with?'

'You got a better one?'

'Stop!' Beth exclaimed, heading off an argument. 'It could work. Like Zeb said, we need some luck ... and a mask.'

'So?' he looked at them. 'Are we all in?'

Bwana cracked a knuckle. 'So long as we take out several of his men, hell yeah!'

They nodded, bumped fists, and followed Zeb out of the park.

SMIRNOV WAS SMART. It wasn't an empty claim. He could join dots faster than most of the SVR or Zaslon agents and could read cases and investigations and interpret them in several ways.

He shut down his screen after he had reread Laskin's notes and the files he had transferred from Ruslan's computer.

Finding out who grabbed or killed Laskin, Golubev or Nikitin might be easier than investigating what happened to them.

He went to Gorshky, who looked up from his screen.

'Did you see what the papers are saying about my speech?'

'Da. It was a great one. I was watching Feder and Thompson's faces when you commented on the CIA and MI6. They were squirming.'

'Fools.' His boss nodded, smiling broadly. 'Did they think they could come to Moscow and we would not ridicule them? What have you got for me?'

'I won't take up Laskin's investigation into Yasimov and Belsky's disappearance.' He added hurriedly, when the SVR chief's face darkened, 'What I mean is, there might be an easier way to find out what happened to them.'

'I am listening.'

'Get the perpetrators to come to us.'

'How?' Gorshky frowned.

'This group is likely to be the same one. The shooters who killed our men in Zakharova's building, the people who kidnapped Laskin, Golubev and Nikitin, and the man who killed Dmitri.'

'Yes. Protesters from the resistance.'

'Dmitri thought they could be former soldiers. Spetsnaz or some elite unit.'

'Da,' Gorshky nodded thoughtfully. 'That makes a lot of sense. But how will you get these people to break cover and come—' He snapped his fingers, his eyes lighting up.

'You'll set a trap.'

'Da.' Smirnov grinned. 'There's one reason that will make them come running.'

46

'A mask?' Zahavy repeated when they had gathered in his office. 'What kind?'

'You know which kind.' Beth shifted on her feet impatiently. 'For disguises. To impersonate someone else.'

'How close will the impersonator be to the target?'

'Very close.'

'So it will have to be perfect, or as accurate as possible.'

'Yeah.'

'Can I see the person? The one you want to impersonate?'

He's an ally. Avichai is a friend.

Zeb nodded imperceptibly when Beth looked at him.

She brought out her phone and showed him Smirnov's photograph.

Zahavy jerked his head back in shock.

'You have lost your—'

'Yeah, that's what we told him,' Chloe grinned. 'But, admit it. It is so outrageous that it could work.'

'And if it doesn't?'

'Then I'm dead.' Zeb shrugged.

Zahavy stared at him for long moments. 'I had heard about

this,' he whispered in shock and awe. 'That you spoke very casually about dying. It's true. You don't care.'

'Do you have someone?' Meghan demanded.

'Of course. We are—'

'Yeah, yeah. You are Mossad. You can walk on water.'

'Not yet,' Zahavy said earnestly. 'But we are working on it.'

SMIRNOV ORDERED Galkin to stay with Tony the Tank, outside Gorshky's residence, when their boss was back at home. He took Bortnik and Orlov with him and drove out of the city.

'We are flying out somewhere?' Orlov commented when the signs to Sheremetyevo appeared.

'Nyet.'

The team leader reached his destination and parked the car on the side of the road.

'How difficult will it be to set up an ambush here?'

His companions checked out the street, which had a few trees but offered unrestricted views from buildings on both sides of the road.

'Why here?' Bortnik chewed gum slowly as he squinted in the darkness.

Smirnov pointed to the apartment building on their right. 'That one is of interest. The people we want to capture will go to it—'

'That should be easy enough. We set up roadblocks—'

'We can't be obvious,' the team leader said irritably. 'Here's what I am thinking. Two vans or trucks on each side of the road, with us inside it. We'll have some non-suspicious markings on them, like company logos. We'll have more men inside the front garden of that building, hiding. When our targets turn in to its driveway, our shooters will open fire. This will make them fall back to the road, where we will get them.'

'How many will there be?'

'We don't know.'

'How many of us should be here?'

'All of us, except Tony. He'll be with the boss. I'll get more hitters from our agency. About twenty of us in total. The four of us in the vans, with shooters, with most of our men in the garden. We'll be more obvious if we have greater numbers.'

'It should work.' Bortnik scratched his jaw. 'They won't be expecting us.'

'One point. We need them alive.'

'Why?'

'They know what happened to Laskin, Golubev and Nikitin.'

'In that case, they shouldn't live.'

'They won't, after spilling everything they know to us.'

47

'Hmmm,' the man said as he looked at the photograph.

They were in the Danilovskiy District, in a workshop that had masks hanging from the walls and ceilings. Masks of Hollywood actors, politicians, anime characters ... they couldn't move about without their heads bumping into a mask.

The man, in his sixties, walked with a hunch, but his grey eyes were sharp, his silvery beard was neatly trimmed, and the long hair on his head was tied back in a ponytail.

ZAHAVY HAD BROUGHT Zeb and the twins to the man's store the next day.

'Mikhail,' he said, introducing the mask-maker, without mentioning a surname. He hadn't spoken their names, either.

Mikhail was a supplier of costumes, wigs and all related accessories to stage artists and movie productions.

'He is the best in the business,' Zahavy had informed them as he drove them there in his fast-food van. The Mossad agent had made no comment when the rest of the Agency operatives followed in their vehicles at a discreet distance.

'He's Mossad?' the elder twin asked him.

'No comment.'

'Which means he is,' her sister snorted.

'How do you embed such people in different countries?' Zeb mused aloud.

'We are Moss—'

'Stop it,' the twins chorused.

'Do you have more than this photograph?'

'Da.' Meghan played the video outside the MOD building on her phone.

'Transfer it to my computer.' Mikhail pointed to a large screen, from which several cables snaked out. Moments later the clip was running in HD.

The mask-maker looked up sharply when he seemed to recognize the demonstration's location and Gorshky's car, but he didn't speak. Zahavy didn't either. The Mossad agent crossed his arms and watched from behind them.

'You captured him from different angles. That's good.'

Mikhail zoomed in on Smirnov's face several times and inspected his features before resuming the video.

'Normal-looking face,' the mask-maker pronounced. 'You will be wearing it?'

Zeb nodded.

'Da, da.' The elderly man rubbed his fingers. 'The sizes of your face and his ... they are similar. Your heights also. How quickly do you want this?'

'As soon as you can. But we want a good—'

'Tch!' Mikhail clicked his tongue. 'Look around you. All these masks ... can you distinguish them from the real people?'

'This one will be different.'

'Da, I know. You want one that you can wear without anyone knowing you have a mask. I can do that.' He took them to an inside room and gestured at the 3D printers, the various rubbers and composite materials stored in shelves and in wrappers. 'I am the best in Russia; that's why Josiah comes to me. You will get your mask.'

He led them out and, as they were leaving, commented, 'I hope you know what you are doing.'

Me too!

'Da,' Zeb said noncommittally.

He made a discreet *all-okay* hand gesture to Roger, who was on a bench sipping coffee.

'I'll drop you back—'

Zeb's phone buzzed.

Yasimov! What does he want?

'Take it,' Zahavy urged. 'I will pretend I didn't hear.'

'You had better,' Beth growled as she leaned over Zeb's shoulder and accepted the call.

'Da?' she asked.

'Where are you? I need your help again. Have you heard what's going down? They will attack—'

'Slow down. Take a breath. What's going down?'

'My people have heard we will be attacked.' The editor made a noticeable effort to slow his words. 'Imminently, tonight.'

It's already dark.

'Attacked where?'

'Belsky's building. Its residents are going to be attacked.'

'By whom?'

'SVR.'

48

'How did you hear this?' Zeb asked tightly.

'We have our network. I have told you about it. Cleaners, drivers, maids, office workers—we have eyes and ears everywhere. One of our drivers is friendly with a bunch of government ones. They told him.'

'Specifically?'

'Da. The other man mentioned SVR and the building.'

'How reliable is—'

'We have survived for so long because of our intelligence. It has never failed us. I could get other protesters to go to their aid, but this is SVR. They are ruthless. They will kill. The resistance's members will be ready to sacrifice their lives, but if you can help, that would be better.'

'Get me more information,' Zeb said. 'How many of them will be there, what time—'

'Do you think they talk that openly? I thought you would help! That's why—'

'We will,' Meghan said calmly. 'If your intel is correct, we will deal with it. Pass the word. Tell the residents to stay inside the building. No kids playing on the lawn ... no one should be out. The protesters should stay away. This will turn ugly, and we don't want to worry about civilian casualties.'

'I will do that. Thank you,' Yasimov said gratefully and hung up.

'There could be a hundred SVR agents there,' Zeb brooded.

'There won't be,' the elder twin scoffed. 'Chloe, Bwana, did you hear that?'

'Yeah,' the petite operative replied.

'Gorshky won't take that kind of risk,' Meghan continued. 'He has power, but he cannot act recklessly. Social media will roast him if his agency turns up in those numbers.'

'How many could show up?'

She chewed her lip thoughtfully. 'More than ten, because they don't know how many of us could be there ... but less than fifty.'

'Twenty or thirty would be my guess,' Chloe added.

'Yeah,' Broker agreed. 'Thirty, tops.'

'There are only eight of us.'

'Eight of us are enough,' Bwana said menacingly.

49

'All quiet,' Yasimov said nervously. 'Residents are watching through the windows, but no strangers have turned up.'

'Lights?' Zeb snapped as he passed a slow-moving truck.

He ran down a mental list.

Our vans' colors changed? Check.

Weapons? Check.

Combat outfits, body armor and disguises on all of us? Done.

They had changed swiftly in Zahavy's base and driven out immediately.

We lost time on that. He gritted his teeth as he honked and overtook another car. *Another forty minutes to go in this traffic.*

'Lights?' Yasimov asked, confused.

'Outside lights, are they on at the building? They should be. Everything should look normal.'

'Da. I will relay that.'

'Call me as soon as you hear anything.'

Zeb eyed his rearview mirror to check Bear's van. It was two vehicles behind him. Beth caught his eye and winked reassuringly.

'We'll get there in time.'

'It's not that,' he huffed. 'I'm worried about those SVR goons taking hostages.'

That would change the game entirely.

Game!

He flicked on his blinker, turned right, and slammed his brakes to come to a halt on the side of the road. Angry drivers swerved, honked; one of them flipped them as he went past.

'What?' Meghan yelled as she gripped the grab-handle.

'What's up?' Bear asked, his van easing up behind them.

'It could be a trap,' Zeb said tightly. 'To sucker us in.'

No one replied for several moments.

'It's a move out of our own playbook,' Beth said, nodding slowly. 'Gorshky must have figured out we are the same folks who killed their men and grabbed Laskin and their two operatives. He doesn't know who we are or what we'll do next.'

'He'll set the field for us to walk in, blind.'

'You mean they weren't intending to attack the residents?' Roger questioned.

'They will,' Zeb asserted, 'if we don't show up. That's their card to draw us in. We can't not go. It's an opportunity to trim down their numbers.'

'Now you're talking.' Bwana grinned.

'But we'll be walking into a trap,' the Texan protested.

'We won't be walking.' Zeb adjusted his side mirror to get Bear in its frame. 'Or, at least, not all of us will be.'

'We'll take to the roof!' Meghan snapped her fingers.

'Yeah.'

'But if we don't show up—'

'Someone will,' Zeb said grimly. He punched a number on his device and put it on speaker.

'Da?' a gruff voice answered.

'Get me Illya Pushkin.'

50

'Your offer still stands?' Zeb asked when the pakhan came on the line.

'Da. What can I do?'

'Shoot up some SVR thugs.'

'With pleasure.' Pushkin's smile could be felt in his voice. 'Where and when?'

'Not so fast. There will be many of them waiting in an ambush. Some of your men *will* die. Think about it.'

'There's nothing to think about. My people are as committed to my cause as I am. They are prepared to die. You wouldn't understand. We are Ukrainians first—'

'Got it. One more thing. None of them can be captured. Even if some are dead, the others must retrieve their bodies.'

'You don't want SVR to know who exactly they are,' Pushkin guessed.

'Correct.'

'Getting bodies out might be difficult—'

'We will help.'

'Where will this be?'

'Near Sheremetyevo Airport. An apartment building. I'll message you the address.'

'When?'

'Right away.'

Pushkin had a muffled conversation with someone and returned to the call.

'I can send two cars packed with my shooters.'

'I need someone to coordinate with.'

'Timur. He is one of my best shooters. He is a leader—'

'Send me his number.'

Zeb hung up and called Yasimov.

'We need to get onto the roof of Belsky's building.' He shifted to make room for Beth's screen between him and Meghan. On it was the street view of the baggage handler's neighborhood.

Buildings on both sides of the road have good shooting angles.

'I can arrange that,' the editor replied.

'No one should be around to see us. Leave any doors open—'

'I get it. It will be done.'

'No residents should go to the roof, even if they hear sounds of shooting. There will be lots of that. They should stay—'

'Indoors. Da. I will pass on the message. They will follow your instructions.'

'You are confident about that?'

'Everyone in that building is part of the Resistance. They know what needs to be done.'

'We also need access to the building opposite the road. To its roof.'

'No problem. I will message you when everything is in place.'

'Does it have parking?'

'How many spaces do you need?'

'Two. No one should come near our vehicles.'

'I will arrange it.'

Yasimov swallowed. 'Those killers should not harm any resident.'

'They won't, if your people follow my instructions.'

'They shouldn't live. I mean SVR's thugs.'

Zeb grinned. *Yasimov is thirsty!*

'We will do our best.'

51

The van rolled to a stop on the side of the road and turned off its lights. It bore the logo of an energy company, and every one of its occupants wore uniformed coveralls.

'Looks quiet,' Smirnov whispered as he peered through the windshield.

Bortnik nodded. 'It's late. People are having dinner. There's school and work tomorrow.'

A second van rolled up on the other side of the street, bearing the same company's signage. A man jumped out of it, went to the junction box on the grassy bank, opened it and placed a traffic cone on the road.

'Go,' Smirnov ordered in his radio. 'Check out the parking lot in the building and make sure there aren't any gunmen.'

Two men walked down the street, dressed casually, carrying gymbags on their shoulders. They went up the building's driveway and disappeared from sight.

'There's no one here,' one of them reported. 'Not even the residents. All the cars and vans in the parking lot are empty.'

'What about hiding positions?'

'There are flower beds in the garden around the driveway. They are recessed in the ground. There are enough spaces for seven or eight shooters.'

'Take your positions. I will send four more men.'

'Nikola,' Smirnov called the CPO in the second van. 'Send your men.'

'Da.'

The four hitters came through in the darkness, individually. One of them pretended to talk on his phone, another jogged with headphones over his ears, the other two walked casually.

'In position,' they checked in.

'You have five men with you, Nikola?'

'Da.'

'The same in my van, not counting me, Kostya and Magar. When those protesters arrive, shoot out their tires. Fire over their heads. If they fire back, shoot at their legs, but don't kill them. Is that clear?'

A chorus of *das* echoed in his radio.

'How will we know it is them?'

'They will have lowered windows with visible guns, because they are expecting us to be attacking the residents. They won't hide their approach. They will drive fast. They will either park on the road or go inside. Either way, we will be ready for them.'

ZEB PARKED his van in the opposite building's lot, pulled his mask over his head and climbed out. He didn't see any residents. No heads poked out of any windows, most of which were lit.

We are disguised, but the masks will help the residents if any of them see us. They will claim truthfully that they can't describe us.

'Go,' he told the twins, who opened the van, drew out their heavy bags and went inside the fire-exit door.

That's the one Yasimov asked us to use.

'Drone is in the air,' Beth announced fifteen minutes later. Her voice was even despite the rapid seven-floor climb.

'And we have thermal confirmation! Two vans on the road packed with bodies .... Ten, no, fourteen men! The one nearest to Belsky's building has eight, the other has six. Armed.'

Zeb leaned against the van while she navigated the UAV.

'Six shooters in the garden. The night is clear. It looks like they have AK74s with them. Three on each side of the drive.'

'No other hostile,' she declared after a wide loop. 'The roof is empty.'

That was the cue for Bwana and Roger to emerge.

'We'll go down that track Yasimov told us about,' the Texan whispered. 'I'll be at the front; Bwana will cover the rear.'

Zeb gave him a thumbs-up.

That dirt path follows the road but is shielded from it by trees. No one in the vans will spot them.

Bear and Chloe slipped out too, fist-bumped him, and raced into the night.

They'll take the cable pipe that goes beneath the road and come up near the electric substation near Belsky's building.

'Second drone is in the air.'

'I'm on it.' Broker thumped his van from inside.

He will be Beth's backup in case she misses anything when it gets hot.

Where are you?

Fifteen minutes away, Timur messaged back immediately.

Slow down. Wait for my signal.

Da.

BEAR SWORE when his jacket snagged on a rough edge.

'It's your fault for being so big,' Chloe chided him.

'Yeah, as if I had anything to do with that.'

The cable track was nothing more than a large PVC pipe

that ran beneath the road. The electric cables were bundled in a metal runway, fastened to the bottom of it. Debris and wastewater made the passage stink.

'The things we have to do,' Bear panted as Chloe helped him out the other side.

'Quiet,' she whispered and looked warily around.

'You're good,' Beth announced in their earpieces.

She made a thumbs-up at the sky, crouched low and ran towards the fire exit. She held her breath as she opened the door. It swung noiselessly.

Someone must have oiled it.

She went up the stairs cautiously her HK ready to fire, with Bear covering her back.

'On the roof,' she grunted.

'I see you.'

She pointed to a firing position on the parapet and helped Bear set up his tripod. She brought her Leupold Rangefinder to her eye and swept the garden.

No wind. Clear sky. Two hundred and eight yards to the targets.

'They're sitting ducks,' Bear said, reading her thoughts.

MEGHAN HAD her eye to the MKII scope on her Accuracy International.

Schmidt and Bender, she thought, recalling the German manufacturer who produced the rifle's scope. *They make the best ones.*

'Quit admiring the rifle,' Beth admonished her.

'I'm not,' she retorted. 'I'm ready.'

'It feels like we're alone up here.'

'We are.'

'You know what I mean.'

Meghan nodded. The building wasn't high, but the absence

of surrounding foliage or nearby construction made it feel like the sky enveloped them.

'Ready,' she whispered in their comms channel.

ZEB WENT DOWN the track Bwana and Roger had taken, but he left it before he reached the end and cut to the road.

'What are you doing!'

He winced at Beth's yell in his earpiece.

'I want to see how they'll react.'

'They will pepper you!'

He grinned at her vehemence. 'Nope. They're killers, but they won't shoot a lone civilian.'

He stepped onto the road and walked towards Belsky's building.

52

'There's someone walking on the road.'

Smirnov turned at Vadim Popov's whisper. He trained his binos through the van's rear window and focused on the figure.

'Who is he?' he wondered aloud.

The stranger was clearly a man. His head was down, and he seemed to be reading something on his phone's screen. The team lead tried to see his face, but he could see only the dark covering of his hoodie.

I should have put sentries at both ends of the road and put a drone up as well, for aerial surveillance. He cursed himself for his carelessness. He had been in such a hurry to set the trap that he had missed out on the basics. He didn't articulate this out loud, however. He was the team leader. He wouldn't admit his mistakes.

'We can take him down,' Popov said.

'Nyet.' Smirnov shook his head as the stranger came closer. He was dressed in dark clothing, some kind of cargo pants and a loose jacket, with its top drawn around his head. 'He must be a local resident. We'll arrest him if he turns inside Belsky's building.'

'I CAN FEEL THEIR EYES.'

'What did you expect?' Beth snorted. 'You are walking in the middle of the road as if you haven't got a care in the world.'

Zeb thumbed his screen as he pretended to read. He drew closer to the vans.

That's the one Smirnov is likely to be in. He turned his head fractionally to the vehicle on his left. It didn't move on its shocks and seemed to be empty from the outside. There was no one behind the wheel or in the passenger seat.

Those side and rear windows are one-way. They can see out; I can't see in.

He drew closer to the second van to his right, which didn't show signs of occupancy either. He looked curiously at the traffic cones, shook his head and walked on. A civilian exasperated at the energy company.

'There's no one beneath the vehicles.'

'We told you that,' Beth scoffed.

'They could have been wearing anti-thermal suits,' Meghan corrected her sister, 'that our drone or our binos wouldn't have picked up. Much as I hate to admit it,' she drawled, 'Zeb's surveillance walk was needed.'

'Are we done, here?' Bwana grouched. 'Can we press play?'

'HE MUST BE from some other building,' Smirnov said, watching the man recede into the darkness.

'Who walks in the middle of the road?' Popov said contemptuously. 'We should beat him up just for that.'

'There is no traffic. There are no lights on the sidewalk. He thinks it is safe.'

'Where are these protesters?'

'They will come. Nikola—'

'We are ready.'

Zeb searched the darkness but couldn't see Roger.

He'll be somewhere ahead of me.

'I'm in a gully next to the road,' the Texan spoke up. 'I can see you.'

'You have good—'

'Yeah. Clear firing lines.'

'Me too,' Bwana growled.

'Us too,' Chloe chimed.

Meghan clicked her mic in confirmation as well.

'Timur.' Zeb went to the side of the road, crossed the sidewalk and hid behind a tree. *I'm out of sight of the vans.* 'Where are you?'

'Waiting for your signal.'

'GO!'

53

Smirnov waited. He scanned the road occasionally and checked in with the shooters in the garden. He didn't pace, drum his fingers or show any signs of impatience.

'They will come,' he said confidently when Bortnik shifted restlessly. He made to speak when a dull glow appeared on the road behind them.

He brought his binos to his eyes instantly.

'It's a car.' His tone was even. 'Be ready for anything.'

The vehicle drew closer. He made it out to be an SUV but couldn't read its brand. It was approaching fast, its lights bobbing as it rolled over the road's imperfections.

'It isn't slowing,' Orlov commented.

Smirnov nodded. He could make out the driver and the passenger, their lower faces covered by scarves. Something protruded from a side window.

He frowned. *What's that?*

'GUNS!' He shouted in warning and threw himself to the floorboard.

The van rocked from the impact of rounds. Several tore through its thin walls. He felt a grunt beside him. An SVR shooter fell, gripping his chest. The roar of bullets faded as the SUV drove past them.

Smirnov looked up cautiously to see its taillights recede and disappear. He looked around him. Three of his men were on the floorboards, clutching their bellies. One shooter was motionless. Popov was unscathed, swearing furiously. Bortnik and Orlov felt his glance and gave him a thumbs-up.

Four of us unharmed out of eight, he thought bitterly.

'Nikola—'

'I have two dead, one injured,' the CPO said flatly. 'We couldn't return any fire. They were past us in a flash.'

'They must have been using armor-piercing rounds.'

'Da.'

'ANOTHER VEHICLE!' Popov yelled.

Smirnov whirled. 'It's an SUV,' he warned. 'Fire if they show weapons.'

'THEY HAVE GUNS!' he screamed when the vehicle drew close enough for them to see the barrels emerge from its windows.

He threw himself to the floorboard again, raised his hand, thrust his HK out of the lowered window and triggered blindly.

He heard the whine of rounds, the smack of bullets against flesh, a choked scream, gasps—and then the roar of firing died away and all that remained was the smell of gunsmoke and the moans of the injured.

Valerie Isaenko had had enough. The instructions had been clear. Stay inside the building, don't look outside the window, don't get scared if there is shooting.

There was a lot of that. She could hear the gunfire in her apartment on the third floor. Raisa, her dog, was scared.

The eighty-year-old woman defied the orders and peered

carefully through the window. She could see the street and those two vans, but nothing else.

Who was shooting?

She cocked her head and strained her ears but could hear nothing.

Raisa whimpered, and that was the decider for her.

She put the leash on her dog, opened the door cautiously and went out. No one in the hallway. Even if there was anyone, she wasn't going to be stopped.

Raisa needed her evening walk, and she didn't care about any shooting. If Rostov accosted her, she would deal with him.

Who did that old man think he was? Did he own the building?

With an angry sniff, Valerie led her dog into the garden in front of Belsky's building.

'UH-OH,' Meghan breathed softly.

'What?' Zeb asked.

'A woman and her dog have come out of Belsky's building. Looks like they're heading to the road.'

That will take her past the shooters. Smirnov could be raging. He might turn his anger on the resident.

'I'll head her off.'

'You'll have to move fast. There's a path through the—'

'I'm on it.'

Zeb sprinted at the line of trees that stretched out from beyond the sidewalk to the edge of Belsky's building. He wasn't worried about the shooters in the vans or in the garden.

Meg and Bear will take them out if they start firing.

'THERE's someone on the approach road,' Popov yelled.

'It's a woman,' Smirnov exclaimed as his binos trained on her. 'With her dog.'

'She'll know who those shooters were! She has come out because she knows it's safe. I'll get her.'

'VADIM, NYET!'

The SVR killer ignored the team leader's instruction and ran up the driveway.

Smirnov cursed under his breath.

'Keep an eye out for any trap,' he rapped out.

He inched closer to the door, ready to fire at the first sign of hostilities.

'Man coming up the driveway,' Beth announced laconically. 'From the nearest van. He'll get to the woman before you will.'

Zeb increased his speed. There was only one reason why the old woman was going to be accosted. *Smirnov will want to interrogate her.*

'Zeb!' Meghan exclaimed, 'I recognize that dude. He's the Meat Cleaver!'

54

Zeb's steps faltered.

Meat Cleaver! That's Vadim Popov!

Popov was suspected of killing the wife of a Russian political leader, an opponent of the President, in London. He had been captured on security cameras but had flown out of the country before he could be questioned. The Russian government denied that he was an SVR agent, despite the credible evidence the British authorities had made public.

The victim's body had been chopped into small pieces with a kitchen knife which was why TV and newspapers had given him the nickname, and it had stuck.

Zeb had read the man's file. *He's ruthless, likes to torture his victims.*

He willed himself to go faster, uncaring that his approach could be heard.

The approach road came into view. The building's lights illuminated it well enough for him to see the woman. A small shape trotting at her feet, the dog. A man racing up the road.

'She's in my firing line,' Meghan said flatly.

'I have eyes on him,' Bear said. 'But he's moving fast. A shot could be risky. It might alert the gunmen in the garden, who could fire.'

'Take them out, on my word.'

'Copy that.'

'Gotcha,' Meghan replied.

Popov was on the woman. His outstretched hand slapped her. She screamed and staggered. Her dog barked. The killer caught her before she fell, his hand drawing back for a punch when he heard the pounding steps.

'NOW!'

Zeb was a spear in the night. He was a missile. He dove at the Meat Cleaver. Saw the flash in his hand and recognized it for a knife.

He went beneath the wicked swipe as he sensed the silent rain of bullets smashing into the bodies of the hidden gunmen, some of whom cried out.

His shoulder caught Popov in the chest, and his strike crashed into his throat as they fell on the ground. The Russian grunted and brought his knife up again. Zeb kicked him high on the thigh, caught the incoming blade, twisted his body around and, using the killer's own momentum, plunged it into Popov's belly. He trapped the killer's knife hand beneath his body, drew out his Spyderco and thrust it repeatedly into the Meat Cleaver's chest until the man shuddered and groaned.

'WATCH OUT!'

Zeb looked up to see a second man run up the driveway.

'THAT'S SMIRNOV!' Meghan warned.

'Don't shoot him.'

He extracted his blade and sheathed it. Lunged to his feet, dragging up Popov's body with effort and shoved it towards the approaching team leader, who flinched when rounds struck the concrete.

He won't recognize me through my disguise.

Zeb drew his Glock out and trained it at Smirnov, who

came forward cautiously, his hands up in surrender, grabbed Popov's body and hauled it back to the van, even as rounds rained around them.

'He saw you.'

'Yeah,' Zeb acknowledged Beth. 'I wanted him to.'

'Why?'

'Because,' he said, watching the vans fire up and drive away, 'now he will know fear.'

55

'Are you—'

Zeb took the slap on his cheek, caught the woman's arm before she could strike him again, and helped her to her feet.

'Nyet, I am not with that man,' he told her gently as the dog yipped and ran circles around them.

'Who are they?' her voice quavered.

'I don't know. I saw him attacking you and came running.'

'Where is the body? I didn't look up after I fell.'

'His friends took it away.'

Smirnov will recover the dead shooter's bodies in the garden before it gets light.

'Please go back to the building and stay there.'

'I thought it would be safe,' she said, trembling. 'Raisa needed a walk. She was cooped up all day.'

'You can go out in the morning. It will be safe then.'

Zeb waited until she was inside the building and then checked the shooters in the garden.

'All dead,' he pronounced. 'Let's get out of here.'

'Timur?' he called when they were in their vans. 'How many casualties did you take?'

'Two men are dead,' the Ukrainian said gruffly. 'Some of us have cuts and scratches.'

'I'm sorry about—'

'Nyet. Did we kill anyone?'

'I don't know, but their vehicles had a lot of holes. There were fourteen men in them, and chances are at least a few of them didn't make it.'

'Good. Let me know when you need such help again.'

'He's talkative,' Beth sniggered when Timur hung up.

'That must be his cheerful mode.' Meghan grinned.

Zeb didn't comment. He drove out, alert, checking the road continually for police vehicles or checkpoints.

He lowered the window and could hear sirens in the distance.

'Weapons—'

'They're out of sight,' Chloe replied.

Both vans had storage compartments beneath the floorboards and in the sidewalls where they could stow their guns.

'Talk,' he told Yasimov when he called the editor.

'Nothing much to tell. The building is quiet again. Valerie, one of the residents, witnessed—'

'Is she okay?'

'Da. Was that you?'

'Tell them to stay inside,' he said, evading the question. 'SVR will return to recover the bodies. They will question everyone. Police should be there shortly.'

'Let them come. We know what story to tell. No one saw anything. The residents heard gunshots but didn't dare to look out. That's what everyone will say.'

'NIKOLA,' Smirnov said, 'what's your status?'

He twisted in his seat to look out of the rear window at the second van, which was a distance away.

'Three dead,' the CPO said bitterly.

'Four in my van, including Vadim.'

'Who killed him?'

'You didn't see?'

'Nyet. Someone was shooting from both the buildings. They pinned us down. We couldn't look out of the windows.'

'Da,' Bortnik nodded from the passenger seat. 'It was the same for us. You followed him. What happened?'

They didn't see what went down!

'There was a masked man in the garden. I didn't see where he came from. He killed Vadim.'

'What about our men?'

'Dead,' Smirnov snarled. 'There was no time to check, but they didn't move, didn't come to my help. I fired at this man but he escaped in the darkness.'

'He didn't shoot back at you?'

'Nyet. I didn't see a gun in his hand. Look at Vadim's body. He has been knifed.'

I won't tell them the man had me at gunpoint. He let me leave with Vadim's body.

'We need to recover their bodies.'

'Let GUVD do that. We don't know if those shooters are still there. We can't afford to take any more casualties.'

'We set a trap for them,' Orlov said softly. 'It was we who walked into it.'

56

Zeb was stretching in a park early in the morning when Yasimov called him.

'The police came at night and took away the bodies.'

'Did they question—'

'Da. They searched every apartment as well, not just in our building but the one opposite. They say there were shooters on the roofs of both buildings.'

'That's on the news. I saw it. Police are blaming the protesters.'

'Who else can they hold responsible?'

'Will they harass the residents?'

'I am sure they will return to question them today also. SVR will also come.'

'Let me know if there's any trouble.'

'There won't be,' the editor said confidently. 'Even if they suspect we helped you, no one will do anything for some time. They have seen how deadly the shooters were. They will not risk any more casualties.'

'Can you find out how many agents died in the vans?'

'Da. I will reach out to the network.'

Zeb hung up and finished his kata moves. A young girl who was playing with her mother stopped to watch him. She mimicked him and ran away bashfully when he showed her a simple block. He wiped his sweat, slugged water from his bottle and sent a text to his boss.

Vadim Popov won't be chopping any more limbs.

He grinned when she called instantly. The director of the Agency seemed never to sleep. She always sounded as if she was at work, even when she was in her DC home.

'You can confirm that?'

'Yes, ma'am.'

'Alex will be glad to hear that, though he would have wished Popov could stand trial. How did it happen?'

'You don't need the details.'

'Right,' she said drily. 'There was some shoot-up near Sheremetyevo last night, wasn't there? Is it connected?'

'Let's say we were in the vicinity, ma'am.'

Once Clare greenlit a mission, she left it to Zeb and his team to work out the execution.

'Are you on track?'

'Looks like it, ma'am. A few more pieces need to fall into place.'

'You went out with twenty men and returned with thirteen dead.'

Smirnov didn't reply. He stood at attention while Gorshky regarded him through hooded eyes.

'Would you call that a success?'

'Nyet.'

'The protesters were smarter than you.'

'Da.'

'They turned the tables on you.'

'Da.'

'You didn't think they would anticipate your trap and set one of their own?'

Smirnov didn't reply.

'Even if you anticipated, you could have avoided so many losses. Do you realize how?'

'Da. By checking the roofs.'

'Why didn't you?'

'I was overconfident.'

'You said you are better than Dmitri. So far, I haven't seen any evidence of that.'

Smirnov didn't counter his boss.

'Vadim was one of our best operatives. The British will be celebrating today ... and you know they would have heard of his death even if we hid the information.'

'Da.'

'Do you realize how humiliating this is for us?'

'Da.'

'He was killed with a knife. You had a gun on his attacker but he got away.'

'He was fast.'

'You are one of Zaslon's best agents. That's why you are in charge of my protection. Was he better than you?'

'He got lucky. He was already escaping when I fired at him.'

'In SVR, we make luck happen.'

'Da, but there are times when the circumstances aren't in our favor.'

'Are you aware we are stretched thin with all the operations we are running and the upcoming events in Ukraine and Belarus ... and you helped reduce our numbers even more.'

'Da.'

Smirnov was stoic. He didn't offer excuses. He had gone into the meeting expecting to be roasted, and the only surprise was that his boss wasn't in a raging fury but rather coldly dispassionate.

'What should I tell the Kremlin? I have a meeting with the President shortly.'

'That we are investigating.'

'We have been investigating the protesters for a long time. You think hearing this will make him happy?'

'The protesters weren't working by themselves. The shooting, the organization ... that was an extremely professional job. They had help.'

'Help? Some other organization?'

'Da. Most of the rounds we found at the scene were from AK74s. Those guns are common, not just with us and our military, but gangsters, too. However, we found several shells from two different rifles. A Barret and an Accuracy International.'

Gorshky leaned forward, a flicker of interest in his eyes.

'You are sure?'

'Da. It is not easy to get those guns in our country. But there is one organization that sells them on the black market.'

He stopped at his boss's raised hand.

'The shooters could be American or British agents.'

'Da, they could, but they weren't. If they were, none of us would have been alive. With those guns, they could have killed all of us in our vans. The shooters on the roofs could have shot me and Vadim as we ran up the driveway. They didn't.'

'Because?'

'They weren't that good. They were not snipers. They were spray-and-pray killers.'

'Didn't you tell me Dmitri thought there were former soldiers, Spetsnaz operatives, who had joined the resistance?'

'Da. They could have been the shooters. Not all of them are great snipers, and they might not be familiar with the guns.'

'This organization—'

'You know which one deals in those weapons. The Pushkin Bratva.'

Gorshky steepled his fingers and pondered his words.

He moved finally and punched a button on his phone.

'Send him in,' he ordered his aide.

The door opened presently and a man walked into the office. He was dressed casually. White shirt over blue jeans, with a tan jacket. A gold watch on his wrist, a chain around his neck, his shades in his left hand.

'Dusan, this is—'

'Da, I know who he is. Sergei Goncharov.'

The pakhan dropped into a chair and smiled lazily at the team leader.

'It's good to be famous, isn't it? Saves us a lot of time.'

'Dusan, Goncharov was here for some business but when you mentioned that other organization, I thought he could help us. Why don't you tell him about it?'

Smirnov nodded stiffly. He didn't know what business his boss had with the biggest of Moscow's criminal gangs, but it looked like they were more than casual acquaintances.

'You've heard about the shooting last night—'

'There's not much else on TV. Your people are taking a beating. These resistance people are outwitting you every time.'

'They have help. Illya Pushkin is supporting them.'

Sergei Goncharov's smile disappeared. His face became cold and hard.

'Tell me everything,' he whispered.

57

The clerk was in a low-level position in the SVR office. He wasn't privy to operational details, but from his seat on the bottom floor, he could see comings and goings in the building.

He had seen Goncharov arrive but hadn't recognized the man. He made a mental note of his appearance and returned to the letters in his hand. There were thirteen of them to be posted, and it was his responsibility as part of the mail office staff to get them delivered.

He went to the bathroom, checked that the stalls were empty, removed his phone's SIM card, replaced it with a new one and fired a text.

Thirteen dead.

He flushed the SIM down the toilet, put back the old one and returned to his office.

THE MESSAGE REACHED Zeb via Yasimov. He showed it to Beth, who shared it with Meghan, who nodded.

'Something I should know?' Illya Pushkin asked him when he stuffed his phone back into his pocket.

'Timur killed thirteen men last night.'

Let him take the credit for all the dead.

The pakhan stared incredulously for a moment and then threw his head back, roared in delight and thumped his thigh.

'Thirteen!' he wheezed. 'We didn't expect that many people to die.'

'Those vans were stuffed with SVR agents. They didn't have anywhere to escape when your cars rolled up.'

'The police didn't report that many deaths,' Pushkin said, grinning. 'The news channels are saying there was violence at the dormitory and a few people are dead.'

'Social media is reporting the shooting,' Beth reminded.

'Da. I got my people to do that. I am sure the residents have tweeted too.'

He smoothed his jacket and snapped his fingers, prompting an aide to refill their coffees.

Silver carafe, gold-rimmed porcelain cups. Nothing but the best for him, Zeb observed as he savored the Jamaican Blue Mountain brew.

'What can I do for you?'

'You're still ready to help? Despite the deaths—'

'Da. My people are heroes. They will be ready to sacrifice themselves.'

They are criminals. Killers. Despite that thought, Zeb couldn't help admiring the Ukrainians' commitment.

'We will need distractions. A lot of them.' Meghan wiped her lips with a paper towel.

Pushkin's eyes swept over her face and lingered on her chest.

'We are in your home, surrounded by your goons. We didn't plant any bombs this time before coming over. But just because you're helping us, don't think we have forgotten you are a criminal. If you look at me like that again, I will tear your eyes out and kill you on your couch.'

It took all of Zeb's iron control to maintain a straight face at Pushkin's reaction. The pakhan stared at the elder twin, initially in disbelief. His eyes swung toward her sister, who was grim-faced too. He flushed in anger. His fists curled. His mouth opened to reply angrily before he caught hold of himself and raised his hands in a silent apology.

'It will not happen again.'

'We need your men to cause distractions,' Meghan continued as if she hadn't just threatened one of the most dangerous men in Russia in his own living room.

'What kind?'

'Car bombs. Explosives in empty buildings—'

'Empty? What's the point of that?'

We don't want to kill anyone.

'You'll find out,' Meghan said steadily.

'Da. Car bombs. Bringing down buildings. Shootings ... anything. We are ready.'

'If your people are identified, or your role is known—'

'We discussed this.' There was a lean, hungry look on Pushkin's face. 'We can handle any trouble that comes our way.'

'We will be in touch.'

Meghan got to her feet and led the way out of the living room. Zeb raised his eyebrows when Pushkin followed them out of the door.

'I have a meeting,' the pakhan said. He waggled his fingers at them and slid into his armored Mercedes.

'We could have called and asked him if he was still in,' Beth frowned when Zeb applied his disguise and drove their van out of the gates.

'Yeah, but I wanted to see him. I wanted to confirm he meant what he said, after losing those men.'

He turned left to slip into the traffic and joined New Arbat

Avenue. The Mercedes flashed in the sunlight, three cars ahead. He searched his rearview mirror and spotted Bwana's van tailing them.

It was when they were slowing at a light that it happened.

Three cars burst out of a side street. One of them jammed in front of Pushkin's Mercedes, another cut off its rear, while the third stopped at its driver's side.

'SHOOTERS!' Beth yelled at the gunmen who jumped out.

58

'MASKS ON!' Zeb roared as he stamped on the gas. 'Doesn't he have a protection team?'

'There were two men in his car, including his driver.' Meghan slipped on her balaclava and tucked her hair beneath it. 'But no other vehicle followed his Merc.'

'Twelve shooters,' Zeb counted. 'Bear—'

'Yeah, we'll stay back. Provide covering fire.'

'And I'll be your secret weapon.' Broker peered out through the sliding window between the cab and the rear of the van.

Zeb honked and brought the van to a sliding stop several feet away from the gunmen, who were firing at the Mercedes. Some of them looked up at his approach. A shooter pointed his arm at them and turned to train his weapon on them.

AK74s. They all have the same weapons.

Zeb dove out, rolling on the ground. A round spat in front of him. Another whistled over his head, and then his Glock was to his eye, front sight on a straight line to the shooter. He triggered. The gun bucked in his hand and kicked up again as he fired a one-two burst that spun the shooter around and dropped him.

'No cops in sight,' Broker said calmly. 'No sirens. It's as if they know what's going down and they're keeping away. Traffic has stopped.'

Zeb rolled towards the van and squeezed tight as the attackers spun around to combat the new threat.

He looked beneath the Mercedes, aimed at the legs in front of them and shot. A body fell and jerked when his round punched through the man's chest.

He snatched a glance backwards when the chatter of HKs filled the air. Bwana, Bear, Chloe and Roger, using the doors of their van as cover, raining death on the shooters.

'BACK!' he heard one of the attackers shout, and the survivors stumbled to their cars, but the hail of bullets got them.

Zeb got to a crouch cautiously. None of the bodies were facing him. *Even if they're alive, they'll have to turn to aim*. That gave him the advantage.

He crabwalked, gun at the ready. Checked the first shooter. Dead. As was the second one.

He saw movement from inside the car. Pushkin's wide-eyed face at the window, his bodyguard holding down his shoulder.

Zeb heard the slither of feet on concrete and threw himself down just as a shooter sprang from the front of the Mercedes, yelling, firing, and his shots went high in the air when his Glock's rounds punched him back, and his body shuddered and jerked when Zeb's friends fired at him.

Zeb looped wide, glancing down at the bodies, kicking away the AKs until he could see in front of Pushkin's car and could confirm no more shooters posed a threat.

'Clear,' he said, at which Bear, Bwana, Roger and Chloe retreated into their van.

He tapped Pushkin's window, which rolled down.

'Don't say my name,' he warned. 'There will be people

recording this on their mobiles. GUVD will be able to lip-read from their videos. Where is your protection team?'

'I didn't need one for today.' The pakhan's voice was strong, unafraid. 'I have my bodyguards.'

'They wouldn't have saved you.'

'My car can take a lot of punishment. I would have called for backup ... but, who knows what could have happened. Thank you. You saved us. Piotr.' His eyes went past Zeb. 'That one is still alive. His body is moving. Get him.'

Zeb stood aside when the bodyguard lunged out, picked up the injured shooter and dumped him into the trunk of the car.

'We'll get answers from him,' Pushkin said coldly. 'Thank you. You need to go. The police will be here soon.' He nodded briefly. His window rolled up and his Mercedes navigated around the attacker's vehicles and resumed its travel down New Arbat Avenue.

Zeb returned to his van and got behind the wheel. He glanced at Meghan, turned to Beth and called out in his mic.

'Any injuries?'

'Nah,' Bwana scoffed. 'We had the advantage. They were out of their cars. They didn't have cover.'

GONCHAROV WAS in his office when the call came. His face was impassive as his man broke the news.

'You have eyes on them?'

'Da.'

'They aren't aware of you?'

'Nyet. We were following several cars behind. We can take them. I have five men with me.'

'Follow them. I'll send more men. Get them.'

59

'We have a tail,' Chloe called out softly. 'A Range Rover, black, dark windows. I can't see inside but it's riding low on its wheels. It's three cars behind our van.'

Zeb turned on his flasher and cut through two lanes to get to the fast one, then hopped onto the Garden Ring, exited it at Bolshoy Devyatinsky and drove out of Arbat District, past the American Embassy and into Presnensky District.

'Still behind us,' Bwana said laconically.

'They must have hung way back,' Beth observed. 'They've got to be with the shooters. The police would have flicked on their lights to stop us.'

'Yeah.' Zeb looked at the street map on his satnav display and went down a side street.

'We'll be trapped there,' Meghan exclaimed. 'That road, Prokudinskiy, it's flanked by roads at either end ... oh!'

He smiled grimly when she understood.

'Bwana, you've got the grenade launchers?'

'Sure do. Are you thinking what I am thinking?'

'Yeah.'

Zeb went to the middle of the street and parked to the right.

Bear followed and stopped to the left, several yards behind them.

'There they are,' Chloe whispered.

Zeb watched the Range Rover drive in behind them. It slowed and came to a stop in the middle of the street, blocking their rear.

'And here comes their backup.' Meghan cocked her head at another SUV that rolled in from the front.

'They're not alone,' her sister commented as a second SUV came behind it. 'We're trapped.'

The attackers didn't wait. They gave no warning.

Windows rolled down as the vehicles in the front spread out and guns started firing at them from windows.

The rounds struck their windshields but didn't break through the armored glass. Bullets whined as they ricocheted off their vehicles.

Zeb felt the van shake on its shocks as Broker moved in the rear. He rolled down his window an inch, thrust his HK out and triggered a long burst.

Pin them where they are.

'I'm down. I've got a good shooting line.'

'So have I,' Bwana said flatly.

Zeb gave the word: 'Take them out.'

'I feel sorry for them,' Meghan drawled when the first GRP20 grenade roared out from beneath them, and seconds later one of the SUVs ahead splintered from its impact. Broker triggered again, and the second vehicle was demolished.

Zeb checked his rearview mirror to see smoke and debris filling the road behind them from Bwana's weapon.

'Got to make sure,' the black operative said almost apologetically and fired again.

'Let's roll.' Zeb punched the gas and crashed through the wrecks while simultaneously firing through his window.

He thought he saw bodies through the swirling smoke, and then he was through, turning a sharp right on Zamoronova and then cutting through several side streets, guided by Meghan, until they came to a tree-lined dead-end road.

'We've got cover here.' The elder twin hopped out.

They replaced the skins on their vans with the signs of a cash-delivery firm. They changed into the coveralls of that company, climbed back into their rides and drove out.

'Those openings in the floorboards,' Broker said, chuckling when they merged into traffic, 'that was smart of Zahavy to equip these vans with that exit.'

'Yeah,' Zeb agreed. He glanced at the twins. 'Any guesses who those attackers were?'

'Nope.' Meghan shrugged. 'But I'm sure Pushkin will find out.'

60

Illya Pushkin found out by watching Timur work on the captured shooter, who screamed at the hot tongs on his flesh and begged to be released and finally broke and confessed who he was.

The pakhan nodded at his man, who shot the killer in the head. Two men grabbed the body and threw it into the pit of an under-construction building, which Timur filled with concrete.

'Be ready,' Pushkin told his men. 'If we are hit, we hit harder.'

He got into his car and made a call as it drove out of the construction site.

'It was Goncharov. His men were the shooters.'

Pushkin was emotionless and expressionless. His Mercedes rocked when his driver shifted in his seat. The bodyguard in the front was alert, his eyes flicking constantly. The bratva himself was still as he spoke from the backseat with his window lowered.

Zeb was in their van, parked parallel, but with the front of his vehicle alongside the Mercedes' rear, so that they could talk.

They were at a packing plant in Veshnyaki District. Men and women in blue overalls carted out slabs of frozen meat and loaded them into delivery vans. No one paid any attention to them or to the perimeter of hard-faced, gun-toting men around the parking lot. Nor did anyone look at Broker, who leaned idly against an empty vehicle, or Bwana and Roger, who were observing the meat carts with interest. Bear and Chloe were out of sight.

'You heard about the second attack?' Meghan asked the pakhan.

'Da.' His lips creased in a thin smile. 'Someone fired grenades at two vehicles. Nothing is left of them. Vanya Baladin, the GUVD chief, has asked me to come down for questioning. He is hopping mad. He wants to know if I have started a war. I told him I know nothing of grenades. I was attacked in broad daylight. I asked him to look into that.'

'No doubt you said you were an honest businessman, and if people like you were shot at, what was the city coming to?'

Zeb hid a smile at Beth's sarcastic comment. Pushkin didn't detect the irony, however. He nodded vigorously.

'Da. That's what I said.'

'Baladin will ask you what you and I spoke of at your car.' He told the pakhan.

'He already did. I told him you asked me if I was okay. I asked you who you were. You didn't reply.'

'Why did Goncharov attack you?'

'His bratva and mine are rivals. They are the biggest in the country. We are not far behind in size, but we are growing fast. It is possible he wants to eliminate me.'

He's no longer hiding the fact he runs a criminal network.

'Or,' Zeb pointed out, 'he might have found out you are

helping the resistance. You are the only gang who sells Accuracy International and Barret rifles. Those were—'

'Da, I watched the news reports. Those were the guns used at the apartment.' He looked out of the window with a distant expression. 'Sergei Goncharov is close to Alexei Gorshky. Very close. The SVR head has bought several dachas extremely cheap because Goncharov's men threatened the sellers and made them drop the price to one-third of market price. SVR and the police don't harass that bratva.' He took a deep breath. 'It is possible Gorshky asked him to find out if we were involved, which was why we were attacked.'

'They'll know now, since we rescued you.'

'Thank you for that. My driver tells me my car wouldn't have lasted much longer if you hadn't arrived. Let them know.'

'Why were you without your protection team?'

'I had one of my bodyguards and the driver. But yes, the rest of my security people weren't with me. My mistress doesn't like it.'

'Mistress?'

'Da. I was going to visit her. She doesn't like it when I come with many men.'

He's utterly serious. Zeb shook his head in disbelief.

'You should change your routine,' he growled. 'Clearly, they are watching your residence.'

'Da.'

'Aren't you worried Gorshky will throw his agency at you?'

'Nyet,' the thin-lipped smile appeared again. 'We will attack his agents wherever we see them. I will expose his criminal dealings. We can protect ourselves.'

'What about your Ukrainian identities?' Beth asked. 'Will they suspect that?'

'Nyet. I have made no secret of my dislike of government interference. I have said many times the politicians should stick to running the country. I have talked of corruption. Everyone knows my views, of my dislike for the government. Besides, I might not have Gorshky in my pocket, but I have other very senior and powerful politicians.'

'What will you do now?'

'We have to respond to Goncharov's actions. I can't be seen as weak.'

'Gang war?'

'Da, but not outright. We won't go about shooting in the streets. You'll hear about what we do. It will be on the news. In fact,'—his teeth flashed—'I will be going on TV today, accusing Goncharov of trying to kill me. I will say no one is safe in Russia—it's the bratvas who are running the country.'

He laughed at their expressions. 'I know. It will be one of the most talked-about interviews.'

'Those guns ... GUVD will question you about it.'

'I have a legitimate business that sells guns. I have nothing to do with military-grade rifles,' the pakhan said with a straight face. 'Let me know if there is anything else I can do.'

And with that, his Mercedes slid away, with the packing-plant workers making room for it.

'The gang war will help us, won't it?'

'Yeah,' Zeb nodded at Beth. 'It will drain investigative resources.'

'And when the time is right,' Meghan said softly, 'Pushkin will direct his attacks at SVR.'

'Correct.'

He drew his phone and made a brief call.

'Greg, how are you folks finding Taiwan?'

'Greg? What do you need from him?' Beth whispered.

'I need you all to do something.' The twins watched him as he spoke to the actor. 'Go to our embassy ... yeah, the US Embassy. I will arrange for you all to be let in. But make sure you show your faces to the street as you go ... yeah, sorry. You folks are actors. I don't need to tell you.'

'Have you worked out why I called him?' he asked the younger twin when he hung up.

'Yeah.' She punched him on the shoulder. 'You're one chess move ahead always, aren't you?'

His smile faded quickly when he fired up the van and drove out.

'Yasimov—'

'I warned him,' Meghan interjected, 'that the police or SVR would harass the protesters. They're prepared for it. I'm impressed by what he said. They have folks who gather around the protesters whenever police or government officials approach them. These *observers'*—she made finger quotes in the air—'record everything on their phones and post them on Twitter and other social media. *See how we are being harassed,* is the overall message.'

'Those will get amplified by the rest of the Resistance and will get picked up by TV and newspapers. However biased and controlled they are, they have to report it.'

'Yeah. On top of that, he says everyone has a verifiable alibi.'

'Mistress!' Meghan drawled, which got them laughing.

'Geez,' Beth chortled, 'we came to get Gorshky and rescue Elena, and here we are in the middle of a gang war.'

61

'What's this?' Gorshky pointed to the scenes on TV as soon as Goncharov entered his office. 'This is madness. Your people were shooting in the middle of one of Moscow's busiest streets.'

'There was no other way to get to Pushkin. He was alone—'

'And that was enough for you to shoot up the street? Do you know the calls I have had to take? The explanations I have had to give?'

'Why are you involved? This is GUVD's investigation.'

'Because everyone in Russia knows you and I are close, and those dead men belong to your gang!'

Gorshky panted after his outburst. A flunky poked his head in to see if his boss needed any help and withdrew quickly at seeing the SVR chief's glare.

'What did you tell the police?' He sat down and gestured at his visitor to take a chair.

'What's there to tell?' Goncharov was unperturbed at his anger. 'I don't know any of those dead men. I don't employ them. I don't run a criminal gang. I invest in real estate, I have oil companies, mining firms … I have many interests, but all my businesses are clean. I pay my taxes.'

'Like they believed you.'

'Whether they do or not does not matter. No one can prove anything.'

'Who were those men? The one who helped Pushkin?'

'No one knows.' Goncharov shrugged. 'My entire bratva is asking that same question. There are rumors that it is a group of protesters from the Resistance. Highly trained.'

'Da. We are investigating former soldiers and Spetsnaz. If it is them, they are responsible for other attacks in the city. Grenade launchers!'

'Nothing was left of my men,' the pakhan said bitterly. 'They were well armed. They were experienced fighters. The location they chose for the ambush was ideal … but they didn't expect grenades.'

'I spoke to Baladin. His people are looking for two vans … but I am sure they will be found somewhere, burned to a crisp and with no evidence. Their license plates were false.'

'At least it proves that Pushkin is collaborating with the Resistance.'

'Proves? Nyet. It does nothing like that. He will deny any knowledge of those men. Don't underestimate him. There's only one way to trap him, and that's to get hard evidence of him talking to protesters.'

He stiffened. 'Your people are watching his building. Have they—'

'Nyet. We can't see who is in the vehicles that enter his residence.'

'Those guns. The Accuracy and the Barrett. We get evidence that his men sold it to the Resistance … that's how we'll nail him.'

'I am working on that.'

'One of your men was captured, wasn't he?'

'He hasn't been found. I am sure he's dead by now.'

'Pushkin will know it was you behind the attack.'

'Da.' Goncharov gave a predatory smile. 'It's open warfare now.'

'Not on Moscow's streets,' Gorshky told him sharply. 'Do whatever you have to do, but do it quietly. And I want proof. Something that connects Pushkin and the protesters.'

'You will get it.'

THE SVR CHIEF rubbed his eyes wearily when his visitor had left.

I have to tell the President something. This shooting, those grenades, they don't make good news. He will want me to control Goncharov.

He shrugged mentally. Of all the things on his plate, answering the President about the pakhan was the easiest task.

He was reaching for the remote to turn off the TV when he froze.

Why didn't I spot that before?

The news channel was replaying a clip of the shootout on New Arbat Avenue.

Goncharov's men at Pushkin's car.

Then the arrival of the two vans. Masked and dark-clothed figures emerging from it to take down the shooters expertly. The single person checking out the bodies before approaching Pushkin's car.

He's a pro. The way he moves, his team covering him ... they are experienced at this.

It wasn't how the man moved or how his crew acted that had really caught his attention, however.

He counted slowly.

Eight rescuers.

He went to the TV, touched the screen and counted again.

Eight.

His hair stood on end.

They are men, he told himself to quell his rising panic. *There are no women.*

Nyet, his inner voice argued back. *The way they are dressed, there is no way to tell if they are men or women. They could be all men or all women or five men and three women.*

Like Carter and his team.

Nyet. It can't be. Vasili said they are in Taiwan.

Gorshky raced back to his desk.

'VASILI!' he roared when his London case officer came on the line. 'Are you sure Carter is in Taiwan?'

'Da, boss. I sent you the pictures.'

'I want proof that they are in that country. Right now.'

'In Taiwan. We don't have that many assets there—'

'I KNOW! Are you telling *me*, the SVR chief, how many agents we have—'

'I will get proof for you.'

Gorshky ordered coffee when the call ended and drank the brew slowly to take the edge off his anger.

He brought up the photographs Vasili had sent. Da, there Carter was in the airport, along with the rest of the team.

He's in Taiwan, not in Moscow. Vasili will get proof.

Which reminded him.

He summoned Smirnov to his office. 'Where are you with all the investigations? Yasimov, Evgeny, Shulga, Karel, and Dmitri's killer.'

'We got diverted by that attack. I have started looking into them today, again.'

'I don't want excuses, I want results.'

'Da.'

He tried to focus on his work. He signed off various requisitions and read intelligence reports without paying them real attention. He skimmed through a brief for the President, which normally he would have spent more time on.

He grabbed his phone at the first ring.

'Check your message, boss,' Vasili said confidently.

Gorshky put the call on speaker and typed hurriedly on his keypad.

The case officer's message came up, attached to which were several photographs.

Carter, in front of a building, his body half-turned. Bwana —there was no mistaking him.

The SVR chief sucked in his breath when he recognized the building. The American Institute in Taiwan, which acted as the US Embassy.

'When was this taken?'

'Today, boss.'

Gorshky exhaled in relief and slumped limply in his chair.

62

It was a closed-door meeting in the Kremlin. That wasn't unusual, but this one was different because of the absence of aides.

The President watched impassively as the Minister of Defense, in full military uniform, poured coffee for him and the two other visitors.

'Spasibo.' The President inclined his head and took a sip.

'Where are we?' he asked them.

'We need some more time,' the Defense man said.

'More time? For what?'

'Our troops are on the border, but we need to have supplies lined up as well. Fuel for the tanks and vehicles, food, ammunition. There is no point entering Ukraine if we have to halt because of lack of those.'

'You need one week? One month?'

'Nyet. We don't need months. We should be ready in two weeks.'

If that was reassuring to the President, he didn't show it.

'What about you?' he shot at the Energy Minister.

'Those extra weeks will help us as well. We have negotiated

with most of the concerned parties in each of the countries. We still need to hold discussions with a few big miners and private companies, but I am hopeful we can conclude those talks in two weeks.'

'How will it impact our energy needs?'

'We won't be affected. That was the brilliance of your plan. The countries we take over will take the impact of this ... which is what we want.'

'And you?'

The Finance Minister spread his hands. 'My job is the easiest. We will pass laws that no Russian can take money out of our country. We will take over the foreign deposits of Ukraine and any other country we invade. That will add to the significant US dollar reserves we have. We have sufficient reserves in yuan as well to mitigate our risks. The laws are ready to be signed off. Once we conquer those countries, all it will take is one announcement.'

The President thought for a moment. 'You are aware that Miroslav Kotenko is calling for a meeting?'

'The President of Ukraine? Da,' his visitors chorused.

'I will meet him.' The President smiled for the first time. 'It will show the West that we are serious about defusing the situation. And then we will invade his country.'

THE MEETING WAS OBSERVED by a clerk, who reported it to the Resistance. Yasimov heard about it and sent a text.

It was also reported by another aide, who sent an encrypted message that reached Clare, who requested an urgent meeting with President Morgan.

63

Zeb showed the message to the twins.

Meet me immediately.

'Yasimov?' Meghan frowned. 'What's he got for us?'

'He could have called us.' Her sister nodded. 'It must be something important.'

'Only one way to find out.' Zeb got up from the grass and folded the word game he had been playing with the twins.

'We're going to Yasimov,' he briefed the rest of the crew, who were spread out in Zaradye Park.

Bwana got to his feet instantly.

'Nope, you folks stay back. Two vans repeatedly going there will raise attention.'

I'll ask Zahavy if he has other vehicles. We need to keep switching our rides.

'You'll need backup,' Bear objected.

'The three of us can deal with anything,' Beth retorted. 'Besides, his building is safe. SVR doesn't suspect it. We haven't seen any police or SVR agents on our cams.'

'The three of you in his apartment—'

'Not us,' Meghan cut him off. 'Beth and I will go to Olga's.'

'Olga?'

'The hair salon in that strip mall. Yasimov said she was close to Elena. We have to talk to her. She might know something about the article.'

'Stay safe,' Bwana growled.

'THEY AREN'T GOING to listen, are they?' Zeb adjusted his rearview mirror.

'Nope.' Beth grinned. 'They'll follow at a distance and will probably park on Michurinskiy.'

Zeb drove into the strip mall's lot and checked it out. A couple of other cars, none of which looked like police or government vehicles.

He remained seated while the twins went out to scan the stores and returned, giving him a thumbs-up.

He climbed out and went up the approach road.

SMIRNOV KNEW everything there was about Laskin's investigations. He didn't want to walk in the missing case officer's footsteps. He pondered for a while and then signaled to Bortnik and Orlov to go with him.

'Nikola,' he told Galkin, 'the boss isn't going anywhere today. Stay here with him.'

'Where are you going?'

'To get some answers.'

He went to the building behind their office, checked out the various vehicles available to SVR staff, and selected a nondescript white car.

'We shouldn't look like we are driving government vehicles,' he told Bortnik and nodded at him to get behind the wheel.

'Where to?'

'Zakharova's building.'

ZEB CHECKED all the cars in the building's parking lot and compared their plates to the list in Yasimov's files. All of them were residents' vehicles.

He went up the stairs and cocked his head at Grusha's door. No sound from within.

Do I tell her Ruslan, Golubev or Nikitin will not bother her again?

Nope, he told himself. *She doesn't need to be involved any more. She'll find out someday, and it might give her some closure then.*

He knocked on the journalist's door in the code they had agreed upon with the editor, removed the seal and went inside.

'You don't need that,' he told the editor, who was holding a baseball bat, ready to attack. 'What was so urgent that you had to get me here?'

'The President had a meeting with his ministers. Defense, Finance and Energy.'

Zeb shook his head, puzzled. 'Yeah, so what? Presidents meet their ministers every day.'

'This was a no-aides, no-recordings meeting.'

'Again, that happens often. It's not a big deal.'

'It is, for Ukraine!'

'GO PAST IT,' Smirnov told Bortnik.

He checked out the approach road when the CPO drove on. Nothing out of the ordinary.

'Turn back. Park on that approach.'

They walked up the road to the building. Smirnov in the lead, shades on his eyes, Bortnik and Orlov flanking him. All of them casually dressed. No suits. Only jackets, which concealed their Glocks.

'Why are we here?' Orlov whispered when they entered the lobby. 'Zakharova's apartment is empty.'

The team leader didn't reply. He waved his hand at the ceiling.

'What are you doing?' Bortnik asked him curiously.

Smirnov opened his palm to show a small EMP gun in it.

'Burning cameras.'

'How did you know they were there?' Bortnik squinted at the lights.

'I don't know. Precautionary measures. Your phones are dead, too. Get new ones when we get back to the office.'

He led the way up the stairs until they reached the landing below the reporter's residence and did his hand wave again.

He pointed to the broken seal and answered Orlov's question.

'Is it empty?'

They drew their guns and went up cautiously.

No sounds from inside the apartment.

Smirnov stood to the right of the door, along with Orlov, and removed his phone from its Faraday case.

Bortnik went to the right.

'Nikola,' the team leader whispered, 'send more men to Zakharova's building. Right now. *Don't ask why!*'

'They'll be here in ten minutes,' he told the men with him as he pocketed the phone. 'We got lucky. Some of our shooters are in a car not far away.'

Smirnov gripped his Glock and crouched, counting down the time in his mind.

'How so?' Zeb asked the editor.

'Elena always thought the President's plan went beyond military invasion.'

'Da, you said she thought it was world-changing.'

'Why do the energy and finance ministers have to be there?'

'This military action will spook the financial markets—'

'What about the energy minister?'

'How do you know this is about Ukraine?'

'Because,' Yasimov insisted, 'all such meetings have been about Ukraine. The Resistance has its informers in the Kremlin. We know about these meetings. They are conducted secretively, without anyone else present.'

Zeb surveyed him.

'You're reaching,' he began and then cocked his head up and gestured sharply at the editor to stay quiet.

'We don't know who is inside,' Bortnik whispered. 'It could be empty. Vandals could have torn that seal. Or, there could be fifty men.'

'There will be a handful, no more,' Smirnov said confidently.

His phone vibrated.

He read the message.

'They are here. On my count of three.'

'Three.'

They crouched and held up their Glocks.

'Two.'

They heard footsteps pounding up the stairs.

'One.'

Several armed men reached the landing beneath them.

'GO!'

Bortnik kicked the door.

64

It was his radar. Some called it a sixth sense.

It was that extra awareness that only someone as experienced as Zeb had, developed over years of navigating through and surviving countless missions in hostile terrain.

It was the faint draft of air on the back of his neck that had alerted him initially. Tree branches, visible through the window, hadn't swayed, however. The apartment was sealed tight.

The barely discernible movement of air could only have come from the gap beneath the door.

From bodies coming up the stairs and moving in front of it.

He didn't have to think about it consciously. His body felt the draft, his mind processed it and came to its conclusions and sent electrochemical messages to his synapses, which fired his muscles to spring into action.

'BACK!'

Zeb roared. A flash of his left hand brought the mask over his head. He didn't bother to pull it down fully. *So long as it covers my eyes and nose.*

His right hand blurred to draw his Glock as he lunged into Yasimov, sending him backpedaling across the living room, into the passageway, just as the door crashed open and two men appeared in its frame.

His gun bucked and kept doing so as he fired a long burst. He heard shouts and yells and felt rounds whistle in the air, and then he was shoving Yasimov into the bedroom at the end of the hallway, locking the door behind them and dragging the bed to jam against it.

'WINDOW,' he urged harshly.

'But—'

'DON'T ARGUE. CLIMB ON THE SILL.'

'BACKUP, NOW!' he spoke in his mic.

'On it,' Meghan replied calmly.

Zeb went to the window and looked out.

Several cars parked beneath, all of which seemed to be empty.

No sign of any hostiles.

They're all inside the apartment.

The bedroom door shuddered as something crashed into it. Holes appeared in its wood.

That won't last long.

He took another look through the window and at Yasimov, who was gasping in fear, sweat on his face, and looped an arm around the editor's waist and lunged towards the window.

65

Glass shattered from the impact as they flew out, with Yasimov screaming.

The bedroom door crashed open.

A figure appeared in the window.

Zeb shot at it as he was falling, holding the editor close.

The man disappeared.

Another shape appeared in an upper-floor window.

'STAY INSIDE!' he roared and twisted his body to crash on the roof of a car, which buckled from their weight, sending its alarm off.

Zeb grunted from the force of landing on his left shoulder.

Got to move!

He threw himself and Yasimov off the mis-shapen roof and landed on hard concrete.

'Are you hurt?'

'I am fine,' Yasimov gasped. 'I fell on top of you. Are you okay?'

Zeb ignored him. A rain of bullets swept over the car, peppering it, searching for them, as he jammed their bodies close to the vehicle.

Can't squeeze beneath, he thought grimly as he peered beneath its chassis. *There's not enough clearance.*

He reloaded his Glock swiftly, his eyes scanning the parking lot.

Shouts and pounding footsteps.

Boots appeared in the lobby.

He shot at them from beneath the vehicle.

The men disappeared and a deadly wave of rounds came their way, shattering the car's windows, glancing off its body and ricocheting in the air.

Zeb heard an engine growl and snatched a look at the approach road to see a dark car race up, its windows lower and guns turn on him.

It's over, he thought bleakly. *That's their backup.*

He prepared to surrender. Started raising his hands when, with an angry whine, a van drove up and crashed into the car and its door slid open and his team poured lead at the attackers, sending them scattering and dropping, since there was no cover.

A relentless burst from within it kept the shooters in the building at bay.

'We've got you.' Meghan waved a gloved hand from behind the van as Bear, at its wheel, revved the vehicle.

That's Bwana and Roger in it. The rest of them are behind.

It was an improvised counterattack that worked because of its unexpectedness.

'Come!' He caught Yasimov's arm.

They crouch-ran and dove inside its welcoming cover, while Bear stamped on the gas and backtracked at full speed.

'Stay down!' Zeb told the editor, caught the HK that Bwana tossed at him, and joined the firing as the van raced backwards, down the approach road.

He went to the rear window when they were out of sight of the building, to see Megan, Beth, Chloe and Broker keeping pace with their ride as they provided backup in case more attackers came up the road.

They dove inside the van when Bear got on Michurinskiy, straightened and drove into the traffic.

The operative drove fast, weaving through slower-moving vehicles until they got to the Ramenskiv intersection, where he hung a left and slipped through side streets and alleys and came to a halt behind a line of cars on a quiet road.

'Come on, slow-poke,' Beth peered inside the van and beckoned at Zeb. 'We're switching rides.'

He helped Yasimov out and followed his team, who hustled towards two white SUVs that sported the logos of a TV station. They stuffed their weapons beneath its floor mats, pocketed their masks and got into the rides, with the editor crouching in the back between Broker and Beth, out of sight from any casual observers on the outside.

'Explain.' Zeb checked that his earpiece was working and glanced at Meghan.

The older twin drove out of the neighborhood and replied when they joined the traffic.

'We got delayed because we had to arrange these vehicles, move our gear from the vans to them, get back to Bear's ride and come to you.'

'Who ... Zahavy! These SUVs are his?'

'Yeah.' Beth smiled.

'He moved fast.'

'He said he's got caches all over the city. There was one near Michurinskiy.'

Zeb worked out the moves they had made.

Meg must have called Zahavy, who must have arranged for his men to drive the SUVs to my team and then taken the vehicles to the Ramenskiy neighborhood.

He felt himself. His ribs were sore and his shoulder hurt,

but it didn't seem that he had torn any muscles or broken any bones.

'Who were those men? I thought I recognized Bortnik, but I wasn't paying attention to faces.'

'Yeah, he was there. Orlov as well. Smirnov fried our cameras—'

'How—'

'I don't think he knew about them.' Meghan's ponytail bounced on her neck as she shook her head. 'He fired an EMP gun as he entered the lobby and did the same on Elena's landing. He aimed it at the ceiling, not at the lights specifically, but the blasts were enough to take out our visual.'

'We could have warned you—'

'You should have,' Yasimov shouted from the rear.

'Da, and what would he have done differently?' Beth countered, nodding in Zeb's direction. 'He and none of us knew how much backup Smirnov had. He couldn't have opened the door and started shooting. Firing on the landing or down the stairs ... anything could have happened. You could have been killed.'

'We could have—'

'You could have gone to the roof, but what would you have done there? Smirnov would have searched the entire building. It was safer to jump out of Elena's bedroom than from the roof.'

'How did you know he would do that?'

Beth squeezed Zeb's shoulder and grinned. 'We know him far longer than you do. He came out of the window with you, just the way we figured.'

'The moment we recognized Smirnov,' Meghan said, glancing at Zeb, 'Beth and I realized warning you wouldn't help much. We spotted the cars and thought you would—'

'You thought right. How did he get past you or Bear?'

'Did you see his ride as we backtracked? It was a white Toyota. He parked it on the approach road and he, Bortnik and Orlov walked up to the building.'

'We missed it,' Bear admitted in their comms channel. 'We were looking out for black cars or vans. He fooled us by taking that ride.'

'You expected him to call for backup and waited until his reinforcements arrived.'

'Da.' Meghan nodded and blew hair out of her face.

Zeb knew what she was thinking.

'We got lucky. Things were ... intense back there.'

'We should have warned you,' she said beneath her breath.

'No. You were right. Nothing would have changed,' he said and meant it. 'You knew I would have held out long enough for you to figure out your moves. Remember—'

'No second-guessing,' she and Beth, who had jammed her head between them to overhear their soft conversation, chimed in together.

'Da. What about Olga?'

'We got our hair done,' the younger twin said, pointing at the stylish cut on her head, 'and got her to talk. She wasn't busy. It was just us. She spoke freely once we said we weren't the President's fans. But she doesn't know anything.'

'Elena spoke to her about her report,' Meghan interjected, 'but only referencing it. She didn't say what she was going to publish.'

'Are they close?'

'Very.'

'Where does she live?'

'Same building. Ninth floor. That's the highest one. She's single, too. You think Elena might have hidden her notes in her salon or apartment?'

'It's possible. But we can't approach either place for a while. Smirnov will post men there.'

. . .

'Zeb,' Bwana rumbled from the second van. 'He and Gorshky aren't dumb. They will have noticed that it's eight masked people who show up everywhere.'

'Da,' Zeb acknowledged. 'They'll work out who we are.'

'And then the fun will begin,' his friend replied yearningly.

66

'They went down the road,' Bortnik told Smirnov, 'with shooters on each side of the van. They pinned down our men, and if we'd had more people come up, they would have shot them to pieces.'

The team leader nodded. He placed his hands on his hips as he watched an ambulance crew tend to the injured shooters.

Four good men are dead, Smirnov thought bitterly.

'That van—'

'It must have been somewhere nearby. We'll have to watch traffic cameras,' Orlov joined in. 'A second van is in front of the shops. Empty. The managers said they didn't see who was in it or how long it was there.'

'They are lying.'

'Da. None of them like us. They don't have cameras either.'

'Yasimov was here all along.' Smirnov bunched his fists as he walked around the building and looked at the window.

'Da. How did you guess—'

'It wasn't hard. No one searched the reporter's apartment after we kidnapped her. We sealed it and assumed no one would break it. Pah! It is a strip of plastic tape. Why would anyone respect it? This entire building is filled with people who hate us. After I read Evgeny's notes and Dmitri's investigation reports, I knew we had to search this place. That man, though —' Smirnov broke off and cursed loudly. He didn't care that several police officers and medical staff could hear him. 'He reacted so fast. We were lucky none of his rounds got us. And throwing himself out of the window ... that was a genius move.'

'He landed correctly,' Orlov said, kicking at a shard of glass while he inspected the wrecked car. 'This man is no ordinary civilian.'

'He isn't,' Smirnov said grimly. 'He is a soldier. Probably Spetsnaz.' He ran a hand through his short hair and surveyed the police and ambulance crews.

'Let's go,' he ordered. 'There isn't anything we can do here. I'll get a team to watch this building.'

'What will we tell the boss?'

'The truth,' he snarled. 'That we were outwitted again by these masked men.'

67

'Do you know how many of them there were?' Gorshky asked when Smirnov finished his briefing.

'At least five. I didn't see all of them but traffic cameras show there were that many in the van on Michurinskiy. Once the shooting started ...' he trailed off and shrugged, as if to say, *we weren't counting.*

'Any of them women?'

'It was hard to make out their shapes. All of them were masked. This man in the apartment ... he didn't have his mask fully over his face. His chin was exposed, but it wasn't enough for me to recognize him. If I had to make a guess'—Smirnov pursed his lips—'I would say they are all men.'

'That was smart thinking, guessing where Yasimov was hiding.'

'Spasibo.'

'Where do you think they will go?'

'Moscow is a big city. The reporter's apartment was an obvious hiding place, but now that they're out there'—Smirnov bobbed his head in the general direction of the city—'there are thousands of places they can hide. It could be a protester's apartment. They know we can't raid all of them. We don't even know how many people there are in the Resistance.'

'Keep investigating.' Gorshky dismissed him.

He returned to the file on his screen when he was alone but swore and exited it.

He had taken several calls from ministers who demanded explanations for why there had been more shootings in the journalist's building.

'It's because that entire place is filled with people who are opposed to our government,' he explained smoothly. 'We have to take hard measures to protect our country. You are aware we have yet to find out what Zakharova was planning to publish. We have to find out where she hid her notes. We have to be tough to make progress in our investigations. Perhaps you can speak with the President to check whether he is happy with how we are approaching matters.'

The politicians retreated at that point. None of them wished to speak to the man in the Kremlin.

Gorshky ordered coffee and, when his aide delivered it, drank it slowly while he consciously cleared his mind.

It didn't work.

Masked people.

Eight of them.

They turn up everywhere.

The quote mocked him from the wall.

He opened the photographs Vasili had sent. There was no doubt. That was Carter and his crew in Taiwan.

Who are these people, in that case?

Was it a coincidence that they were eight as well?

None of the security cameras at any international airport had alerted him of Carter's arrival in the country.

He won't show his face to them. He's smarter than that.

The thought struck him like lightning. He shivered. Coffee sloshed over and spilled on his wrist. He felt the burn dimly.

Why did Carter show himself at JFK? And in Taiwan?

'Send me one of the geeks,' he barked at his aide.

Washington DC

'You summoned this meeting,' President Morgan said, looking dubiously at Clare, 'for this? The Russian President met with his energy, defense and finance ministers. What's special about that?'

He wasn't alone in his skepticism. Jill Dalton, the Veep, showed her doubts too.

Catlyn Feder, Director of the CIA, Daniel Klouse, National Security Advisor, Clayton Farley, Secretary of State, Jerry Polson, Secretary of Defense, and Mike Hoosier, Director of National Intelligence, were in the Oval Office as well.

'We got the same reports, sir,' Feder announced. 'Yeah, the President meets his cabinet regularly, but this one was unusual. No one was allowed to sit in on it, no notes were taken—'

'I conduct lots of meetings like that!'

'You do, sir,' Clare agreed, 'but in none of our meetings do any of us enter the White House through side entrances, nor are the cameras turned off so they don't record arrivals. Entire floors of the Kremlin were cleared so that there wouldn't be witnesses to this meeting's participants. Our asset got lucky. He spotted the ministers in a bathroom.'

'Ours saw them in the parking lot,' Feder chimed in.

Zeb has confirmed, too. Clare didn't mention that, however. Catlyn, Daniel and the President knew about his operation, but no one else did.

'This wasn't the first one, sir. There have been a few more with the same stakeholders.'

'Okay, what does this mean?'

'The Russian President is thinking beyond Ukraine.'

'We know he wants to restore Russia to the old size of the Soviet Union.' The President didn't look convinced. 'But even he can't fight several wars at once. He could turn off the gas to Europe, I guess, but that would hurt Russia too. There would be economic sanctions; global stock markets would go into meltdown, which would affect them, too.'

'He is aware of that, sir. Perhaps his ministers have plans too—'

'Such as?'

'Develop a financial system that will insulate Russia from the economic storm.'

Moscow

'It isn't the first time such meetings have happened.'

'You've mentioned that a few times,' Zeb told Yasimov. 'I've reported it to my boss. They will work out what it means.'

'What it means? It's disaster for Ukraine and any other country Russia invades,' the editor fumed.

'A military invasion by itself would be damaging. What do you suggest we do with this information?'

Yasimov opened his mouth, but no words came out. 'I thought you would know what to do,' he said weakly, finally.

'We do. We have reported it to people smarter than us, who will analyze the implications and get back to us. Nothing has changed for us, however. You need to be in a safe house.'

'What about Elena? You seem to have forgotten her.'

Zeb's patience snapped. He swung around at the editor.

'Nyet,' he said coldly. 'We are working on rescuing her. We will get her out.'

Yasimov looked away from his stare. His shoulders slumped. He ran his fingers through his straggly hair.

'I don't have the right to ask you anything. All of you have risked your lives—'

'Enough of that,' Meghan drawled. 'We said we will rescue her. We need your help, however. The Resistance's.'

'Anything. Ask anything of us, and if we can do it, we will.'

'We will let you know what we want.'

They drew up into an automotive garage in Khovrino District and parked alongside a jacked-up vehicle.

None of the mechanics looked at them as they got out, but one of them lowered the shutters immediately.

'We'll stay out,' Roger said softly. 'We'll warn you if hostiles turn up.'

Zeb acknowledged him with a double-click and checked out the inside of the garage. It was a large one, with a line of ten hoists with buses, vans and cars on them. Men and women in greasy overalls went about replacing wheels and driveshafts, working efficiently. A beatbox in a corner played tunes. A woman's ponytail danced on her back as she bopped to the music.

Zahavy emerged from an inside door, wiping his hands on a rag.

'There you are—'

He broke off and did a double take at Yasimov.

'The whole country is looking for you,' he said, whistling softly.

'Does that mean you can't put him up?' Zeb asked him.

'Nyet. I didn't say that. We are Mossa—'

'Don't start,' Beth warned him.

He grinned at her and beckoned them inside and led them to a rear office.

'You will stay here,' he told the editor and pointed to the bed. 'Kitchen sink, refrigerator, which is stocked, your own bathroom.' He pointed to a door. 'Wi-fi. If you need something, tell anyone outside and they will get it for you. Every one of them is an experienced agent. They will protect you.'

'Who are you?' Yasimov asked, bewildered.

'You didn't tell him?' Zahavy looked at the Agency operatives.

Zeb shook his head. 'We thought you would want to boast about yourself.'

'We are Mossad,' the Israeli said proudly.

'Mossad? In Moscow? These many agents?'

'There are more of us, and we have other places. Moscow is our base for Eastern European operations.'

'Why Russia? What has my country—'

'You supply arms and expertise to my country's enemies. Russia is a threat to world peace. Which is why we are here.'

'All those mechanics—'

'Are Mossad agents.' Zahavy smiled. 'You are in the safest place in Moscow. They will die before anything happens to you.'

He means it.

'I am safe,' Yasimov whispered to himself and collapsed on the bed, shivering.

Beth squeezed his shoulder and draped a blanket over him. 'Get some rest,' she told him gently. 'You have our number. We'll be in touch.'

Zahavy glanced at the room when they were outside and turned to Zeb.

'That mask, Yasimov ... you are aiming big.'

'Not as high as Mossad, I'm sure,' Meghan said sarcastically.

Zahavy mock-winced and then snapped his fingers.

'Come, we have a meeting.'

'With?' Broker asked.

'Mikhail.'

68

The geek looked the way his kind was portrayed in movies.

Stringy hair, thick glasses, pale skin, as if he didn't spend much time in the sun.

He doesn't.

Gorshky had an entire floor of technicians in the basement. Some of the smartest software programmers in the country, who built facial-recognition algorithms, systems for manipulating social media sentiments, cyber-hacking initiatives and various other cutting-edge technologies that made SVR the leader in foreign espionage.

The geek wore blue jeans and a faded white Tee with the image of an American rock band on it.

The SVR chief thought of rebuking him for it.

Don't we have our own bands? Why do all of these people follow American music?

He didn't mention it, however.

He turned his computer screen toward the man and showed him the Taiwan images.

'I want to know if this man'—he pointed to Carter outside

the American Institute—'is the same person as this one.' He brought up a surveillance photograph of the operative in New York.

The geek adjusted his glasses and bent towards the screen.

'They look similar. Email me—'

'Why would I call you here if I wanted to do that?' Gorshky growled. 'Do whatever you need to do in my office. Those photographs do not go anywhere else.'

The technician bit his lip and then nodded. 'I will have to use your computer to access some programs.'

'Do it.' The SVR chief got out of his chair, poured himself a warm beverage and went to the window. He raised its shade to look out at the floor on which several flunkies worked. A few of them spotted him and bent zealously to show they were hard at work.

They feared him, which pleased him.

He turned at a sound from the geek and went back to his desk.

'What is it?'

The technician pointed at his screen, on which both images were laid out side by side, with nodal points to show the differences in the two men.

'They are not the same men.'

69

'Faces that don't have many features, like no scars, no marks ... those are harder to make,' Mikhail said as he opened a drawer and brought out a package.

He unwrapped the opaque film and drew out the mask. 'Such faces have nothing to draw attention to, so they have to be perfect. Normally, I require several images of the person; I'll bring them in for a sitting, where I can measure their face ... but you gave me only a video. Josiah provided me with a few more photographs.'

Zeb looked at Zahavy, who shrugged. 'We have our surveillance database. That man was in them.'

'I think I did well, if I say so myself.' Mikhail held the mask to the light.

Beth took it from his hand and fingered it.

'It's not plastic. Not rubber. It is a composite material that will rest easily on the skin, allowing it to breathe. Think of it like a human skin. Da,' Mikhail nodded. 'That will help you understand. You can wear it for days or weeks and it will not feel uncomfortable. Your skin will not itch. You will not get rashes. You will not even feel that you are wearing a mask. Try it.'

Zeb removed his prosthetic disguise and laid its parts on the table.

Mikhail reacted with a grunt but made no comment.

He now knows what I look like.

It was a risk they had to take. *If the Mossad trust him, so can we.*

He put the mask over his face, helped by Beth and Meghan, and pressed it firmly.

'No adhesive needed,' Mikhail said. 'It uses the skin's moisture to create a seal.'

Zeb ran his fingers over his new appearance. He could see through the eyeholes and breathe through the new nose without hindrance.

He went to the mirror and drew back in shock.

Mikhail laughed. 'Da, that's the first reaction people get when they try my masks.'

I look just like Smirnov!

He looked closely at his reflection and saw that the eye and mouth openings had been cut out expertly to reveal no extra skin.

Just like the masks we manufacture in our labs.

Meghan, reflected in the mirror, gave him a thumbs-up.

'What about ears?' Beth frowned.

'I've made those too,' the mask-maker chortled. He handed out a pair of prosthetic ones, which Zeb tried on.

These fit as well. I'll keep using them instead of the ones I have.

'You'll pass,' Zahavy nodded. 'But what about DNA imprints?'

Don't need them. I won't be entering SVR's offices.

He removed the mask and ears and stuffed them carefully into his backpack.

'Do you have soldering irons?' Meghan cleared a table and plonked her backpack on it.

'Da,' Mikhail's eyebrows drew together, puzzled. 'On that counter, over there.'

'Clear the room, please.'

'What?'

'We need to be alone.'

Zahavy and Mikhail looked at Zeb, who shrugged. 'She's the boss. Wait outside. We'll join you in a while.'

'Why did you get them to—' Bwana began.

'Your disguises,' Beth pointed to the table. 'Put them here.'

'Why?'

'Do it.'

They did her bidding.

Beth and Meghan took the false noses, ears, cheek pads and eyebrows, made small slits and soldered silicon chips in them, while the rest of the operatives watched.

'Clare sent these over a couple of days ago,' Beth informed them. 'Through the CIA channel. Those chips are more advanced than the previous ones. The older ones used to blur the masks for cameras and interfere with infrared waves ... but that could be investigated. These chips project false nodal points invisible to our eyes. Those create new faces. Like invisible masks over our faces that only the cameras can detect. What's more, the projections keep changing so we have new, random faces at intervals.'

'That sounds like Hollywood stuff.' Bear scratched his chin.

'We'll find out how good they are,' the elder twin said cheerfully.

Zeb fingered his prosthetic disguises when she handed them to him.

'They won't feel any different,' she said, smirking.

'Yeah, I know that, smartass.' He grouched and slipped

them on and, when everyone was ready, went out to join Zahavy and Mikhail.

The mask-maker looked at them curiously and sniffed at the faint soldering odor, but didn't make any comment.

'I'll get more vans for you,' Zahavy said as he fist-bumped them. 'Use the SUVs for now.'

'Da,' Zeb replied.

'Do you need our help?'

'You have helped.'

'I mean when you go hot.'

Beth lowered her shades and looked at him scornfully. 'That'll be the day!'

She turned to Zeb when they had driven out.

'You have a plan, don't you?'

'I do.'

70

Gorshky dismissed the geek and sat at his desk watching the images until the churning in his belly had settled.

He fooled us, he thought bitterly. He used body doubles. *I have assets in America, we have hacked into many of their security systems, but he used actors to dupe us.*

It was an old saying in the espionage business. Technology had greatly enhanced intelligence gathering, dissemination and surveillance. But there were times when low-tech beat high-tech, and Carter had shown just that.

The SVR chief waited till his hot rage turned to cold fury and then grabbed his phone.

'Dusan, get to my office.'

'Have you heard of Carter?' he asked when Smirnov entered.

'Da. Who hasn't?'

His expression changed. 'He's here? He can't be. I read the report. He's in Taiwan.'

'That's what I thought, too.' Gorshky turned his screen

toward his team leader and showed him the two photographs. 'Those people in Taiwan are body doubles.'

Smirnov bent down and observed for a long time.

'Eight people,' he whispered. 'It's always eight. Pushkin's rescuers, the attackers at Zakharova's building …'

'Da.'

'That's why they were always masked.'

'Da.'

'He killed Dmitri. He was the fake businessman in the nightclub.'

'Yes. He may be one of the few men capable of taking out Dmitri.'

'I am sure they are responsible for Evgeny, Shulga and Karel's disappearance too.'

'You didn't find anything?'

'Nyet. Belsky has dropped out of sight. The airport does not know where he is. His only family is his sister and niece. They're gone too. Dead cameras at the last restaurant he was at. I told you about them. But no witnesses. People are either scared to tell us what they saw, or don't want to, or genuinely didn't see anything.'

'They don't want to,' Gorshky growled. 'They want to see us humiliated.'

'How did they come into our country, though? None of our surveillance cameras or teams spotted them.'

'I don't know.'

'We are assuming a lot, however. Those attackers could be resistance people. The Spetsnaz soldiers Dmitri was investigating. We don't think there were any women in that team.'

'Have you lost your senses?' Gorshky snarled. 'Don't you know how easy it is to hide body shapes beneath combat outfits? Their hair could be easily tucked in. You really think it's not them?'

'Nyet.' Smirnov sat down in a chair. 'No one else could carry out those attacks. We found cameras in Zakharova's building. Hidden in the lights. That's how they were watching Zakharova's apartment. I didn't know about them, but I suspected there would be some kind of surveillance, so I used the EMP gun and fired it at the ceilings.'

'That was Carter with Yasimov.'

'Da. Who else could it be? He was caught unaware when the feed died. I don't know why his team didn't warn him of our arrival ... we nearly had him.'

His expression changed. He leaped up from his chair, went to his boss's computer and, without asking for permission, searched for a video clip on the internet and brought it up.

'This man outside the Ministry of Defense building ... it must be Carter.'

'Nyet.' Gorshky looked at the figure carrying away the struggling protester. 'It doesn't look like him.'

'That's because he and his entire team are wearing disguises. Some kind of high-tech ones that fool our cameras.'

'Da, I am aware of that. But there's no reason for him to expose himself there. I wasn't attacked. Nothing happened at the event other than those protesters gathering. We checked out that woman, too. She's part of the resistance but is not a danger to us. Nyet. That man isn't Carter.'

'Why is he in Moscow?'

'To get me.'

'No,' Smirnov waved dismissively. 'Your security cannot be breached. He can't get inside this building.'

'Have you forgotten he was here, in this office—'

'I read that report. That was some time ago. We have upgraded our security since then. We replaced the entire Zaslon team and brought in Dmitri, me and all the others. Besides, he had a lot of luck that time with the power outage. We have taken care of that, too. Generators that will make sure our building and others within a half-mile radius will never have an outage. Nyet. There's no chance he can get to you. I am sure he knows that too. He's after some other target.'

'Zakharova!'

'She's in Lubyanka. No one can get her out of there.'

The two men sat in silence, trying to work out the American operative's mission.

'He's not unbeatable,' Smirnov mused after a while.

'No one is,' Gorshky scoffed. 'He is good, very good, but he has also been lucky.'

'He has a weakness. He helps weak people.'

'What are you thinking?'

'Set a trap.'

'We tried that before and failed. At Belsky's building.'

'I didn't know who I was dealing with then. I know, now.'

'Who will you use as bait?'

'We can't go after random resistance members. He won't fall for it. Yasimov ... I am sure the editor is hidden somewhere safe. Unreachable from us. He doesn't have family in Russia. But Belsky ... he has extended family. We put pressure on them, and they will crack. They will tell us where Belsky is. He or his family, or both, will be the bait.'

Smirnov broke into a wolfish smile and got to his feet.

'Carter might have been the deadliest enemy you've encountered, but I am better.'

'Don't be overconfident,' Gorshky warned him sharply. 'Dmitri thought that too, and look what happened to him.'

'I am not. But I am sure of myself.'

They turned towards the TV which was showing a newsclip of protesters.

'It would be simple if we tortured Zakharova, extracted her information and killed her.'

'Don't you think I have thought of that?' Gorshky ground his teeth angrily. 'But the President doesn't want that. He says it will create too many political challenges. He is right, in a way.

Her article hasn't leaked yet. It looks like no one has it. All we need to do is wait for this event to be over, and then we will deal with her.'

'Which event?'

'Didn't you read the news? Our President has invited the Ukrainian President for a meeting in Moscow.'

71

With the new disguises, Zeb took the risk of getting all the operatives together in the same restaurant. They had been under the same roof before, but this time they were seated closer.

Beth had chosen the venue in Arbat district, a joint popular with tourists, an environment where Bwana could blend in.

'Any update from Clare?' Roger asked softly as he scanned the menu.

'No. She briefed the President on this meeting and he has asked them to prepare for every contingency. That's a tall order, since we don't know what the Russian President's game is.'

'Tell us what you have in mind,' Bear said impatiently, after he had given his order to the server.

They turned to the TV at the sounds of clapping and cheers.

'Ukrainian and Russian Presidents to meet in Moscow,' Broker read the headlines. 'In an attempt to de-escalate the situation.'

Meghan gasped. She whirled towards Zeb.

'That!' she said urgently. 'That's your plan!'

'I knew you would work it out,' he grinned.

'You've lost us,' Chloe complained. 'Explain—'

'I got it.' Beth's eyes lit up. 'This is how it will go down.'

She explained rapidly, and when she had finished, they turned again toward the TV, showing more scenes of the Red Square protesters.

'A lot of parts have to fall in place,' Roger commented.

'They will,' Meghan asserted, 'with Yasimov's help.'

'That exfil route—'

'Clare will talk to President Morgan about it. I'm sure he can swing it.'

'It could work,' Bear brooded, 'but y'all are forgetting something.'

'What's that?' Zeb asked him.

'Gorshky and Smirnov won't be sitting idle. They will have worked out who we are by now. They'll be hunting for us.'

'Yeah, I know that.'

'You don't seem concerned.'

'I am.'

'You know where they'll strike?'

'They won't come after us directly. They'll get us to walk into their trap.'

'Trap? Who's the bait?'

'I don't know,' he said helplessly.

It was Chloe who came up with it when they were in Zaradye Park, later.

'We aren't thinking like them,' she said as she plucked a blade of grass and played with it. 'Gorshky knows by now that we'll go to protect the Resistance. We did that at Belsky's building; we rescued Yasimov. He'll use that.'

'There are thousands of protesters in Moscow alone,'

Bwana pointed out. 'How will we know who he plans to use as bait?'

'It will be someone we know. We wouldn't help some random Resistance worker. We can't. Like you said, there are too many of them.'

'Belsky's building's residents?'

'That's a possibility. But they tried that once. They may not—'

'Belsky!' Zeb sat up straight.

THEY GATHERED in a fancy hotel's lobby in central Moscow and spread out on couches and chairs in the cavernous interior.

'He's safe,' Zeb briefed them. 'I checked with Zahavy. He and Yasimov are both in the safe houses. No hostiles around. His sister and niece are—'

'I'm looking into that Odintsovo motel that Jelena Vorishnov, his sister-in-law, runs,' Meghan whispered in their comms channel. 'It's owned by a holding company …' She trailed off and spoke aloud to herself, after a moment. 'Registered office in Moscow. Directors are two men. Who are they?'

Zeb checked out the lobby as the sisters worked their magic. A tour group at the check-in desk. He could hear English, German, French and Afrikaans being spoken. A burly man's roll-on clattered to the marble floor, drawing everyone's attention. He waved a hand apologetically, and the rhythm of the hotel resumed. A dark-suited man in a corner.

Security. He's no threat to us.

His eyes returned to his team when he didn't detect any police or SVR men present.

'Okay, I've got the link,' Beth said. 'One of those directors is the sister-in-law's school friend. The other is from her previous employer, a bank. She must know them really well to have them on the company.'

If we can make the connection, so can Gorshky. That motel is outside Moscow, in a less populated area. He'll work out it would make a great hiding place.

Bwana got to his feet and popped his knuckles. His biceps strained against his Tee when he stretched.

'Let's see if SVR is thinking the same way as us.'

72

Odintsovo was the administrative headquarters of the Odintsovksy District in Moscow Oblast.

'Just over a hundred thousand people,' Beth narrated as Zeb drove the SUV through quiet streets, past apartment buildings that looked the same wherever they went.

'Sleeping districts,' Broker quoted.

Zeb nodded.

The city's suburbs were called so because many people went out to work and returned to them only in the evenings, to sleep. The buildings looked identical. *Soviet-era construction for workers who came to factories in Moscow to work. Pre-fab blocks of flats, the largest industrialized housing experiment in the world.*

The neighborhoods were designed to be identical, with parks, daycares, schools and health centers, and were the precursors to the *mikrorayons*, micro-districts.

The motel wasn't in such a suburb.

It was in the commercial center of Odintsovo: bus station, supermarkets, banks, restaurants, hotels and various entertainment and commercial establishments.

The place was contained in a square, around which the

Sovetskaya and Svobody streets looped. At the back end of the city center was a major road, the Mozhayskoye Shosse, bustling with traffic. A police officer leaned against a prowl car and looked disinterestedly at them when they drove past.

'I don't remember all of this,' Zeb commented.

'We took a different route,' Meghan pointed out. 'There, that's the motel.'

It was in a corner of the commercial square. He recognized it immediately from the faded sign and the tired-looking parking lot.

That's the only building that's got vehicle access. No other establishments near it. It's got an exit to Svobody.

They checked the center out on foot, he at the front and the rest of the operatives splitting up, pretending to be tourists.

There were bigger hotels in the town center, but none had its own parking lot.

Sister-in-law must have greased some palms, or something went awry with the center's planning and the motel got its own parking space.

He sauntered to the rear of the building. A concrete boundary wall that left enough room for an alley for the deliveries entrance. Beyond the wall was a tree-lined grassy bank that trailed away to Mozhayskoye. To the left of the motel was an entertainment arcade.

'A shootout here would be dangerous during the daytime,' Meghan said as she came up to him and peered through a store window. 'There will be people around in the evening, too, until the town center closes. But the bus station ... that operates all night. There will be pedestrian and foot traffic.'

'Yeah.'

'On top of that,' Beth said, sidling up to them, 'we don't know when Gorshky's men will arrive.'

'*If* they do,' Broker added. 'They might not. Our thinking might be wrong.'

'They will,' Zeb said confidently. 'We'll use their trick on them. We'll let them know we're planning to move Lara and Petra.'

'I DIDN'T KNOW Odintsovo had such nice-looking women,' Orlov said, leering when a young woman passed their restaurant window.

Smirnov followed his gaze at her retreating back. For a moment he thought they looked like the twins in Carter's team and that other woman, Chloe. He stared hard at their profiles.

Nyet, it isn't them.

He scowled when Bortnik whistled softly as two more attractive women went past.

'We are not here to look at women,' he said harshly. 'That motel—'

'Da,' Bortnik nodded apologetically. 'I went inside it and asked if they had spare rooms. They don't. They are full. But our—'

'Geeks hacked into its reservation system,' Orlov completed. 'Belsky's sister and niece aren't registered as guests.'

'They wouldn't be,' Smirnov replied. 'Or, they could be entered under false names.'

'Da. We checked that out. All the women staying at the motel are genuine. We tracked down their identities. But there's this,' Orlov said triumphantly. 'There are three rooms at the back of the motel that aren't rented out. They're likely for staff and owners' use.'

'The sister and her daughter could be staying there.'

'Da.'

'That was smart work, identifying this place as a likely hiding place for Belsky's relatives,' Smirnov said, complimenting the two men. 'We can arrest Jelena Vorishnov for tax evasion. But does she work here?'

'Da.' Bortnik beamed. 'There is a security camera at the reception. We have accessed its footage. She is the manager, even though her name is nowhere on the motel's records. What's more, she is there right now.'

'Finish up.' The team leader wiped his hands on a paper towel. 'Mount watch, or find a way to check out those three rooms. We need to confirm if Belsky's sister and daughter are there.'

'Where are you going?'

'To get more men and to start the rumor that we will be capturing those women.'

'Rumor? Aren't we going to grab them?'

'We are.' Smirnov bared his teeth. 'And Carter as well.'

73

Zeb's team took the easier route.

Beth and Meghan fired up drones when darkness had fallen, while the rest of them changed into tactical outfits. HKs strapped to their thighs with easy-draw snaps, fastened such that the barrel swung freely beneath their knees.

It wasn't their preferred position to carry their weapons. It made sitting uncomfortable. However, they couldn't risk slinging the weapons across their chests or shoulders, since it would be obvious.

Dark Tees, beneath which they wore lightweight armor, which in turn was reinforced by their tactical vests. Crye Field Pants without any logos. Custom-designed trainers with Vibram soles on their feet.

Every piece of gear dark, black or a deep shade of blue. No logos. The only identification they carried was the fake cards in their wallets.

Seven pm.

Zeb squinted out of his SUV, which was parked in a supermarket lot one street away from the motel. Bear's ride was several cars away. He could see it rocking on its shocks as his friends geared up.

'I'll take over,' he said, tapping Beth on the shoulder.

He occupied her seat as she squeezed past and went to the rear. He took the screen control of the drone and continued flying it towards the motel.

'You take the rear,' Meghan told him. 'You have more cover. I'll check out the rooms at the front.'

'They're camo-enabled, right?'

The UAVs were coated with Stealth paint and also with silicon chips and reflectors that allowed them to change their appearance to blend with the background.

'Yeah, but we'll be flying low and there's still foot and vehicle traffic.'

It's getting dark. We could have waited, but we need to know that Lara, Petra and Jelena are in there, right now.

He flew the drone across the highest floor, using its thermal imaging to see whether there were occupants and, if there were, using its night-vision camera to zoom in through cracks in the curtains.

'There's this room, which is sealed up tight.'

'I should have stayed with the drone,' Beth sighed. 'Teaching him will take more time.'

'Thermal?' Meghan looked at him.

'Yeah, there's one occupant.'

'Size identifier?'

He looked blankly at her.

'See that corner image on your screen, dumbass. That's Werner telling you whether it could be a man or a woman in there. It runs an algorithm automatically that—'

'Don't get into the deets,' her sister scoffed. 'He wouldn't understand.'

'It's a man,' Zeb said defensively.

'Move on to the next room, in that case,' Meghan told him sharply.

'But what if the curtains aren't open?'

'Then we try to listen in, and if that doesn't work either—'

She broke off and stared at him when he brought out his phone.

'Who are you calling?'

'Belsky. He can ask his sister where she is and if Jelena is in the motel. Why didn't you think of that? What—'

She snatched the phone from him and ended the call.

'We. Did. Think. Of. That.' She spat out the words: 'Belsky would have called his sister to check ... did it occur to you Gorshky's people could be monitoring calls? Even cell phone ones. It's not hard. A fake antenna to spoof the phones into thinking it's a tower ... his sister would definitely ask him how he was. He could give away his location and Zahavy's involvement inadvertently. That's why Beth and I launched the drones.'

Zeb didn't reply.

Bwana chuckled over their comms. 'I'll say it. Zeb's getting old. He's not thinking the way he used to.'

I deserve that! He smiled ruefully and took back the phone. Turned his attention back to the screen and the drone and continued checking out the rooms.

It was Meghan who found them.

She had finished the front rooms and flown her UAV to the side of the motel that overlooked the parking lot. She snapped her fingers in the silent SUV.

'Middle room on the second floor. Window's open ... probably to let in natural air. Petra's combing her hair, and there's her mom, on the bed!'

'What about Jelena?'

'We know what she looks like,' Beth interjected. 'She's got social media accounts.'

'Yeah. She isn't in any room. Maybe she's at the front desk?' Her sister bit her lip thoughtfully. 'We can't check that out with our drones. There are too many obstructions.'

'Her social media,' Zeb straightened. 'Does she have any videos? Any clips where she speaks?' We can call the front desk and compare the voice—'

'Maybe you aren't that old,' Meghan acknowledged. 'It might be someone else who answers, but it's worth a try.'

Her fingers danced over her keys.

'There are videos,' she muttered beneath her breath. 'Several of them. She's a gardener. She's got a channel for growing stuff.'

She dialed the motel, said she was a traveler and needed a room for two nights.

She fist-pumped at the reply, thanked Jelena, the speaker, and said she would go to the motel in person to book the accommodation and hung up.

'That's her.'

'Keep the drones flying.' Zeb moved out of his seat to let Beth take it. 'We need eyes on the motel as well as the surroundings.'

He went to the back of the SUV and fist-bumped Broker, who was playing with a pack of cards.

'Ready?' he asked his friend and eyed the weapons on the floor. Spare HKs, magazines, blood packs, two grenade launchers—everything that they could possibly need.

'Yeah. I'll go to Bear's ride when the women come here.'

Zeb nodded, removed his HK and placed it on the floorboard, then got out of the SUV.

'I'll check out the neighborhood.'

'No signs of hostiles,' Meghan informed him when he circled the square.

'I can't see any folks either,' he confirmed.

It's nine pm. Light traffic, but none of the parked cars on the streets seem to be occupied.

'You saw the Twitter posts. Someone has started a rumor that SVR will make some arrests tonight in the Moscow Oblast area.'

'That's by Gorshky's people. They couldn't have made it any clearer that they are targeting Belsky's family. Setting the trap for us.'

'One that we will walk into.'

74

Zeb walked casually, pretending to speak on his phone, and went into the bus station. He looked up timings on random bays and watched a polished aluminum coach back into one. Several passengers came out, wheeling their roll-ons. He went out of the coachway, checking for anyone who didn't belong.

There were families, couples coming out of a nearby movie theater, a bunch of teenagers, but no one who had alert eyes or carried their hands close to their bodies.

'We've responded to those rumors?'

'Yeah,' Beth confirmed. 'Through our anonymous Twitter accounts.'

That will tell Gorshky and Smirnov we'll be here. Where are they?

By ten pm, he had completed two more circuits and hadn't spotted any shooters.

I'll stick out if I continue to wander aimlessly.

'No suspicious vehicles on our drones' feeds, either,' Meghan told him.

He nodded and went to a lone traveler in the bus station. A brief conversation. The man's surprised look changed when Zeb produced a thick roll of bills and the passenger's roll-on changed ownership.

'I'm going in.'

ZEB WALKED UP to the motel like a tourist double-checking his address, pulling his bag behind him. He went through its revolving door, put on a smile and went to the check-in desk, behind which sat a woman in her forties. She wore the motel's uniform. Dark Tee with the logo on her chest, dark trousers, hair swept back, a half-empty mug of coffee next to her.

That's the sister-in-law.

'I have a reservation,' he told her and pushed forward a sheet of paper.

She took it and frowned when she read it.

YOU, Lara and Petra are in danger. You need to come with me, right now. I am Vlad Belsky's friend.

'WHAT—'

'Check my name and date.' He leaned forward. 'Turn off the security camera.'

She looked at him with a confused expression but her hand went to the keyboard automatically, responding to the authority in his voice, and punched a button.

'You are in danger. SVR is planning to pick you up any moment. They are hunting Vlad and think you know where he is. You have to get out of here.'

'Who are you? What are you talking about—'

'Come with me to Lara's room.'

'Wait! You can't go—'

She cursed loudly, came from behind the counter and hustled behind him when he went up the stairs.

'Who do you think you are?' she called out angrily when he hurried down to the landing. 'What's this nonsense you're talking about—'

'Quiet! You'll wake up the entire floor.'

Zeb knocked on Lara's door as the sister-in-law came up to him, fuming.

'I am calling the police.'

'If you do that, they'll arrest you.'

Belsky's sister opened the door. She frowned.

'Jelena, what is it? Who's this—'

'Take your purse. Nothing else. Take her.' He nodded when Petra, in her sleep clothes, joined her mother. 'We have to leave right now. SVR is coming for you.'

'Do you know this man, Lara?' the sister-in-law said angrily. 'He's talking this nonsense. He—'

'Nyet. I haven't seen—'

'I and my friends rescued Vlad and Petra a few days ago, when SVR men had captured you. Three women in my team. Two large men. One man—'

'Let me talk to them,' Meghan ordered in his earpiece.

Zeb gave the disbelieving sister his phone. She took it hesitantly.

'Da?'

She listened intently, looked at the screen, and scrolled through a Twitter page. Her skepticism gave way to a look of fear. She nodded several times and returned the phone.

'He's right,' she told Jelena. 'We have to leave right now.'

'But—'

'There's no time. They know about your ownership in this motel. Get your purse. Don't take anything else. Petra, honey, change quickly. Wear your jeans and jacket.'

'Are bad men coming, Mama?'

'Lara!' the sister-in-law said fiercely. 'How can you believe this man? Who was on that phone? What's this about—'

'Jelena, I trust him. They saved us.'

'YOU SAID YOU DIDN'T KNOW HIM!'

Lara caught her sister-in-law's shoulders and looked deeply into her eyes. 'Everything he said is the truth. If we don't leave now, we will be caught and tortured. We have to leave right now.'

She didn't wait for a reply. She went inside the room, snatched her handbag from the bed, helped Petra with her shoes and came to the door.

'Behind me,' Zeb told them and went down the hallway. 'If strange men come toward us, drop to the floor.'

'Why?' Jelena challenged him.

'Because there will be shooting.'

Zeb jabbed the elevator button, but instead of waiting for the car took the stairs.

He heard a gasp behind him when he drew out his Glock but didn't look back. The lower-floor landings were clear. He peered cautiously into the lobby. No one in it. He looked through the revolving doors. Lights from various establishments. Cars in their bays. He counted them.

No new vehicles have arrived. None have left.

He motioned to the women to join him.

'Take your bag,' he told Jelena.

She went behind the counter, reached down and slung a stylish purse over her shoulder.

'Give me your phones.'

'Why?'

'Oh, Jelena,' Lara said impatiently as she fumbled in her carry bag, 'why do you have to be so difficult. Give it to him.'

Zeb removed the batteries from their phones, crushed them beneath his heel and threw the carcasses into the trash bin.

'Come.'

Smirnov looked at the screen Bortnik held up.

'Their phones have gone offline.'

The team leader's eyes glinted.

'The trap has been set.'

75

Zeb went to the door and looked out.

'Clear,' Bwana spoke in the comms channel.

He nodded unconsciously. *They're spread out, covering the parking lot. They'll take down any approaching hostiles.*

No one accosted them as they hurried across the lot, squeezing through cars, and got onto the sidewalk on Svobody just as Meghan raced up in the SUV. Its rear passenger door slid open, and Beth helped the women inside. Zeb got into the front and pulled on his mask, and the elder sister floored the gas while he buckled in.

'Why are you all wearing those?' Jelena asked fearfully.

'Because we don't want to be recognized by other people.'

'I don't like this—'

'Jelena,' Lara said impatiently, 'I told you ... they are good people. Our friends. They saved Vlad and Petra.'

'Petra said those men were wearing masks.'

'You want to go back to the motel? Go!'

Jelena didn't move. She turned her face away when she met Zeb's eyes in the rearview mirror.

'Did we read it wrong?' Meghan asked him when they passed the first set of lights.

'I don't know. We have them,' he said, jerking his head backwards, referring to their passengers. 'Who else could SVR have been referring to in those tweets?'

She didn't reply. She drove expertly down the quiet street, a look of fierce concentration on her face. They got onto Mozhayskoye.

Not much traffic here, either.

'What's that? Are you playing a game?' he heard Petra ask behind them.

'Nyet, honey. We have a drone flying above us. It is sending us pictures. We can see if any bad men are following us. No one is.'

They passed another set of lights and a roundabout.

'All quiet behind you folks,' Roger said softly.

Zeb saw the second SUV come up behind them. He reached down and strapped his HK to his thigh, letting his fingers linger on its stock.

A side street passed. Another came up.

Street lights, dim on the road but giving enough illumination for them to make out details.

The snow removal truck came out of the darkness. Its plow lifted them up, brought them crashing down on the driver side, and pushed them across the road.

76

Zeb felt the door buckle from the impact. Metal shrieked. Petra screamed, her mother joining in the shouting.

He tugged furiously at his seat belt, felt it release. He was sprawled on his left side, across the central console. Felt Meghan move, kick up to free herself.

'THERE'S A DITCH BEHIND US! THEY'RE SHOVING US TOWARDS IT.'

He caught the grab handle, found purchase on the seat and hauled himself upright.

'Beth?'

'I'm good.' Her voice strained. 'None of us are hurt—'

Metal ripped as the plow tore through the chassis. Zeb brought his HK up with difficulty and broke the window with its butt. Rolled it around to make a clearing and thrust his head up. Jerked back inside when rounds splattered the SUV.

Hostiles on foot behind the snow truck. Bear's truck attacked as well. Ten feet to the ditch. If we end up there, we'll be sitting ducks.

'HERE!' Beth yelled.

He reached out blindly and caught something cool, round and heavy.

The grenade launcher.

He felt it blindly. It was loaded.

No time to aim.

He shoved it out of the window, braced himself with one foot on the dash and the other on an armrest, felt Meghan's hands at his waist to support him, and fired.

His ears rang from the explosion in the closed space. Petra screamed again.

We've stopped moving.

He let go of the launcher and reached for his HK. Winced when his neck caught on the window's jagged edge. Fired in the general direction of the approaching men.

'PETRA! NYET! DON'T GO THERE.'

Zeb looked down the vehicle.

The back door was open, and through the opening, he saw Petra scramble out and run onto the road.

He fired at the hostiles. Heard their shooting falter. The SUV shuddered when Meghan kicked at the windscreen. He felt movement from within and risked a glance out to see Beth lunge out of the vehicle.

She raced behind the child, her left arm outstretched, her right arm firing her HK. A concentrated burst of shooting came from the second SUV, which had taken out its snow truck, too.

A shadow moved.

Zeb shot at it and kept firing, replacing empty magazines in practiced fast-change moves, uncaring that he could be stomping on Meghan.

All that mattered was to cover Beth, who was nearing Petra.

And then the younger twin jerked like she had been shot.

She stumbled and fell face down and didn't move.

77

Zeb heard someone exclaim in his earpiece.

Meghan moaned.

It felt like the night grew sharper, where he could make out every detail: Beth's leg angled out just so, the fraying edge of her trouser leg, her hair spilled out on the road, and her body lying so still.

He saw a man rush towards the child.

He blew out the hostile's head.

A round smacked into the buckled door. Paint chips flew in his face. A bullet whistled past his head.

He didn't move. He didn't duck. He didn't let up from shooting at the SVR men, who had fallen back into the darkness, leaving nothing on the road but Petra, who was running away from them, and Beth, who lay motionless on concrete.

And then Lara burst out of the SUV and ran screaming toward her daughter and two men came out from behind their cover and went at her, and the hostiles resumed firing to pin Zeb and the second SUV's occupants back.

He ducked down and peered through the jagged tear in the chassis, next to Meghan, whose face was angles and edges and who didn't turn to look at him. He thrust his HK through the tear and joined her firing, knowing the angle was bad and their rounds flew off harmlessly in the night.

He thrust his rifle down with all his strength, hoping to make the tear bigger, but it didn't work, and a dim part of his mind, where thought was still possible, realized that Bear and the rest of them in the second ride had the same problem.

They were hunkered down with not enough firing angles.

One of the men reached Petra. Caught her just as Lara reached them, and the second man slapped the mother away, and Meghan, with another moan that carried the weight of the world's grief and anger, crawled out from the back, and Chloe, who escaped from the other SUV, lunged to the mother's rescue, the older twin firing from her hip, her rounds ripping into the second attacker's chest while the petite operative dove at the first man and shot him in the face point-blank, all the while as bullets whispered through the air.

Beth moved. Her HK straightened.

'I'm okay. It was my vest.'

Her voice was croaky but strong.

And the earth started rotating and revolving again.

The younger twin fired at the hostiles, crawling back as she did so, with Meghan and Chloe adding to the protective fire, Zeb thrusting his head out of the shattered window and triggering as fast as he could, and to his right, Bwana and Bear joining the shooting.

The hostiles ducked for cover under the concentrated rain of lead that kept pouring their way. They fired back intermittently seeking out the women, but Meghan and Chloe, crouching low in front of Lara and Petra, with Beth reverse-crawling and shooting, made sure none of the attackers' rounds got close.

'I've got control of the drone.' Broker. Voice rasping like

sandpaper. 'There's a line of vehicles on their side. A ditch, too. That's their cover.'

Even as he finished, a grenade flew out from his SUV and tore into metal. Zeb ducked down and brought up his launcher and fired two more GRP20s at the SVR killers' defensive vehicles.

'We aren't out of it yet. There seem to be more than twenty shooters behind their cover. We have dropped a few with our grenades, but they outnumber us. We have six more coming up the ditch behind us. Three hundred yards down the road, on their side, there's a car with three warm bodies in it. They've got binos; one of them is on a phone.'

Smirnov! It's got to be him, directing the attack from a distance.

Zeb threw down his grenade launcher, picked up his HK and wriggled down his ride.

'Stay down,' he told Jelena, whose face was pinched with fear, her eyes large.

Petra came inside and crawled to the sister-in-law, who hugged her tight. Lara followed and then Beth, who gave a thumbs-up to Zeb.

He wanted to hold her. Check her out. Shake her angrily for her reckless move.

He swallowed and edged past Meghan and Chloe, who crowded inside. None of them questioned where he was going.

They knew.

Got to take out the attackers in the ditch, or they'll trap us.

78

A sinuous dark shape crawled out from behind the second SUV.

Bwana!

Zeb raised a clenched fist at him, got an acknowledgement and crawled to the line of trees that marked the edge of the ditch.

'Careful. They're in a spear formation,' Broker warned.

Which meant one man ahead, the rest strung out towards the back, to minimize casualties and at the same time attack effectively.

'That ditch is large. About twenty feet wide, ten feet deep.'

Must be used to collect or move large quantities of water.

Zeb crouch-ran to the tree line. Dull whumps behind him as the team kept firing grenades at the attackers' main force.

No cop sirens, no civilian vehicles. Smirnov must have taken care of that. The night is his.

'Fifteen feet to Bwana's left.'

That's about thirty feet from me.

Zeb was closer to the edge than his friend. He dropped to his belly and crawled rapidly to risk a glance over the ditch's lip.

The earth collapsed, sending him tumbling to the bottom.

He lost his HK in the loose soil.

He heard a shout, and a round slapped mud next to him. Another struck his chest with the force of a tree-trunk, knocking him to the ground.

'Vest,' he panted and drew his Glock out, and then Bwana was diving down, presenting himself as a target, his HK chattering, filling the ditch with a deadly hail, and he fell down and Zeb reared up on an elbow and emptied a magazine at the six hostiles, two of whom dropped. The rest bent low and fired back, but they were still outnumbered, and firing in a tight channel with no cover was an easy way to get one's ticket punched. And then Bwana's hand moved.

'Duck,' he growled, and Zeb looked away as the flame and sound rocked the ditch and another explosion signaled a second grenade.

Zeb lunged forward as the ground stopped shaking from the blasts. He weaved from side to side as he approached Bwana, firing at the shapes on the ground. He dove over his friend, who reared up and joined in the shooting until they had emptied several magazines at the six-person team.

'Careful,' Bwana hissed when Zeb got close to the first body.

It was torn by the grenade, as were the next two, and the remaining hostiles were riddled with bullets.

One was still alive when Zeb got to him, the angry glare in his eyes fading, his breath sighing out until he stilled.

'That was nowhere like a textbook operation.'

'Nope,' Zeb agreed.

'We could have tossed grenades from the top.'

'That was my idea. The ditch had other plans. Why did you go Superman?'

'You thought I dove in to save you?' Bwana's teeth gleamed in the dark. 'Nah. The soil broke on my side, too. I fell.'

No, it didn't. He threw himself deliberately, to make himself a target.

He squeezed his friend's shoulder hard and got a back thump in return.

'Beth?'

'Didn't talk to her.' Zeb hurried down the ditch. 'She looked okay.'

'You took a round, too.'

'The vest did. It looks like the shooters are using standard rounds.'

Bwana nodded.

'They want us alive if possible.'

'Yeah.'

'You'll have to cross the road to get to the car,' Broker directed him. 'That's twenty feet of open stretch, at your ten-o'clock.'

'Copy. Sitrep?'

'Looks like the grenades have done the job. Hardly any return fire.'

Zeb climbed up the ditch carefully, seeking toeholds, until he could see the surface across the road at Smirnov's vehicle, which looked boxy and dull in the reflected street light.

They'll be armed. They'll know the ditch team has failed. We've got to move before Smirnov calls for backup.

He couldn't ask his team to break out and cover him.

Bwana and I will have to do it ourselves.

'No shooting,' he warned and got a sound of disgust in return.

He held up three fingers, folded one and then the next, and on the curl of the last one burst out of the ditch, zigging and zagging across the road, feeling the earth shake from Bwana's pounding steps behind him. Smirnov's vehicle drew close, a face turned towards them from the front, two more looked in their direction from the rear seats, their windows rolled down;

guns appeared and Zeb dove beneath the incoming fire, slapped away the barrel from the driver's window and jammed his Glock in Smirnov's teeth.

'Keep shooting,' he snarled at Bortnik and Orlov, whom he recognized from Yasimov's files, 'and I'll make holes in your boss.'

They stopped firing. Bwana snatched their AK74s and tossed them away. He yanked open their door, at which Bortnik lunged out with a Glock in his hand, but the Agency operator had been expecting such a move.

Bwana caught his gun wrist and twisted it, almost lazily, to snap it, then shoved Bortnik backwards to crash into Orlov, who looked like he was drawing a handgun.

Bwana caught the first man by his neck and smashed his face on the car's roof. He pulled Orlov out, backhanded him across the face and pounded his head on the trunk until the man collapsed limply.

Smirnov licked his lips and turned to Zeb, who gestured at him.

'You are still useful to us,' he told the team leader and knocked him out with his Glock's barrel.

He and Bwana crushed their phones and dragged their bodies deep into the darkness.

Zeb got behind the wheel, fired it up and drove toward the wrecks of their SUVs.

'Clear,' Broker greeted him.

Zeb stopped the car behind his SUV to provide some cover.

'Get in,' he told Lara. 'You, Petra and Jelena. We'll get you to a safe house. How's—'

'I wasn't scared,' the girl sniffled. 'I would have hit that man. I am learning boxing.'

The memory escaped from the tight vault in his mind. Another young child, along with a woman with smiling eyes.

He forced it back away and dropped to his knee in front of Petra.

'There are many bad people in the world. You will come across some of them as you grow up. But there are good people, too, many more than the baddies. What happened tonight … you may not forget it, but try not to let it define your life.'

'That's heavy, Zeb,' Beth drawled, and he looked up to see her wink and knew in that instant that she wasn't hurt in any way. He wanted to hug her, to reassure himself that she wasn't injured.

Later. We need to get out of here.

He got to his feet, feeling lightheaded, and helped Petra inside. He was aware of Lara and Jelena's curious glances as they scrambled into the back seat, flanking the girl.

'It will be tight,' the younger twin grinned as she squeezed in next to the sister-in-law. She took the screen from Broker's hand and got control of the drone.

'There's another one—'

'We won't need it,' Broker told her.

'You know what to do?' Zeb asked his friend as they transferred their gear from his SUV to the car's trunk. It was a Toyota Camry, custom-designed to have more storage, into which he and his crew dumped their spare HKs, magazines, grenade launchers and the remaining gear.

'We'll empty our ride and jog up the ditch towards the city.'

'Fly a drone. Beth's idea is good.'

'Nah,' Chloe pushed back a tendril of hair. 'That will slow us down.'

'Stay in touch. I'll arrange vehicles.'

'We will.'

Bwana and Bear leaned down and looked at Belsky's family.

'You'll be safe,' the black operative said.

'Nothing will happen to you,' his friend nodded.

They stood there, each of them with their HKs slung casually over their shoulders, dirt smudged on their shoulders, rock-solid in their presence, lethal ability packed into human frames. Lara trembled and a tear rolled down her cheek.

'Spasibo.' Her hand reached out and Bwana cupped it in both palms and squeezed it gently.

'Nothing will happen to you,' he repeated, then straightened and stood back.

Zeb got behind the wheel with Meghan next to him, her HK in her hand. He glanced once in the rearview mirror and stamped on the gas.

79

'I need vehicles,' he called Zahavy as he drove down Mozhayskoye. 'The SUVs got totaled.'

'Where are you?' the Mossad operator asked.

'Moscow Oblast. Outside Odintsovo, about a mile away from it.'

'Why there?'

'I need safe houses, too,' Zeb said, ignoring his question. 'For three people.'

'At this rate I'll have to start charging you rent,' Zahavy said, laughing.

He sobered when Zeb didn't respond.

'Are you on foot?'

'No, we borrowed a car. But that's the only ride we have. The rest of us are—'

'Can you get to Kuntsevo?'

'Da.'

'I'll send you the address. Two vans will be there, along with me and my team in half an hour.'

'We'll be there. The rest of my team—'

'We'll circle back to them and pick them up.'

Zeb ended the call and gave the phone to Beth.

Meg needs her hands free to deal with attackers if they show up.

The younger twin double-tapped her mic to confirm Zahavy had sent the message.

THE RENDEZVOUS WAS in a residential neighborhood, on a tree-lined avenue.

Zahavy was there, with three men next to an SUV, two vans behind him.

'Vlad is under his protection,' Zeb told Lara when Belsky's family joined him.

'I will take you to him. Here.' He brought out his phone, dialed a number. 'Give the phone to our guest,' he told someone and then handed the device to Lara.

'VLAD!' she shouted when she recognized her brother's voice, tears rolling down her face. 'We got attacked! Petra was nearly killed!' She described what had gone down through her sobs, and then Zeb took the phone gently from her.

'We can't spend too long here. It's me,' he spoke in the phone. 'Do you recognize my voice?'

'Da. What happened? Why were they attacked? Are they hurt? Where—'

'We are bringing them to you. They will stay there until this blows over.'

He ended the call.

'Are you with some bratva?' Jelena asked them.

Zahavy's lips twitched. 'Kind of, but not a criminal one.'

'How can we trust you?'

'Do you have a choice?' Beth challenged her. 'SVR is looking for you as a way to get to Belsky. They found you at the motel even though you had hidden your ownership of it.'

'If my brother trusts them, I do too.' Lara wiped her face and helped Petra into a van. 'Let's not waste time.'

Zeb got behind its wheel, while Beth climbed in beside him.

'I'll take the other one,' Meghan told him.

'We'll drive it,' Zahavy protested. 'We'll get your friends.'

'Nyet,' Zeb interrupted. 'We'll join you at your safe house. The fewer people seen together, the better.'

'What happened? What went down?'

Zeb stared at him and then at Beth.

'You don't know?'

'Why would I ask if I did? I checked the news before we left. Nothing ... but it's clear you have been in a firefight.'

SVR sealed the news. They must have gotten the social media platforms to delete any posts about the attack too.

'We'll brief you later,' Zeb told him, then glanced back to check their passengers were buckled in, and set off.

THEY PICKED up the rest of the operatives in the Moscow Oblast side of the MKAD, near a golf club.

'Any trouble?' Zeb asked when Meghan climbed out of her van and Bear got behind its wheel.

'Nyet,' Bwana said disappointedly.

'You got a lot of action tonight.'

'It ended too soon. I was just getting warmed up.'

'He wants to fight some more?' Jelena asked from behind when the black operative got into the van and Zeb wheeled out to take the lead.

'He eats enemies for breakfast.' Meghan turned and winked at Petra. 'And for lunch and dinner.'

'They will be hunting you,' Lara observed after a while. 'SVR. You killed several of their men. GUVD will be searching.'

She glanced out of the windows and gnawed at her lip worriedly.

Whittling down their numbers is part of our plan.

. . .

At the Mossad fast-food front, Zeb watched Belsky unite with his family. Hugs, tears, and Petra cuddled and swung onto the baggage handler's shoulders.

'I can't thank you enough—'

'Nyet. We brought this trouble to you.'

'No,' he protested. 'I helped Boris escape. That started it all. Is he—'

'He's safe, too.' Zeb turned to Zahavy. 'Is there enough room—'

'Da. We have a couple more rooms here.' He directed his men to lead the new arrivals inside and turned to Zeb with a speculative look.

'There are some rumors that there was a shootout on Mozhayskoye.'

'Rumors?'

'Nothing in the news yet, but I made some calls. A few nearby residents say they heard loud explosions and guns. The police are denying such reports.'

'There might have been something we got involved in.'

Zahavy grinned. 'I've been hearing stories about you ever since I joined Mossad. Once the ramsad starts talking about you folks, he doesn't stop.'

Ramsad. Mossad's Director. Avichai Levin.

'You don't have a family. You have been doing this for years. How do you keep going on? What drives you? I'm sure I won't be able to do this as long as you have been. In a few years I'll be suffering from burnout.'

Zeb felt his face freeze. Beth called it his Sphinx expression. *I like him*, he thought dimly. *He's a good friend, but not as close as Avichai is. He doesn't need to know my story.*

He brushed past the Mossad agent and went to his van.

'What?' Zahavy frowned. 'Did I annoy him? Was that too personal?'

'Josiah.' Meghan cut her eyes to him. 'You keep saying how great Mossad is, the best agency in the world. We aren't in a competition. Maybe you are a better outfit than us, maybe you aren't. But I'm sure of one thing. You don't have anyone like Zeb in your agency.'

She went past him, too, leaving Zahavy scratching his head.

'I didn't mean to offend you all,' he told Beth. 'What she said, though ... she didn't answer my question.'

'She wasn't trying to,' the younger twin scoffed.

She didn't utter it, but *dumbass* hung loud and unsaid in the air.

80

Zeb couldn't control himself anymore.

He led their convoy to the banks of the Moscow River in Ramenki District and stopped in a public car park.

'What's up?' Meghan climbed out and watched as he opened the rear door and beckoned at Beth.

'Why are we here?' the younger sister asked as she got out.

The second SUV rolled up and the rest of their crew joined them.

'Where were you hit?' Zeb demanded.

'On my sternum. I told you, the vest took the impact. See?' She poked her finger through the hole in her jacket and raised it to show the disfiguration on the vest.

'Chloe and I checked her,' Meghan confirmed, 'when you were with Zahavy in Kuntsevo. She has no injuries.'

'It hurts like hell, but I'm fine.'

'You didn't move,' Zeb said in disbelief.

'That's because I fell on my chin. I was dazed.' She caught his palm and squeezed it between her hands. He looked into her green eyes searchingly for a long time as the tightness between his shoulders finally started easing.

'That was a dumb move, going after Petra like that.'

'What we said,' Chloe nodded.

'As if none of you wouldn't have done the same,' Beth said scornfully. 'I moved faster, that's all.'

None of them had an answer to that.

'You were hit, too.' Bwana looked at Zeb's chest.

'In the belly.' He rubbed his jacket absent-mindedly. He raised his eyebrows when Broker brought out a flask and poured coffee into several cups.

'Zahavy. He had them in our van. He wasn't meaning anything with that question. He was curious. You know how Avichai is.' He grinned. 'He describes us as legends.'

'Yeah,' Zeb acknowledged.

I'll apologize when we meet.

'Gorshky will be fuming.' Roger grinned. 'We've come out on top yet again. What do you think he'll do?'

'He'll ask Smirnov to lie low. The Ukrainian visit isn't far off.'

'You think the Zaslon dude will do that?'

'No.'

81

Alexei Gorshky stared at Bortnik and Orlov when they came into his office, along with Smirnov.

'You look worse than last night,' he exclaimed. 'I saw you in your car, but I didn't realize you looked this bad.'

Smirnov had called him the previous night and briefed him. The SVR chief's fury at the failure had abated by the morning.

'They took a physical,' Smirnov said quickly. 'I supervised it myself. They are fit. They will stay on the team. Unless you want them replaced.'

'Nyet. That's not necessary. If you say they are good to be on duty, I have no problem.'

'Kostya has several broken teeth, Magar has a broken nose, but their injuries will not interfere with protecting you.'

'Aren't they in pain?'

'They are on medication, but those drugs haven't slowed their capabilities. I witnessed it myself.'

'They look fearsome. That alone should desist anyone who's coming after us. You saw Carter up close?'

'I think it must have been him and one of the large operatives who came to our car. They were wearing masks.'

'Did they speak English?

'Nyet. Russian, like natives.'

'They used grenades on you. That's the second time they've used those weapons. Why didn't you—'

'We want them alive. I told our agents to use light arms only, standard rounds. We thought we had killed one of them, but that operative—'

'It looked like a woman. Our man said that one, and the others who rescued that girl, had smaller builds,' Bortnik mumbled through swollen lips.

'Beth and Meghan Petersen and Chloe Sundstrom. It has to be them.' Gorshky sat down in his chair and looked broodingly at his phone. 'Do you know how many calls I made to Vanya Baladin to make sure GUVD was in control of the scene? To make sure no police officer leaked details to the media?'

'Our agents have sealed that road. We have told residents there was a gas explosion.'

'You think they bought it?' Gorshky's voice started rising. 'Do you think people are so dumb? No, don't answer. We have lost so many good men that I have lost count. None of your traps for Carter have worked.'

'We came close this time, really close.'

'Da, I will give you that. Where is he, though?' The SVR chief made a show of sweeping his office with his eyes. 'Sit tight. Do nothing. We have to be alert for the Ukrainian President's visit. We can't take any more losses.'

'Are you expecting trouble?' Orlov asked.

'Trouble?' Gorshky glowered at him. 'Don't you follow the news? The Resistance has promised to flood Moscow's streets with people in support of the Ukrainians. There are bound to be riots. And, we can't do a thing because the eyes of the world will be on us. NYET,' he thundered. 'Don't do anything. We will deal with Carter when our visitor leaves.'

'The American might be planning something during this visit.'

'Nyet. No one knew about it before it was announced a few days ago. That wasn't enough time for him to plan anything. Besides, what can he do? The army, the police, Spetsnaz teams from all over, our operatives. GRU, FSB, everyone will be on the street. Security will be so tight that there's nothing he can pull off and get away with. Go! Sit in your office. I need to work out how much to tell our President.'

SMIRNOV RETURNED to his desk in a sulk. His head throbbed from Carter's blow, but the pain was nothing compared to the humiliating rage he felt.

Eight Americans against thirty of us. We snow-plowed them and still they escaped! And only I, Kostya, Magar and four others survived.

He had ordered his agents to prowl through surrounding streets and neighborhoods after he regained consciousness. Got Moscow Police to help, too. SVR operatives and GUVD personnel had pored through hours of traffic-camera footage, but there was no sign of the Americans.

They have vanished.

He fingered his temple, and his fury mounted when he recalled Carter's words.

What did he mean by that? How am I of use to him?

82

'How did they figure it out? Where to ambush us?' Zeb asked as he joined a tour group outside the Kutafya Tower, the main entrance to the Kremlin.

There was another entrance through Alexandrovsky Garden that had a smaller line, but that didn't interest him. He broke away from the security gates and stood aside to let other visitors pass.

Cameras, gun-toting guards, metal barriers, rapid-response teams ... nope, this isn't suitable.

He retraced his steps and came onto Manege Square, the pedestrian, non-traffic zone, and joined Mokhovaya Street, where lines of coaches disgorged travelers.

He spotted Meghan, Beth and Chloe as they walked ahead, snapping photographs, playing the part of tourists. He adjusted his shades to take in Bear and Bwana, towering over pedestrians far behind him. *Roger and Broker will be somewhere ahead of the twins.*

They had changed their disguises, with the sisters replacing the chips in their prosthetic attachments to give an additional layer of protection.

'We worked it out.' Beth, smug, in his earpiece. 'They must have had watchers in the surrounding buildings. They—'

'I didn't see any. Our drone didn't spot any suspicious cars, either.'

'I said *inside* the buildings. Smirnov must have threatened some of the businesses and occupied their offices. Or the bus station's building. It's got that tower that oversees the motel's parking lot.'

'They didn't intend to stop us,' Chloe agreed. 'Once they saw Lara and Jelena come out, they would have—'

'Those snowplows needed to be in place,' Broker argued. 'They couldn't have driven them in so quickly.'

'Svobody joins Mozhayskoye, no other way to go. And that main road ... we could either go left or right. I'm sure Smirnov had a second set of snowplows at another location if we had taken the other turn. Our SUVs ... they knew which one had the women. There was hardly any traffic on Mozhayskoye, and once we approached their ambush, they knew which one Bear was driving.'

Zeb nodded thoughtfully as he navigated past a bunch of travelers. *Makes sense.*

'Smirnov is smart,' he admitted. 'We came out on top only because we used grenades. If he had given his team shoot-to-kill orders, we would have been toast.'

He stiffened at a double-tap.

'What?'

'Check out your two,' Meghan hissed, 'on the other side of the road.'

Zeb looked past the traffic, at the intersection of Mokhovaya and Tverskaya Streets. A dark car beyond the junction had stopped near the sidewalk. A suit emerged from it, and he knew why the occupants didn't care that they were violating parking rules.

'Dusan Smirnov,' he whispered.

'What?' Bwana exclaimed. 'He's here?'

'Yeah, three hundred yards from me. Bortnik and Orlov are with him as well.'

'They don't look in great shape,' Chloe said, smirking.

'Shall we take another crack at them?' Bear asked eagerly.

'Stand down,' Zeb said. 'We need them alive. Why are they here, though? Is Gorshky around?'

'Can't see any other SVR car,' Meghan commented.

Zeb saw the women cross the street and did the same. They fell in behind the SVR men and watched from behind as Smirnov and his men strode down the sidewalk.

'They're going towards Lubyanka,' he said, working out their direction. 'Why?'

The men barely glanced at the prison-turned-museum building, outside which a few protesters had gathered. *Those Resistance members don't know Elena is there, beneath their feet, underground.*

Andropov had sent him an encrypted message to confirm the journalist was still alive, unharmed, in the basement.

'They are cutting towards Red Square,' Beth announced.

Zeb stopped at a food van and bought three coffees. He handed two of them deftly to Bwana and Bear when they came abreast.

'There will be more security down there,' the black operative said, sipping his drink.

'Yeah. Back off,' he declared in his mic. 'Let's go back to our route.'

Back to checking out attack points.

He couldn't stop thinking about the SVR team leader, however.

Why is he there?

. . .

SMIRNOV HAD FELT SUFFOCATED in the office and, after checking out the message Gorshky had sent him, went to Bortnik and Orlov.

'Let's go.'

'Where?'

'Kremlin.'

Galkin reached for his jacket, too.

'Nyet, Nicola, you stay here with the boss.'

The operative's face fell.

'Why can't I join you?'

'You want to check out buildings and traffic?'

'Is that why you are going?'

'Da.' Smirnov showed them Gorshky's message. 'Only our team knows about this. We have to recon it and make sure—'

'Go,' Galkin backed off with a grin. 'I can't think of a more boring job.'

Which had led to Smirnov and his agents arriving on Mokhovaya and walking down the sidewalk.

'You really think the protesters will do anything here?' Orlov asked doubtfully.

'Nyet, but we cannot take chances.' Smirnov glanced behind him but saw nothing other than tourists and traffic. His gaze swept past three women and down the street to where two men were drinking coffee. His eyes sharpened at noticing their height.

Was it ... nyet. It wasn't anyone who looked like Carter's team.

They wouldn't dare show themselves so openly and follow me.

Smirnov clicked his tongue impatiently when the men crossed the street and drifted out of sight.

I have important things to do.

He turned back to his men and pointed out side streets.

'We will need more men there. Soldiers. Our operatives will be deployed at key junctions.'

Orlov scratched his chin.

'You talk as if the boss will be out here.'

'We don't know, but we have to be prepared.'

'DID HE SEE US?' Bear murmured.

'Yeah,' Zeb replied. 'But Bwana had dropped behind by then. If he had seen the three of us, he might have become suspicious.'

He checked the rearview projection on his lenses. No signs of Smirnov or his men.

'That intersection,' Broker spoke from far ahead. 'Cars will slow down. It's a natural chokepoint.'

'The one with Tverskaya? It's too close to the Kremlin, and Gorshky's team will be prepared for it.'

'There's a long stretch of road before it crosses Garden Ring,' Roger said.

'We can be in alleys or side streets,' the elder operator added.

'No. We take him on a flat stretch of Tverskaya. That's when the security might relax.'

'Here.' Meghan jerked her head sideways at the avenue they were on. 'After Georgiyevskiy Street. It's straight ahead for a while.'

Zeb took in the buildings on either side. Offices, retail stores, coffee shops. He pictured it in his mind.

There will be crowds. Protesters and soldiers. Police vehicles on the road, between which will be the convoy. Close to the Garden Ring won't work. There will be more traffic, and that will hinder us.

'This will work.'

'Now,' Chloe said drily, 'how are we going to pull it off? How will we grab Gorshky from the security around him? And how are we going to get Elena out of her prison?'

'Gorshky will do that last part for us.'

83

They worked out the plan and went over it repeatedly.

Beth made a list of gear they would need.

'Smoke bombs, fireworks, signal jammers—'

'They should be localized,' her sister interrupted. 'Otherwise, the security teams will suspect the attack.'

'We have all of those,' Chloe said. 'But I still don't know why Gorshky would let Elena be taken out of Lubyanka.'

'He will be forced to. Check your Twitter feed.'

Is Elena Zakharova in Lubyanka?

Meghan posted the tweet.

Bear whistled softly. 'That account—'

'Is one we have created. Russian intelligence agencies believe it to be a Resistance poster.'

'You think that single post will be enough?' Bwana asked doubtfully.

'Nope. The Ukrainian President's meeting is the day after tomorrow. By then, there will be a social media storm. And we'll help create it.'

'Helped by Yasimov's friends as well,' Broker caught on. 'The protesters will threaten to storm the prison ... which will force Gorshky to act.'

'The timing has to be right, however. We have to leave it to the last minute.'

'Got it.' Bear snapped his fingers. 'And everything comes down to him.'

Zeb shrugged when they looked at him. He took a long slurp of his juice and pushed away his empty plate.

'It will work. It has to. But there's something else we have to try.'

'What's that?' Bwana asked.

'If we can get Elena's notes or unpublished article, we'll know what the Russian President is planning. Once it's out there—'

'There's no surprise. Diplomatic pressure can be applied. He might back off.'

'Yeah, and they might release Elena.'

'We'll still need to grab Gorshky, though.'

'We will.'

'How do you plan to get her notes? Yasimov doesn't know where they are. We've searched her apartment. There's nothing in her cloud account. We haven't found any place she might have—'

'We didn't search Olga's apartment.'

'No! You can't be thinking of going there!' Meghan exclaimed. 'Smirnov will have people around it. There's no way you can—'

'Why can't we ask her? Why do we need to search it?'

'She won't trust us.'

'Yasimov—'

'Smirnov will be particularly careful, after the setbacks he's had. He'll tighten security. She and the rest of the residents might be watched. Their phones might be tapped. Nope, a covert search is our only option.'

'EIGHT MEN,' Zeb observed, peering through his NVGs at Elena's building. 'They aren't hiding themselves.'

'Why would they?' Beth said scornfully. 'Everyone knows they're SVR men. I'm sure they've identified themselves to the residents.'

TEN PM. Zeb and the twins beneath a thick bush in the trees behind the journalist's apartment. Bear and Chloe in two SUVs on Michurinskiy, their getaway rides. The rest of the operatives ranged around them with long guns.

The Agency crew had crawled to their hiding place in the evening, with a couple of drones overhead to alert them of any danger. It had been slow going, but they hadn't encountered any threat.

'They must be the night shift. I can take them out.' Bwana spoke from behind a fallen tree.

No one told him shooting SVR agents wasn't their objective. They knew him well enough.

Zeb watched the men patrol the yard and parking lot casually. *They're relaxed. One of them is smoking as well.*

That didn't mean they were low-level door kickers.

Gorshky has had too many setbacks. He would have pushed Smirnov to deploy good shooters.

'She's in her bedroom. Alone, sleeping.' Beth read out the thermal image from the drone.

'How low can you get our bird?'

'You want to check for cameras?' Beth asked.

'Yeah.'

'Hold tight.'

Her fingers moved on her night-effect screen, whose glow couldn't be seen beyond a couple of feet.

'In the parking lot ... nothing there.'

The UAVs were equipped with an array of sensors and receptors for radio wave, infrared, and UV wave detection, among many others in the spectrum. Werner analyzed their feed in real time and could spit out details on the presence of any surveillance device almost instantly.

'Nothing,' Beth said.

'Why wouldn't Smirnov mount cameras in the ceiling?' Zeb wondered.

'Because we've fooled the SVR team several times. He's relying on his agents to spot and stop us or any other threats. I'll take the drone inside once you're ready to—'

'I won't be going up the stairs.'

The twins looked at him. Meghan checked out his dark suit and the gloves on his hands.

'You're scaling the wall,' she guessed. 'There's a drainpipe that goes up the building. You'll use that.'

'Yeah.'

'That faces the approach road,' Beth objected.

'Which is why he arranged for the distraction.'

'Correct.'

'When were you going to tell us?' Beth fumed.

'I just did.'

He winced when she jammed her elbow in his ribs.

Eleven pm.

Can't delay it. SVR know we tend to strike late at night.

'Bear?'

'Yeah.'

'Go.'

Three cars in the parking lot outside the strip mall, which had been parked there by Zahavy's men earlier in the evening, suddenly had their alarms go off.

The SVR agents in the yard looked in their direction, then drew together and conferred softly.

'I can lower the drone further to listen in,' Beth whispered.

'No. Let's not risk it.'

'It's silent, and it's invisible in the dark.'

Before he could reply, three men broke off and trotted down the approach road.

'Need more of them to split up.' Zeb grimaced. 'I won't be able to get past six men. Chloe?'

'On it.'

Several loud explosions sounded on Michurinskiy. Car bombs that they had planted in pull-offs. The blasts were strong enough for windows to rattle. Several apartment lights turned on in the building, but no heads emerged from windows.

The residents don't want to risk stray fire.

Three more men ran down the approach road after furious gesticulation.

'Olga is still asleep. Doesn't look like she has moved on her bed,' Meghan confirmed.

Zeb rose to a half-crouch, fist-bumped the twins and hurried towards the building.

'This is a bad idea.'

'You got a better one?' he panted at Roger.

The Texan didn't reply.

'Those two shooters, in the parking lot,' Beth whispered in his earpiece, 'are looking down the road. One of them is making a call.'

'For backup or for instructions.'

'Go wide on your left.'

Zeb skirted the yard using the cover of vehicles. He crouched behind a wheel well and peered at the men who were speaking on their phones.

Checking with the six men.

He burst out of cover when more explosions sounded and circled the building, his feet whispering on concrete, until he went behind the lobby, down the side and to the front of the building.

They'll have to come out to see me.

But anyone coming up the road would spot him.

He caught the drainpipe with both hands and tested it. It held.

He gripped high and hauled himself up quickly, a dark figure going up the equally dark side of the building.

THE KITCHEN WINDOWS were dark on his side, three feet to his right. No curtains or blinds.

He climbed swiftly, his hands and feet levering up the side of the building, until he came to Olga's window.

Double-glazed glass in a PVC frame. He ran a finger beneath it, and it swung out wide.

She must have cracked it open for ventilation.

He pulled it wider and peered inside. Sink on a counter in front of him. Gleaming utensils on one side. He leaned inside, braced one hand on the top and hoped it would hold his weight.

It did. It took awkward maneuvering for him to slip inside without clattering into plates or bowls, but he was finally on the floor, inside the apartment.

He sucked lungfuls of air through his mask as he centered himself and lowered his chi until he became the night.

Zeb had just turned to the window to pull it shut when the light snapped on.

'Who are you?'

Olga confronted him from the doorway, brandishing a cane.

He hurled himself at her.

84

She shrieked and swung the cane. He went beneath it, slapped a palm against the light switch and turned it off.

Zeb winced when the cane struck him on the face on its return.

'I am not here to hurt you,' he said as he caught it firmly.

'I'LL CALL THE POLICE. WHO ARE YOU? HOW DARE YOU—'

'I am Elena's friend.'

He released the cane and went to the window.

No one on the approach road.

'Sitrep?' he asked softly in Russian.

'No change. Six dudes are still out. Our two men are where they are. No signs of more operatives. What's—'

'WHO ARE YOU TALKING TO?'

'Uh-huh,' she said, grinning. 'Deal with that.'

Zeb turned to Olga, who swung at him again. He took the blow on his shoulder.

'Friends. If I was here to attack you, I wouldn't let you hit me.'

The cane faltered in its downward arc. Her furious eyes narrowed.

'You are masked. You are dressed in black ... like a killer. You expect me to believe that?'

'I am masked so that you can't identify me. So that those men below—'

'SVR pigs,' she spat.

'Da.' He grinned beneath his mask. 'So that they can't recognize me.'

'Are you wanted by ...' her mouth turned into an O. 'Are you one of those Resistance men everyone is talking about?'

'Something like that.'

'Why should I believe you?'

'I'm the one who rescued Yasimov.'

'Boris? You were in that shooting?'

'Da. I and my friends.'

'Anyone could say that. That doesn't prove anything.'

Olga stood there, a foot shorter than he, with swirling red hair, in a Tee and loose cotton pants, bare feet, but no fear on her face.

He could see her biceps flex as she twirled the cane and wondered if she worked out.

'I asked you a question.'

'I can't prove anything to you without revealing my identity. That would be dangerous to you and me. I don't have much time. I came here to search your apartment—'

'Why?'

'To see if Elena hid her notes here.'

'She didn't. Why would she hide them? She could have given them to me. She didn't do that either.'

'Giving them to you would have compromised you. Did she say anything about them?'

'She said she had hidden them safely, and if I came across them, I would know what to do. In case she wasn't alive.'

'What would you do?'

'Give them to Boris,' she said, as if it was obvious. 'He's the—'

'I know who he is. She didn't give them to you because she knew GUVD would have questioned—'

'They did, several times. FSB, SVR, all of them. Pigs.'

'She could have hidden them without your knowledge. Did she stay here alone at any time?'

'Da, many times, when I was away on vacation, went to visit my family. We had keys to each other's apartments. *Have*,' she corrected herself fiercely. 'I know she's alive.'

'She is.'

She looked at him sharply.

'Don't lie to me,' she warned.

'She is alive. But she's a prisoner. I can't say more than that.'

'Those notes will help get her out.'

'Da.'

'Do you drink coffee?'

'What?

'Do you drink coffee?' she snapped impatiently as she brushed past him, filled the kettle with water and turned it on.

'Da.'

She took him in silently as the water boiled.

'Are you one of the Resistance soldiers?'

'We went through this.'

'Elena told me it was important to be persistent.' She grinned, her face lighting up, which made her look young. The smell of coffee filled the kitchen as she brewed it and poured it into two cups.

'Drink,' she ordered, 'and then we'll start.'

THEY RETURNED ninety minutes later to the kitchen, perspiring.

'What is that?'

'This?' He held up the wand he was stuffing in his backpack. 'You saw how it worked. It uses temperature differences and radio waves to see through walls. Once I plug its feed into my phone, some fancy software will stitch it together to tell us what's behind the walls.'

'But we didn't find anything,' she said disappointedly.

'Nyet.'

'Maybe she hid it in my shop,' she said hopefully. 'She has keys to that, too.'

That was my thought as well.

'I'll search it tomorrow.'

'Nyet. You could be watched.'

'I'll go at night.'

'That would be suspicious as well. Please don't do anything. I will find a way.'

'If you destroy my shop—'

'I won't. By the way, how did you know I was here?'

'I am a heavy sleeper, but wind wakes me up. I felt the breeze from the kitchen window and got up.'

'You should go back to sleep.' He slipped the backpack on his shoulders and tightened its straps. 'If you get questioned, you should deny you saw anything—'

'Of course, I will.'

He surged towards her, hit her on her carotid and kept applying the pressure. He caught her as she slumped and carried her to her bedroom.

I'll apologize the next time we meet. This will help her alibi if she is questioned. That someone entered her house and knocked her out.

He laid her out on the bed, covered her with a sheet and returned to the kitchen.

'Exfil,' he announced and climbed onto the counter.

'All quiet,' Beth told him. 'Looks like the six men are investigating the explosions. They haven't returned. The two men near the lobby are still there.'

Zeb climbed onto the counter, leaned out of the window, caught hold of the drain pipe and swung himself out. He pushed the window back with a palm and slithered down the pipe.

He was below the third floor when he heard voices coming up the approach road.

Bear and Chloe are on Michurinskiy. They must have pulled back deep when these dudes started investigating. They couldn't have seen these men. Drone—

'Three men. Coming up fast. More behind them. GO!'

Zeb slid down as fast as he could as the voices grew louder. He glanced behind him. The men came into view, talking loudly.

They drew closer to the front yard.

The weight of his eyes must have warned them.

One of them looked up.

He stared for several seconds.

'HEY!' He reached for his waist.

85

Zeb lunged off the side of the building, kicking against it to power his flight. He twisted in the air to face them, his Glock coming to his hand as if it had a mind of its own.

It spat once. His round tore into one man's shoulder, dropping him, and then he was on them, crashing bodily, bringing all three to the ground.

He struck savagely with his gun, felt its barrel strike flesh. Got a return blow to his head that made his head swim.

Shouts. A shot.

He snatched a glance.

Three more men running up the road. The two in the lobby shouting orders, their guns raised.

'EYES!' Bear said cheerfully, and with a slash of his Glock, Zeb squeezed his eyes tight and rolled away from the men.

The flashbangs they used were modified to impair vision for a few moments. Their bangs had been altered to sound at subsonic levels that didn't produce loud explosions but interfered with human senses and left the victims dazed for several minutes.

Zeb felt the flash behind his eyelids even though he had turned away. His ears grew dizzy. His breath shortened. He stumbled to his feet blindly when another flash lit up the night and then felt a hand on his shoulder, guiding him.

'Stay with me,' Bwana growled.

He thought he heard rounds whizzing in the air, but he couldn't be sure.

He ran mechanically with Bwana, felt another body come up alongside, and heard a Texas drawl.

'What a waste of rounds.'

THE FIVE-MINUTE SPRINT to Bear and Chloe's waiting SUV cleared his mind. It sped away the moment they were in it.

Zeb gratefully took the water bottle the petite operative tossed at him and took a long slug.

'Thanks,' he said hoarsely, wiping his chin. 'How —'

'Your friendly neighborhood cavalry to the rescue,' Bwana said with an elegant bow. 'We broke cover the moment we saw those men approach. Bear came up the road behind them and tossed those bangs. Then, it was a matter of pinning them down with fire while we hauled you away.'

'Fire?'

'From us,' Beth panted.

Why's she gasping? It came to him immediately. *She, Meg and Broker are getting away from their hideout.*

'You killed any?'

'Nah,' Bwana said disgustedly. 'You got one in the shoulder, but he's alive.'

'Waste of rounds,' Roger repeated, shaking his head, but his broad smile showed his relief at their escape.

. . .

'NOTHING IN HER APARTMENT,' Zeb briefed them when they gathered in a deserted street.

He took in a long swallow of water and capped the bottle. Checked that his Glock was in its holster.

It was just past midnight. The distant sound of traffic. He rolled his shoulders and felt his friends' eyes on him.

'To the salon?' Meghan asked.

'Yeah. We can't leave it to the morning or the following night.'

'Smirnov will put it together,' Broker cautioned.

'He will. Which is why we'll have to improvise.'

86

They planned swiftly.

They couldn't drive back to the strip mall's parking lot.

'Smirnov's men will see our vehicles. They'll come to investigate.' Zeb outlined the plan. 'We'll have to go on foot. Bear, Chloe, you'll be in your pull-off.'

'Yeah,' the petite operative nodded. 'We're good there. No one saw us.'

'The rest of us will go to the parking lot on foot—'

'And get onto the roof,' Broker said.

THEY DROVE BACK TO MICHURINSKIY, where Meghan parked her SUV in a neighboring apartment building's lot, while Bear and Chloe cut away to go to their location.

Zeb filtered through vehicles and navigated the road between the building and the strip mall until he could see the front of it. Lights on top of some of the shops that illuminated the front area.

He turned to Elena's building.

Those men are still there, he observed through his NVGs. *Why haven't they called for Smirnov?*

'They aren't sure if they should report it,' Beth guessed. She was a shadow to his far left.

'They will. We have a small window.'

He clipped his binos to his belt and snaked up the road until he came to another residential building behind the shops. A wired fence at the edge of its parking lot overlooked the backyard of the mall. A small downhill slope from the chain-link to the backyard.

'Cameras?'

'Fried the two of them in the building,' Meghan said drily. 'None at the front of the shops, and our drone hasn't detected any at the back ... but we'll blast EMP rays to be safe.'

'No lights at the back of the shops.'

'No one uses that rear yard at night. We have some visibility from this residential building.'

A dog barked somewhere as he ghosted across the parking lot. He tensed and turned, but no apartment lights turned on. He caught the chain-link fence with his gloved fingers and scaled it swiftly. It teetered under his weight but held, and it bent alarmingly when Bwana went over it, but didn't collapse.

They spread out. Zeb behind the salon, stepping carefully over the trash and debris at the back of the shop; the rest of the operatives ranged out.

He got to the wall and peered through the window in the back door. Cardboard boxes and plastic sacks heaped on the floor, visible through the dim light from the building behind them.

Zeb wedged a foot on a jutting brick in the wall and powered himself up to catch the low roof. He rolled onto its flat surface and winced when plastic beneath him crackled. He lifted himself up carefully, brushed away the debris and went to the skylight in the salon's roof that they had noted during their first visit to the strip mall.

Shadows spread out around him. Beth and Meghan on either side, Broker next to the younger twin, while Bwana and Roger remained on the ground, taking cover behind the shops.

He broke the glass with his Glock and made a hole big enough for him to drop through.

'Go,' Meghan said in irritation when he looked around to see if the noise had attracted attention. 'We've got our bird. We'll alert you if there's a threat.'

He jumped through the opening.

87

Zeb landed on shattered glass. He slipped, steadied himself and started searching.

The obvious places, initially. Drawers, beneath the vinyl flooring, the undersides of chairs, behind the mirrors. A flashlight clipped to the holster's strap illuminated his search. The smells of creams and perfumes filled the salon.

He checked the small bathroom and the kitchen.

Nothing.

She's smart. She wouldn't hide it in places that obvious.

He removed the thermal imager and started scanning from the front door.

'You thought of telling me only now?' Smirnov yelled into his phone.

The office had a handful of people that late at night. He, Bortnik, Orlov, Galkin and a couple of flunkies. Gorshky was in his apartment, on the top floor of the building.

It was a second accommodation for the SVR chief, one that

he often used during emergencies or on critical missions. The Ukrainian President's visit was one such event, which meant Smirnov and his team were camped out in the office as well.

'What happened?' Galkin rubbed his eyes.

'Carter, at Zakharova's building.'

His men woke up instantly at that.'

'Do you know where they went?' he asked the caller, and his fists curled at the reply. 'Stay there. I am coming there myself. Don't let anyone in.'

He hung up, grabbed his jacket and slipped it on. 'Nicola, you and Kostya come with me. Magar, stay here.'

He dialed another number. 'I need twenty shooters. Right now. Ask them to meet me in the garage.'

He briefed his men on the incident as they went down the elevator.

'We need to use Carter's tricks. We can't roll up in vehicles. We have to be on foot. I am sure they have a backup vehicle on Michurinskiy. We need to identify it and block it.'

'You said Carter escaped. If that's the case, why are we going to the building? And why was he in Zakharova's apartment?'

'Nyet. He wasn't there. He was in that salon owner's flat. I am sure of it. I should have thought of it.'

'But he's gone now!' Galkin protested. 'What good will it do—'

Smirnov's eyes narrowed. His lips split in a thin smile.

'I know where he'll be. In Olga's shop, to see if Zakharova hid her notes and articles there. We should have searched it!'

THERE WAS nothing in the salon's walls, roof or floor.

'We're running out of time,' Beth told him.

Zeb nodded and returned the imager to his backpack. He surveyed the shop again, pushing away his rising disappointment. He went to the kitchen and opened the cabinets and drawers randomly. Olga's neatness struck him again. Every bottle was labeled. Sugar. Coffee. Tea. Milk sachets. They were arranged in rows. Cutlery gleamed in their drawer slots. The counter was clean, with not a single dish in the sink.

He went to the bathroom, saw the same tidy arrangement in its cabinets. Fresh towels neatly folded. Spare detergent bottles on the lower shelf, Soaps, handwashes, tampon sets in their plastic wrapping.

He ran a finger idly on the lower cabinet door, leaving a mark on the film of dust.

Hasn't been cleaned or used in a while.

He opened it to see to more supplies. *Backup stock if the upper cabinet runs out, which is why it hasn't been opened recently.*

He crouched and checked out the shelf.

Olga is into neatness. Why's that toilet roll package out of place? Everything else is arranged properly.

It was on the bottom, with another shrink-wrapped set of rolls on top of it. It was out by about an inch but, given the tidiness in the shelf, it jarred.

Zeb brought it out and inspected it.

Store brand. It wasn't opened. The plastic covering was intact.

That doesn't mean anything. Those can be resealed and made to look like they're store-fresh.

He hefted it in his hand.

It didn't feel heavy.

Here goes nothing.

His Spyderco ripped it open with ease. He brought out the rolls one by one and inspected them.

Nothing hidden in them.

He made a sound of disgust and tossed them away. One of the rolls started unfurling on the floor and, after a long length, a note appeared on the inside surface.

. . .

'You,' Smirnov directed five men, 'come up from behind the shop.' His finger stabbed the map on his screen.

They were in a building's parking lot half a mile from the strip mall. Ten men arranged around him, Bortnik and Galkin, all of them in combat outfits, armed with HKs and AK74s.

'Three of you,' he said, turning to the remaining men, 'find that backup vehicle. It will be on Michurinskiy, I am sure of it. This time of night, no other vehicles will be there.'

'Two of you will come with Kostya, Nicola and me. We will go up the parking lot. We want them alive.'

'What about the other ten?' Galkin asked, puzzled.

'They will show up when we have been captured.'

Zeb stared at it for a moment and then reached for the roll.

The note was folded to the size of the toilet paper and pasted to its inside.

THIS IS FOR OLGA. OLGA, YOU KNOW WHAT TO DO WITH THIS.

The first sheet had nothing else on it. He got to his feet and sent the roll unfurling down the floor to reveal more sheets.

He began reading the first one and then clicked his tongue impatiently.

Not here, not now.

He removed all the notes, realizing they were pages torn from a notebook, which when put together were half an inch thick. There were several photographs among them, too. He arranged them neatly and stuffed them in his backpack.

Tidied up the bathroom and was finishing up when his comms squawked.

'HOSTILES!' Meghan yelled.

88

Bear reacted instantly when the car rolled up in front of them.

'Get out!' he told Chloe and punched the gas. He rolled down his window and fired his HK at the shooters who emerged as his partner dove out of the SUV and disappeared from sight.

CHLOE USED the open door as cover and darted to the rear of the vehicle. No other hostiles in sight.

She heard Bear shooting and the crunch of bodies as the car crashed into the men, and then she was climbing up the bank and was onto the top of the rise, from which she could see the parking lot.

She crouched-ran, hearing Beth and Meghan's shouts in her comms, and threw herself to the ground when she was a hundred yards away from the strip mall.

Her HK came to her shoulder. The lot filled her scope. Her finger curled over the trigger and she waited.

. . .

BWANA SIGNALED TO ROGER, and they moved to the bottom of the slope, on top of which was the chain-link fence.

'Who's shooting?' he growled at the sound of shots.

'Me,' Bear growled back.

'How many shooters?'

'Three at my end. Two of them are pulp. One of them has surrendered.'

'*Pulp*? How did that—'

'Quit talking!' Meghan hissed. 'Five hostiles coming up. Doesn't look like they've seen us on the roof yet. Don't shoot until I say so.'

'Everyone tells me not to shoot,' Bwana complained.

He crouched close to the slope and clenched his fist at Roger, who gestured in return.

LOOSE SOIL FALLING near him was the first sign that the hostiles were near the fence. He didn't look up.

Roger and I can't be made out from the top. We blend in with the slope and are hiding in depressions.

A body flashed past him, and then another one.

Bwana uncoiled himself.

A whisper of movement gave him away.

The SVR man whirled. His weapon came up.

His first shot went wide when Bwana slapped away his barrel, and his second shot slammed into earth, and then the Agency operative's HK crashed into his throat.

Bwana tossed him away as if he weighed nothing and staggered back when a round struck his shoulder. With a yell that reverberated in the small space, he charged at the second shooter and yanked at his AK, a move that caught the hostile by surprise. Before he could react, the Agency operative's blade was buried deep in his neck.

'You good?' he asked Roger, who was finishing off a third hostile.

'Yeah, you took a round!'

'The vest did.'

Bwana cocked his head at the fence.

'Beth, Meg, Broker, what's—'

'All clear. Two hostiles on top are dead.'

'Five, in the parking lot.' Chloe's voice rang out.

'THAT'S SMIRNOV,' Meghan whispered. 'Along with Galkin, Bortnik and two other men.'

Zeb tried to find a gap in the shutter at the front of the store but couldn't.

Why are they approaching openly? They must have heard the shooting.

'Shall we pepper them?' Broker seemed to be chewing gum.

'Let them get closer.'

Zeb searched the salon for a wrench to break the locking bolt from inside but didn't find one. *I'll have something in my backpack, but it will take too long.*

He rolled a chair beneath the skylight, climbed on it awkwardly and leaped high to pull himself up through the opening.

'What—' Beth whirled at him.

'I'm going down to meet them.'

'Are you crazy—'

He crawled to the front of the roof, jumped to the ground and began walking towards Smirnov.

The team leader yelled in surprise. The shooters with him spread out and aimed their weapons at him.

'I can take them out,' Chloe whispered.

'Shoot into the ground.'

Smirnov jumped when the round spat near them and ricocheted into the air.

'You are surrounded,' Zeb told him. 'Drop your weapons.'

The team leader didn't react for several moments. His men looked on expressionlessly.

And then Smirnov smiled. He laughed.

What's gotten into him?

He heard Meghan exclaim in surprise and Beth shout.

'Look behind you,' the team leader said triumphantly.

Zeb turned to see five men standing in the parking lot, their guns trained on his team. He spun back at the sounds of scuffling. Chloe, dragged by her hair by one of five more men coming up the Michurinskiy bank.

Where's Bear?

'*You* are surrounded,' the SVR man smirked. 'You have troubled us too much. It ends here—'

The night lit up in a series of explosions on the approach road. Windows shuddered from the blasts.

Zeb dove sideways. His Glock came up, bucking in his hand in a long roll to take out Bortnik, Galkin and the two shooters with them. They were bunched together and hadn't reacted fast enough to get out of the way of his rounds.

He fell on his shoulder. Slapped in a new magazine and fired at the men holding Chloe, who twisted, whirled and fell, with a killer on top of her, which gave more room for Zeb, who felt returning shots search for him. He lay still, presenting himself as a target while he reloaded and emptied a magazine at the SVR killers.

CHLOE REACTED INSTANTLY at the explosions. Her hand swept up to dislodge the gun at her neck. She tripped the man holding her, twisted her body and dropped to the ground, dragging him with her. As he fell she brought her knee up into his groin. A brutal finger strike to his throat finished the man. She didn't move from beneath him but caught his AK74, reversed it swiftly and, using his dead weight as cover, fired at the four men who were diving away from Zeb's shooting.

BEAR HOSED the men standing at the chain-link fence with a long burst. They were two hundred yards away but were illuminated by lights behind them, and he had his Leupold scope to his eye while they were distracted momentarily by the explosions.

Easy targets for him.

They dropped to the ground.

He fired more rounds into their bodies and kept his gun trained on them.

The shooting died.

He heard voices and snatched a glance to his left.

Chloe, yelling that she was safe.

Zeb, talking to Smirnov.

SMIRNOV STARED, aghast, at the carnage.

Those explosions—where did they come from? Didn't my men see who set them off?

How had Carter's men reacted so quickly? One moment he had the American surrounded. The next, the operative was diving away and his men had fallen. He looked at Bortnik and Galkin. They lay motionless, face down.

Carter did that even as he was diving.

The two killers with him were dead, too.

They were elite men. *But not as good as the Americans*, he thought bitterly.

That woman, Chloe, was checking that the five men who

had held her were dead. She signaled to Carter, who came close to him.

'You had us,' the American said softly.

He was close enough for Smirnov to see his features, which looked nothing like the surveillance photographs they had on him.

'But you make the same mistakes.'

The SVR team leader wanted to ask him what Carter meant by that, but the slashing Glock knocked him out.

89

'That was your doing?' Zeb asked Bear, who came up into the parking lot.

'Yeah. Those five men ran up Michurinskiy and climbed up the bank. I tried to warn you folks, but my mic didn't—'

'Signal jammer,' Beth said bitterly. 'They took out our comms and EMP-ed our drone. Meg and I were figuring out why the feed died, but by then those shooters were on top of us.'

'I tossed grenades on the approach road,' Bear continued. 'I thought it would give us an opening.'

'It did,' Zeb squeezed his shoulder. 'You—'

Chloe nodded soberly. 'I'm fine. Four of those guys who were holding me were aiming at you. They thought the fifth man could deal with me.'

Zeb looked at the fallen bodies and shook his head.

That was a close shave. If Bear hadn't come up with his ruse, we would have been captured. He looked at the wire fence. 'They—'

'Won't give us any trouble,' Broker said grimly. 'We checked.'

Zeb looked at Beth and Meghan, who looked furious at themselves.

They're feeling guilty they let us down.

'Stop that,' he said fiercely. 'SVR is one of the deadliest agencies in the world. We caught Gorshky's men by surprise the first few times, but they were always going to smarten up.'

Roger broke their somber mood.

He cocked an eyebrow at Bear. 'How does it feel, knowing you saved our butts?'

'I'll never let you folks forget it.'

Meghan laughed reluctantly and returned Chloe's hug.

'Beth and I'll destroy the drone. It must have fallen in that building's parking lot. We'll meet you in Michurinskiy.'

'No,' Zeb shook his head. 'No more splitting up. We go together.'

'Any luck in the salon?' Broker asked him.

'Yeah.' Zeb reached into his backpack and brought out the notes.

They stared at him.

'You found them?' Beth's face lit up. She shoulder-punched him. 'You should have led with that. What's in it?'

'I didn't read it,' Zeb said as he jogged towards the chain-link fence. 'We have to get out of here. Someone might have called the police.'

'Elena's article,' Bwana growled. 'That makes it worth almost dying.'

90

They drove their SUVs to the Mossad garage, where expressionless men took in the state of Bear's ride and thumbed at two identical-looking vehicles.

Zeb and his team transferred their gear and drove out. They changed clothing and disguises while driving and arrived in the lobby of a swanky hotel near Red Square, where a tour bus had just disembarked its passengers, giving them cover.

Zeb rented several rooms for them under a false name, and they gathered in the largest one. He removed the notes and spread them on the bed.

Beth slapped Roger's wrist when he reached for a sheet.

'Hold up. Let's photograph this first, so that we have a back-up.' She and Meghan snapped pictures of all the sheets on their phones, and then she began reading.

She took the first sheet, finished and passed it to Meghan, who handed it to Chloe in a relay, and by the time the eight of them had finished reading Elena's notes and article and had gone through her photographs, they wore shocked expressions.

'You remember what Yasimov said?'

Beth Petersen had faced down organized criminal gangs.

She had taken out ISIS terrorists. Zeb had never seen her scared, but in that hotel room, with the sheets spread out on the bed, he read fear on her face.

'World-changing,' the younger sister continued. She bobbed her head at the notes. 'This will do that. We've got to tell—'

'On it.' Zeb drew out his phone and dialed Clare's number.

'Ma'am, are you alone?'

'Yes,' their boss replied. 'Are you safe? Where are you? I've been trying to reach you—'

'Yeah, we're good.'

'You haven't heard?'

'Heard what, ma'am? We've been off our phones for a few hours. Haven't turned on the TV either.'

'Russia invaded Ukraine an hour ago.'

Beth sprang from the bed to turn on the TV.

They watched in shocked silence at the rolling news coverage on the conflict. 'Troops entered Donbas region,' she translated hollowly. 'Tanks and convoys from Belarus into northern Ukraine.'

'War has started,' Clare confirmed. 'You have to get out. It's no longer safe for you to be there.'

'Zeb?'

'ZEB!'

He started, and found his friends looking at him while their boss called out his name.

'Yeah, I'm here, ma'am. I was trying to work out why the Russian President decided to attack without any warning.'

'He made a long speech in which he said this is an act of self-defense. He said he would de-Nazify Ukraine. He claims he doesn't intend to occupy Ukraine.'

'De-Nazify?' Chloe laughed bitterly. 'What does that even mean? Not occupying Ukraine! He's lying!'

'Be that as it may, you folks need to leave, now!'

'No,' Meghan shook her head.

'What?'

'We aren't leaving, ma'am.' The elder twin glanced at the team and got acknowledging nods. 'We're here on a mission. We won't leave until we complete it.'

'Meghan—'

'She's right, ma'am,' Zeb said, turning off the TV. 'If anything, the events could play out in our favor. The entire country's attention, all its agencies' attention, will be on Ukraine.'

'Zeb,' Clare said in a strained voice. 'You're in a country that has attacked—'

'Yes, ma'am, we're aware of that now. But we're staying put. It isn't the first time we've been in such circumstances. It won't be the last.'

The Agency Director's sigh reverberated through his phone.

'You're still determined to go through with the mission?'

'Yes, ma'am.'

'Ma'am, we found Elena's article,' Meghan spoke quickly. 'It could help President Morgan.'

'Lay it out.'

'Elena has everything on this invasion. Donbas, Luhansk, Donetsk, plans of attack, convoy movements ... she has interviews with soldiers, officers, photographs of equipment, voice and video recordings—'

'She has all that?'

'Yes, ma'am, but that's not all. Russian hit teams are in Ukraine right now to kill or capture the entire cabinet and the military leadership. They're waiting for a signal to act.'

'WHAT?'

Beth couldn't hold back. 'And once they take over the country, Russia will allow unrestricted mining of crypto-currencies.'

'Ukraine is already a haven for miners,' Clare thought aloud. 'But a free-for-all will kill its energy capacity.'

'Yeah. On top of that, Russia will get Ukraine to declare crypto as its default payment system.'

'Default? Elena's article says that?'

'Yes, ma'am. She's got a witness statement and a recorded interview from a high-ranking official in the Energy Ministry.'

'El Salvador already accepts crypto but still has the US Dollar as its main currency. Ukraine is bigger, has more political impact ... this will—'

'Destabilize world markets, but also, along with the mining, destroy Ukraine's economy.'

'You haven't told me everything, have you?'

'No, ma'am.' Beth took a deep breath. 'Azerbaijan. Russia has similar hit teams in that country to kill or capture its President, Veep and the cabinet and install a puppet government. Those replacements have already been identified.'

'Azerbaijan?' Clare's voice rose a shade, which was the equivalent of an ordinary person yelling. 'That doesn't share borders with Russia. Why ...'

She trailed off when it came to her. 'Gas. Russia is a major supplier of gas to Europe, but those countries have been looking to Azerbaijan as an alternative source because of these tensions.'

'Yes, ma'am, that's what we figured, too. If Russia controls Azerbaijan, then it controls the gas supply to all of Europe. And if it encourages unrestricted crypto-mining and usage, energy prices will go up. There will be a ripple effect throughout the world. Inflation, social unrest ...'

'You said there was a signal. What is that? Did Elena find out?'

'She did, ma'am. The Ukrainian President will be captured once he arrives in Moscow tomorrow. That's the signal.'

91

Dusan Smirnov came to consciousness and found several people looking down at him. A stranger murmured softly and helped him up.

He got to his feet and looked around. Took in his fallen men and the people gathered.

'Who are you?' His voice came out weaker than he wished.

'From that building,' the woman pointed to the one behind the chain-link fence. 'We heard the shooting and came out to see what was happening.'

'We called GUVD,' a man told him.

'Go back,' he told them. He straightened his shoulders and showed them his identity card. 'I will handle the police. Don't tell anyone what you saw or heard. I will make life difficult for you if you do. Understand?'

They nodded silently and trudged back to their building.

Smirnov's head throbbed, but he presented a cold, grim face. He was SVR. He couldn't show he was weak or hurting.

He checked Bortnik and Galkin. Dead, as were the rest of the shooters. He didn't bother to check those behind the strip mall or at the fence.

Carter's people would have killed them.

He looked at the approach road and tried to figure out what had caused the explosions.

GUVD will find out soon enough. I'll have to convince them not to report this.

He had enough seniority and clout in SVR that his order would be obeyed by the police.

He heard sirens in the distance, and as he surveyed the parking lot, he knew what else he had to do.

He had to lie to Gorshky.

I can't tell him I failed yet again.

92

ashington DC

'Have you read it?' President Morgan asked his team in the Oval Office.

'Yes, sir,' Mike Hoosier replied. 'It's ... hard to believe.'

'Elena Zakharova's notes and article are extensive,' Catlyn Feder said. 'She has photographs of the hit teams, which we have verified, a dark-web link on which she has uploaded her interviews with the Energy and Finance Ministry officials, interviews with special-ops soldiers—'

'Can Russia carry this out?'

'Yes, sir."

Clare sat on the edge of the couch, watching, listening.

He's been on calls and meetings every moment since the news broke out. With us, with the Treasury Secretary, the Pentagon, European leaders, business leaders ... he's been working non-stop ever since the invasion.

. . .

Following Zeb's call, she had requested an emergency meeting with the President, along with the CIA Director and Daniel Klouse. She had shared her team's findings with them. The President had ordered a second meeting two hours later.

During which time he wanted us to verify whether Russia's plans were feasible.

'I agree with Catlyn, sir,' Jerry Polson said hoarsely. 'These are hit teams. Russia fooled us with their overt moves. Small teams of assassins could have moved across the borders easily. Into Azerbaijan, too.'

'Why does he need them? He has invaded the country! He can install his puppet government once Kyiv has fallen.'

'There's no certainty about how successful his military move will be, sir. He can take out both the Ukraine and Azerbaijan governments with these killers.'

'The Russians have had years to plan this.' Daniel Klouse said somberly. 'They know how we will react. We don't want another war. We've just come out of Afghanistan. Our people don't want to see soldiers committed to another country. We'll go down the economic sanctions route. The President and his oligarchs have so much hidden wealth and investments around the world that our moves won't really bother them. Our sanctions will hurt the Russian people, but they don't care about that.'

'Daniel is right,' Clayton Farley agreed.

'Are you saying they've won, Clayton?' President Morgan asked angrily.

'Sir, we are in react mode. They have the advantage for now. And unless we are ready to commit troops to battle, there is little we can do to stop the Russian army. Their President is testing us. He wants to see what our limits are. Once he sees we won't engage militarily, he'll go on to the next country. After

Azerbaijan, if he dares to challenge NATO, the Baltics. Finland could be next.'

'Even on sanctions, sir,' Feder added, 'we are hardly united. I'm sure the British will be slow to act.'

'Londongrad doesn't want to lose its money,' Farley said bitterly, referring to that capital's colloquial name. 'The United Kingdom, over the years, has allowed Russian oligarchs to buy properties, hotels, buildings, turning a blind eye to how they acquired their wealth. It is the Western world's money-laundering city.'

'And Germany, they're reliant on Russian gas.' Hoosier traced an imaginary pipeline route on the table. 'France, too.'

'I'm not hearing solutions,' the President growled. 'We cannot allow Russia to occupy independent nations. China might do the same next.'

Clare leaned forward. *We need to be alone*, she mouthed silently, angling her face for only him to read her lips.

President Morgan nodded.

'Come back to me with options.' He got to his feet, signaling the meeting was over. 'Clare, Catlyn, Daniel, stay back.'

'Now, what did you have in mind?' he asked the Agency Director when it was just them in the Oval Office.

'I want someone's opinion, and I didn't want to ask for that in front of the others.'

'Whose?'

'Zeb Carter's.'

93

Moscow

They were still in the hotel room.

Still watching the news unfold on TV with disbelief and anger.

Meghan reached for Zeb's phone when it buzzed. She turned it on speaker.

'Yeah?'

'Meghan, is Zeb there?'

'We're all here, ma'am.' She straightened and snapped her fingers to get the operatives' attention.

'I am with the President and Daniel, in the Oval Office.'

Zeb sat up, reached for the remote and turned off the TV.

'Yes, ma'am. Sir. We're listening.'

'Clare tells me you didn't know the invasion was taking place,' the President said.

'No, sir. She broke the news to us. We're shocked. Still

processing it.'

'How is it on the ground there?'

'We haven't gone out, sir. The Russian propaganda machine has started. The TVs here are relaying only the state channels, which are claiming the country acted in self-defense.'

'Which is nonsense.'

'Yes, sir. I don't think the people believe it either. We ordered room service and the server took one look at the TV, shook his head and said *lies*.'

'How is it in Moscow, Zeb?' Clare asked.

'Doesn't look like anything has changed, ma'am. The hotel is working, public transport is running. It doesn't feel any different.'

'You know Russia as well as any diplomat, Zeb. Do you believe what Elena wrote? That the President will hold Kotenko?'

'Yes, ma'am. He believes in audacious moves. In doing the unexpected. No one in the world is even thinking of this. He will capture the Ukrainian President.'

'Zeb,' President Morgan's voice boomed into the room. 'What do you suggest we do?'

Me? He was thinking, taken aback. *He's surrounded by advisors and military and political strategists.*

'It's not a trick question,' Clare said, reading his silence.

'Buy twenty-four hours, sir. Get elite operatives to take out those hit teams in Ukraine and Azerbaijan and protect the targets. Get Kotenko to cancel his visit. If he's still coming.'

'He is. I spoke to him. He won't back off. It wouldn't be good optics.'

'The Russian President,' Beth burst out and visibly bit back a curse. 'He's played this so smartly, sir. His tanks and soldiers roll into Ukraine today. Tomorrow he invites Kotenko for discussions, as if they aren't the aggressor country.'

'Agreed, but let's focus on our Ukrainian friend. How can

we get him out of Moscow?'

'Wire him,' Beth interrupted.

'Excuse me?' President Morgan asked, with an amused-bewildered chuckle.

'Get Kotenko to wear a wire, sir. One of the fancy ones the CIA has developed that will not be detected by any Russian security. Record the meeting and publish it instantly if he is held captive. That will expose the Russian President's hand.'

Smart. Zeb grinned and gave her a thumbs-up.

'And,' Meghan added, 'those hit teams ... publish their photographs and identities in every newspaper and TV channel and expose what they intend to do. That will stop them, even if our teams aren't able to neutralize them.'

'Why don't y'all,' President Morgan said seriously, 'come and work with me in the White House.'

'No, sir!' the Agency operatives said in one voice.

'Even that might not be enough, sir,' Zeb said soberly. 'That will stop the assassinations and the takeover of the Ukraine and Azerbaijan governments, at least for now, but Russian forces will continue advancing.'

'We're working on a package of economic sanctions. Those will hit Russia hard.'

'Those might not be enough, either, sir.'

'I am aware of that. We will provide weapons and fighter aircraft to Ukraine. There are no limits, short of going to war with Russia directly. I am in constant discussion with other world leaders. We're working on a range of punishments of escalating severity.'

'Are our European allies on board, sir? What about the British?'

'They are. This has taken all of us by surprise. They need to work with their cabinets and come up with proposals. I will talk to the Azerbaijanian President, too, to not only assure his safety but also accelerate the gas delivery to Europe. As for the

British,' he said grimly, 'they need us more. Trade deal. I will convince their Prime Minister to support us in the strongest possible way.'

'Sir, the elections, public opinion—' Zeb began.

'I'm in my second term. My party might lose the next election, but I didn't get into politics to win them. I wanted to do right ... I know that sounds a little grand, but that's really the reason. As for convincing the American people ... there is nothing but shock in every home in the country. I'm sure they will support what I propose. We aren't going to war. That isn't on the cards. This isn't an attack on NATO, and let's not forget, Russia has nuclear weapons. Of course, economic sanctions will hurt us and our businesses, too. American businesses will be affected. They won't be popular with everyone. But this is about freedom. It is who we are. What are we if we don't stand up for it? Who are we, if we don't help our friends? But,' he smiled self-deprecatingly, 'I am practicing my speech on you. How is it on the ground?'

He's asking about the mission.

'We should be ready to go hot shortly, sir.'

'If you can pull it off, rescue Elena, that alone will be a major blow to the Russian President. It will show he isn't invincible, that we can strike successfully in the midst of his military operation. Elena's findings will help contain the invasion. The Russians will think twice about invading another country—not when their President's plan is revealed.'

'Yes, sir.'

'And the second target as well,' Clare added.

'No pressure,' Beth said when the call ended. 'Why did you ask him about the elections?'

'I wanted to see how far he would go.'

'You got your answer.'

Zeb nodded.

'I wonder what he'll tell Kotenko.'

94

ashington DC

President Morgan didn't waste time. He got Hoosier, Polson and Farley to rejoin them and briefed the arrivals quickly on his plan of action.

Everyone in the room was on board.

He knew he would still have to sell his sanctions package to the opposition party and to the American public.

I'll do that, too. There's no backing down.

He got his office to ring Kotenko and put it on speaker.

'Miroslav, how are you, my friend?' he greeted the Ukrainian President when he came on the line. When his team made to leave, he motioned for them to stay.

'I am still alive, President Morgan, since our last call.' Kotenko smiled grimly on the video feed. 'Our forces are prepared for a long and hard war. As if recognizing Donetsk and Luhansk as independent countries wasn't provocation enough, now Russia's President has invaded us directly. And he claims he wants to *de-Nazify* us!'

'Yeah. I'm following developments closely. What about Moscow? Are you still going tomorrow?'

'Yes, sir. Can you believe his gall? He attacks us and then expects me to show up for de-escalation talks! I'm sure it's no more than a publicity stunt.'

'He's going to arrest you. You will not be allowed to leave. And at the same time, your entire cabinet and the Azerbaijan government will be either assassinated or captured.'

Kotenko gasped.

'What are you saying?' he breathed out in disbelief.

'It's true. You heard of Elena Zakharova?'

'Yes. Everyone has. She's like a folk hero in our country.'

'We got her article and her research papers. She has proof on everything I said.'

'But ... isn't she missing?'

'Yes, but we managed to get her report. We'll send copies to you securely. She uncovered the Russians' whole plan, and it goes beyond Ukraine.'

The President went through the journalist's article.

'He wants to destroy my country! Azerbaijan as well. I know he won't stop there. He will go after the Baltic countries once he's occupied us.'

'Yes, that's our guess, too.'

'I will cancel the meeting!'

'Do that, if you think that's the best choice.'

'You think I should go?' he asked incredulously.

'If you can go and buy us some time, it will help.'

'For what?'

'For NATO, US and European special forces teams to neutralize those hit teams, maybe slow down the invasion.'

'You would do that for us?'

'Yes, my friend.'

'In that case, I will go ahead with that meeting. My life means nothing—'

'It won't come to that,' President Morgan said, though he couldn't help smiling at Kotenko's words.

'How can I buy time?'

'By appealing to the Russian President's ego,' Clare said.

'Who is that?'

'One of my trusted advisors,' President Morgan said and gestured at her to continue.

'Mr. President,' the Agency Director said, 'In less than twelve hours, a special team will be with you. They will fit you with a microphone. It will not be detected by the Russians, we guarantee that. It will record your meeting.'

'They will jam all signals.'

'Yes, but this will record passively and transmit when you are outside.'

'How do I get out, though?'

'Tell him you know what he is planning. That with his army already in your country, he should try to capture you in your office, in Kyiv. Taunt him in a way that strokes his ego—tell him that will show how powerful Russia is, not holding you captive in Moscow.'

'That might work. He likes dramatic moves.'

'If it doesn't, Miroslav,' President Morgan said, 'you will be held prisoner for a few hours only. Because we will release your recording to every news outlet in the world. We will publish Elena's article and research. The Russian President will be exposed. Even his allies will not be able to support him.'

'I'll get my military to protect my cabinet.'

'Don't do that. Best to be careful about who you share this information with. Your country is filled with Russian spies. Trust me. The US, NATO and our European friends will deal with that threat. You will have a team to protect you as well. I will warn the Azerbaijanian President as soon as we finish this call.'

'Yes, Mr. President. Now, on the invasion, we need a no-fly zone over our country. I am grateful that NATO teams will protect me and my cabinet, but we need more than that. We want it to join us in the war. We want to join the European Union—'

'We had this discussion earlier, Miroslav. None of those are my decisions alone. NATO committing troops would be an act of war on Russia, which could escalate very quickly. He has already threatened to use nuclear weapons. I'm sure you don't want to see that. But don't get the impression we will do nothing to help you.'

President Morgan's voice hardened. 'I have been calling world leaders ever since this attack happened. America and European countries will go all-out to help you in every other way possible. We will provide you with every type of arms, missiles, aircraft, food and medical supplies, whatever we can do without committing NATO to war.'

'Some European countries are opposed to even that kind of help,' Kotenko said. 'These moves will be unpopular with your opposition party, with many German citizens and many others in Europe.'

'That was before the invasion, Miroslav. I will be calling the Chancellor after this. I'm sure their views will have changed almost instantly. You're going to see a level of support from all countries that the world has never seen before, not even during the world war.'

'The West will go to that extent for us?' Kotenko asked.

'It will. This isn't about just Ukraine, Miroslav. It is about the values we cherish. Those are worth defending; otherwise, what are we?'

'Thank you, Mr. President.'

'Things are going to get nasty over there. Your life is at risk as long as you are in Ukraine. The United States will gladly offer you refuge—'

'Sir, what kind of leader would I be if I left my people to fight while I fled for safety? How could I ask them to resist if I took the easy way out? What would I see if I looked in the mirror? No, sir. I am staying, and if I am arrested or killed, so be it.'

'Let's hope it doesn't come to that,' President Morgan said softly and ended the call.

I hope I would be as courageous as him in those circumstances, he said to himself.

95

'Coordinate with the Pentagon, NATO and the Europeans. Decide which agency will take the lead on this,' President Morgan addressed his team. 'I don't want any turf wars. I want results. By the time Kotenko lands in Moscow, I want those hit teams out of the picture. Am I clear?'

'Yes, sir,' the CIA Director nodded.

'Am I asking mission impossible?'

'That's what we specialize in, sir.' Polson smiled thinly. 'We know who these killers are from Elena's notes. We will make their details public as soon as our teams are in place in Ukraine and Azerbaijan. Their names will be plastered on TV. Every airport, seaport and bus terminal in those countries will be alerted. Our teams will protect those countries' officials. It will work. It will need precise coordination.'

'Jerry,' the President growled. 'We put the first human on the moon. If we can't coordinate to that extent, why are we the world's biggest superpower?'

'Yes, sir.'

'Clayton, call every nation's Ambassador. There are a

hundred and ninety-three countries in the United Nations. I want us to reach out to all of them and get as many as possible on our side. If they merely speak out against Russian aggression, that will help. We are going to isolate that country like the world has never seen before. And we are going to squeeze it hard.'

'Will do, sir.'

'I need to call European leaders. We are not backing down. We are not playing wait and watch anymore. Our defense budget is well over seven hundred billion dollars. It's time to flex that muscle. We need to arm our Ukrainian friends.'

96

Moscow

'WHAT'S TWITTER SAYING?' Zeb leaned back on the bed and crossed his arms.

'About the war?' Beth asked. 'There's little else being discussed.'

'About our post.'

'Lots of reaction. Comments, retweets.'

'We need to increase that discussion by several fold.'

She typed on her screen for several minutes and looked up.

'That may not be enough, however.' She pulled out her phone and began dialing when Zeb stopped her.

'You're calling Yasimov?'

'Yeah.'

'There should be no mention of storming Lubyanka. Not today.'

'I'll make it clear to him.'

Kotenko's meeting is scheduled to finish at twelve pm, Zeb recalled from the schedule that Russian state media had published. *He should be out of the Kremlin about half an hour after that.*

If he's allowed to leave. Our entire plan hinges on that.

We can still make it work if he's captured.

Not all of it, he argued. *You might get Elena but not Gorshky. If Kotenko is captured, the SVR chief won't leave his office.*

He shrugged. *Can't have contingencies for every development.*

That wasn't how the real world worked.

If we get out with Elena alone, we'll have to return to Moscow later for Gorshky.

'Kotenko?' Chloe looked at him. 'Everything rests on him?'

'Yeah.'

Washington DC; Chievres, Belgium; Mons, Belgium; Brussels, Belgium; Paris; Berlin; Baku, Azerbaijan

President Morgan called the German Chancellor. The man was newly elected, relatively inexperienced in comparison to the previous leader of the country, but had a very good grasp of ground realities.

They discussed the attack, and then the American leader briefed him on the list of US sanctions on Russia.

'We are going to cancel Nordstream 2,' the Chancellor said, referring to the gas pipeline from Russia to Germany. 'It's not yet public news, but I will be announcing it shortly.'

The American leader rocked back in his chair. *That's a major U-turn by the Germans. That pipeline would have secured their energy needs. At the same time, they would have been even more reliant on Russia.*

'We have started exploring alternate supplies. We will also

release a range of sanctions. We will freeze oligarchs' assets, work on kicking Russian banks out of SWIFT, encourage many of our businesses to stop their Russian operations—'

'Those alone might not be enough.'

The German leader caught his meaning.

'Ja, we have been debating that. My people are reluctant to commit to military action. You know our history. You know why many of our politicians and citizens don't want to get involved in armed conflict. We don't even export weapons to conflict zones.'

The American President knew. He kept silent.

'However, we will reverse history today. Germany will increase our military budget significantly. We will send Stingers, anti-tank weapons, whatever we can, to Ukraine. This is as big a threat as any we faced in the 1930s. But I will need your help, sir. With Azerbaijan—'

'I'm talking to their President shortly. I can virtually guarantee that country will step up their gas supply to you. I will also talk to the Saudis and the UAE, get them to speed up their discussions with you on energy.'

'President Morgan, I know you had a very close relationship with my predecessor. I hope, with time, you will find that I am as capable and worthy of your trust.'

'Stephan.' The most powerful man in the world smiled briefly. 'With time, I hope you will find that I don't compare state leaders in that manner. I am sure we will develop a very strong relationship. The United States will always stand with Germany. Political leaders will come and go, but that relationship is immutable. There is something else you should know.'

He briefed the Chancellor on Elena's findings and heard him draw a shocked breath.

'My people will be sharing all those notes with you.'

'Whatever you need, we will provide.'

'I will be briefing the Secretary General of NATO. It is best we all coordinate with that organization. They might need some of your special forces teams. NATO alone might not have enough operatives to protect that many people. We will be sending teams from Ramstein Air Base as well.'

'Our KSK and KSM units are on standby,' the Chancellor said, referring to the German special forces teams. 'We will act as soon as NATO greenlights the operation.'

His next call was to the French President, with whom he was close friends. He switched to that country's language, which he had learned to speak well during a couple of years as a student in Paris.

'Things are not good eh, mon ami?'

'No, William,' the French leader said. 'But we will ratchet up the pressure.'

'There is something else you need to know.' President Morgan broke it down swiftly. When he had finished, he was unsurprised by the French leader's response.

'Whatever it takes. My military is ready for anything. My armed forces minister is already coordinating with NATO. Protecting Kotenko and Azerbaijan, helping Ukraine. Money, weapons, seizing of Russian assets ... there are no limits to what France is ready to do, without actually going to war.'

He called the Azerbaijan President.

'President Aghayey, you and your ministers, sir, are facing imminent threat of capture and assassination, within the next day. No,' he said, smiling grimly. 'I am not joking, nor am I making a threat. The danger to all of you is real, but from Russia.'

He briefed the Azerbaijanian leader on the contents of Elena's notes. He exclaimed several times in shock and surprise and expressed gratitude for President Morgan's support. He promised to accelerate gas supplies to Europe.

'Send me everything from Elena,' Aghayey added. 'I will

make sure those photographs get published once you give us the signal. We will stop those killers, with your help.'

President Morgan went on to speak to NATO's Secretary General, the British Prime Minister, and several other European leaders. By the time he had finished his list, he was exhausted.

'We need to share Elena's findings,' he said tiredly.

Catlyn Feder looked at the rest of the team, who still hadn't left the Oval Office. 'Clayton, your people should take the lead in sharing this information.'

'We'll do that.'

'But it needs to be coordinated. Our friends should make it public only when Kotenko is in the meeting.'

'Got it.'

She stayed back, along with Clare and Klouse, at the President's gesture.

'The President turned to the Agency Director. 'Zeb. Do you know how he's going to pull this off?'

'No, sir. He doesn't share operational details. All I know is it will go down tomorrow.'

'Does he have a chance? Moscow tomorrow will be sealed so tight, escape will be impossible. And how's he going to get Elena out of Lubyanka?'

'I don't know, sir, but if anyone can succeed it's him and his crew.'

'And if they don't?'

'Then,' Clare breathed deeply, 'we have to be prepared for the worst. The Russian President and Gorshky will want to humiliate us. They will put Zeb's crew on public trial and won't hesitate to execute them.'

97

Chievres, Belgium

THERE WAS nothing distinguishable about the forty men. No scars, no tattoos, no distinctive facial features and no fancy hair styles. They were dressed casually in jeans and Tees or half-sleeved shirts.

They had one common feature, however. All of them were hard-bodied and had alert eyes.

Some were from France's 1st Marine Infantry Parachute Regiment, RPIMa, an elite special forces unit. There were members from Kommando Spezialkrafte Marine, KSM, a German elite unit. Men had arrived from the US 1st Battalion Special Forces Group, based in Panzer Kaserne, Stuttgart, and the rest of the group was drawn from NATO's special forces.

'None of you know why you are here,' said Colonel Brewster, of NATO's Supreme Headquarters Allied Powers Europe,

SHAPE, addressing the group in English as he began his briefing. 'You are the spear that will protect Europe.'

By evening, the men had split up into teams of twos and threes and were driven to train and airport stations, from which some would go to Azerbaijan and others to Ukraine.

Berlin

ANOTHER THREE-PERSON TEAM set off from an apartment in Mitte, Berlin. With their backpacks and easy laughter, they looked like office workers.

Only a close observer would note their thickly corded forearms and the way they moved: easily, but warily.

They took a cheap flight from Berlin Brandenburg Airport to Boryspil Airport in Kyiv, where crowds of panicked people were clamoring for flights out in the wake of the invasion. They hired a cab at the airport to Bankova Street, where the President's office was located.

They went through the security screening, after which an aide was waiting for them.

'Mr. Smith?' he looked at them.

'That's me,' one of the men replied. 'Jones and Rogers,' he said, introducing the other two.

No first names.

They went down the carpeted hallway, where the aide knocked on a large door and nodded at them.

'President Kotenko,' Jones said, greeting the man behind the desk. 'You should have been briefed about us.'

'Did you have any trouble getting to Kyiv?'

'No sir. Flights are still getting in at the moment. But everything going out is full, sir.'

'Do you blame our citizens for fleeing? We didn't want this war.'

'No, sir.'

Rogers removed a plastic case from his backpack and laid it out on the polished desk.

'Your wire, sir.'

Kotenko looked at the tiny device, which was no larger than a shirt button.

'That will do it?'

'That, along with these two.' Rogers laid out two more devices on the table. 'They go on your sleeve cuffs. Which shirt will you be wearing tomorrow, sir?'

'That one.' The President pointed out to a neatly ironed shirt laid out on a couch. Next to it was a suit on its hanger. 'I have been sleeping in my office for several days.'

The men didn't comment.

Smith and Jones brought out more devices and went around the office methodically.

'Searching for bugs, sir.'

'My office is swept every day. It's clean.'

'We can confirm that, sir,' Smith said politely after a while.

The men didn't speak. They stood easily while Rogers removed a button on the front of the shirt and those on the sleeve, and sewed on the replacements.

'They will record everything said within a twenty-meter range and relay the feed as soon as there is a satellite signal. Everything is built into them.'

'In such small devices?'

'Yes, sir. Who do you trust most in your office?'

'Victor, my aide. He's the one who brought you here.'

'Please call him here, sir.'

Kotenko frowned but did as he was asked.

'You know how to search a room?' Smith asked the aide when he arrived.

'Yes, everyone in the President's office does.'

'Please scan this room for listening devices.'

Victor looked at the arrivals and then at Kotenko, who nodded. He went out and returned with gear and carried out the search.

'The clothing, too.'

'There's nothing here,' the aide said, puzzled.

'Good. You may go.'

Smith ran his wand over the shirt and showed it to Kotenko.

'Even our equipment does not detect them, sir. The Russians won't, either.'

'If they do?'

'Then we all are screw—. Stuffed, sir,' he corrected himself.

'Aren't you staying?' the President asked when the team zipped up their backpacks.

'No, sir.'

'But what about my protection? President Morgan assured me—'

'That will be a different team, sir. It should be arriving any moment.'

They left as silently as they had arrived.

Kyiv, Ukraine, Baku, Azerbaijan

THE VARIOUS HIT teams were in place by the time Smith, Rogers and Jones were on their return flight from Boryspil. The ones tasked with protecting Kotenko identified themselves to Victor, who was in the loop, and stationed themselves next to the President's room.

Meanwhile, Aghayey's team inserted itself within his security detail and waited.

They all checked in with Brewster, who relayed the information to SHAPE's commander, who in turn passed on the information to a handful of people on both sides of the Atlantic.

98

M*oscow*

ZEB HADN'T MOVED from his position on the bed—propped up against the headboard, staring at the wall—for several hours.

His friends didn't disturb him. They knew he could lie there, in that state, for days. They could, too.

He didn't join in their conversation. He went through his plan yet again and grimaced inwardly at the holes in it.

We can't do any better. We've got to roll with our odds.

He stirred, finally.

'What's social media saying?'

'Steaming,' Beth replied. 'Big demonstrations tomorrow in Kotenko's support and against the invasion. The Russian government has banned protests, but the protesters are going ahead with them There is talk of tearing down Lubyanka and freeing Elena.'

'Red Square will be flooded with demonstrators,' Meghan added. 'It wouldn't take much to start a riot.'

Which is what we want, but it should happen at the right time.

'Boris,' he said in a call to the editor, 'are you seeing what's going on Kotenko's Twitter?'

'Da. I am proud of the Resistance.'

'You are in contact with all the leaders?'

'Da.' He chuckled. 'Some say I am one of them.'

'They have been posting about going to Lubyanka. They shouldn't do that until I give you the signal.'

'You are going to bomb it!'

'You don't need to know the details. The protesters should move towards it only when I or my team tell you to.'

'What will that do? We need to—'

'It will help free Elena.'

'It will be done. The leaders might be reluctant, but I will convince them.'

'The military or police might open fire. You are aware they have outlawed demonstrations.'

'Da. Nothing is going to stop us, though. What the President has done deserves to be condemned. We know many of us might be arrested tomorrow or die. Everyone who joins the Resistance is prepared for that.'

'DA?' Illya Pushkin growled when Zeb called him next.

'I need you to carry out some bombings.'

'Have you seen what's happening in my country? I will set them off myself! Where do you want us to attack? The Kremlin? But my President will be—'

'SVR's office.'

'Da,' the bratva leader said chillingly, 'that we can do. We might not get near it, but we can fire rocket launchers—'

'That won't be necessary. Set off several car bombs. Arrange them so that the first one is far away, the next one is closer ... you get the picture. I or my team will give you the signal for each blast. Don't set them off before you get that. Clear?'

'Da.'

'We need similar bombs to go off at Lubyanka too—'

'Why there?'

'Can you do it?'

'We can bomb the whole of Moscow. Just give me the word.'

'SVR's office and Lubyanka are sufficient. We need to start a riot at the second location, too. Can you help with that?'

'Da.'

'There will be protesters. I don't want civilian casualties, either in the bombings or the riot.'

Pushkin paused a beat. 'We can place the bombs in cordoned-off areas and parking lots. There won't be anyone nearby. But the riots ... I can't promise there won't be injuries.'

That's a risk we'll have to take. Yasimov said the protesters are aware of the danger. They are prepared for it.

'Aren't you forgetting something?' Pushkin asked.

'What?'

'What if the police or soldiers open fire?'

'I am hoping they don't. The entire world will be watching. *Russian Soldiers Slaughter Peaceful Demonstrators*. That's not the kind of headlines the Russian President wants.'

'Do you think he would have attacked my country if he cared about headlines?'

'You have a point. But remember, if there is shooting, some of your people might die.'

'I am ready to die myself.'

99

K*yiv, Ukraine*

It was bright and sunny, but the weather did little for President Miroslav Kotenko's mood.

'I might not return from Moscow today,' he said, addressing his cabinet in an early meeting. 'You might see me again only on TV, as a prisoner. Or, I might even be killed by the Russians.'

'What?' his finance minister exclaimed. 'Do you know something we don't? Is Russia planning to—'

Kotenko held his hand up to silence his visitors.

I can't tell them about the killers.

'All I am saying is, we have to be prepared for all contingencies. If—'

'We will choose a leader. Quickly. But it will not come to that.'

'I hope so.' He looked at the defense minister and nodded. 'Begin.'

He dismissed his team ninety minutes later and made several calls to various European leaders, apprising them of the current situation. He made a televised address to his country and warned his citizens to stay vigilant.

'Many of us will die. I myself will bear arms to defend Kyiv. I may not live. Our blood will redden the soil of our country. It is a price we will all gladly pay, however. We are a sovereign, democratic country. We are a free country, and we will defend ourselves till the last one of us is standing.'

'The media are saying your approval among voters is soaring like never before, sir,' his aide whispered when he returned to his office. 'Every TV channel in the world is praising your leadership.'

Kotenko grunted. 'You've known me for a long time. Do you think that's important to me?'

'No, sir. But I have to ask ... you had a good life before entering politics. You were famous, popular, rich ... do you regret it? You could have escaped Ukraine and lived in Europe or America if you hadn't become a politician.'

'You know I am divorced—and that my former wife lives in Switzerland with my son and daughter?'

'Yes, everyone knows that.'

'President Morgan said I could seek refuge in America. I said I wouldn't. What kind of person would I be if I fled my country and left our people to fight for themselves? There are not many times we look deep into ourselves and work out who we really are. I have been doing that over the past few days. I have found I am an ordinary person, just one who believes in what is right and is prepared to stand up for it.'

'Aren't you afraid, sir? I'm scared by what's happening to us now.'

'Yes, I am. Who wouldn't be? I want to see my children grow up. I want to see our country prosper. I don't want to see innocent people die. But what good is fear if we can't turn it into something useful? I will channel that, to tell the Russian President today that, yes, they might take over Kyiv and arrest or kill me. They might even occupy us. But then they'll be trapped in Ukraine, with *us*. They should be afraid of that. Very afraid.'

Kotenko slipped on his jacket and went to his armored car, which drove him to the Presidential aircraft at Boryspil International Airport.

He buckled in as they started rolling, and when his flight left the earth, he fingered the buttons on his cuffs.

I hope those devices work.

I pray Ukraine remains free.

Moscow

ZEB WAS IN MISSION-READY MODE. The TV in his hotel room was muted but turned to CNN International, which was covering Ukraine, live.

He adjusted the sleeves of his jacket and felt for his Glock in his shoulder holster.

Beth came to him and gripped his forearm.

'Your mic works?'

'Yeah. It takes some time getting used to it.'

He was wearing a tooth microphone that was clipped to one of his molars. The device worked based on bone conduction technology, whereby sound was transmitted through vibration into the inner ear. Voices would be heard as if they were inside his head instead of from the outer ear. The device could be linked to Push-To-Talk, PTT, controls and to any other communication devices such as encrypted phones or tactical radios.

'You'll be always-on,' she warned.

He nodded. *Can't risk PTT. It could be detected.*

He checked his team out. All of them in jeans and Tees and

lightweight jackets, over their body armor. Backpacks and gymbags held their gear.

He went inside the bathroom, removed his prosthetic disguise, put on the mask Mikhail had made. Dusan Smirnov emerged from the bathroom.

He looked at the TV, which was now showing Red Square. An angry, seething mass of protesters.

'Those numbers will go up,' Meghan commented. 'We're in touch with Yasimov. He said there are hundreds more Resistance members waiting to flood the square and Lubyanka Square.'

'Let's go.'

ALEXEI GORSHKY WAS JUMPY. He knew there was no reason to be, but still, he was on edge. He swore beneath his breath and saw that there were new operatives taking the place of Bortnik and Galkin. Smirnov was in his seat but he didn't ask the team leader about the replacements.

I have enough on my plate.

He closed the door to his office, checked the news on TV, and made calls. The first was to the President, to whom he listened respectfully, nodding several times.

'Da. Nothing will go wrong,' he said and hung up.

He went through various reports, but found he couldn't concentrate and gave up. He turned up the TV volume and started following coverage of Kotenko's visit.

'KOTENKO HAS ARRIVED,' Beth informed them as they weaved through people and made their way to their ambush point, near the intersection of Tverskaya and Georgiyevskiy streets.

A prowl car went past them as they sauntered on the sidewalk. The street was some distance from the Kremlin, but it had several protesters who carried Ukrainian flags and placards with Elena's name on them.

'Police,' Chloe whispered. 'Lots of them, strung out. Armed as well.'

Zeb stopped at an office building that had a TV in its window. He joined the crowd that had gathered around it and watched the coverage.

'I'll do it,' Beth said softly when he reached for his phone. 'You'll be busy later.'

She sent the first text to Pushkin.

Detonate!

Meghan sent a message to Yasimov.

Move towards Lubyanka.

ELENA IS A PRISONER IN LUBYANKA! FREE HER!

Chloe posted the message on Twitter, where it was picked up by several bots that retweeted it, and soon, hundreds of accounts amplified it.

'BOMBS—'

'I can see that,' Gorshky said irritably when Smirnov burst into his room. He pointed at the TV that was covering Kotenko's visit. A rolling banner reported the explosions. A journalist appeared on the scene and reported breathlessly that it was too early to tell if there had been casualties.

'Two blocks from our office and from Lubyanka,' the team leader said.

'The police will investigate.'

'There are so many protesters in Red Square and near the prison. I have never seen that many people. I got reports that the Resistance people are moving towards Lubyanka.'

Gorshky's lips tightened.

. . .

'I WISH I could say it was good to see you, sir,' Kotenko said to the Russian President, who rose at the far end of a lengthy table in his Kremlin office. 'It would have been a pleasure in different circumstances.'

The men didn't shake hands. There was no one else in the room. Nothing but fifteen feet of highly polished wood between them.

Kotenko had held his breath while being searched as he entered the Kremlin. The security man had looked at him quizzically when he had expelled it audibly.

Those bugs haven't been detected.

'What better circumstances?' the Russian President asked bluntly.

'When your troops retreat from my country.'

'They won't. It was never an independent country, you know. When Lenin gave you autonomy, you thought it meant you were independent. You weren't. Ukraine belongs to Russia, always has and always will.'

Calm down, Kotenko told himself. He wants you to be angry. *That might be when he summons his guards to arrest me.*

TWO MORE EXPLOSIONS, Beth messaged the bratva leader. *Closer to the locations.*

Zeb heard one of the blasts. Several people in the crowd heard it as well. A murmur ran through the watchers. A man next to him held up his phone and peered intently at it.

LET'S BREAK INTO LUBYANKA AND FREE ELENA.

He showed Chloe's post to his friend, who nodded, and the two men drifted away. The crowd filled in their spots.

Zeb backed away from the watching people, crossed the street and took up his position. Bwana and Bear on the edges of his vision, the rest of his team on his other flank.

Waiting. Ready.

. . .

'THAT WAS CLOSER,' Smirnov whispered. 'Our windows rattled.'

Gorshky shifted uneasily on his feet. The TV showed coverage from a chopper. The protesters were an angry, seething mass of people that seemed to spread for miles. The camera zoomed out to show smoke from the bombs.

'Car explosions. No one hurt,' his team leader said, breaking away from his phone.

The SVR chief glanced at the quote on the wall, and a chill raced through him.

'Carter is setting them off. He's coming here.'

'But—'

'It's his style. He'll distract attention while he slips inside.'

'We have the best security—'

Gorshky was beyond hearing.

'Let's go.' He slipped on his jacket and rushed out of his office.

'Go where?'

'We'll join Kotenko's convoy. We have to be out there.'

'He's still with our President!'

'STOP OBJECTING,' Gorshky roared.

Just as another explosion could be heard.

THE CLERK in the mail office saw them leave. He messaged the Resistance. Yasimov relayed the information to Meghan, who conveyed it to Zeb, who didn't react.

He kept looking down the street, like many of the protesters, waiting for Kotenko's car to arrive.

Yasimov has people on the road from Yasenevo to the Kremlin. He'll tell us if Gorshky is joining Kotenko's convoy.

Everything depends on that happening.

Where else would he go? He would want to be close to the action.

He waited.

'You are misinterpreting history,' Kotenko replied. 'We have our own language, our own culture, and we became an independent country in 1991, thirty-two years ago, after the collapse of the USSR—'

'Lies. You came under the influence of the European Union and NATO. They corrupted you. Ukraine was always part of us and will be again, just like Donetsk and Luhansk.'

'Sir,' Kotenko said forcefully, 'what you are saying is wrong. Your recognizing those two regions as independent countries is wrong. Russian troops entering sover—'

'DON'T CRITICIZE ME IN THE VERY HEART OF MOTHER RUSSIA.'

Kotenko got scared. *Is this it? Will he arrest me now?*

'AND DON'T PRETEND YOU CAN TELL ME WHAT TO DO.' The Russian President pointed his finger at the Ukrainian leader. 'YOU. SURRENDER. HERE, NOW. That is best for you. Otherwise, our tanks will be forced to shell Kyiv, reduce it to rubble. We will conquer your drug-addled Nazi government and restore Ukraine to her rightful place.'

'Gorshky is heading to the Kremlin,' Beth relayed.

'Set off two more bombs and get Pushkin's men to join the protesters near Lubyanka.' Zeb's lips barely moved.

'Done.'

The SVR chief's eyes were glued to his phone screen. His armored ride and Galkin and the rest of his protection team, in another vehicle, sped down the near-empty street.

He heard Smirnov speak to the police to get an update.

'No casualties.' The team leader frowned. 'All the bombs have detonated without injuring anyone. That doesn't sound like Carter.'

'It is just like him,' Gorshky snapped. 'He's not like us. He won't kill innocents. Are you seeing these social media posts? The protesters aren't just talking about the war, they're discussing storming Lubyanka to free Zakharova.'

'No one can breach it.'

'You know better than that. Any building can be breached if people are prepared to die. These Resistance people ... they don't have fear. How much longer?'

'Twenty minutes more to the Kremlin. Are we going inside?'

'Nyet. We will join his convoy outside, near Tverskaya.'

'I am not sure we should be there.'

'Carter will not expect us with Kotenko. We'll make sure the Ukrainian President departs safely and then return.'

I can tell the President I personally made sure Kotenko left unharmed.

'You have already declared war on us, sir,' the Ukrainian President said. 'Surrender? That will never happen. You want to capture me? Why don't you do it in Kyiv, in my office? It is very easy, cowardly even, to arrest a visitor when they come to your office or home. If Russia is so powerful, demonstrate it. Let the world see the true nature of your aggression. I will personally pick up a gun and fight your soldiers. The world will see which country is in the right.'

With that, Kotenko stood up. He hurried out of the office, expecting the Russian President to call him back.

He went down the hallway briskly, aware of aides and soldiers eyeing him curiously. The hairs on his neck prickled, but he didn't look back. He strode quickly, wishing he could run but careful to continue looking statesmanlike. He couldn't show fear.

He reached the end of the hallway. Soldiers at the door. They didn't stop him.

He ran down the steps and climbed into his car, slammed the door shut and yelled at the driver.

'SHEREMETYEVO AIRPORT!'

100

'Kotenko is out,' Beth said.

A roar burst from the protesters. Many people in the crowd shook placards in the air.

Zeb checked out the police officers ranged along the crowd, containing the protesters to the sidewalk.

Twenty-foot interval between them. Rope barrier between us and them.

They were hard-faced, their hands on their AK74s, watching the street as well as the protesters.

Will they shoot once we go hot?

He hoped not.

Bear and Roger came in front of him, blocking him from being seen from passing vehicles.

'Start the riot. Explode the rest of the bombs near Lubyanka.'

Meghan double-tapped her mic in acknowledgment.

Applause and yells broke out from the crowd.

'Motorcycle outriders,' Broker announced.

The blasts sounded before Zeb could reply. He felt the crowd shifting, murmuring as people checked their phones.

The police officers spoke into their radios but didn't move from their positions.

The outriders rolled past them.

A police vehicle followed.

An ambulance came next.

A black car nosed around the corner and entered Tverskaya.

A loud roar filled the air.

'Kotenko,' Meghan said softly. 'It has started.'

'What?' Zeb frowned and then it came to him. 'The arrests?'

'Yeah, news reports are coming thick and fast. Arrests made in Kyiv and Baku. The identities of the assassin teams on TV.'

'What about Kotenko's recording?'

'Not yet released. Our side must be waiting to see if he gets clear.'

Makes sense.

The Ukrainian President's vehicle grew closer.

Zeb could see between Bear and Roger's bodies. Dark windows. A pale face behind the wheel. He stood on his toes and looked behind it.

Where's Gorshky?

'Go faster,' The SVR chief barked, his face pale, his eyes on his phone's screen. 'Something big is going down. We need to get close to Kotenko.'

'Riots have broken out near Lubyanka. More bombs have blown—'

'I know. I am following the reports. Did you see about the arrests in Baku and Kyiv? Russian agents who were supposed to capture or kill the Azerbaijan and Ukraine cabinet and military leaders. I didn't know our President was planning that.'

'Da, I have been reading the breaking news. Do we stop Kotenko?' Smirnov asked.

'I haven't received any orders yet. That's why we need to get closer.'

'There.' The team leader pointed. 'He's ahead, on Tverskaya.'

'Take over command of his security. Wait. Let me do that.'

'Baladin,' Gorshky spoke authoritatively when the GUVD chief took his call. 'SVR is taking over Kotenko's security. I and my security team leader, Dusan Smirnov, are behind him in our car. Smirnov is the point man. Patch him into the communications channel.

'No, don't argue,' he thundered when Baladin protested. 'Are you following what's happening? I am ordering you to stand down. Take your complaints to the President; I am acting on his authority.

'Done,' he said after listening for a few more moments and hanging up. 'Take over.'

He watched Smirnov introduce himself to the police outrider on his radio. He looked up sharply at movement ahead of them.

'WHO'S THAT MAN?'

He pointed at a man who walked out in front of Kotenko's car.

LUCK CAME their way in the form of the protester who jumped over the rope barrier and darted towards Kotenko's car, cheering, waving his placard, which slowed down the Presidential vehicle and got Gorshky's ride to draw closer.

Two police officers reacted swiftly.

They clubbed him brutally, dragged his body to the sidewalk, and dumped him behind the rope barrier.

'He didn't act on our instruction,' Beth whispered. 'We didn't tell Yasimov to get someone to run in front of the car.'

Zeb didn't reply.

He was counting down in his mind.

Kotenko's car went past them.

The nose of Gorshky's vehicle, fifteen feet to their right.

Bwana exploded the first smoke bomb. Chloe and Broker triggered several more at their feet.

Protesters yelled and covered their mouths and noses with whatever they could find.

It's not tear gas. It's harmless smoke.

Gorshky's car drew abreast, and that was when Bear and Roger acted in the thick, vision-reducing fog.

They lunged over the barrier and plunged syringes into the necks of the two closest cops, who were drawing up their AK74s.

Broker pounded on the SVR vehicle's passenger window.

'THERE'S A BOMB BENEATH YOUR CAR!' he yelled.

The car slowed to a stop.

The window rolled down a couple of inches.

Smirnov's face appeared. He narrowed his eyes against the smoke and coughed.

'There are lights underneath your car. It looks like a bomb,' Broker said urgently.

The SVR team leader frowned. He opened the door and got out.

Broker pointed to the ground and stepped around him to block the view from the partially open door.

Bear and Roger came forward in the heavy smoke, grabbed Smirnov and pulled him to the side.

Zeb sprang to take Smirnov's position. He bent down, shook his head, felt the team leader's phone slide into his palm, gripped it and climbed into the car with his elbow over his face, coughing hard.

'Keep going!' he wheezed. 'Get closer to Kotenko. Stay ten or fifteen feet behind that car. No one else should come between us unless I order it.'

Is there a privacy window? He searched swiftly. *There, that button in the central console, above the aircon vent.*

'Bomb? Did that man say—'

'Nyet.' He lowered his elbow and looked at Gorshky, who was waving his hand to dispel the smoke that had entered the car. It was the first time he had been that close to the SVR chief. 'It was a child's toy with lights on it. The fool didn't recognize it.'

'YOU LEFT THE CAR!' Tank exploded from the front seat. 'You exposed the boss! Anyone could have—'

'Da!' Zeb yelled back.

He didn't notice the switch, he thought triumphantly.

'Because I am the one responsible for his security. I had to check out the toy, and it was a split-second decision. Nicola is some distance behind us, and he wouldn't have been able to help if it had been a real bomb. Drive! The boss and I have to make some calls.'

He jabbed the button, and the privacy screen rolled up between them and Tank.

'What calls?' Gorshky asked, puzzled.

'Call Lubyanka. The riot cannot be contained. We should not risk keeping Zakharova there.'

I hope that's how they refer to her.

'Get her to be moved in a van. It should join us. We'll take her with us while we figure out where to keep her.'

'What happened to your voice?' The SVR chief looked intently at him.

'The smoke,' Zeb coughed again. 'Someone must have set off some kind of fireworks or smoke bombs. Not tear gas. The police are dealing with the protesters.'

I'm trying to imitate Smirnov's voice. Looks like I didn't get it right.

His explanation satisfied Gorshky, who returned to his phone's screen and shook his head.

'Everything has fallen apart.'

'The arrests in Baku and Kyiv?' Zeb guessed.

'Da. Our killers' pictures and details are all over the news.'

'Did the President call?'

'Nyet. He must be busy with his cabinet and advisors. They must all be working out what went wrong. I don't know if we have to kill Kotenko—'

Zeb froze.

He looked ahead, past Tank's silhouette and through the windscreen.

The Ukrainian President's vehicle was still ahead, still being driven to Sheremetyevo. It didn't look as though the driver had received any other instructions.

'Why would we have to do that?'

'Dusan, don't you see it? This was the President's plan all along. Kill Kotenko and the Azerbaijan leaders, install puppet governments who will better serve our interests.'

'Da, I follow that. But why would he get *us* to kill Kotenko? In any case, let's see if he calls you. Please order Elena's—'

'Da, da.' Gorshky dialed a number and spoke rapidly. His voice rose. 'Don't you know who I am! Do you want to spend the rest of your life cleaning toilets in Siberia? Put her in a secure van with a team, and send it to join us!'

'No other vehicle,' Zeb whispered, prompting him. 'We can't draw attention to it.'

'No other vehicle,' the SVR chief repeated.

'Ask them to coordinate with me.'

'Coordinate with Dusan. Yes, do it now, before those Resistance duraks break into the prison! Da. I know they will be killed, but if hundreds storm inside, what are you going to do? Do as I say! Take down Dusan's number.

'Fools,' he said bitterly, after ending the call. 'Our President's plans have turned to ash and these men are daring to disobey me. I will transfer every one of them out of Moscow. I will—'

Zeb leaned into him and jabbed him with the syringe that was taped to his left wrist. He held the plunger down until its contents emptied into Gorshky's neck, withdrew it, threw it to the floorboard and crushed it under his heel.

The nerve agent left its victims in a passive state. They were aware of what was happening around them, but their muscles wouldn't act on brain commands. Their bodies obeyed external instructions and kept carrying out their normal functions.

The twins called it the Zombie Drug, a name that had caught on in the clandestine world they operated in. Bear and Roger had injected the two police officers with the same agent.

Smirnov's phone in his hand vibrated.

'Dusan?'

That's Galkin.

'Da?'

'What happened? That smoke ... you stopped. We were too far behind to see what went down, and by the time we got close you were rolling.'

'The smoke was from some kind of homemade bomb. Some protester must have set it off. The man who knocked on my window was warning me of a bomb ... I checked. It was a kid's toy.'

'That's good,' the SVR man sighed in relief. 'Why are we following Kotenko? Where are we going?'

'To Sheremetyevo, to make sure he gets on his flight safely.'

'Have you heard what's going on in Kyiv and Baku?'

'Da, the boss told me. He wasn't looped into these plans. He didn't know our army was actually moving into Ukraine. The President kept the plans to himself. The boss thinks only a few ministers would have known about it.'

'Do you think NATO will join the war?'

'I don't know,' Zeb said sharply. 'Our job is to keep the boss safe and follow his orders.'

'We heard all that,' Bwana drawled in his tooth mic. His voice rumbled inside Zeb's head. 'We're drawing parallel to you, on Bretskaya Street.'

Were you able to get away? Zeb messaged his team.

'How do you think we're on our way?' Beth replied. 'Those smoke bombs worked as designed. The fog dissipated in seconds, which helped, otherwise the other police officers would have come to investigate.'

Did the media cover what happened?

'Nope. Several protesters moved forward when Bear and Roger did. They blocked what went down. There aren't helis in the sky. No aerial coverage. We took out the nearby CCTV cameras. We are good.'

What about those officers Bear and Roger injected?

'They must be still on duty. They were in their positions, last we saw of them.'

Didn't the other officers react?

'They did. They beat up the protesters and then went back to their positions.'

They didn't suspect anything?

'Nope. The switch happened in eight seconds. I timed it. The smoke was very thick, but it took forty-two seconds to dissipate. Less than a minute. There was no bang, no flash ... no reason for them to think it was anything more than a prank.'

Smirnov's phone buzzed.

'Da?' Zeb took the call.

'Somov Georgiy, SVR Team Leader at Lubyanka. You are a legend. It's my honor—'

'Later, Georgiy. Have you got Zakharova?'

'Da. We are forty minutes behind you.'

'Catch up with us once we cross the Garden Ring. We will slow down for you.'

'Da.'

'How do we get Kotenko's car to slow down?' Broker thought aloud. 'We can't get to his driver or to him.'

'I know someone who can,' Meghan said confidently. 'Clare.'

101

Miroslav Kotenko's heart was still pounding. He was following the rolling news on his phone but didn't dare call his cabinet or the Azerbaijan President to congratulate them on their escape.

My call might be tapped.

His phone vibrated.

A text message from a number he didn't recognize.

This is from your tailor. Don't reply to these messages.

Tailor? He frowned. *I don't ... it's President Morgan!*

Ask your driver to slow down. Give any reason. Your vehicle should take all the time it can to get to the Third Ring.

Kotenko waited, but no other message appeared.

He lowered the privacy glass.

'Can you slow down, please?' He smiled at the driver and hoped the sweat on his forehead didn't show. 'This might be the last time I see Moscow. I want to admire it.'

The driver looked at him in the rearview mirror and nodded.

The car slowed.

Kotenko's phone vibrated.

Please take extra passengers with you.

Which passengers? he wondered, but there was no further explanation.

'BINGO,' Beth chortled.

How does she know it's slowing? She and Meg have a satellite feed, dummy, Zeb admonished himself.

Zeb fired a text message to Meghan.

Get Zahavy to bring Yasimov to us. Rendezvous with us at the airport. Ask Belsky if he and his family want to join.

'Will there be enough room in the aircraft?'

Yeah.

'Dusan,' Galkin called him. 'Why are we slowing down?'

'Because Kotenko's car is slowing.'

'Why?'

'I don't know.'

'Does the boss—'

'He's been on calls all along. I can't disturb him. There is nothing to be worried about. We will be joined by another vehicle—'

'Another vehicle? Why? Which one?'

'I'll tell you, if you let me finish,' Zeb growled. 'Zakharova. A team is bringing her from the prison to join us. The boss decided we can't leave her in Lubyanka. The protesters might free her. The boss has arranged for more SVR men to join us. They will be in Zakharova's vehicle, and one of them will be with Tank. For reinforcement. Clear?'

'Clear. Who are these men?'

'I don't know. They aren't Zaslon. The boss pulled them from other SVR teams.'

'SMIRNOV?'

Where's that voice coming from?

Zeb searched between his seat and Gorshky's and found a radio jammed into a crevice. He inspected it briefly before pressing the PTT button.

'Da?'

'Bera Danilov.'

'Danilov,' the man said impatiently when he didn't respond. 'The lead rider in front of Kotenko. We spoke when your boss made you in charge of security.'

This is the radio for the comms channel with the police outriders and vehicles in the convoy.

'Da. A lot is going on. I am juggling—'

'Why has Kotenko's car slowed down?'

'We want it to. We will be joined by another vehicle in the convoy, between his ride and mine. We'll be having more men join us as well.'

'Another vehicle? More men? Why?'

'Who is in charge here?' Zeb reminded him coldly. 'I am responsible for security. This is an SVR operation now. You don't need to know the details.'

Danilov hung up sullenly.

IT HAPPENED at the intersection of Skakovaya with Tverskaya, just before the Third Ring.

'We are approaching from the left,' Georgiy warned Zeb.

'Da. I have eyes on you.'

He watched the van nose out of the side street.

'Tank, slow down,' he spoke into the car's microphone. 'Let that van get ahead of us.'

'Why?'

'Because I say so. It has the journalist Zakharova. We will guard her.'

'We are taking her to the airport?'

'I have no time for your questions. Be prepared for a passenger. Leonid from SVR. He will be joining—there they are, the SVR team, on the road.' He nodded at his team as they ran across the street towards the vehicles.

They've changed into Russian combat outfits.

'Danilov, we have our guests.' He switched to the radio, heard the officer's acknowledgment, and switched back to Smirnov's phone.

'Nicola, we have—'

'I see them. I don't recognize those men.'

'I don't, either.'

He hasn't seen through Beth, Meg and Chloe's disguises.

The van inserted itself smoothly between Kotenko's ride and his car.

Bear raced to the passenger door, opened it and climbed inside. The armored car sank an inch from his weight.

Zeb heard his muffled conversation with Tank, but his attention was on the van. Broker and the women were getting inside through the rear door, Roger at the front.

Bwana will follow us on the side street.

His ride shook. He saw a body slump at the wheel and another climb over it.

Zeb lowered the privacy screen to see Bear shove Tank's body to the seat he had vacated. The large operative's teeth flashed in a grin.

Missed me? he mouthed.

Zeb nodded and pointed at the road ahead.

Bear floored it and followed the van.

'SVR,' Broker said curtly as he held onto a grab handle. 'Who's Georgiy?'

Five armed men on two bench seats on each side of the van.

Elena Zakharova, chained to a steel rod that rose from the floor and joined the roof.

Her face was deeply lined, gaunt; worry and fear filled her eyes. Her clothing hung loosely on her and her hair was unkempt.

'That's me.' A stocky man raised his hand.

Broker shot him, then took out a second man while Beth and Chloe killed the rest. Meghan searched their bodies, then removed their phones and radios and crushed them all, except the ones on Georgiy.

The partition to the front cab slid open and Roger glanced sideways.

'Clear?' Broker asked him.

'There were two in the front.'

'Where are they now?'

'Dead.'

'The van didn't swerve while you attacked them.'

'That's how good I am.'

He slid the panel back and continued driving.

'Who are you?' Elena said, licking her dry lips.

'Friends,' Beth told her.

102

'We have control,' Meghan spoke in their comms.

Zeb grinned when Bear punched the air.

We aren't out of the woods yet, he told himself. *We still have to make it to the airport. The President could block our way and arrest us.*

'Danilov,' he called the police outrider, 'peel away. My car will be taking the lead. Return to your base. Take the ambulance with you.'

'What? Those aren't our orders.'

'I am giving them now. Have you forgotten?

'I need to check with Baladin.'

'Check with him, and then be ready to face insubordination charges, because you are disobeying a direct order from a superior officer.'

'Order received,' Danilov replied tightly.

'Who is Kotenko's driver? Is he—'

'This is Fyodor Pasternak,' a voice replied. 'I am on the comms channel. I am the driver.'

'You know who I am,' Zeb told him. 'My vehicle will be

taking the lead. The van will be behind you. Our guest will be safe between us.'

'Da.'

'GUVD out,' Danilov said expressionlessly, and a moment later the outriders, the police vehicle and the ambulance had left them. Zeb looked back to confirm the motorcycle escorts peeled away, too.

'DUSAN!' Galkin called him. 'The police are leaving!'

'I ordered them to.'

'Why?'

'Because the boss received orders from the President.'

'What orders?'

'I will shoot Elena Zakharova in front of Miroslav Kotenko.'

103

Zeb heard Chloe gasp. Bear's eyes met his in the rearview mirror.

'WHAT?'

'You heard me. The President wants her executed in front of the Ukrainian. He wants it to be recorded. That video will play on our state media. That will be our lesson to Kotenko, that we will stop at nothing. It will teach the West, too. They foiled our plans. This is what they get in return. You need to drop away. Return to the office. Follow the developments from there.'

'Why? We cannot leave the boss!'

'You fool. Use your brain. Stop talking and listen. Learn to take orders. Do you know why I am commanding you to go to the base? Because my face will be on that video. I will be the most wanted man in America, France, Germany—all those countries. They will be trying to figure out who else was near that killing. That's why the boss ordered those other SVR men. He doesn't want Zaslon's strength to be reduced by having you around as well.'

'What will happen to you?' Galkin whispered.

'Nothing, for now. It depends on how the West reacts. But once they identify me, I'll have to disappear.'

'You are a hero, Dusan,' Galkin said, awestruck. 'You are—'

'GO!' Zeb ordered.

He turned back to see the SVR vehicle flash its lights and turn into a side street.

He tapped Bear's shoulder, who nodded, passed Kotenko's ride, and took the lead.

'The convoy is ours,' Beth declared.

Except for Kotenko's driver, Zeb thought.

104

'Pasternak,' Zeb called the driver. 'Let's go quicker. The sooner Kotenko is on his plane, the better for us.'

'Da.'

Bear, listening in, punched the gas. Their vehicle leaped forward. Kotenko's car kept pace, and behind it, so did the van.

'We're following police chatter,' Beth said. 'Nothing about us or Kotenko. Officers beat up several protesters at our grab site, for the smoke, but they aren't investigating it.'

Danilov must have reported to Baladin that he's no longer in the convoy, but as long as Gorshky is with us, everyone will assume this was an SVR operation all along.

Zeb weighed Smirnov's phone in his hand and realized he hadn't explored it.

Didn't have time, before.

Most of the recent calls were to and from Gorshky and the rest of the protection team. A few to other SVR and Zaslon agents. He opened the secure messaging app and grimaced when it asked for iris recognition.

Any luck with SVR phones? He messaged his team.

'Yeah. We hacked several of these guards' devices. Nothing

much on them. Authorization from Lubyanka's commander to take Elena out of prison, on Gorshky's orders. Chatter about what's unfolding on the news, about Kyiv and Baku.'

What about Elena's article? Has it been published?

'It will be, once Kotenko is out of Russian airspace, along with the meeting recording.'

Where's Smirnov?

'Bwana knocked him out, flexi-cuffed and gagged him, and dumped him in a trashbin. He won't be discovered for a while.'

'I wanted to kill him,' the black operative complained, 'but Beth and Meg talked me out of it.'

Where are you?

'He's taking the inner roads,' Beth replied. 'Driving parallel to us. Zahavy called. He'll meet us at Sheremetyevo. He's got Yasimov with him. Belsky stayed back. He said Russia is their home.'

'He can't go back to his job.'

'Yeah. I'm sure he knows that.'

Zeb checked on Gorshky, who was staring blankly ahead.

He's still out. The drug's effect should last for another hour.

He straightened when the car went over rumblers.

They were approaching Sheremetyevo International Airport.

Bear leaned sideways and straightened Tank's body in the passenger seat. He buckled the dead man and adjusted his jacket. Finally, he placed a pair of shades over his eyes.

'His face is damaged,' he said, looking critically at the body, 'but a casual look won't show he is dead.'

105

The VIP entrance to the airport was a discreet side road that broke away from the main approach, swung around maintenance hangars and drew up to an iron fence.

'Our bird is in the air,' Meghan commented as Bear drew close. 'Two guards. You can see them at the gate. A vehicle nearby, with three civilians in it. Probably maintenance staff, in case the President's aircraft needs attention. No one else nearby. Crew is in the bird.'

The armed men came out on the road on each side of their ride. Zeb lowered his window and showed Smirnov's identity card and held his breath, waiting to see if they would ask Bear to lower his window.

They didn't.

'We are escorting President Kotenko,' he said harshly to the soldier close to him. 'That's him, in the car behind us. That van is with us, too.'

We're winging it here. We couldn't find out what the protocol is for his departure.

Bear moved in his seat.

He's got his hand on his HK.

We'll take Kotenko and Gorshky hostage if we are surrounded by hostiles.

That was their exit if the mission went south. It wasn't ideal. It was high-risk and would mean a firefight, but it was the best they had come up with.

And it might not work.

The guard went to Kotenko's car, looked at him and returned to him.

'What's in the van?'

'*Who*, not what. SVR officers, with a prison exchange with Ukraine.'

'We were not told of that.'

Zeb leaned forward and jerked his head at Gorshky. 'That's Alexei Gorshky, head of SVR. I am sure you have heard of him and our organization. We are responsible for escorting President Kotenko out. Is my boss looking at you? No. Do you know why? Because you don't matter. Your opinion does not matter. All you need to do is obey orders. Got it? Now open the gate and let us enter.'

The guard nodded stiffly and pressed a button to slide the gate back.

'Security cameras fried,' Beth whispered.

Bear drove inside and stopped close to the Gulfstream that was painted in Ukraine's national colors and bore its flag on the tail. The President's car followed, as did the van.

The civilian vehicle didn't move from its position. Three men in the front, visible through the windshield.

'Is that it?' Broker, amazed. 'No red carpet. No officials to see Kotenko off?'

'Does it look like we know how presidents are seen off in the middle of a war?' Chloe, querulous.

'Besides,' Meghan whispered, 'this is Ukraine's leader. I am sure the Russian President wants to humiliate him, show how little he thinks of Kotenko.'

Zeb got out of his car. He hurried around the back of the car and opened the door for Gorshky, held his shoulder and helped him out.

The SVR chief followed his nudge automatically.

Zeb guided him to Kotenko's car, aware of Broker and Roger drifting towards the sentries at the gate.

They'll take those soldiers out. Doesn't look like the civilian vehicle can see the guards, which will make it easier.

Zeb opened the door to Kotenko. Smiled at the President and shook his hand when the Ukrainian leader emerged.

'Guards out,' he heard the Texan in his head.

Zeb introduced Gorshky to him, confirmed that Pasternak couldn't hear them, and whispered softly in Russian.

'Smile. Nod. Don't say anything else. Don't say any names."

Kotenko's forehead creased momentarily. He smiled broadly and pumped the SVR chief's hand.

The van's doors opened. His team emerged, with Elena among them.

Where's Zahavy?

Where's Bwana?

Zeb searched the gate. No sign of approaching vehicles.

'Wait here, sir,' he told the President and left him with Gorshky.

He heard Kotenko trying to make small talk with the SVR chief as he went to the President's car.

Pasternak lowered his window.

Zeb chopped his neck with the edge of his palm and squeezed it until he collapsed.

'Take your time,' Bear murmured. 'Those civilians can't see you. We're obstructing their sight line.'

Zeb gagged the driver, cuffed his hands to the door and removed his gun, radio and phone.

He went to the President, who quickly concealed his look of shock.

'You!'

Elena, terror on her face. She stumbled backwards, away from Chloe. Meghan and Beth were stowing away their screens. Bear, Broker and Roger ranged behind them, cutting off the civilians' view.

'You said you were friends. That's Gorshky and Smirnov! They are after me—'

'We'll explain later,' Zeb said hurriedly. 'You need to get into the plane.'

'Nyet, I won't—'

'DUSAN!'

Zeb whirled at the voice, to see Galkin with ten men at the gate, striding towards them.

106

They must have parked some distance away and come on foot. Our drone had to have seen them, but Beth and Meg put away their screens.

'Nicola?' Zeb asked, surprised. 'What are you doing here?'

'What are *you* doing? We were halfway back to the office when I looked up Leonid. There's no such agent in SVR. That made me wonder—'

'NICOLA, WHO ELSE DID YOU TELL?'

'No one. We turned back. I got seven agents to join us, but I didn't tell them why.'

Zeb recognized the two men with Galkin. *They're from Gorshky's protection team.* All ten were armed, the Zaslon men with handguns, the rest with AK74s.

'What's going on? I thought you were going to kill Zakharova in front of Kotenko. Why are you talking to them?'

The Ukrainian leader exclaimed in surprise. Elena moaned and started backing away.

'What's happening?' Galkin stopped several feet away. 'Why is the boss looking like that? He hasn't spoken.'

'You have to return. You have messed up this operation. You—'

'No, something isn't right, Dusan. I can feel it.'

Elena fled.

A soldier reacted and brought his AK up.

Zeb dove at her, yanking at Kotenko's jacket as he was moving and brought him down hard.

He body-slammed into the journalist to throw her onto the ground and landed on top of her.

A round struck him in the chest. Another blew past his head, and then he lay still, over her, protecting her, as he triggered rapidly at Galkin's men.

His shots went wide, but they got the hostiles to scatter. They dove behind the van and shot from its cover.

Beth and Meghan sprawled on top of Kotenko, their faces tight, intent, HKs chattering, seeking targets. Broker on top of Gorshky; Bear, Chloe, Broker and Roger ranged further out on the ground, firing. A line of blood on the Texan's temple. Broker jerked, winced, but kept shooting.

We have no cover. We are outnumbered.

Zeb snatched a look around desperately.

His and Kotenko's cars were just a few feet away, but with bullets flying in the air, they were as good as miles away. The civilian vehicle was backing away rapidly.

Nothing to it but kill them. We'll get hit, but we'll have to deal with it.

'Stop moving,' he growled at Elena, who was squirming beneath him, and shot at a hostile.

He grunted when another round hit his vest and his Glock wavered. The journalist screamed when a bullet splat near them.

The shooting became louder and then lessened. Fewer rounds came their way, and then they stopped.

Zeb aimed at the van, searching for movement.

'Hold your fire.'

His shoulders slumped at Bwana's voice.

His friend came from behind the van, a wide grin on his face.

'You are welcome,' he bowed briefly.

Zeb looked at the civilian vehicle, which was reversing.

'Rog—'

'On it.' The Texan burst into a sprint, with Chloe following him. They shot at the vehicle's tires, reached it and knocked the men out.

'They didn't call anyone,' Chloe panted when they returned. 'It happened so fast that they didn't think of it.'

'Aircraft mechanics. We secured them. They won't be alerting anyone.' Roger wiped his forehead and frowned at the blood on his fingers. 'A scratch,' he said.

'Sure?'

'Yeah.'

'Broker—'

'I'm good.' The elder operative got to his feet. 'These vests saved us.'

'I played a hand, too,' Bwana replied.

Zeb hauled Elena up. She looked at him and Gorshky in confusion. She made to speak, but he ignored her and went to Kotenko.

'Sir, are you okay? I am sorry I had to pull you down like that.'

'Nyet.' The leader dusted off his suit. 'I am fine. I was covered by these two,' he said, nodding at the twins. 'Who were those—'

Zeb spun on his heel and stood in front of him at the sound of an approaching engine.

A dark van. A hand waving out of the window, signaling the occupants weren't hostile.

Zahavy climbed out carefully, aware of the guns trained on

him. Two men came out from behind. They spread out to reveal Yasimov.

'BORIS!' Elena yelled and ran towards him. She hugged him hard and led him back to the Agency operatives.

'Do you know what's going on? Why are Gorshky and Smirnov here? I don't understand—'

'There's no time for those questions,' Zeb cut her off. He pointed at the aircraft. 'Get inside, please. Quickly!'

'*You* are the extra passengers,' Kotenko smiled.

'Sir?'

The President waved his question away and led the journalist and editor to the Gulfstream.

Zeb was going to Zahavy when the man stepped out of the guard hut with raised hands.

'Grigor?' he gasped.

'Da.' The spymaster came to him, his eyes flicking over the bodies on the ground. They took in Kotenko, who had stopped to look back, and Yasimov and Elena.

'You were here all along?'

'Da. I worked out why you were in Moscow. I've known you long enough to figure out how you would get away.'

More men came from behind a hangar. Lean, loose-limbed. They didn't appear to be armed, but Zeb knew appearances were deceptive.

'And you're here to stop us?'

'Nyet,' Andropov smiled grimly. 'How can you even think that? I will help you get away. I will clean up. I will deal with those men,' he said, pointing at the mechanics. 'I will come up with a plausible story. I have already taken care of the cameras.'

His smile grew warmer when he looked at the twins. 'You didn't need to fry them. The shooting ... unfortunately we didn't have good angles, and by the time we were in position,'—he pointed at Bwana—'he had saved your bacon. That's what you would say, da?'

'Correct, sir,' the black operative nodded solemnly.

'You said you wouldn't take a hand.' Zeb reminded him.

'I said I would move against you if you went after our President.'

The spymaster looked hard at Zahavy, who returned his stare.

'I know you.'

'I run a fast-food—'

'That's not all you run.'

Zahavy's face sharpened.

'We are on the same side. Sometimes. You are of no interest to me. Shalom.'

Zahavy's lips parted in surprise. He stood motionless for a long time and then nodded.

'Shalom,' he said. He gestured at his men and drove away.

'Looks like Mossad isn't as great as it thinks it is,' Chloe drawled.

'What's that?' Andropov asked.

'Nothing important, sir.'

'Why?'

The spymaster understood Zeb's question.

'Because there are some things bigger than country borders and national interests. Go, moy drug,' he said with a tight hug. 'Fly out quickly. You have a small window before Gorshky and Smirnov's disappearance is discovered.'

'WHO IS THAT?' Kotenko asked when they were taxiing.

Zeb watched as his friend's figure shrank into the distance as the Gulfstream defied gravity and parted with the earth.

'A friend, sir.'

107

It was a tight fit in the Gulfstream, which had only ten seats, an office space and a folding bed.

Zeb, on the thickly carpeted floor, with Bwana, Bear and Roger beside him, smiled briefly as the pilots cheered from the cockpit when they cleared Russian airspace.

'Who are you?' asked a man whom Kotenko had introduced as Victor, his aide.

'You were in the aircraft all along?' Beth asked him.

'Da. The Russians wanted a no-aides meeting.'

'Check the news, first.' Chloe held up her phone.

The President looked puzzled, as did Victor, Yasimov and Elena. The aide pressed a button on a remote, and a TV slid up from one of the work tables.

'CNN,' he said unnecessarily.

That was the only word spoken for several minutes as the broadcaster interrupted its war coverage to break Elena's article, her research, and Kotenko's recording, and linked all of those to the killer teams in Azerbaijan and Ukraine.

'The Russian President is exposed. His ambitions are there for the world to see. He wants to build Russia to the size it was during the Soviet Union. He will achieve that by whatever means necessary, including invading Russia's neighbors. Elena Zakharova has revealed the extent he is willing to go to. Destroy Ukraine militarily and economically, hold Europe hostage to the Russian gas supply—'

Victor turned off the TV at Kotenko's gesture.

The Ukrainian leader went to Elena and hugged her. 'You did this.'

'Not just me,' she said, smiling through her tears. 'Boris helped too. And these people ...' she trailed off when she looked in Zeb's direction. She shuddered when she took in Gorshky, who was handcuffed to the bed, his mouth taped, still under the influence of the nerve agent.

'Remove your mask, dumbass,' Beth sniggered.

Zeb lowered his face and unpeeled his disguise. His crew removed their prosthetic fittings, and the twins and Chloe freed their hair.

Elena stared at them. Yasimov smiled, as if some secret had been confirmed.

'You got my message! You came.'

'Of course, we would.' He held her tightly when she came over and sobbed on his shoulder.

'You are American!' Kotenko exclaimed.

'Da.'

'But the way you speak Russian ... you saved my life. I can't thank you enough.'

'You helped us too, sir,' Roger drawled. 'We hitched a ride on your plane. That was our exfil plan. We would have been stuck in Moscow if you hadn't let us join you.'

The President looked searchingly at them. His smile faded.

'This won't stop the Russian President. I met him. I have seen the person he is. Treaties, allies, friends—nothing matters to him other than expanding Russia.'

'Ukraine is not alone, sir,' Zeb began and stopped at Kotenko's expression.

'I know it isn't. We are lucky to have support from all over the world. I know our friends have started putting financial pressure on Russia. But it is my people who have to stop the Russian soldiers. It is my people who are dying.'

He's right.

'We will make them regret coming into our country. The Russian President thinks we are a small country with an insignificant army. He might be right. But what he is going to find out is we have the biggest hearts in the world, and as long as they beat, we will not give up.'

108

Kotenko and Victor were on calls continually until they landed in Kyiv.

'Take the Gulfstream,' he said, squeezing Zeb's hands with both palms. 'Take Elena and Boris to safety. She will be staying with his family, da?'

'Da.'

The politician's lips twisted in a grim smile. 'In any case, I won't be needing it. I am not going anywhere.'

It was Elena who voiced their fears when they took off for Berlin.

'Will we see him alive again?'

None of them had an answer.

THE NEWS BROKE when they landed in Berlin's Brandenburg Airport.

Kyiv, Kharkiv, and Donbas were being shelled.

'Civilian deaths are already being reported.'

'I'm surprised it took them that long,' Meghan said soberly as they climbed into three cabs.

'The Russian President was working out how those killer teams got identified. He must have thought there were leaks in the Kremlin,' Zeb guessed. 'Kotenko might not have been on his mind at all. That was why we could get away.'

BY THE TIME they drew up in front of a residential building in Berlin's Templehof, the world had acted.

The European Union, the US, countries around the globe, including nations such as Singapore and Japan, had condemned the aggression and imposed a brutal range of sanctions.

Russian assets owned by oligarchs were seized. Bank accounts were frozen. Russian banks were kicked out of payment messaging systems. Exports to the country and Russian holdings in foreign countries were blocked.

'We failed,' Elena whispered when she got out of the cab and held onto Yasimov's arm. 'All that investigation, interviewing contacts, finding out about those hit teams ... what was the point?'

Zeb watched a woman and a girl come out of the building.

'Papa!' the child cried and ran at Yasimov, her arms outstretched.

'Are you going to stop writing for *The Reality*?'

'Never!' Elena shook her head. 'Boris and I spoke about it. This has made us more determined than ever to keep the newspaper going.'

'Then,' he said, giving her a squeeze, 'you haven't failed.'

ZEB LOOKED at the twins and Broker when they were back in the cab, heading to the airport. They were all deep in their own thoughts, reflective.

The younger sister flicked her hair back and smiled

absently when she sensed his gaze. Her eyes didn't have their usual sparkle. Her smile was absent.

He knew the mood would be similar in Bear's cab.

They all feel like Elena. That we failed.

Do you feel that way too? he asked himself.

He searched himself deep down and shook his head unconsciously.

No. I was always expecting the Russian President to attack. Besides, Clare was right. Our team wasn't there to stop the war.

He didn't say anything to his team, however.

They have to work it out for themselves.

THEY ARRIVED at the airport and boarded the Lear that had arrived from New York to pick them up.

Gorshky, who had recovered and was secured in a seat, snarled and attempted to kick them when they passed.

'Don't, dude,' Bwana said tonelessly at him. 'None of us want to deal with you.'

The aircraft spun a lazy circle in the sky and headed towards the Atlantic.

Zeb's phone buzzed when they were mid-ocean.

'Put it on speaker,' Clare told him.

He punched the button and beckoned his friends to gather around.

'I can guess how you all are feeling,' she said. 'Whatever I say may not make you feel better. Listen to the President, however. He's live, addressing the country. Here, I'll put him on.'

President Morgan's voice boomed out of Zeb's phone.

The leader of the free world outlined the various measures that had been brought against Russia. Economic, military, diplomatic, even the sporting arena. The Russian President had been personally targeted in many of the sanctions.

'I know some of us, maybe many of us, in America, Canada, Germany, France, in all the countries that have come together, will be wondering, why are we doing this? This isn't our problem, you might say. Ukraine isn't close to our country. It does not affect us.'

'To you I say, look out of the window. You'll see the sun or the moon. You'll breathe and inhale air.

'Freedom is like that.' he thundered. 'It is there, like the elements. It isn't granted by a person or by a state. It is there the moment we are born, and because it just *is*, it is as precious as sunlight or the air.'

'Freedom isn't an American concept. The right to live our lives the way we want to is for everyone, not just for those in rich or privileged countries.'

'Ukraine is currently facing the dark Russian cloud, but just as nature's clouds always part to bathe us in sunlight or moonlight, I promise President Kotenko and our Ukrainian friends that the United States of America and our allies will do everything we can to restore to you your inalienable rights.'

Beth broke down. She sobbed on her sister's shoulder. Meghan had tears in her eyes, too.

Zeb knew it was due to the power of the President's words and the weight of events.

He also knew they were crying with hope.

109

*oscow*

One Week Later

Sergei Tuzov tested his chair and decided he liked it.

'I will keep this,' he told the movers in his office. 'This desk will stay, too.'

He directed them to shift the couches and coffee table to his liking and then dismissed them.

Chief of SVR.

He liked the title and the power that came with it.

The President had appointed him the previous day, and he had immediately sat in on a series of meetings. The Ukraine invasion wasn't going as they'd wanted. Kotenko had inspired his people to fight for every inch of territory and become a worldwide hero.

The Russian economy was suffering. The ruble had tanked against the dollar and showed no signs of recovering. The personal assets of many of the cabinet ministers and the rich and the powerful had been frozen. Tuzov's own offshore accounts in the Cayman Islands had been sealed off.

He didn't dwell on that for long, though. He was determined to enjoy his position and wield his power ruthlessly.

The quote on the wall caught his eye.

'Dusan!' he yelled.

Smirnov trotted into the room.

He had kept the Zaslon man on despite the humiliation he had endured. Outwitted by Carter, his principle snatched from him and tossed in a garbage bin, Smirnov had endured hostile questioning until Tuzov had rescued him and reappointed him to his previous position.

'How are you feeling?'

'I am good. Thank you for—'

'You are a good agent,' Tuzov said magnanimously, 'and I know you won't make the same mistakes again. Tell me about that quote. Why did Gorshky put it there?'

He went to the wall and inspected the words.

'To frighten visitors. To convey his power.'

'I like that.' Tuzov beamed. He wiped the dust off the lettering with his sleeve and blew on it.

He shrieked in fear as the frame clattered to the floor.

'Why is that happening?' he asked hoarsely, the letters fading with wisps of smoke.

'I don't know.' Smirnov's voice shook.

Tuzov felt a wave of panic sweep through him when new words emerged on the frame.

The Devil Is Closer Than You Think.

MORE BOOKS

Click here to download *The Watcher*, a novella exclusive to Ty Patterson's newsletter subscribers

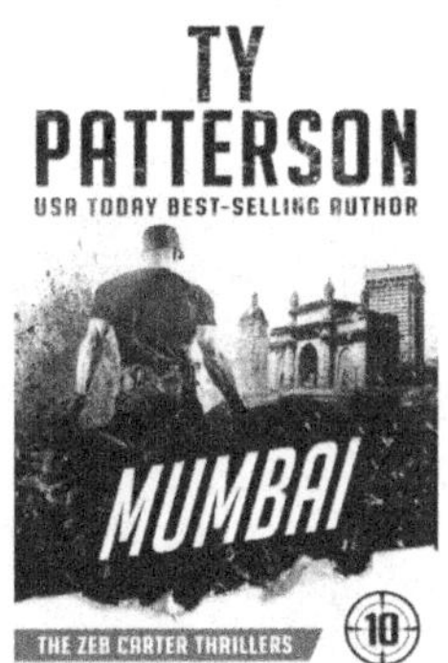

Check out *Mumbai* here, the next Zeb Carter thriller

Check out Paris, here, the previous Cutter Grogan thriller

Join Ty Patterson's Facebook group of readers, here

BONUS CHAPTER FROM MUMBAI

Mumbai

Zeb wandered through the Crawford Market, one of the largest of its kind in Mumbai. Vegetables, poultry, fruits and fragrances —the market had them all.

He wasn't there to buy anything. He was following his team members, who were browsing through the stalls. Meghan, negotiating with a vendor for a scarf, Bwana, trying on a turban, he took them in, enjoying the warmth, the sounds and smells of India's largest city.

They were vacationing in the country. They had been invited by his close friend, Vikram Kohli, Special Agent, Research and Analysis Wing, the country's secretive foreign intelligence agency.

'Warm weather, very warm. Good food and the opportunity to get away from it all.'

That had been Kohli's spiel. Bwana and Roger were sold instantly. The twins agreed, too. Chloe arm-twisted Bear into accepting. Zeb looked at Broker, who had shrugged. 'We have nothing else to do.'

That had nailed it.

The sisters planned their visit, and there they were in Mumbai, sampling the wares in the market.

It was the man's sudden turn that alerted Zeb.

He had noticed him behind them and thought nothing of it. The man looked like a Westerner, in his patterned shirt and loose shorts, but there were thousands of tourists in the country and many in the market.

Zeb's casual look back seemed to have prompted the man to swivel suddenly, which caught Zeb's attention.

Is he following us?

Zeb fingered a shawl, asked its price, nodded politely at the storekeeper and moved to another shop.

The stalls were irregularly aligned. Some shops ran straight; others angled out with various wares.

He cut to another row of shops and inhaled perfumes from display bottles. From an ornate plate's polished surface, he saw the man following him.

'Zeb!'

He looked up to see Kohli hustling up.

The RAW agent was beaming. He weaved through the crowd easily, using his height and presence to part the shoppers.

Zeb looked beyond his friend.

Saw his tail raise his hand. Made out what he was holding.

'SHOOTER!' he yelled.

The explosion threw him back against a stall's counter. His ears rang. Smoke filled the market.

A second blast sounded, and he heard nothing else.

~

AUTHOR'S MESSAGE

~

Thank you for taking the time to read *Moscow.* If you enjoyed it, please consider telling your friends and posting a short review. Sign up to Ty Patterson's mailing list and get *The Watcher*, a Zeb Carter novella, exclusive to newsletter subscribers. Join Ty Patterson's Facebook Readers Group, here.

BOOKS BY TY PATTERSON

Zeb Carter Series

Ten Books in the series and counting

Cutter Grogan Series (Zeb Carter Universe)

Five books in the series and counting

Zeb Carter Short Stories

Three books and counting

Warriors Series (Zeb Carter Universe)

Twelve books in the series

Gemini Series (Zeb Carter Universe)

Four thrillers in the series

Warriors Series Shorts (Zeb Carter Universe)

Six novellas in the series

Cade Stryker Series

Two military sci-fi thrillers

ABOUT THE AUTHOR

~

Ty has been a trench digger, loose tea vendor, leather goods salesman, marine lubricants salesman, diesel engine mechanic, and is now an action thriller author.

Ty lives with his wife and son, who humor his ridiculous belief that he's in charge.

Made in United States
Orlando, FL
15 February 2024

43730310R00264